I0784291

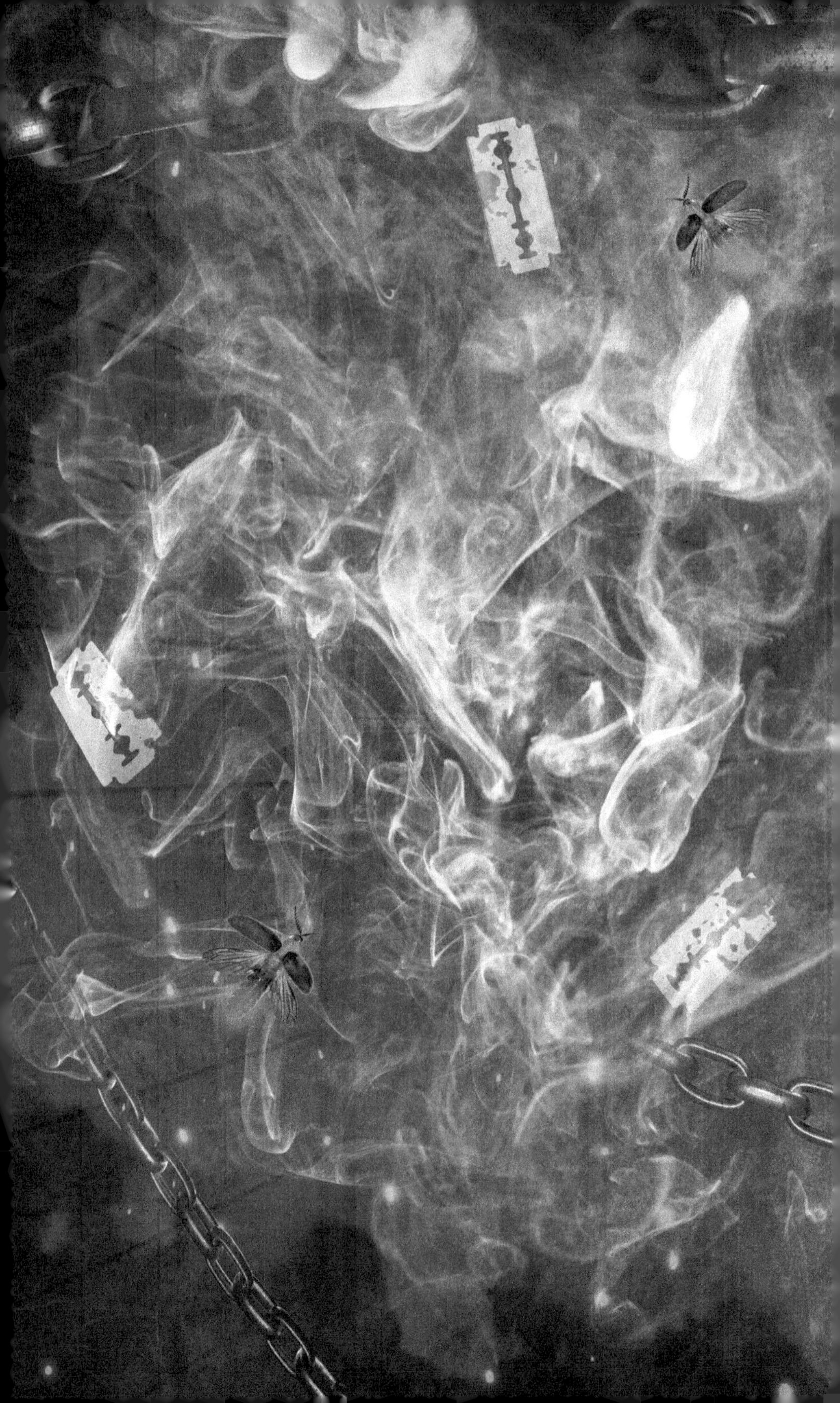

BOOK 1

ALAMORT

JAINE DOE

PRIYA

I killed my sister.
Not really, but when our school goes up in flames, all fingers point at me. It gives my parents the green light they needed to get rid of me. Sending their fire enthusiast child away to Cox Academy and throwing away the key for good measure. Insert meeting my real first friend and newfound enemies, "The Demons," who seem determined to make my life hell at every turn. Add in the Shadow Man who sneaks into my room at night, not to mention the creepy letters I start receiving. Little do they know, no one hates me more than I hate myself.
I thought losing my sister was bad. This might push me over the edge.

THE DEMONS

"An eye for an eye."
When our adopted brother is killed in a fire on the other side of the country. There's nothing that will stop us from getting our revenge. There's no better option than having the accused sent to a school for teen criminals ruled under our thumb. What starts as avenging our brother's death becomes sticky with betrayal, deceit and secrets. What happens when the past comes back to haunt us? Will we be able to face the crack in our foundation together?

For the girls who fought their war mentally and suffered silently

TRIGGER WARNING

This is a dark romance. Reader discretion is advised. That includes but is not limited to, misogyny, physical, mental, and verbal abuse, self-harm, child abuse, attempted SA, victim blaming, dubcon, odaxelagina, blood play, knife play, Dom/submissive play, depression, anxiety, suicidal ideations, torture, an inaccurate portrayal of Dissociative Identity Disorder. Your mental health matters! If any of these are triggering, please do not continue.

4 YEARS AGO

CHANGE (IN THE HOUSE OF FLIES) - DEFTONES

When I was younger, I was afraid of the dark. Of the monsters in the closet, under the bed, the things that go bump in the darkest part of the night. Afraid of the unknown. Everything changed when I realized it was people like me, is who I should've been hiding from.

Plink. Plink. Plink. Something wet hits my temple before trailing lazily down my face. I draw in a deep breath to do an automatic physical body check for any damage. Breathing hurts my ribs, bruised but not broken. Nothing feels like it needs immediate tending to. An ache lingers in my fingers when I open and close them, as if I had strained them by clenching too hard, too long. It wouldn't be the first time he's left me a mess. The effort of rolling onto my back causes my arm and leg muscles to scream in protest.

Plink. Plink. Plink. That leaky pipe needs to be fixed. If he ever found out, the consequences would be far worse than a beating. My insides shrivel at the thought of being locked down here and losing my only water source.

I give my eyes a minute or two to adjust to the darkness, picking up the familiar sound of tiny claws scurrying on the floor, hinting there's a small rodent nearby before ultimately leaving me in the suffocating silence.

There's nothing I hate more than being stuck inside my mind. That this is what I have to look forward to for the rest of my life. I sniff back the tears that sting the corner of my eyes, a whiff of the distinct familiar odor of the basement, mildew and earthy. I pause, my muscles tensing... The undertone of sweet, rancid decaying smell of death causes my stomach to roll. Gradually sitting, flakes of mud fall off my jeans, excluding the damp patches on my knees.

I rotate my head left, damn near jumping out of my skin at a dark mass less than an arm's reach away, hovering next to me. My mouth waters, that feeling when on the verge of vomiting, the glands salivate, and everything spins. I swallow it, my palms slick with sweat, the stickiness clinging to my skin.

"Hey," I whisper to the shadow. Expecting a response that doesn't come, "I promise I won't hurt you." After a second, I add "I used to get scared when he put me down here too."

Hoping to establish a sort of camaraderie. We don't have to suffer alone if we're down here together. My first mistake was thinking another person was here for a punishment. It's highly unusual he'd place me down here with someone. It would disrupt my alone time for 'self-reflection'.

I'm met with dead air. Sticking my hand out to brush against the mass, I touch cloth, something crusty flakes off at each brush against the fabric. Gritting my teeth through the pain, I push myself up from the unforgiving half-finished concrete ground, wincing as the sharp edges of small rocks pierce my palms. I dust myself off and inch my way towards it as if it were a cornered animal. In a way, it is. We both are.

"Hey," I speak softly, my hand tentatively reaches out to shake them. The chains rattle with the force, the body it's holding vibrates from my shake, unable to move an inch from being held taut. Not to hold the person back... but holding them in a Vitruvian man position I've come to know well. I run my quivering hands along their spread arms, shivering at the coldness beneath my fingertips. It's a person.

Was a person.

"No." My heart sinks to the pit of my stomach. "No. No!" gradually getting louder. "Please." I whimper, warm tears gather on my lashes. I should be used to it after of years of being molded into his "protégé". But his victim taints my only safe space. The thought makes me as sick as it did the first time.

This is *my* space. He's supposed to leave me alone here.

"You fucking monster! Come out and own up to what you did!" I yell, spit flying from my mouth. My body heats. I respond by puffing out my chest, a subconscious attempt to protect myself from displaying vulnerability. He feeds off of fear. It's what he wants. From the furthest corner, laughter echoes through the hollow room.

"I've been watching and waiting." He pauses dramatically. "Look at this masterpiece! At what *you* created!" His eagerness and excitement are palpable in the air.

Shaking my head at the shadows, "No. You sick fuck. You did this." I would remember harming someone. My stomach sinks and my palms sweat. I think I would remember.

"I brought you this gift. But this? You did this. She screamed so beautifully for you. Begged so prettily… like you used to. Do you remember?" His reverence for our history brings a full-body shudder as he flips on his lantern. The sudden harsh light causes me to flinch and my eyes to water.

I want to shut them again because nothing in this basement will take away this feeling of deep pitted dread. With hesitation, my eyes open to look at the hanging girl. She's disorganized chaos. Her head lays limply against her chest. Blood mats her dark long hair. Every single fingernail and toenail, missing. Hundreds of cuts, all different depths and lengths, cover her body. Someone deliberately flayed her skin on one side of her cheek for maximum damage, so she'd remain conscious despite the excruciating pain inflicted upon her. A centuries old torture method *he's* been obsessed with for as long as I can remember.

Burn marks left by something small litter her exposed body. The worst part was the lack of clothing, in her bra, her panties around her ankles. Her shirt is cut down the middle and gathered at the sides of her exposed, bloodied torso.

I've watched him do this countless times, too many to count. One after another, I've had to clean up his messes, girl after girl.

Slowly backing until I hit the stone wall, looking down at my hands. Blood covers my skin. There isn't a clean patch to be seen.

"You should be proud. This? This is your best work yet. If I would have known that you had a soft spot for a certain incentive, I would have done it a lot sooner," he says thoughtfully. As if I'm the answer to all of his problems.

Bile crawls up my throat. When was the last time I ate?

I'm going to be sick.

My hands rip at the strands in my hair, the sting of it being pulled at the roots, some false semblance of punishment as he delves into the details of the gruesome scene around me.

"You should have seen the way she cried when you pulled down her …" his voice trails off as my knees buckle under my weight and I retch violently. The horrors of what happened to the young girl are muffled through the blood roaring in my ears. It sounds like a drum being banged over and over.

Panic grips my chest as my breaths come out in short, choppy gasps in my attempt to get oxygen into my lungs that no longer want air.

I'm tired. Pressure pulses in the back of my skull.

Plink. Plink. Plink.

I am so *tired* that sleep couldn't take away this feeling. The world fades into the comforting darkness I know well.

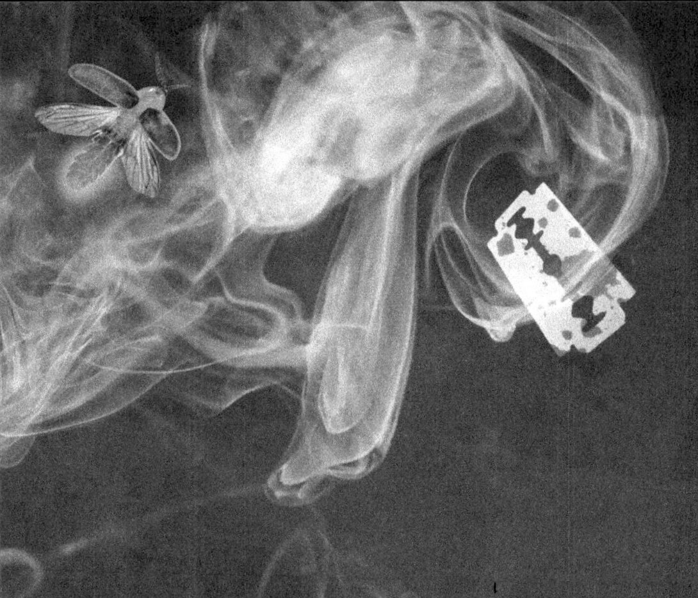

Unbearable pain. My head's going to explode from the pressure. I could hear him yelling at me, but the ringing muffles it in my ears. It reminds me of the cartoons. When the character gets hit, stars pop up around their head, and their body sways because they're dizzy. I think the stars represented the flash of light in the darkness when someone was hit and the loss of balance that accompanies it.

"Daddy! Stop! Please! She didn't know!"

I'm unable to pinpoint the sound of the muted yell from around me. My hands fly to my face to soothe the stinging from the backhand I received from our father. Tears gather in my eyes, knowing I disappointed him again.

It'll only anger him more if he sees my tears, so I keep my eyes fixed to a point on the marble floor, tracing the vein as it expands and branches off, reminding me of the creek beside our house. My sister's perfect blonde head of

*tamed curly hair pops in front of me as she crouches down to check on me. I
avoid eye contact. That's all it'll take from me to crumble.*

Dad has never struck her.

I wish I could be as perfect as she is…

Blinking, I pull myself out of a memory of my best friend,
forever my savior.

Growing up with a sibling who was a year and a half older
than me meant we were inseparable. It was always her and I
against the world. I tell her everything. We do everything together.
I personified the harmful carbon dioxide, while she embodied the
life-giving oxygen. Feeding off each other to survive. When our
parents first started using food as a punishment, she would be the
one to sneak me some of her dinner so I wouldn't go hungry. Our
mother didn't have a "favorite" child. She just hated me more
than my sister. I could use that to distract her from giving Addison
a verbal lashing by doing something worse to earn her wrath.

Addi would help me avoid our father by letting me know
where he was and what level of anger he seemed to be at for the
day. On the off chance I found myself in his presence, she would
be there to diffuse the situation, giving me a chance to escape
fairly unscathed.

Around the time I turned 12, I fully grasped the significance
she held in my life. My parents were incapable of loving anyone
other than themselves. So how my sister was able to love and give
her undying loyalty to me without ever receiving it is beyond me.

I throw my head back against the headrest and grab the book
of matches out of my pocket to rub each of the edges clockwise,
then counterclockwise. The sides of the white cardboard are already beginning to fray. I don't think I've had it for more than a
week.

I pick up my phone to no missed calls. Not even a text. I
would have thought one of my parents would care about the well-
being of their remaining child.

I'm grasping for crumbs at this point. Unable to face that they
couldn't care less about what happens to me. I'm naïve to sit here
and miss the parents I never had. Yearning for some sort of

connection to fill the one I've lost. What type of trauma is that? The excuse, "they're still my parents" rings a bell. And when will it no longer be good enough?

Flipping open the book of matches, I count them individually, touching each white tip, finding comfort in the routine. There's tension building up inside me. Inflating like a balloon that would need an outlet soon before it popped and I, characteristically, self-destructed. Another flaw, add it to my ever-growing list of why I'm a fuckup.

That and the fact my parents blamed me for my sister's death.

Silently drowning in anger and heartache from the hole in my heart, add in a dash of the abandonment from my parents shipping me off to a new school during my last year of high school like I'm a burden they could give away when life got too hard.

They had turned their noses up and threw money at me, treating me like a dirty secret that needed to be hidden. I did nothing. This time, anyway. Pulling me out to make an appearance as the "perfect" family for their own benefit. Only to be tossed to the side when I've done my part. But now? My parents think I had something to do with the deaths at the school. Not just anyone died, though. My entire world and a boy she was with. That I would be as careless and selfish to put not one but two people in danger. My mother's Botox-injected face held pure revulsion. She refused to look at me. If she hadn't liked me before, the look on her face made it a concrete fact now—but that could be the Botox.

Trying to distract myself from needing a release so soon, I slip my matches back into my front pocket and attempt to make conversation with my designated driver, or prison guard for the day. He looks like a poster child for the mafia. Tan, a bald head that has black tribal tattoos starting at the base of his beefy neck and disappearing beneath the collar of his suit, but his head… it's so shiny it looks like it was spit-shined. He has massive arms the size of my thighs and his legs have to be tree trunks. I wonder if he's ever squeezed the life out of anyone.

"Hey, Baldilocks, have you ever killed a person? You're abnormally huge, like how I'd imagine Goliath would be." I say, staring at the back of his bald ass head with a smirk. Goliath died from David, hitting him with a stone on his forehead before decapitating him. Deflect your pain with a bit of humor, right?

His lips press into a firm line, "Today could be the day." The leather steering wheel creaks under his scarred hands.

My eyes widen and I sink back into the black leather interior while trying to make myself as small as possible. That wasn't quite the answer I was looking for. I've never met this guy, and he's already had enough of me?

Well, he should get in line to join the club. Rolling my eyes, I sit up straighter, clearing my throat, "Can we stop somewhere? I have to use the bathroom."

"No. Your parents said straight to school from the flight."

"Baldie, if you think I won't piss in this seat to prove a point, you're sadly mistaken. Plus, I want some snacks …. I'm starving." I say as nonchalantly as I can muster, hoping he doesn't see straight through my lies.

"You literally just ate on the plane. I was two rows behind you." He scoffs.

Hmm. Okay? I didn't know I had my own personal stalker to accompany me to a fucking school, not death row. That should raise a red flag, but regardless, I need to make this stop.

Leaning forward and resting my elbows on my knees, to glare at his fat head until his shit brown eyes meet mine in the rear-view mirror. Usually, I'm timid but, things change and I refuse to back down from my last stock-up before I'm locked away in a school where I have no idea when I'll be allowed to leave campus. He relents, breaking eye contact first.

"Fine, but make it quick. I don't want to turn this into an all-day trip."

Hurrying to cover my smug smile, I grab my phone and slip in my wireless headphones to lose myself in my "Pity Party" playlist. Feeling lost and definitely in the mood to feel sorry for myself, I click "Summertime Sadness" by Lana to have some background music and lay on the seat, propping my feet on the door panel and drown myself in my gloomy thoughts.

At this point, I might as well dye my hair black, get some face piercings and all-black clothes with how life's been going. I snort at the imaginary breakdown my mother, Anna, would have if she were ever around.

This morning when I left, my parents didn't even say goodbye or see their only remaining child off. I woke up to the familiar stillness of the lifeless, cold estate. When I asked Miranda, my mom's assistant, she condescendingly looked down at me and informed me that both my parents had very important, unmovable meetings and had left the night before. They never made time for me, so I wasn't sure why I thought my leave of absence would be any different.

I spent the rest of the morning emptying my stomach in the toilet until only acidic yellow bile remained. I couldn't bear the idea of leaving my sister behind. Or maybe I was throwing up the last remnants of trying so hard to fit in with this family. That's when it hit me. I am truly alone.

It wasn't always like this though. The first time our bond solidified was when Addison saw the bruises on my body and my split lip from our father. Something that day had broken in her. She held me and rocked me back and forth in her arms while crying for hours, as if the pain I couldn't voice aloud was her own. She forced me to sleep with her for a week until I convinced her I would be okay in my own bedroom. I could tell she felt accountable for not being able to fend off the monsters that haunted me.

Shortly after high school started, it got worse whenever I was alone with our father, as if my presence itself enraged him. Simple backhands became full-on beatings. Addison would try to make sure I was never left alone with our father, always putting herself in his path and diffusing the situation before it escalated. As time passed, a sense of responsibility fell on me to protect her, just as she had protected me. Robert got more careful to not damage my face, and I became more cautious and withdrawn to keep her away from the guilt she felt each time she saw me knowing she wasn't able to prevent his bad temper.

By internalizing the pain, I could gather enough strength for both of us. All the times she rushed home from school, skipping practices, staying at home instead of going out with friends to make sure I was safe, sacrificing a piece of myself for her happiness was the least I could do. So, for her, I pretended.

I found a different way to cope. Cutting to bring myself a sense of a different kind of relief. Sometimes to deal with the pain, other times the guilt I had from hiding it from Addi.

My parents have been looking for any excuse to get rid of me, even before Addi. She was the final push they needed to pull the trigger. I tried to be the perfect child. I really did. Not for them, but to shoulder the worry my sister constantly faced on my behalf.

But the more I tried, the more resentment poured from them. I got good grades, but Addison had a 4.0 GPA, so I enrolled for extra credit, which involved tutoring. My sister was a cheerleader, so I joined extracurricular activities. It was never enough.

I wasn't enough.

After hearing the news of my sister's sudden and tragic death... I couldn't believe it. I went straight into denial and currently live there.

One cheerleader had gotten ahold of me that day, asking if I was okay because there was a fire at the school. I knew she was reaching out only for gossip, but she was asking the wrong sister.

I texted and called Addi repeatedly. My messages went undelivered, and my calls, straight to voicemail. My heart beating out of my chest with every unanswered attempt I made. Begging a God I didn't believe in to tell me it wasn't true, only to be met with silence.

When I got to the school, the library was in flames. The sight mesmerized me, in awe of the destruction, the flames licking the sky before putting two and two together. Realizing the severity of the situation when I saw the fire pouring out of the library windows and eating up the sides of the building, with police and firefighters failing to contain it.

I spent the rest of that night screaming and destroying whatever I could get my hands on. Trying to piece everything together to make it make sense.

The thing about grief is it's never beautiful. It's a melancholy that became a permanent fixture, haunting my every step and never letting go. An ache soul deep that never ends.

There are moments when it feels like a sudden, unexpected blow to my chest, leaving a gaping, exposed wound.

Grief is brutal and ugly. Addison's absence left a void in songs. They now lack the magic of her voice. The sun lost its luminance, and the flowers wilt a little more without her presence. At times, her smell taunts me like a whisper. It's by far the most painful thing I've lived through. A black smoke slowly seeping its way into all aspects of my life. The memory of losing everything replays in my mind, as vivid as if it were happening all over again.

I'm in a personal time loop, stuck in my version of hell.

My parents blame me for the fire that I didn't start. Their first assumption was the only person they knew that lived for the havoc and destruction fire causes. They blamed me. My fingers tighten around my phone, my veins fill with bitterness, eating me from the inside out.

The heat wells up in my chest, a rage that starts softly and pulses like its own entity.

I'm angry Addison left me here to fend for myself. She left me alone. She allowed me to love her the way I did, that she became the center of my world and fucking left me here in a world without her. One where I've never had to live a day without her by my side. Her laugh and smile echo around every corner, taunting me with what I'll never have again.

I want to die with her. I want to be buried right next to her in the same soil that will cover both of our graves because we are so intertwined in life that we are in death. So why couldn't she just take me with her one last time? Why —

"Motherfucker! Did no one teach you how to drive? Jesus Christ!" I yell, rubbing a spot on my forehead that bounced off the doorjamb and smacked the back of his leather seat.

Shrugging like he probably didn't just give me a minor concussion, "I told you three times to put your seatbelt on." Does this guy only have two emotions? Asshole or nothing at all? Roughly grabbing at the seatbelt and pull on it until I hear the click indicating I won't go flying out of the windshield the next time he decides to break check me. If I die, it'll be on my terms not some asshole who can't drive.

I snatch my headphone off of the middle seat to place it back in my ear and stare off at the highway through the illegally tinted windows that block out the light, making it look just as dark as I do inside.

PRIYA

HELP I'M ALIVE – METRIC

The car rocks to a soft halt and the doors click to unlock. Taking my time to open my eyes, I unbuckle and raise my arms into an amazing stretch, releasing some tension in my muscles as I sprawl over the backseat.

"How long was I out, Baldie?" Asking mid yawn. Frowning, I pick up my phone to no missed texts.

"An hour and a half. Now hurry up and get your snacks. We have 45 minutes left until we get to the school." He practically growls, irritation rolling off of him. Scrunching up my nose at his attitude, I can definitely see the award-winning personality he has going on.

Letting out a sigh, I slide out of the black SUV, grabbing the precious gift Addi gave me, a mini black backpack with time worn expensive leather and a zipper nearly broken from the grief and anger that threatens to break free.

I take in my surroundings. The hair on the back of my neck stands, accompanied by a prickling sensation that makes my skin feel like bugs are crawling all over me. The sense of eyes watching my every move. Not just being watched. The lingering presence that has me uneasy.

Taking a quick look around, I realize the only things in sight are a run-down convenience store, a pair of neglected gas pumps, and tumbleweeds stubbornly clinging to the pump hose. A desolate gas station in the middle of nowhere with sparse trees scattered around.

This is the beginning of a horror movie. I can feel it.

Approaching the—probably used to be white—building, I tug on the stubborn door. A crumpled missing persons ad with a young girl on it draws my attention. **"Have You Seen Me?"**

Megan Riley, a seventeen-year-old with brown hair, has been missing for four years. It could be my paranoia, but as I look at her, I couldn't help but notice the similarities — curly brown hair, blue eyes, and the same age as I am now. And for me, that is close enough. I've watched enough "Cold Cases" and "Criminal Minds" to make me a detective. Although my personal amount of solve rate of any case is zero.

Addi always teased me for my excessive worrying, claiming that I'd easily succumb to mass hysteria if given the chance. My intrusive thoughts seem to win more times than not, leading me to have hypochondriac tendencies.

I'm not too keen on the similarities of seeing a missing person at a gas station in the middle of bum fuck nowhere that's 45 minutes from the place I'll be calling home for the next nine months.

Feeling my frustration rise, I inhale deeply to regain composure before I lose my shit, exerting all my strength to wiggle the door open, almost losing my balance. The *ding* announces my arrival in this clearly empty store, cue horror music. I straighten myself out and move away from the deserted front counter, making my way through the dingy aisles towards the to the back of the store where the restrooms are located. Immediately seeing the women's restroom, I make a beeline and quickly lock the flimsy, brown door. Letting out a relieved huff of air, a tingling sensation spreads through my fingertips, anticipation building. The 'dirty-rundown store' seems to be an ongoing theme, continuing here in the bathroom.

My gaze shifts upwards, and I can't help but notice the ceiling, a patchwork of holes, pipes, and wires with no cover panels. There doesn't seem to be any fire detectors, which is ideal. Quickly grabbing the matches from my pocket, I take two black paper sticks and snag a couple of cardboard-looking paper towels, then walk towards the grungy sink that could use a deep cleaning.

My hands quiver with anticipation as I flick the comb against the matches. The orange flames leap up, eagerly engulfing both white tips. I carefully place the matches on top of the brown paper towels in the sink, adding some paper from my bag to intensify the blaze. The heat, the smell of sulfur dioxide, and the small flame. A perfect trifecta.

The only thing that could make this better is some gasoline to make it touch the ceiling until eventually, the entire store burns to ashes. A shudder of relief goes through me as I watch it burst up in flames and unceremoniously die down. The worries of my trip washing away momentarily.

See? I set *controlled* fires. I am responsible. It's either this or my blade writing my story through my skin. I'm working on it.

'It' being myself. I'm determined to get clean of both vices. Just a long ongoing process and trying to figure it out by myself is a little harder than I expected.

Turning on the cold water, I empty the nasty basin and wash the evidence off my hands. Someone wrote all over the mirror in black sharpie, "M+O=4ever", and "Call Brad 4 a good time" with his number listed underneath. Through the words, I catch a glimpse of my reflection. I visibly cringe at the thought of looking homeless and repulsive. My mother would be disgusted by my appearance. Sleeping in a car has left my long brown curls disheveled, while my usually lifeless, blueish eyes appear dilated.

Quickly drying my hands, I waste no time in heading straight for the snacks. Hopefully, someone is in the back and heard me come in. It would raise Baldilock's suspicion if I came back empty handed. A small smile tugs at the corner of my lips, thinking of how embarrassing it would be for him to lose his first fight to a seventeen-year-old girl.

Grabbing a few things like chocolate, some chips, and Addi's favorite bottled sweet tea. I head to that section that every convenience store has of miscellaneous stuff. My fingers wrap around the cold metal of the lighter fluid, its faint familiar smell filling my nose. The sound of the can rattles as I wrestle with the decision to take one or two. Throwing in a pack of condoms in case he sees me, not by the snacks. It's better to be safe than sorry, then I make my way up to the register.

An older man limps toward the counter with a stained, worn yellow t-shirt. Honestly, it could've been white in its past life. The sight of his greasy white hair and the gaps in his front teeth immediately draws my gaze. He shuffles his way to the counter. His beady eyes are anything but subtle, openly ogling me. His eyes roam over my figure before settling on my chest, where my black V-neck tee showcases a glimpse of my breasts. Wrinkling my nose at the smell wafting from him, it smells like piss and cigarettes. I'm second guessing my snacks because of the cleanliness of this store and its employees.

"Is there anything else I can get you?" Never once taking his eyes away from my chest.

Giving the politest smile I can muster, "Can I also get a couple of books of matches?" He nods his head while reaching under the counter. I discreetly grab a black lighter and put it in my bag as he lifts his head and sets down two white sets of matches.

"Anything else for the pretty lady?" Ugh, I'm going to puke. Is there a sign on my forehead for creeps?

I clear my throat through the lump forming, "Maybe a little

more… please?" Pulling out the extra cash I've stashed away from tutoring.

Walking out feeling giddy and lighter since the unfortunate turn of events in my life, I jump into the SUV and buckle up to avoid questioning.

Sucking in a deep breath of the new car smell, I look at Baldie, "I'm ready!" Smiling so big my cheeks hurt. With narrowed eyes, *Bald*win puts the car in reverse and we continue on our merry way to my new prison. I pull out my phone and go to Addi's messages, seeing all of my unanswered texts in the past 9 months and still open a new message.

ADDI

One of your hugs would be nice right now. Iloveyou and I miss you. I don't know what I'm going to do without you. Will keep you updated as soon as I'm settled. xoxo

I give my phone a watery smile, remembering when she said we had to spell I love you like that so nothing can get in between us. I miss my sister.

PRIYA

CLICHÉ – SUB URBAN

Pulling up to my new "school", my first impression is it's the prison I've been envisioning, minus the concertina wire that's found on some prison walls. A massive stone fence, at least three times my height, goes further than my eyes can reach, surrounded by trees. The vibrant green moss that camouflages the worn cracks in the stone. A wide open, thick black steel gate swings freely, granting us access alongside a guy stationed in a security booth. I'm barely able to make out his giant shadow that fills the entire area. With a quick pull through the gates, a gasp escapes my lips, audible in the car's silence. This is some Hogwarts shit. A gothic castle-like structure, complete with multiple crooked towers, stands as the centerpiece of the keep. It's hard to believe that this is actually a school. Let's hope no one tries to kill me because I could live without any more villains in my life.

Baldie pulls into a vast stone Porte cochere, its sleek design contrasts with the gothic castle. Baldwin jumps out to open my door. Huh, he didn't have that politeness when I went into that creepy ass store though, did he? Probably only doing it because he is "representing" my father.

"Why thanks, Archibald!" I shut the car door quickly behind me, my tone dripping with sarcasm. He wants to act all proper because we're in front of people with money, so why not give him a fitting name? From the way he's clenching his teeth, it's clear that he doesn't like it, which makes me even more determined to use it. I file that away for another time. It'll come in handy if I ever see him again.

"Someone will be here to collect your bags and bring them to your dorm room."

"You're not coming with?" My arms wrap around myself as I shift my weight from foot to foot. I may not know him very well ... or anything about him, but I mean come on, during these few hours we've grown pretty close, right? Me and Archi had some good bonding on the way here. Did a part of me think that I wouldn't be facing this alone? Yeah, kind of. It seems a bit harsh to drop me off and dip.

The finality of my situation is sinking in. The metaphorical chains clicking in place, tightening their grip on my freedom.

"My job was to make sure you get to the school from your flight. You." He points at me. Then to the castle. "School."

Did you know... that some chips are flammable? They can set a car seat up in flames within a couple of minutes. I never tried it before. I was starting to feel bad for experimenting, but his attitude has me taking back any guilt I felt.

Swallowing the lump in my throat, I manage a shaky smile that feels more like a grimace and start towards the ancient castle. I'm able to procrastinate by taking a minute to appreciate the two massive dark stained portcullis doors with medieval stained glass that span over both openings. Maybe new beginnings won't be so bad after all.

Determined to maintain a positive mindset, I place my hand firmly on the handle, ready to embrace my fresh start. It swings open, barely missing me. A girl with short, icy blonde hair emerges, her face bearing a cunning resemblance to that of a fox. A smile that reminds me of a shark in… a fucking school uniform. She narrows her dark blue siren eyes. Of course, we wouldn't want students to show any sort of individuality.

"Welcome to Cox Academy. I'm Amber Astor. I'll be your guide today for extra credit and then you can feel free to fuck off." Looking down at the crisp paper in her hand and then at her brightly painted pink stiletto nails. My insecurities creep in as I notice my chipped nude nail polish. Then, a car alarm goes off in the distance accompanied by panicked yelling, has me moving toward her. Even though this girl is giving off a 'mean girl' vibes and her presence is smothering. Baldwin's death threat from earlier lingers in the back of my mind, reminding me I have got to get as far away as possible.

Giving her another once over, she seems the type to smile in someone's face, then stab them in the back to rank higher in the hierarchy.

"Looks like you're in the Cox dorms." The distraught voices grow closer to the front of the school gets my ass moving.

How was I supposed to know he'd take forever to see the fire?

"I'll take you over there and then you can get your student handbook. I'm sure you're a *big* girl and can figure the rest out from there." She eyes me up and down, her nose wrinkled as if she smelt something bad. My head jerks back and my eyebrows shoot up at her unexpected hostility. Also, did she just comment on my weight? What happened to "body positivity"? I'm not super model thin like my sister was or even super thick either. My boobs are about a little more of a handful and that's only because I have small hands. My hips are wider than they should be according to the "ideal body". If anything, I would think it's because I slept in the car and was on a six-hour flight. Not my body measurements. Glad to see my mother's voice follows me everywhere. This fucking bitch. I swear she just wants to press my buttons to see what sets me off.

Blinking slowly at her twice, because she must have grown two heads to start a conversation like that with someone she just met. "That's one of the most socially unacceptable statements I've ever heard someone say coming from our backgrounds, and you went with that? You can do better. Next time, try some underhanded comment or insult instead. But props to you, I don't think I've ever made an accurate assumption about someone right off the bat. Glad you could be just as stereotypical as you appear." I sweeten my words with a smile.

Bristling at my comment, Amber takes off at a brisk pace, her uniform skirt swaying with each step. I guarantee she assumed I'd bow down and surrender without a fight. Shaking my head, I continue walking on the cobbled path around the castle, enjoying the peacefulness away from the commotion of Baldwin's shouting from the entrance of the school, presumably from the bag of chips I set on fire in the back of his SUV.

I inhale the crisp air. It's absolutely beautiful. I'm not fond of the outdoors, unless there's a chance to start a fire, yet being surrounded by nature somehow soothes my soul.

The vibrant green of the courtyard grass stretches out before me. The smell of recently trimmed blades filling the air. Trees become more abundant as we get further away from the academy and closer to the dorms. Dark red, yellow, and burnt orange leaves scatter the path to signify that fall is on its way. Amber's slender frame slows as we approach a much more updated building surrounded by more stone walls and a forest of trees. I'm unable to see directly inside. It's likely built of tinted glass, at least three stories tall.

"No boys allowed in the female dorms. The bathrooms are communal. Theodore Hall serves all meals. They check and inspect bags before returning them. But it looks like you're .... on the third floor." Her voice trails off. The wheels turning in her pretty little head, connecting the dots. I'm not well known but my father and his money are. "So, it looks like you won't have to worry about the bathrooms after all." Her voice gets a little more tense as she shoves the paper she was holding towards me, plastered with the fakest smile I've ever seen.

Shrugging and debating on saying 'thank you' out of habit, she walks off instead. Good riddance. She reminds me of this one girl I used to go to school with. Her name was Leticia. I swore she ruined everything. Not on purpose, she just … did. She'd go on group outings, something would always happen, or she'd constantly complain the entire time. Far from the life of the party.

What I really want is to get to my room to decompress from this trip. A hot bubble bath with music sounds heavenly. I make my way directly towards the elevator and press 3. The doors shut and a slim hand with matte black nail polish slips through.

"Wait! Hold the door, please!" she shouts. Startled, I also pointlessly stick my hand out for the door sensor to prevent it from shutting.

"Thanks," she says breathlessly. "You're Priya. Right? The new girl?"

I don't understand people. Do I respond to that if it's clear she knows who I am? Who is she?

"Uh… yeah. That's me." Looking at her uniform paired with chunky black platform boots. They're far from the stilettos Amber was wearing. Her big doe brown eyes lined with thick black eyeliner, the color of hot chocolate, comforting and warm after running inside to stave off the chilly air. It feels homey. A complete opposite to Amber's soul sucking presence.

"Cool! I'm River Walton. Are you going up to 3 too?" I look up at the only lit up number on the elevator showing I indeed did press floor 3. "It's only us up there. They usually give the biggest donors the best rooms. I would've been here sooner to greet you to our floor, but some black car was in flames at the front gate and everyone and their mother had to go see for themselves." Her megawatt smile would be contagious if I wasn't feeling so tense.

The elevator dings and we step out. She takes it upon herself to show me to my room, as Amber Astor should have. There are four doors, two on the left hallway and two on the right. I'm assuming hers is the door that's personalized with an ombré rainbow of colors all the way at the end on the right side of the hallway that matches her bubbly personality, but not the gothic appearance.

She reaches for my hand. I suppress a flinch by clenching my teeth as she drags me to the door across from hers. Soft touches aren't something I'm entirely used to aside from when my sister was being a mother hen and even that has been nine months since it happened.

"I saw them bringing luggage into this room. Do you have anyone to sit with for dinner?"

"Nope." I pop the 'P' while trying to determine her intentions. "Amber gave me the lovely tour to the dorm and it pretty much ended there," I tell her as if I don't care and not like my anxiety is going to put me in a chokehold on the ground like a WWE fighter if I don't figure out when and where I'm supposed to be.

"Okay, I'll let you get settled and then we can meet out here to walk to dinner at 5:30? I'll give you the rundown on everything. Oh, and after school hours and weekends, you can wear whatever you want." Good thing I didn't plan on changing.

Bouncing on her toes, I can tell she's eager. She's cute, in an "I want to squeeze you" kind of way. Her bubbly personality reminds me of Addi. A familiar ache forms in my chest whenever I think of her. Letting some of my appreciation show for her kindness, I softly smile.

"Sounds like a plan. See you in two hours, River."

The RFID locking mechanism looks like the ones from hotels where you place a card on top to unlock the door. I assume the employees finished searching through my belongings and brought them up, leaving the door open. Time to see what my new jail cell holds.

Opening the door, I'm pleasantly surprised. It's like a studio apartment. The interior of the bedroom looks like the inside of a magazine. It's smaller than my room back at the estate, but it's just as updated as the outside of the dorm. The expansive floor-to-ceiling windows on the back wall offer a panoramic view of the lush trees that encircle the dormitories. Off to the left is an en-suite bathroom, which I'm forever grateful for, so I don't have to share with all the other students. Along the same wall is a kitchenette that seems to be stocked. To the right of the bedroom is another door, probably the closet and desk with papers stacked so high it could be its own book.

The bed is staged center to the bedroom, pulling me in like a magnet. On that note, two hours is plenty of time for a nap and I can freshen up after. Walking up to the bed, I face plant into the cream-colored duvet and grab a pillow to put over my head to filter out noise and light. A content sigh leaves me. This is nice. I could probably die right here, right now and be okay with it. Well, anywhere really. This school could be a new start. No one knows me. Maybe my family name and their success. But no one knows Priya Carter, the black sheep and hidden child of the Carters.

PRIYA

Bang. Bang. Bang. I jolt out of bed, causing myself to fall on the floor, knocking the wind out of myself. Gasping for air, my heart is thudding out of my chest, thinking of the last bad thing I did that could have upset him. Trying to take a lungful of air to catch my breath to calm my racing pulse, I go for whispering to myself.

"I'm not home. I haven't done anything wrong." Trying to self-soothe with words while digging my nails into my palms to ground myself.

I'm not at home.

I'm not at home.

I did nothing wrong.

The incessant sound continues. Huffing in irritation, I step to the door, ripping it open. River stands in the doorway bug eyed.

She looks skittish. A frightened kitten ready to spook. I watch her mask her emotions with a pasted on smile.

"Ready?"

Looking at the clock, it's 5:30 exactly. Shit, I should've set an alarm. Guilt stirs in my gut knowing I've frightened River with my misplaced anger.

"Shit, sorry River." Throwing her a smile and pulling on my favorite boots and a hoodie to keep warm. I spot the white key card that locks and unlocks the room and put that in my bra. "Ready." Pasting on my best friendly smile.

River loops her arm through mine and points out buildings, classes, the study hall and eventually where the dean's office is at on the way to Theodore Hall.

"Tomorrow you should have your meeting with the dean for classes. Probably pretty early if you looked over the papers in your room." She looks at me from the corner of her eyes, biting the corner of her cheek, suppressing a smile. I have a feeling she knows I slept the full two hours, considering how flustered I was when I answered the door. The second my head hit the pillow, I was out. The grimace on my face is a response to her assumption. Not the best start to getting ahead this semester.

"Breakfast, lunch, and dinner are all served at the Hall. It stays open at night and you can still get food after. Causal clothes are all allowed after 5:00 and on weekends. You should have five school uniforms in your closet. Any black shoes will work, hence my choice of shoe." Sticking her leg out to show me as if anyone could miss them. I chuckle continuing our walk until we reach the hall. It looks exactly like a high-end restaurant. I had to learn from my sister or when I was severely reprimanded by my parents. Since I was the black sheep, they only brought me out when it was necessary.

She leads me to a secluded table in the back corner, away from prying eyes. It eases some of my anxiety from being singled out. There are a few people scattered around, but most tables are empty. I'm sure they will start filling up as dinner approaches. I've never seen a school cafeteria laid out like a five-star restaurant. Tables with linen cloths on top, rolled and polished silverware.

She grabs the tablet lying on the center of the table and selects something before passing it to me. A variety of foods, desserts, and drinks are all on display.

"You have everything at your fingertips! It's so cool! My freshman year, I was in awe of all the technology they use here."

"I can easily say I've never ordered anything with this level of sophistication," murmuring while mindlessly scrolling through the choices.

"Your figure is important. If you get something greasy, like you're a heathen who is starving, you'll be running it off in the gym for the rest of the night until you've thrown up every calorie you've eaten."

My mother's nagging voice is like nails on a chalkboard, making me feel disgusting for thinking of a piece of greasy pizza. When did I eat last? The plane, I think.

Deciding to take it easy, I choose an avocado salad with lime and a nice large glass of water. Regardless, I'm starving, so anything will do.

My fingers tap lightly on the stiff linen of the table. I need something to take my mind off of my mother. She isn't here. My eyes drift to River, who's oblivious to the internal conflict I'm having.

Breaking the ice, because I'm awkward. "Tell me about you, River." I steeple my fingers under my chin. The most cliche question to ask like I'm on a blind speed date. She takes it in stride and doesn't point out my obvious lack of socialization.

She hums, "My parents are the world's biggest marijuana distributors and were pretty well-known Cannabis Activists until it was legalized. Then they clearly benefited from it. They're hippies, but rich hippies, if that makes sense. I mean, they named me River." Her cheeks tinge a pretty shade of pink at the mention of her name. I think it's cute. She continues, "This may be an academy, but realistically, everyone was sent here as a last resort. The last acceptable school for troubled teens that won't ruin our parents' reputation. I don't recommend asking why people are here. They tend to be a bit touchy about the subject." Clenching my jaw to hold in a scoff, I busy my hands with tracing the cloth napkin of my silverware. My parents really see me as a reject. That feeling earlier with Baldwin? Accurate, to make sure I didn't give him the slip. He was up my ass to make sure I got here. It makes sense now.

I'm being falsely imprisoned for a crime I didn't commit. Lock me away and throw away the key for good measure. That makes me wonder… What is River in here for? Giving her a closer look, she gives off an air of innocence. She looks like she couldn't hurt a fly, let alone commit a crime. Sitting crisscrossed on her chair, big doe eyes, small nose, fragile and doll like.

"So…" River draws out fidgeting with a strand of her straight black hair, "You've met Amber." It's not a question. I told her who 'showed' me around.

"Yeah, I don't like her. She gives off 'pick me vibes' with an inflated sense of importance." I shrug, unraveling my silverware to keep my hands busy. She also made that offhanded comment on my body, but I keep that insecurity tucked away to obsess over later. There's no bigger critic of me than myself.

"Well, we call her and her minion Ember the 'Brr's for the frigid, cold bitches they are." She does an exaggerated shudder, "They don't play nice with others. As evil and vindictive as they come. Whatever you picture, picture that and then times that by 100. So, that's a pretty spot-on observation. They call themselves the 'Angels of Cocks'" I choke on my water, trying to muffle the wheezing and talk at the same time.

"Excuse me? Did you say the Angel of Cocks?" I grab the linen cloth to pat my face. "Like dick?" I manage to get out in between my sputtering. What the fuck kind of girls would want a name like that?

River fails to smother her laughter behind her hands. "*Cox*. Like the founder of the academy. But it could mean that too. They've claimed the 'Demons' of the academy for themselves. Don't look, touch, or talk to them." Air quotes and all, but that gets my attention. Is there a God I should know about, too? What about Adam and Eve? Amused at the fact girls would go as far as to name themselves after men they're tripping over each other for. "Ookay. And these 'Demons'?" I urge her to continue. Waiting for her to elaborate.

"They're the founders' adopted sons. There used to be four. I guess one was accepted to a better school. They're the most delicious, most sought-after men. They have the money, power, status, and on top of all that, drool worthy. Rumors have it they're killers for hire." Now I laugh.

"At 18? If they meet all the checklist rich boy requirements, then why would they kill people for money?" She shrugs a shoulder with a contemplative expression, chewing on her bottom lip.

"I don't know, but allegedly Saint skinned a man alive and left him to bleed out on his front steps for the family to find all because he thought the guy disrespected Crew. And if you take anything from this conversation…It's not to offend Crew or gain yourself the comeuppance of Saint. Sometimes you can catch him playing with his knife. Just twirling it, over and over." She pauses for dramatic effect. I blink slowly at her. That's kind of… gross. The skinning people thing.

Well…there are a couple of people I would like to skin. The dark thought comes as quickly as it goes.

"Anyway, the Brr's call themselves the 'Angels' because they believe they will take at least one of the guys. Wed and bed him, have kids, make it out richer, and all that. Besides, I'd say to watch out for the Demons, but the Angels seem to take it upon themselves to do the dirty work before they've ever had to step in."

Our food arrives before I can ask more questions. The smell of melted mozzarella and marinara sauce from her pizza makes my mouth water as the waiter places my dull salad in front of me. To not feel disappointed, I rationalize my food choices by telling myself I'm not that hungry. Mid bite, the mindless chatter of the groups around us ceases. Looking up from my salad, the hall has grown crowded with people. Everyone's focus is on the two guys who have walked in.

Oh, River forgot to mention there are Gods amongst the Angel and Demon cliques because I've never seen a more flawless human being in my 17 years of life. The first guy walks in with a white shirt and blonde hair that's almost shoulder length, giving off a surfer aura with his broad shoulders and lean figure. His smile has two deep dimples and is so bright that I'm feel like a moth to a flame. Inexplicably drawn towards it, even if it means death, I'd gladly burn alive. The genuine smile he has gives me a warm buzzing feeling inside.

"The tan blonde is Saint D'Angelo. Italian last name, but clearly doesn't look Italian." My eyes move over to the guy next to him. A flashing warning sign is the first thing that comes to mind. Mocha colored skin with dark hair, a jawline sharply chiseled that it could slice through marble like butter.

His dark hair, curly at the top and shaved at the sides. He's delicious, dark and definitely dangerous. Both take their seats with their backs to the wall. Interesting... I'd think they'd take the center table where they can watch over their Kingdom of Hell and survey their cast away sinners.

Finally, a third walks in. I do a double take of him and then his identical replica that joins him at the table. The only thing different is the hair and clothing styles. His hair is more of an undercut with an edgier style, wearing a hoodie and leather jacket over it. I look at River for an explanation.

"Crew and Bennet Demonio–identical twins. Far more unapproachable than Saint. That's not entirely true. Bennett can be... nice?" She cringes as she says it. Leaving me to believe otherwise.

Pieces start clicking together. "As in Demon?" I look over with a bored expression.

"Demon, Saint, the Angels, Cocks. Got it. It all makes sense now." Letting out an unlady like snort, the flames I felt earlier? Doused out with cold water by the amount of importance people place on themselves is the biggest turn off. I have experienced it my entire life, and I'm glad that I am recognizing it sooner instead of being blinded by foolishness.

Men with money always think people should bow at their feet.

Judging from the way they walked in and the way the room stopped for them, I doubt they're any different from the monsters I grew up with. Conversations slowly pick up around us while we finish our food. Amber, my pleasant tour guide, makes her way towards what I'm deeming the "Demons' lair" and puts on a show while she straddles and not so subtly grinds down on Bennett's lap. Or is it Crew? His hands go to her ass and squeeze while pulling her down into him as he whispers something in her ear. She visibly melts against him.

A flicker of annoyance crosses his twin's eyes before he hides it with the mask of indifference that he walked in with. Over Amber's head, the twin grinding her up and down on him throws a wink in our direction. I wrinkle my nose in disgust. Only an asshole would flirt while his girlfriend is dry humping his leg.

Exhausted and ready to collapse into bed, I long for the sweet release of sleep to wash over me. I look over at River's sweet face.

"I'm going to head to bed. Have to meet up with the dean and the jet lag is killing me. Thank you for sitting with me and giving me a proper tour. I mean it." Shooting her a grateful smile. River goes to hug me, and I recoil when her hands wrap around me, pressing into the aching bruises littering my torso. Addi was the only person who's ever shown me affection. My parents weren't affectionate people. I don't think I can recall them ever hugging their favorite daughter, let alone each other. Her brows crease.

"Not a hugger?"

Trying to laugh off the tears welling in my eyes, recalling the last time Addison's arms wrapped me up safely when I dropped her off. "No, but I can be." I stiffly move in for the hug myself. She smells like lavender and honeysuckles. It puts me more at ease to make the first move. Air kissing her cheek, because that's what people do, right? With one last glance at the Demons of 'Cocks', I make my way outside.

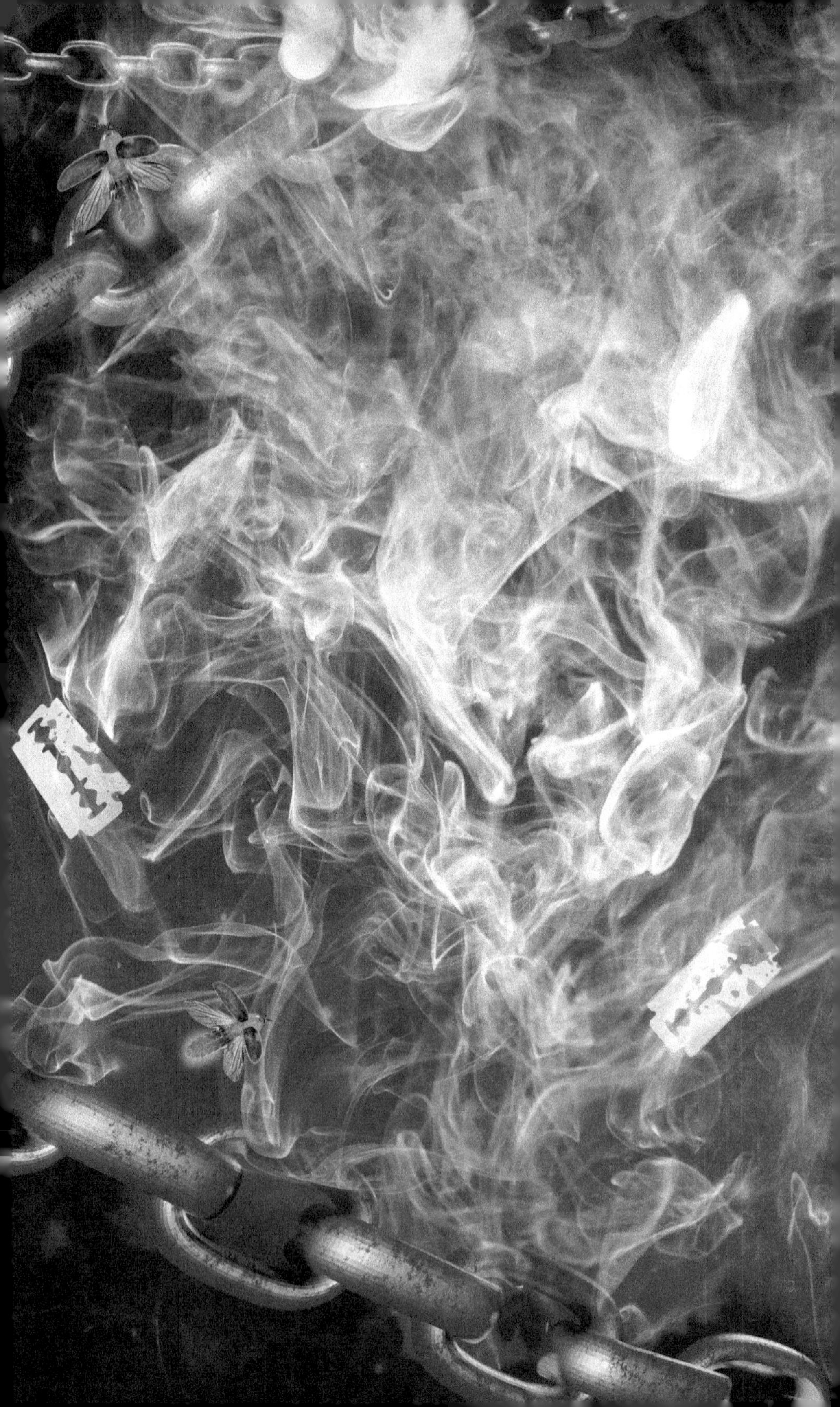

PRIYA

The chilly night air embraces me, nipping at my exposed skin, causing me to regret not bringing a thicker coat. In-ground lights are the only sources of illumination for the cobblestone pathways. The door shuts behind me, silencing the constant chatter of everyone's summer stories. I begin my trek to my nice warm, cozy, and completely silent dorm room, along with a mental list of things I need to accomplish for tomorrow.

I need to go through my manuscript of papers for the school and see what time my appointment is in the morning with the dean. I hope he isn't an entitled prick. That would be a great way to start my school year with an asshole who thinks he's holier than thou.

My mental checklist is interrupted when an arm abruptly yanks me off the path and drags me behind a tree. I let out a shriek that's quickly stifled by a leather gloved hand that covers half my face. A small, sharp object pokes at the side of my throat. Terror has me frozen in place for a second before an eerie calm replaces it.

I don't care if they kill me. Do me the favor and put me out of my misery. Compared to what I endure daily, it would be bliss. Always on edge around people because I have ingrained the belief that every sudden movement could pose a possible threat. The thought of people's hands on me makes my skin crawl. Constantly living in fear.

The perfect contradiction of living without being alive. Pretending to be someone I'm not to people who couldn't care less about me. Pointless conversations about who I am and how I'm doing when no one cares.

Every day is the same, wash, rinse, repeat. I let out a harsh, muffled laugh that makes me sound insane. Who am I kidding? I'm just as fake as all the people I complain about. Can't even properly fake a smile. The irony.

Who would miss me?

My heart stutters, remembering the only person who would care is missing *from* me. Addison.

An irritated sigh leaves me at the obligation to continue on for my other half.

I don't know how much more of this I can do, Addi.

I'm tired of feeling too much or nothing at all. My laughter fades and my thoughts sober. I try to think about what all those shows tell you to do. Usually, they play dead after they've been stabbed, but I've noticed that in most cases, the ones who fight the hardest end up inflicting the most damage to themselves. If I faint, would that work?

The smell of leather, sandalwood, and lighter fluid permeates the air. My mouth waters at the smell, and arousal flushes through my body, sending mixed signals. It's the lighter fluid smell. It has to be. He inhales a path from the base of my neck up toward the carotid artery that houses my fluttering pulse. Pausing to lick the shell of my ear. A shudder runs through my body at the foreign touch. He lets out a dark chuckle at my body's response, leaving goosebumps where his warm breath touches.

"I'm gonna release your mouth if you scream… I'll slit your throat from cheek to cheek. Have you choking on your blood before the first syllable of 'help' gets out." He nips at my earlobe. He has some sort of accent. British? I rack my brain thinking if I've overheard anyone today with anything other than an American accent during dinner. I didn't notice anyone following me outside. I was too busy in my head to take much notice of my surroundings. Pity.

Was he… was he waiting for me? It dawns on me that my razor blade is tucked into the bottom of my black bag in my room. There goes the plan of stabbing my way out of this. My shoulders slump at the difficult situation I put myself in. I nod so he'll release my mouth.

"Hands behind your back." He instructs. At least he smells good, right? I cringe at myself trying to find a silver lining in a shitty situation.

Reluctantly, I slowly place my arms behind my back as he ties them together with no slack. The sting across my wrists has me sucking in a breath between my teeth. In an attempt to relieve the pressure on my wrists, my shoulders are pulled back and my breasts push out.

"Good girl," he praises, petting my hair. I squeeze my eyes shut when warmth floods through me at the approval. Ew. I justify my reaction by realizing I never received praise from my parents that I desperately searched for growing up. That has to be why two simple words are having this effect.

"Why?" I whisper. I swallow when he places the knife back at my throat. Ignoring me, his hand slips up my hoodie. I lean away from his prying hands, resulting in resting further into him. Realizing my mistake too late and giving him better access to dip under my bra and cup my breast. The gloves are icy from the air. He's gentle at first, then roughly twists my pebbled nipple, drawing a shocked gasp from me. I move away from the pain, but his forearm flexes and tightens around my chest.

"Barely anything to grab onto."

My face burns with humiliation. "Then stop fucking touching me!" I seethe between clenched teeth. I can feel his smile through my hair. This is just a game to him.

"I'm more of an ass man. Watching the way it jiggles as I pound into you from behind while you're begging me to stop." He grabs a handful of my jeans, emphasizing his words, squeezing to the point of pain before releasing.

His large hand roams up towards my throat, not enough to restrict my airflow, but enough to send me on the verge of a panic attack to a trip down memory lane. I struggle to breathe, my vision blurs at the edges. Picturing my father's hands around my throat, in front of me, spewing words of hatred before I'm lost in the darkness.

He buries his nose into my hair and then inhales deeply. Is he smelling me?

"You're so much more beautiful than we thought you'd be." His knife traces almost lovingly down my collarbone, pulling me out of my memories. It feels sensual, a whisper on my skin. Wait, 'We'? Who is 'we'?

"But sadder than we expected." His words are like a pebble thrown in, disturbing my calm. The long drawn out pause letting the words settle over him has my hackles raising. His head tilts like he's listening for something. "Your eyes say more than your mouth ever will." Another dramatic pause from him before he continues. "The eyes never lie. A poetic twat. He needs to mend and coddle it better. Attracted to broken things." He shakes his head. The irritation is clear in his tone. This guy is crazy. Certifiably. If there's a 'we', why is he the only one tasked with doing the dirty work? Who are the others?

I strain my ears, listening to hear if there's another person around with us, or even farther away. Only to be met with the chirping of crickets and whispers of the wind on my skin. The hoots of an owl are the loudest, and I count it out twice. Holding my breath, I wait for the third hoot to bring the superstition of death to fruition.

"Are you going to kill me?" I need to know the answer, whether to give myself peace of mind or mentally check to see if I'm okay with it as I claim I am. I'm saved from having to do self-reflection when he thinks it over.

"No, not today, unfortunately. Today is a social call." Relief floods through me. His hand lets go of my throat, wandering down my body to the waistband of my jeans, slowly using the knife to tease underneath the button.

"A reminder that you're exactly where we want you to be." As soon as it pops open, I clench my teeth to keep myself from doing or saying something stupid. We're cheek to cheek. The stubble on his jaw scratches my skin. In tune with how he's clenching his in response, my every exhale he greedily inhales like his own personal life source.

Loosening his grip a fraction, it gives me some breathing room. A jerk of my hair followed by a snip. Uh ouch? What the fuck? I use that minor distraction to my advantage, hopefully making contact with something that'll allow me to get closer to the path of the dorms. Using whatever strength I can muster, I bring my leg forward and rear it back as hard as I can. Only to connect with air. His hand that was unzipping my jeans quickly moves and squeezes my throat much harder this time, while pressure is applied to my pelvic area. A reminder of the sharp knife pushing back into my skin, hard enough to leave a cut. A hiss leaves at the sting.

"I'll give you a reason to scream if you don't stop kicking about."

I struggle against his hold, now banded across my abdomen. His knife sinks in deeper before the pressure leaves momentarily to grab something from his pocket as I suck in a lungful of air. My breaths come out short and shallow. Dread forms a hollow pit in my stomach.

What is his plan? The pain isn't an issue. I can deal with that. It's second nature at this point. Not knowing how far he plans to go, *that* makes my stomach turn. A loud rip and a thud hits the ground behind us. Tape covers my mouth. His arms are a strait jacket wrapped around me, plugging my nose over the tape. If I thought I couldn't breathe before, he *really* made sure I'd have a problem doing so now.

He sinks his teeth into the juncture of my shoulder. I screech behind the tape. He broke skin. My breaths come in ragged gasps, fighting to keep the tears from streaming down my cheeks. "Don't cry, don't cry" is on repeat. Years of abuse coming in handy for once.

"Are you going to cry? I hope you do," he coos. The preparation for this is obvious. My lungs burn, my head is light and dizzy until he suddenly releases my nose. I draw in as much air as my nose will allow, cursing him under the tape. It comes out as nothing other than a muffled complaint, that he blatantly ignores.

His teeth scrape roughly at my pulse point and goosebumps rise across my skin. The bite now feels entirely numb. It has to be bad if it's numb. Or it's the adrenaline masking the pain because he's trying to fucking suffocate me. My mind is slow and sluggish, but every nerve feels like it's on fire. It could be the feeling of being so close to death. It's closer to my sister, would it be that bad knowing I'll see her?

I shake my head at the heady feeling of what he's doing to me. Is it wrong to feel this way?

His hand slowly disappears into the front of my jeans, my stomach erupting with butterflies. The scrape of a pointed edge causes my breath to hitch. Slowly inching lower where no one but myself has been. I focus on a fixed point on the ground to stand stock still. I'm not about to get carved like Freddy fucking Krueger's plaything. He pulls out the knife and brings it to his lips. From my peripheral vision, his tongue flicks out to lick the flat part of the blade. The tip covered in blood where he nicked me. My thighs squeeze together simultaneously, my eyes shut, trying to sort out my body's response.

Removing the knife from his mouth, "Oh? You like that?" There's a smile in his voice. I shake my head like my life depends on it. "Then why can I feel the heat of your pussy through your jeans?" His voice is husky as he whispers in my ear. "Why is your heart suddenly racing?" His tongue pushes against my pulse to prove his point. "Are your nipples hard? I don't like liars. There's nothing wrong with liking it. We all have our own kinks. Yours just happens to be outside in the middle of the woods with a stranger."

My stomach drops. I don't know what made me think he wouldn't notice when every part of his body is resting against mine. Shame burns my cheeks. My brain continues making excuses to exculpate my reaction, anything to not think about his fingers.

"Does it hurt?"

I nod frantically, hoping that'll put a stop to this. "Good." He chuckles darkly. My thighs rub together an effort to alleviate the tingling. His body pushes me roughly against the tree, face first. The hardness hidden behind his jeans pushes up into me, causing a spark to ignite in my core. Putting more of his weight onto my body, the bark of the tree cutting into my skin along with the finger he slowly pushes deeper into the front of my jeans. Inch by agonizing inch.

I stand on my tiptoes to quicken his pace. I might as well get it over with. Then he abruptly stops, sliding to finger the side where the string of my panties rest on my hip. The knife dips into the side of my jeans, nicking the soft skin, leaving a slight tingle in its place before he does the same thing to my other side. The fast movement is far more uncomfortable than the knife. Quickly ripping my panties from my jeans, rubbing against my skin like a fucking rug burn.

My face is the color of a tomato. How horrifying to be pushing him closer to -. I stop, unable to admit to myself what I was doing.

"In case you thought of running to the 'headmaster' as he likes to call himself, you'll find that he answers to us. And you don't want to upset *me*." His threatening words contradict his soft tone. "Or do. I'd like to play again."

Then he shoves me down to the ground. I curl up in fetal position, making myself as small as possible to seem unthreatening.

When what I really want to do is castrate him. Show him what I can do with my razor. He cuts whatever was holding my wrists and I bring them over my head.

"Eventually I'll mark your skin where everyone can see it." Pressing down roughly on the bite mark, I flinch, holding back a whimper. He seems to get off on my reactions. "If it was up to me, we would have had more fun tonight... Next time." He promises, his footsteps slowly recede into the night.

I blink in disbelief.

What the fuck just happened? My body and mind are at war with each other. I don't know what I feel. It was wrong. I want to get back to the safety of my bed to hide from the world. On shaking legs, I hastily zip my jeans since he cut the button off, and sprint as fast as I can to the dorms, avoiding being seen or stopped by anyone.

A cold sweat breaks across my flushed skin as I feel inside my bra. Hoping the key card to get into my room is still there. I slow down when I get to the glass doors that lead to the common room of the dorms. My heart is racing. The feel of eyes on me crawl over my body. The same slimy feeling I got at the gas station. I peek over my shoulder once more to make sure no one is behind me and slink into the safety of the dorms.

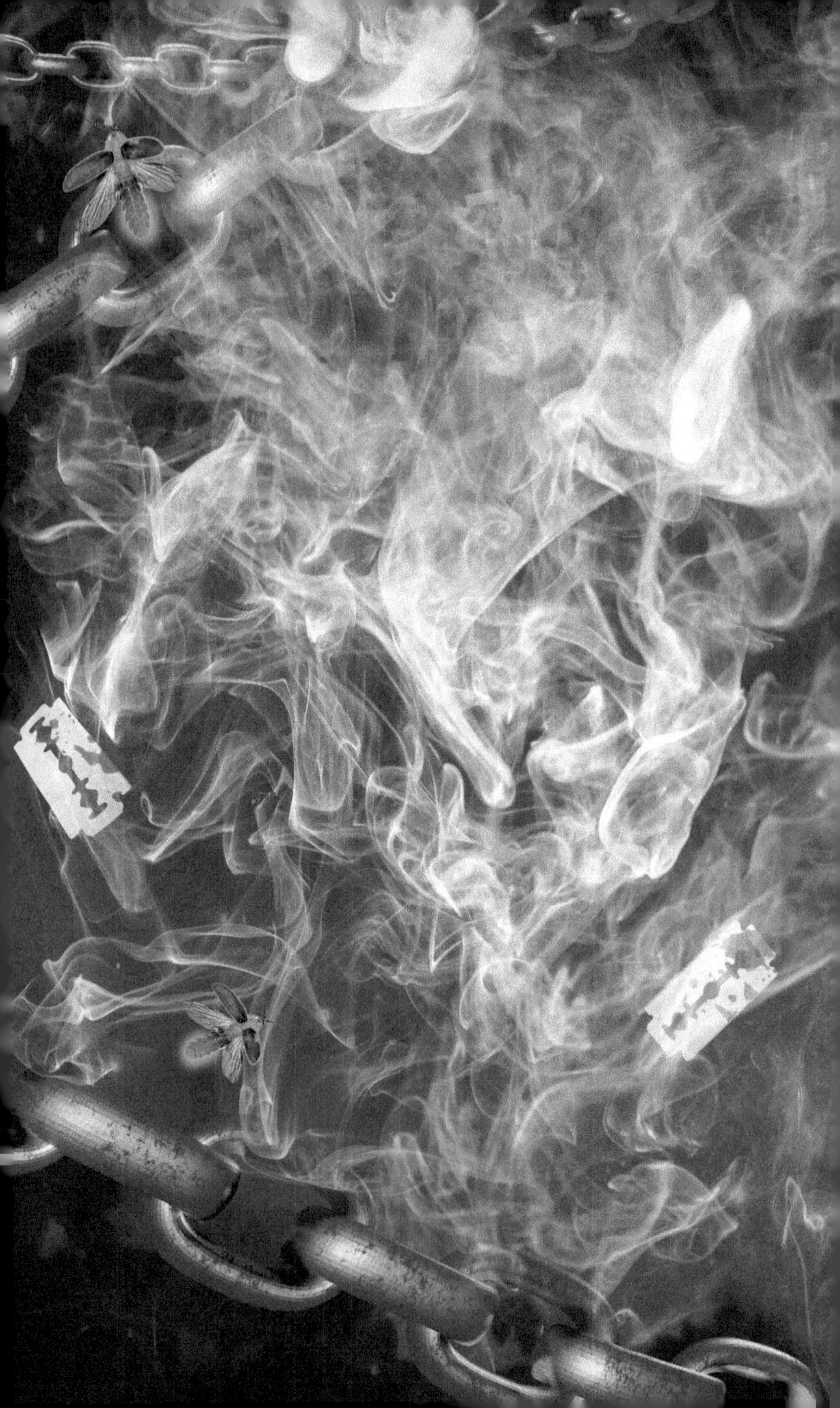

PRIYA

SINNER, PT. 2— PHORA

Conflicted thoughts bounce around my head like Newton's cradle, "for every action there is an equal and opposite reaction". I pass through the doorway feeling like a shaken-up soda. Pressure that's building up inside my head, ready to explode the second air hits.

With shaking hands, I pull my matches out of my jeans, starting clockwise and going counterclockwise to rub at the frayed edges, repeating the action until the elevator dings on the third floor. I peek my head out, looking both ways. I'm not up for any unnecessary surprises or unwanted conversations.

Quietly making my way to my door. The gears click into place, the light on the door turns green. As soon as my hand hits the door, relief washes over me. That feeling is short-lived.

"Hey! Priya! You're back—," River stops. I don't have the

strength or mental capacity to explain or deal with anyone tonight. I push my door open and go to shut it behind me, meeting resistance. My heart races. Is the fight or flight finally kicking in?

I catch my reflection in the window. My eyes widen at the look of my not so clean face. My hair is more disheveled than when I had seen myself at the gas station. Dead leaves and bark are stuck in my hair and clothes. Spinning around, I come face to face with River. Her hand pushes against the door, preventing it from shutting. Her eyes widen and her mouth drops open. She must see something in me that makes her remain silent. It would have been comical if I wasn't so drained.

"That bad, huh?" I say with a halfhearted laugh. She closes her mouth. She gives my body a once over as she takes stock of the visual damage. I've had my fair share of judgment, envy, disgust, admiration, hate, and even snobby sneers from the people I've had to associate with in my "privileged life". But pity is not an emotion I'm familiar with. It makes my skin itchy. Do I really look that pathetic?

She does as she did earlier, wiping off any emotion and pushes inside my room, allowing the door to softly click closed. She heads straight for the bathroom. The water turns on and splashes against the tiles.

I chew on the inside of my cheek, debating on telling her I'm not up for company tonight. She reappears in my bedroom, standing in front of me before gesturing towards the running shower. Taking the hint, I grab my black bag and rush to the bathroom, locking myself inside. The white marble with grey veins reminds me of home. An enormous mirror covers the wall, and I hurriedly turn away from it. I can't stomach to see myself weak.

My mother would be so disappointed, my father furious. What would Addi say? Frowning, I strip off my clothes without looking, reach into my bag, and step into the shower. Grabbing the handle of the faucet to turn the water up as high as it can go. Then, I sink down to the ground to do my ritual.

I swear, I try to talk myself out of it by thinking of Addi, but that only makes it worse. I could be with her if I wasn't such a pansy. We'd be together in death, just like we were in life. I look at my upper thighs. My body bears countless self inflicted scars. The ones from the day my sister left puckering, turning pink and the older ones resembling deep white stretch marks. The familiar sting of the blade pushing on to old cuts brings out a shuddering breath of sweet relief.

How am I supposed to go on when my reason for being here is gone? Knowing I'll never see her smile at me or laugh again? Or even roll her eyes at my paranoia and say I'm dramatic? Who is going to tell me it's going to be okay? Even when I know it's not.

Clinging to that thought. I push deeper on the next one.

I'm so tired. I'm tired of being here. I'm tired of waking up. A sob bubbles in my throat. I taste the salt on my lips, only to realize I'm already crying.

I want my sister. I cry harder and push deeper to form a new line on my skin.

It should've been me. I should've been the one to die.

Another cut for being here.

After everything I've been through, why do I have to live with this feeling of hopelessness and loss? Why me? Why is it always me?

One more for pitying myself.

A relief floods through my veins. My head much clearer than it was before. Physical pain always cancels out the mental anguish I'm suffering through. My gut churns with guilt. Guilt from cutting. For not being stronger like my sister would have wanted.

I wouldn't wish this pain on her, I know that.

The guilt of not entirely hating what happened tonight. Did I like it? Am I mad at him or am I mad I finally felt something other than anger and sorrow? Who was he? It was too dark off of the path and I didn't want to chance looking at his face in case he'd change his mind on wanting to kill me.

Or maybe I didn't want to know.

His accent and his smell. It's so vivid, permanently stuck in my nostrils. I decide to fully disinfect my body.

The next hour I spend washing my body repeatedly, trying to get the feeling of shame to cleanse myself of sin. My head is pounding, exhaustion hits, everything hurts, and I just want to sleep.

I am the epitome of tired. Life was tolerable, at best, when I had a reason to keep getting up every day. I'm tired of pretending, acting like I'm happy when I'm anything but. Begging for the bare minimum of being seen, loved, or cared for. I'm broken down and not even time heals the permanent wounds that never seem to stop bleeding. It's the lack of hope that I'll forever be stuck in this never-ending cycle no matter where I'm at.

There's a soft tap on the door before a lock clicks. At some point I ended up back on the shower floor with my arms wrapped around my knees. Staring at red tinted water being sucked into the drain. River peeks her head around the lip of the wall that's covering me and hesitates a second before walking over and gently gathering my hair to wet it.

"You're getting wet." My voice sounds as emotionless as I feel.

"That's okay. I'll borrow some of your pajamas." Her voice is as gentle as her hands running through my hair and lathering it with the school's soap. I get a lung full of coconut. River clears her throat.

"You don't have to talk about it and I won't pry. But I don't think you should be alone right now. I'm not going to leave you." She states as she conditions my hair. I'm thankful for the spray of the water covering the tracks of my silent tears as the organ in my chest constricts.

Soon after I'm being wrapped in a fluffy white towel. I brace for the nausea that accompanies me as I look at myself in the mirror. There's something to be said about hating myself to the point that seeing my own face makes me ill.

The left side of my face is red from the tree rubbing against it. Indents of teeth are visible, clotted with blood at the juncture of my neck.

My old bruises are on display across my back where River has a VIP ticket to the shit show of my life. I look at River through the mirror. Any hopes that she doesn't know what happened is out of the question.

"Do you want my help getting dressed?"

I shake my head, turning on autopilot. I just want to sleep, sleep the emptiness away.

Gathering the little strength I have to not just take a nap in the shower. I wait until she walks out before digging for a bandage to keep my new wounds clean. Looking around, I spot pajamas neatly folded and laid on the counter. My eyes water from Rivers' kindness. The pain wells up inside me once again.

After disposing of my mess, I gather myself to head to my room where I find River is propped up in the middle of my bed, surrounded by the decorative throw blankets. Her hair in a messy bun and wearing a set of my pajamas, as promised. She pats the bed in front of her, indicating for me to sit and drapes a blanket around my shoulders. River's gentle touch begins to brush the knots out of my hair. She needs to stop being so nice before it breaks me. I don't know if she knew my sister because they're exactly the same person and it hurts.

It hurts so much I want to hate her.

Halfway through my hair, she breaks the comfortable silence we had.

"When I was younger, before my parents came into money. They sold weed to provide for our family, a good chunk of change." She pauses, hesitating, before continuing. "They had a couple of regulars that came around a lot. One was around more than the others and became a close family friend. It started slowly, with a few uncomfortable touches here and there. I thought nothing of it. Rationalized it as accidental. It eventually escalated to where he started to find ways to get me alone. Hide and seek outside, store trips in the car. One night, he snuck into my room, but it didn't stop. Not after the first time, or the second. He kept coming." I didn't realize she had finished my hair and already had it in one braid. As I face her, the sight of her far-off gaze in her wet eyes throw me off.

Softly, I reach for her hand and have her lie beside me, our faces close enough to feel each other's breath. There's no way what we went through is the same. The disturbing feelings I'm emotionally digging through aren't comparable to what she went through as a child.

"It's okay", I whisper. "You don't have to talk about it. I'm not going to pry." Using her words from earlier, hoping it brings some comfort that she won't have to continue to relive her past.

Her eyes are wet as she grabs me and tugs me into a suffocating hold, disguised as a hug.

"I just don't want you to feel like you're alone." She sniffles. "It took me a long time to tell someone. I'll support you in whatever you choose to do." Her warm embrace slowly lures me to sleep. It's almost been nine months since Addi left me, and that was the last time I had any positive physical contact other than a handshake. I would have never thought a stranger could show me so much kindness. My heart squeezes. It's not Addi, but this is the next best thing to feeling cared for. My eyes grow heavy when she runs her hand through the top of my braid and I fall into a dreamless sleep.

MALICE

THE KILL (BURY ME) – THIRTY SECONDS TO MARS

I still smell her on my skin. The sweetest wildflower I've ever smelt. There's a pep in my step and I'm on top of the world. The only thing that could make this better is if I could've witnessed her expression at my favorite knife drawing lines across her ivory skin. My body trembles in delight at the thought of her skin opening up beautifully under it, blood running down her body, my dick throbs with anticipation. One day.

I head to my room on the second floor to beat off in the shower with her sounds and whimpers fresh in my mind. She could've put on whatever façade she wanted. It wouldn't change that, I know. She doesn't want to die. Even though I don't know what she has to live for. Maybe her parent's money or maybe there's something else. Something the Demons haven't looked into.

After the time we spent together in the woods tonight, I don't believe she's capable of what they're claiming she is. Priya lies to herself to get through the day. She's too …soft.

Stepping into my room, I'm met with the twins. Bennett lounges on the bed while his replica sits all prim and proper on a chair. Not even a minute to fantasize about my Little Monster in peace. A name fit for the person she hides inside. Everyone has a darkness lurking inside them, a shadow that sits beneath the surface, waiting to come out and play.

I pass by with the intention of ignoring them and the twenty questions they're going to jump me with. There's something I need to take care of before their shake down. Strutting into the bathroom, I grab the back of my shirt and pull it off in one fluid movement met with two sets of identical dark eyes staring at me.

"Did you get it done?" Crew impatiently prods from the doorway. I toss my shirt and let out a laugh, resting both hands behind my head. There's nothing more fun than getting underneath the skin of the brother with a stick shoved so far up his ass that he has to taste it some days. That's a thought. How long would it take to die from impalement like that?

Usually, it's Bennett's job to poke the bear, but watching Crew get worked up just feels refreshing.

"Is my name Bennett?" It's just as entertaining to plant the seed and water the idea of getting them to bicker. They're easy to antagonize. "Do I look like I fuck around?" Throwing a quick glance at Ben. "You told me to scare her. It's done. Now fuck off." Scoffing at the insinuation that I can't get a job done properly. The twins' have known us since we were 12. A scrawny little kid then looking for a way out. I level him with a look to leave it at that before I stab someone.

Crew throws a glare at his brother. He would have fucked it up, as usual. I admit, I'm good at what I do. Good at taking orders. Bennett must see the impatience on my face, ignoring his brother entirely. He walks up with a shit-eating grin and pushes his hand deep into my pocket to pull out my monster's nude lace panties.

"Did you fuck her?" Crew asks calmly. Bennett's eyes light up. The little wanker gets off on shit like this.

"If you had a certain task in mind, don't be vague next time. I don't care about your need for control of a situation, Crew. I *allow* you to use me for the sake of Saint's best interest. Don't get it twisted where my loyalties lie." I don't owe him or anyone else anything. Not giving him a straight answer to his question will drive him insane.

"What did you tell Saint? So we're all on the same page." Unfortunately, Crew isn't scared of me. We're about the same size, 6'2, and around the same build. It doesn't mean I'll ever stop sizing him up and from the look in his eye, he's always ready for the challenge to draw blood. Aren't we all?

Shrugging, "I told him we were just going to scare her. Reminded him of her purpose and what's been lost. He gets attached easily, saying 'her sadness calls to him'." Saint is gentle, caring, and lives in his own bubble. He's too soft for the things we do. The blood we crave. But he understands the need for revenge even if it isn't the way he would like. "She didn't see my face at all during the... altercation." A malicious smile spreads on my face at the reminder of her half assed attempt to get away. To rile the boys up, I inhale her scent off my fingers before licking up. I didn't quite touch her the way I wanted to, but her skin itself? "Divine as fuck."

Bennett's lips part and his pupils dilate. Snatching the panties from his hands, I inhale them and unzip myself from my black jeans.

"Now, if you don't mind, I have some business to take care of, but you're welcome to stay and watch if you'd like." Giving them a wink, my pants drop. Crew takes the hint while Ben hesitates before walking off, wanting to smell her himself.

Turning on the hot water, I finish undressing and look in the mirror. Scars mutilate my body, from my throat to my legs. Ink covers most of them from Saint's eyes, but the memories are clear as day. Everyone who knows about us considers me to be a psychopath. Some have said I was a sociopath. There is no conclusive evidence or medical decision that's been made. Having to live through what we have, I couldn't protect Saint through everything in our past. I think that's the closest thing to regret I'll get for anyone. That's a feeling, right?

Bringing her panties up to my face, I turn and get into the shower, my thick length throbbing for attention. One last inhale, I fist my cock, running the rough fabric of her panties over my hot, hard flesh. I squeeze to relieve some of the pressure. Creating a slow building ache that spreads through my body. I'm going to destroy her. She'll be done when *I* say she is. Her screams and tears will be owned by me. Once the guys get their head out of their asses and realize their misguided intentions, it'll be too late. Fuck, she's going to be more of a problem than we expected. It's going to be fun to watch the chaos she'll cause.

PRIYA

UNDER THE BRIDGE – RED HOT CHILI PEPPERS

An alarm blares in my ear. Reaching over to snooze it using the button on my phone, I click it twice until I hear the screen shut off. With a grunt of frustration, I raise my head when the sound continues. The noise finally shuts off. Falling back on the pillow, I contemplate my existence and wonder if it would be so bad to drop out of school and live on the streets. My parents will disown me either way. A stripper? I hear they make good money. The scars on my thighs might disgust a lot of people. I'll think about it. Put a pin in it.

The bed dips down and the scent of coffee wafts in front of my nose. "Mmmmm. If this is how you wake me up. You can just move in," I tell River.

"Goooooddd morning sunshine!" Oh God. She's a morning person. I cringe mockingly, making sure it's noticeable behind my first sip of coffee. Which earns me a beaming smile in return. With how bright and happy she is, she looks like sunshine. Does she look like that when she wakes up? A model. Pretty sure I look like Anna from Frozen, hair everywhere, drool running down my face.

"I took the liberty of finding out your appointment time with the dean and set my alarm. I laid out your school outfit. I'm not sure what you want for breakfast—" My hand up, I stop her because first thing is first, I need at least a couple sips of coffee before I can face today and pretend like last night didn't happen. Sweeping it under the rug is the healthiest way, right?

"You're doing too much." A little light fades from her eyes. Her sad eyes make me feel bitchy. After last night, I can tell she has a thing for taking care of people. "It's not a bad thing." Quickly trying to amend my statement. "Coffee is my breakfast…" There's a good, awkward pause. The one where I'm trying to fill in the blank with something. I lean towards honesty. "I'm just not used to it. Thank you…" Those words are definitely in need of dusting off. "For the coffee and making sure I make it to the dean on time." I give a small smile.

"I can tell you're not used to being taken care of, but that won't deter me. Get used to it." I tilt my head, humming my agreement. I don't take her statement to heart because I've learned that no one stays around long enough.

"Coffee or an energy drink is my breakfast usually. It's quick and gets me out the door faster." And away from my parents' wrath. "My favorite color is pink, but the baby pink. Not that hideous hot pink. I'm a loner and I hate being around people." I figured if she's going to be around, letting her peek into my head *a little* wouldn't hurt. As long as it's nothing too detrimental. I'm used to dealing with mean girls and hostile people with ill intentions. I've had no one take an interest in me or go out of their way to make sure I'm okay, other than my sister, of course. Having friends would mean more secrets and lies to cover up for my father. I'd rather suffer than benefit my father in any shape or form.

Allowing myself to make a friend… that's unfamiliar territory. I hope this isn't a trick. A frown pulls on the corner of my mouth.

After 45 minutes of trying to tie a damn school tie, and three seconds of River tiring of my attitude. Like when I'm putting my hair up in a bun and can't get it quite right and I get so pissed off my blood boils? That's where I'm at. At that point, she stepped in and seven movements later, she was tightening the black and green plaid tie.

I check myself out in the mirror that came with the room, and the collar of my fresh white button-up that completely hides my bite mark. Accompanied by a black high waisted skirt, the hideous tie, and my black Mary Jane chunky heels to complete the look. It's ingrained in me to dress up and play a part. River dresses comfortably. I glare at her outfit longingly on the way to the door. I make sure to grab my black bag this time. Wishing we could switch places. My look isn't as sneaky as I thought.

"You're a new student and knowing who your family is, I'm assuming being the show pony isn't far off. So, while you're uncomfortable…" She trails off when we reach to the elevator to get to the first floor. She clicks the ground level button as she continues, "I will be suffering in my pajamas. I'm doing this for you, otherwise, I would be laid up comfortably in bed binge watching '*That 70s Show*' high off my ass on edibles." I tsk as the elevator door dings and we step off into the common area. Before I can come up with a smart-ass retort, we're stopped by my pleasant tour guide, Amber Astor.

It's too early for the snotty look on her face and the words about to come out of her mouth. She is the type of girl who refuses to leave anywhere without makeup on. Not a hair out of place on her head as if it was hair sprayed that way. Her makeup is flawless. The "fuck me" red lipstick she wears is difficult to miss.

"Already cozy with the lesbian of the school, I see." Amber

gives River a once over before dismissing her and angling her body to me. Anger heats my body at the cold shoulder River receives. River looks ready to fold in on herself. I have to say it doesn't suit her bubbly personality and that pisses me off more.

"Good morning to you too, Amber. Glad to see you woke up on the right side of the bed this morning." River shoots back at her.

"I was talking to Priya," she sneers.

"Be careful. Your face will get stuck like that." God, I sound like my mother. I grab River's hand and walk around the eerie carbon copies to move on with our day, knowing I'm damn well not going to be late over anyone's cattiness. Before we breeze past her, Amber's arm shoots out, jerking River to a halt. My eyes widen. Who the fuck does she think she is?

"Make sure she knows the rules, dykopath or neither of you will like the consequences." The threat is obvious. River shakes her off, pulling me to the door that leads outside as if nothing ever happened.

She's going to let her talk to her that way? I stare at River. Really take a look at her as we're walking. She puts on a brave front, but at times she seems timid. Outgoing when she needs to be. I'm not one for confrontation unless it's someone I care about. She's a gentle soul.

"I understand if you don't want to hang out with me." She won't look at me, opting to stare off into the distance. Her sadness encompasses me like it's my own and maybe it is.

"What are you talking about? Because you're into girls? What does that have to do with me? You were a lesbian before me. I don't swing that way, but I'm not going to treat you differently. You did more for me than anyone has last night. Actions speak louder than words and yours were deafening." I give her a reassuring smile. Comforting people isn't a strong point for me. I slip my arm into the crook of hers and continue to the dean's office.

"Now, what was she talking about 'rules' and 'consequences'?" I mock Amber in a deep, ominous voice.

BENNETT

MEMORIES! – 347 AIDAN

My mind wanders away from the irritability with my brother as the permanent marker in my hand sketches away my worries.

I remember the first week I was separated from my 'older' brother, by 4 minutes, but "every minute counts". Cue the eye roll.

I'd always been his shadow. It's never bothered me because that's where I was comfortable, safe, and protected. The hopelessness that accompanied being ripped away from my literal other half, my protector. That was damaging.

That's when I had to learn to survive. I clench my fist around the marker, my knuckles ache, thinking of our abusers. Some people survive to grow from it, and others survive and silently fight their inner demons. The latter has worked for me. Well, personally, I like physically fighting it out with my demons.

Mostly, I take it out on Crew. They say, "You're the most hurtful to the people who you know will love you unconditionally". I know he was a victim of the same circumstance as I was. It wasn't his fault, not really. When everything I knew was ripped away from me, I did whatever it took to make it through.

The door clicks shut and the room's energy shifts. Nervousness pollutes the air. Taking a deep inhale, relishing the smell of fear. Like a shark drawn to blood in the water. The school's dean clears his throat.

"Mr. Demonio! To what do I owe the pleasure of your presence?" Barely refraining from rolling my eyes. He's always given me a bad vibe. Crew swears he's good for our cause. That he'll be helpful to us as long as we can use him.

"Brian!" I clap my hands together with false enthusiasm. "Have a seat." I point to the uncomfortable student's chair across from me. Quite the cozy setup he has here. The leather winged back chair is more than comfortable. Under different circumstances, I might relax in it.

That's a lie. I'm not good at staying still.

A single floor to ceiling window is the only outside source of light. It seems more opulent than it really is. He's even added a little chandelier.

My eyes flick up to meet his. Sweat covers his upper lip and forehead. Why would he be sweating if he's done nothing wrong? Sitting back, my eyes narrow in suspicion. I scan his office, looking for anything that appears out of place.

"I'm here to remind you of our agreement regarding our new student." Relief flashes through his eyes and his posture relaxes. My lips purse, interesting. "All discipline will be approved through us. Her whereabouts reported to us. Her medical records and her class schedule need to be sent to Saint." I continue to use his desk as a canvas. "Anything other than doing so will cause a rather unfortunate outcome." Not that unfortunate. Killing him might be what I need.

I give him my charismatic smile, one that comes across as easygoing, but this isn't an option or even a suggestion. This is a delicate operation. I'm not about to let this idiot fuck up everything we've worked for. The number of favors that had to be called in. The strings that had to be pulled. "It would be a shame if your wife found out you were bending the nurse over your desk every Thursday during your weekly 'meetings'." I stopped fucking her when I caught wind of Brian's interest in her, which helped in our favor with blackmail to ruin his primary source of income.

His wife, Maria, is a beautiful Mexican woman. Crew said she's in with the Mexican Mafia. But he wouldn't give me any more details than that. I doubt Maria's crazy ass would be happy to hear about his extramarital activities.

He gulps loudly in the otherwise silent room. The sweating has begun again. Applying the finishing touches to my drawing, I sit back and admire my work. Satisfied with an explicit depiction of his sweaty ass nailing the nurse over a desk in a 1950s nurse outfit for all to see. In case they weren't sure who it was supposed to be. I stand to leave with the mental list of Crew's tasks for the party tonight.

"I don't need a reminder of what's at stake." He seethes. The anger quickly concealed. He's going to be a problem. I'm calling it now. One that will be fun to get rid of.

"We sign your paychecks that keep your lifestyle and …. Extracurricular activities sustained. Don't think the nurse is the only one we know about. You're replaceable." My voice turns cold to solidify the end of our conversation.

The door clicks shut behind me and I pull out my phone to update Saint on my progress and whereabouts. If I were to respond to Crew's million texts, it would take away the satisfaction of driving him crazy by *not* answering. I roll my eyes at his latest batch of texts, asking if I'm ignoring him. I take my time exiting out of my brother's texts to click on "Nehalem," smirking at the nickname. I think I'm pretty clever. It's suiting with the whole biblical shit the school has been going on with for years. Nehalem, the spawn of an angel and demon.

BENNETT

"Headmaster" is aware and enlightened.
Keep an eye on him, something isn't
adding up.

NEHALEM

You mean the dean? Is it bad?

Is it bad? No, it's nothing Saint couldn't handle. No matter how much I secretly despise Saint for taking my brother away from me and inserting himself as my *twin's* best friend, he still is the one that holds us together. Malice, he's the extra baggage that came with our long-time friend. He kind of grew on us, like herpes. Sometimes people forget it's there and then *boom!* It just pops up out of nowhere, reminding us he never left just, slumbering temporarily. That's what Malice is. That little bugger just keeps popping up and we can't get rid of him. On the other hand, he's helpful, more times than he's not. He can stomach the part of our job that Saint could never do.

BENNETT

He seemed … sweaty, I think he's doing
something. And not just the nurse. He
might be a problem, let Crew know.

NEHALEM

Got it, I'll look into it.

BENNETT

Wait, why can't you let Crew know?

Before I go into more detail, a small body bounces off of me, and my arms automatically shoot out. "Watch where the fuck you're going." I growl. Taking my agitation with Brian's slippery self out on whatever unsuspecting soul has crossed my path.

My arm wraps around a tiny waist. The other steadying her to keep her from tipping over. A whiff of something floral and clean with a hint of coconut. Summer.

"Whoa, there. Are you okay?" When I realize who it is, I

switch my tune to mock concern. Wide, bright, teal-colored eyes with green near the iris stare up at me.

"Oh my gosh. I'm so sorry," Priya sputters.

My hand travels up to finger a piece of curled chestnut colored hair. Her body tenses at the contact. The pulse point in her neck is fluttering, affected by our proximity. Her hair is like silk. The feeling is pleasant, almost comforting. She's a tiny thing. I tower over her by almost a foot. I contemplate on how to play this. Being sweet would reel her in faster or I could off the bat be an asshole. The former would work better in the long run.

"Where are you headed to in such a rush?" Crew set up her meeting with Brian. I'm just here to play a part.

"I have a meeting with the headmaster. I'm running late." She answers shyly. Refraining from rolling my eyes at Brian's self-appointed title of "headmaster" because it sounds more opulent to him. Instead, I focus on her. Freckles dot her nose and cheeks, her full, pouty lips pull down into a frown. She has an ethereal beauty that reminds me of innocence and purity. Like an angel.

But even Eve sinned for Satan.

My thumb makes circles on the small of her back, attempting to entice her.

My next move usually does the trick. I give a half smile, enough to where my only dimple on the left side shows and look at her lips before moving in a little to close the distance. She licks her lips and gently clears her throat before anger enters her delicate features.

"You can let go now. Thank you…" Asking for a name without asking. Taken aback by her request, I give a rough tug on the strand of hair I have wrapped around my finger when I really just want to wrap my fist around it, then carefully release her and take a step back. I can still save this.

"I'm Bennett Demonio." Her eyebrows raise.

"That makes sense."

My brows furrow confused, "What does?"

"The fact you think your charm or your looks would get me to do anything other than thank you." She finishes with a scoff. I can confidently say I've never been turned down, regardless of single or not, young or old. I'm easily able to manipulate people into doing what I want, mimic who they need me to be.

Challenge accepted.

Giving my million-dollar smile that's gotten me far and move out of her way with my arm out like a grand gesture.

She brushes past me. "Your girlfriend wouldn't appreciate that." She mutters under her breath. I let out a little of the hatred I have for her show through my eyes. She wants me to be an asshole.

"I'd be careful who you run into. Everyone is a wolf in sheep's clothing. It'd be a shame to see you broken so soon," I murmur as I walk towards my one true love, Mindy.

PRIYA

Speak of the Devil and he shall appear. After the initial shock of face planting into Bennett, it quickly morphed into annoyance. The warmth of his hand seeped into my tense muscles. The rubbing luring me to a false sense of security. Having daddy issues followed by lack of physical affection, it seems I'll take any "nice" touch.

Shaking my head, I may want love and attention, but I'm not stupid enough to go after someone who sleeps around with anyone who has a vagina. I'm better than that. After going without sex for all my life, I'm not about to give it up to the first person who shows me an ounce of attention. The audacity of him, being that close when he's dating Amber. Makes my blood boil.

I'm pretty sure this violates Amber's rule of "leave my boyfriend alone". But to be fair, he ran into me. I didn't ask for his nearness to linger any longer than a deserved "sorry". The shock on his face that I didn't just drop my panties was hilarious. It must not be a response he gets often. He's manipulative. Slipping on different masks. I don't care to know what all of them are.

River's speech was, 'The Demons are off limits and anyone who disobeys gets a lashing from the Angels'.

Good thing I plan to stay far away from them. The type to ruin anything they touch. The goal is to keep my head down and mind my business.

I knock on the door labeled "Dean Bush". Why the hell have I been calling him "Headmaster"?

"Enter." Walking in with my head up, these people feed off of fear like a wraith in waiting. Everyone at this school is ready to pounce on any weakness. "Please sit." Headmaster or the Dean patiently waits until I'm seated. Off the bat, he makes me uncomfortable. His dark, beady eyes remind me of my father's associates. Greed lies behind his authority. He's heavier set, no chin and his head has been eaten by his neck. His smarmy smile only makes the pedophile mustache more prominent.

"I just wanted to give you a personal welcome, along with your class schedule." He pushes a paper in front of me. I reach forward and his hand brushes against mine. I seal my lips closed. Repulsed at the feeling of his touch.

"None of these are remotely the same courses I was taking at my previous school." His face transforms from trying too hard to be welcoming to huffing and narrowing his eyes.

"We both know why you're at this school. This is a last resort before you're disowned or in prison. What were your charges?" He pulls out a file that I'm assuming is mine. "Two counts of involuntary manslaughter and..." His sausage finger pretends to search my file. "Ahh, yes. Aggravated and reckless arson. Does that sound right?" I bite my tongue to refrain from defending myself. It hasn't helped yet. Both charges contradict each other. But no one will listen. Especially when I'm sure almost every person in this shithole says, "It wasn't me!" I cross my arms across my chest, finally getting away from the sliminess oozing from him, to sit back and listen. That's what they want from me, right?

"I won't tolerate any fires on school grounds. Doing so will result in you serving your full sentence presented by the court. Miss Carter, acting accordingly, is expected. And in this school, being saved multiple times won't prevent your consequences from catching up with you."

With a tense smile, I appease him. "Of course." I'm hoping I don't have to pay him any more visits. He's not the worst I've had to deal with. Lingering looks and touches are already enough. Let alone having to be in his presence more than necessary. "Is that all?"

Happy with himself like a kid at a candy store, "Yes, that'll be all. Please see yourself out."

Scooting my chair back to stand, I spot a crude drawing on his desk. Squinting to make out the picture. A large man with a pig nose and tail, shirtless with only a tie on, his pants and underwear are around his ankles. A nurse is bent over, holding onto his desk and a word bubble hovers over her head. "Your three inches feels so good, Headmaster!" Glancing up, his face is flushed red and then down at the gold band on his finger. He rushes to cover it. The inside of my cheek bleeds from preventing the laugh that threatens to escape as I rush over toward the door. Of course, this sleazeball would step out on his poor wife. Disgusting.

The door shuts behind me. I'm immediately face to face with River, who's buzzing with excitement. Her eyes are lit up, bouncing on her toes. She grabs my arm, practically drags me outside, opposite the dorms.

"So, tonight is a party thrown every year to start off the school year. Everyone is invited." I put my hand up to silence the word vomit. I'm not going. I don't do parties, and I tell her so.

Her eyes narrow. "We're going." Her tone has no broker for arguments. I try to think of a good enough excuse to get out of it. I don't like to be surrounded by people. They're unpredictable, and dangerous. Plus, someone sent us all here for something. A bunch of criminals banded together sounds like a disaster waiting to happen.

Cringing, "Riv, the party scene isn't for me."

"Priya! It'll be *so* fun! We're going together and that's final. Plus," she adds in a little voice, "it'll be my first time not going alone."

I chew on the inside of my lips, giving her the side eye, way to work me. It's hard to tell her 'No' with her big puppy dog eyes. It might have a little to do with feeling like I'm in debt from last night. I hesitate but decide to give in. Do I want to go? No. I also don't want to leave her alone after what happened this morning with Amber. The thought of her not standing up for herself makes me uncomfortable. Caring for someone else's feelings has me uneasy.

I relent, "Fine, I'm only going for a little and then I'm leaving." She starts dancing, which is alarming itself. "As long as you stop doing that!" Giggling, she slips her arms into the nook of mine and begins chattering about getting ready. At the ass crack of dawn.

"Okay, we have to get ready. I have the perfect dress for you to try on. There is food in my room. I've been on a Ramen and siracha kick…" her voice trails off as we pass the trees from last night. My body lights up with awareness. A slideshow of porn and dirty images flips through my mind.

"Hey!" River drags my attention back to her. She flicks her gaze into the woods and back to me with concern.

"You okay?"

Clearing my throat, "Yeah."

Her eyes turn to slits, unbelieving.

Laughing it off, "I'm fine. Just tired. I think I'm going to need a nap. Last night wasn't enough." Sleep is always a good excuse to get out of things. We make the rest of the way in silence, soaking up the morning rays of the sun peeking through the clouds.

Clicking the third-floor button, realizing I don't remember walking through any doors.

"Where are we?" Stunned, I haven't thought to ask before I was dropped off here and forgotten.

"In Maine. Somewhere past Port Clyde, hidden away." She turns to give me a hug before pulling back.

I smile and move on. She squeezes me tightly before retreating into her room. Letting out the breath I was holding, I step into my room when something on the floor catches my eye. A small black envelope with blood red calligraphy. My hands shakily go to open it. Foreboding skates up my spine.

What does someone else take before you can get it?

Wiping my hands on my skirt, the fabric sticks to my sweaty palms. I don't understand. I reread it at least a hundred times. My brain trying to piece together the meaning. Spinning around my room to make sure everything is where it should be. My heart skips a beat when I see the only physical copy of a photo my sister took of us. The night of my 17th birthday, after a horrible dinner party for my father's business associates. I was bummed because I secretly held out hope we could do something together as a family, like I pathetically do every year. Even though I never spoke it out loud, my sister knew. She always knew.

The last picture we took together when she took me to her spot for the first time.

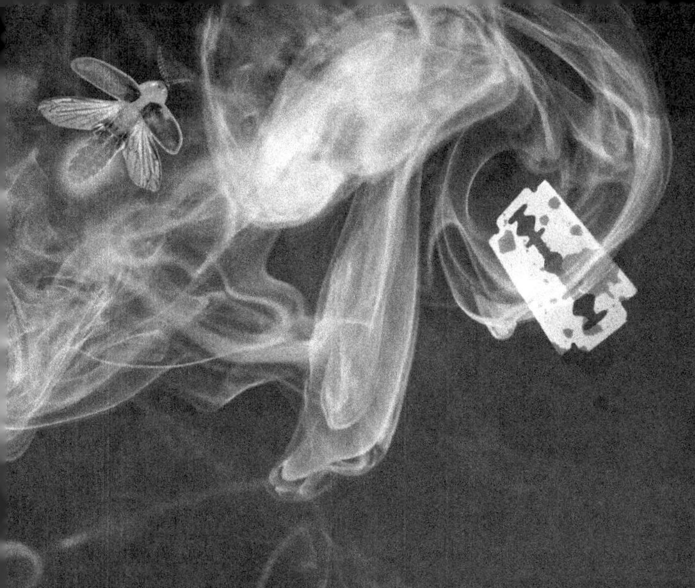

PRIYA

We had just made it through the clearing, the moon illuminated the cliff's edge. As we neared closer, she closed her eyes, breathing in deep, taking in the smell of pine trees and the earth after a rainstorm. The sparkling from the stars reflecting off of the water gave off an otherworldly feeling of peacefulness.

"Yugen." I place my hands over my mouth to whisper like a secret.

"Hmmm?" Addi opens one of her eyes, a hint of a smile playing at the corner of her naturally pink lips.

"It's a Japanese word. Sometimes the world is so intense that the words we try to use to convey what we're feeling aren't able to be said. But you can feel it. It's indescribable."

She hums her agreement "Is that your word of the day?"

"I think it has to be." I take another moment to admire the beauty of my sister. Her eyes closed and face tilted upward to the moon. Her light blonde hair, which is lightly rustled from being kissed by the wind, is out of its usual updo. She looks to be at peace for the moment before her brows furrow, looking troubled. She reaches for my hand, intertwining our fingers, staring out over the water.

"Firefly?" I roll my eyes at the nickname she gave me when I was six, pretending that it bothers me. But I love being special to her because she's everything to me. She said I'm her light in the darkness. I give her hope. Which is ironic because she's mine.

"Do you ever feel so twisted up about something? You know what you have to do. But you're scared?" Her voice breaks, spoken so softly that it feels like it's a confession. My body goes taut at the pain radiating off of her. I'm scared to ask a question that I'm not sure I want to know the answer to.

"That's called bravery, Addi…" I shrug. She's the bravest person I've ever known.

"I'd do anything for you, you know that, right?" She takes my hand and gives three squeezes for 'I love you,' something we've done since we were little. "For you to be happy. Even if the cost was myself. I know you think you have to hide things to protect me. But I'm supposed to do that for you. I'm your older sister. You've always held me as untouchable, invincible even." Silent tears stream down her face at the confession. Alarm bells are going off in my brain. Every hair on my body is standing on edge.

"Addison!" She ignores me and continues to stare ahead. "Addison! Look at me!" I all but scream. She's scaring me. There's been nights where we've held each other and cried. Where she promised everything would be all right, tracing the veins in my arms until I fell asleep. This feels different. Like a goodbye.

"You can't break up with me. We're sisters." My voice wavers. I search her face as a gentle smile appears. "There's no me without you. We're two peas in a pod. I can't do this without you. You've lived without me, but I've never been in a world without you." I stare harder at her to force her to feel my feelings. The ones I have a hard time saying but, hope she can see.

"I'm scared," I whisper. "You're scaring me."

She pulls me into a bone-crushing hug that takes my breath away, but I return it all the same. She's only an inch or two taller than me. Her lips kiss my hair and I breathe in her lavender and coconut scent.

"Don't leave me here." The whimper works its way up my throat.

She backs up and looks down at my pinky finger extended and my thumb out like a "hang loose" sign. Wrapping her pinky around mine and kisses her thumb to meet mine over the top. I repeat the gesture. We've done this sacred pinky promise since we were little. For as long as I can remember, she's never broken a promise. She leans in conspiratorially. "Want to do something crazy?"

Actually, yes. Anything to get out of this depressing mood. I nod vigorously. She undresses to her bra and panties. I look around towards the pitch, black trees behind us, thinking of all the marks on my body. Contemplating if she'd be able to make them out in the moonlight, before doing the same.

She grabs my hand again. "Don't think. Just do."

Adrenaline pumps through my veins. Anxiousness, nervous jitters, and pure excitement are all in the pit of my stomach, building up and radiating throughout my whole body. My breathing picks up. I know what she's thinking.

"One..."

Dizziness from the excitement begins. It has to be about a 60 foot drop. My muscles twitch in anticipation.

"Two..."

My heart is a steady drum in my ears. We take off, running toward the edge of the cliff.

That saying, "If your friend jumped off a bridge, would you?" And the answer is to scoff like it's the most ludicrous thing to say.

I wouldn't if a friend did. But I'd follow her to the ends of the earth. Bridge included.

We leap off the edge. My mind goes blank when the wind rushes past my ears. Thoughts of my sister's words, my shitty parents, or even the fact I've never had a birthday aside from my sister making it everything I needed it to be, is absent. It reminds me of a rollercoaster. The free fall of my organs plummeting.

When the freezing October water, our hands are ripped apart from the impact. I let my arms drift around me, my hair floating up from my quick descent into the water. I sit still for a moment, allowing the belly of the water to hold me as I settle.

If only it could always be like this: calm, peaceful. No fear hovering over me, constantly looking over my shoulder. No disappointments and expectations. What a wonderful way to feel, just nothing.

The moon is a beacon, calling to me. I stay seated in the water until my lungs protest for air. The burning pushes me forward. I break the surface, letting out a loud whoop of victory. Then dissolving into uncontrollable laughter of the fear I didn't realize I had. I'm met with Addi's responding laughter as she drags me back up the rocky slope of the cliff. She takes a picture of us, pure joy and happiness. Unburdened, unlike she was moments ago.

My breathing comes out in rapid, shallow pants. My face is numb, and I'm on my knees, rocking back and forth. Telling myself to breathe as if I'm not already trying to. Addison's face the day I dropped her off is burnt into my mind. My fast-paced breathing turns into choking sobs. I can't think straight. The ache in my chest feels as open as it was the day it happened. A gaping wound that never healed. It hurts. It fucking hurts to think of her.

This is a sick joke. I don't know who knows about my sister, or why they would think this is funny. My anger quickly takes over my sadness with the cruelty of someone who clearly knows no loss. I sneer at the card and shove it in the drawer of my nightstand. I'll figure it out, and when I do… I'll decide then. It's better not to act in the heat of the moment. But that's all I have. If not anger, then sadness. Maybe I'm overreacting and River went through my things. I'll ask her and until then I'll busy myself by unpacking my room a little more. River will be ready soon. Before I unpack, I pull out my phone and start my daily undelivered text to my sister.

Amentalio. That will be our word for the day. It's the sadness of the realization that you're forgetting memories of someone who's no longer here. The days pass and I'm fighting myself to remember the sound of your laugh. Was it high pitched? A cackle like a witch? Did it always reach your eyes?

I'm scared Addi. I'm scared to forget you, your voice. Pictures and a couple videos aren't the same as having you. I'd give anything to switch you places. I pinky promise with a kiss to seal it. On a lighter note. The Dean is probably a pervert. Mom and Dad sent me to a place filled with criminals. There are weird ass cliques here. Oh! The "Brr's" I feel like you'd have fun with them. One is definitely a "Leticia". I met a girl named River... you'd like her. She reminds me of you, some of the things she does.

As usual, Iloveyou and miss you. -Your Firefly

I smile at the text she'll never get and pretend she's busy doing something. Probably not the healthiest coping mechanism, but it works.

My hands rest on my hips, thinking of where to start first. Probably look for a hiding place for my contraband that the head-master warned me about. I walk into the closet, looking at what I have to work with. It's a pretty large closet for a school, not the normal cupboards I've seen in movies.

Gathering a few of my clothes and place them on all black hangers. The corner of the closet houses a built-in safe box. It doesn't seem unusual for an upper-class room. I put in the universal code 0000 and it opens! The space is about the size of the ones I've seen in hotels before, completely bare. I wouldn't leave anything in here. Everyone must know about the placement of it. It would be stupid to think otherwise and leave something important.

An idea pops into my head as I skip to the desk with the school handbook that's as thick as the Bible itself. Skimming over the "Welcome!" Part of it to rip the paper out. Digging through the sleek organized drawers, I find a black permanent. Perfect for my current task and draw a terrible middle finger to secure in my little vault. I wince at the rough, rough drawing. I'm going for knowing what the drawing is, not an art exhibit.

Dashing back over to my side project, because who doesn't get distracted while doing something else entirely? I leave the lovely drawing in the middle and set the code. A smug smirk pulls on the corner of my lips. 0713. Addison's birthday, my little Cancer baby. Then resume my task of hanging clothes. Four white hangers. All for her clothes. She always used the white hangers and I, the black. It's fitting to use the same color scheme as we did before. Some things just make sense.

After I'm finally finished, I plop down with a whoosh of breath, feeling accomplished. I glare at the handbook. I need to read it. Throwing my head back, I let out a loud groan mixed with an "ohmifuckinggod". This is going to be such bullshit.

Flipping open past the ripped page. Oh! And look at that! The first line states, "We respect all student's privacy and therefore expect each student to respect each other's." Right, because my things were searched before they were taken to my room.

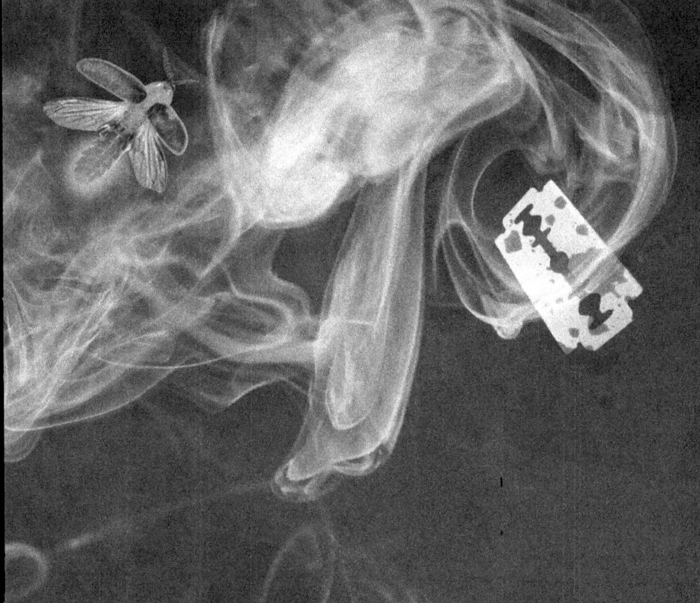

SAINT

STRESSED OUT – TWENTY ONE PILOTS

Thud. I wait for the sticky blue ball to peel itself slowly away from the ceiling before gravity claims it back into my hands. A troubled feeling settles over me. I'm not sure if it's from trying to figure out what's going on with Brian or the fact I'm getting stuck in my past.

I'm aware of what Mal has been through. What *we've* been through, I guess. It's more like watching a movie clip of something where I am the main character in a situation that's never *actually* occurred to me. But still carry the hurt and anger of it happening to someone I love and care about. Damn, my father did a number on him.

Thud. I lift my head up to stare at the computer screen across the room, making sure the software downloads to mirror the phone on a second device so we can see what she's doing at all times. That's my goal tonight. Install a tracking device I created to keep tabs on her, hear any and all phone calls she has in real time.

The guys say she's ours now… but I think Malice takes it more literally. A possession he owns.

They're all worried about me, because they think I'm soft. I keep all the 'good' parts about me by seeming more optimistic. But it's Malice who we should be worried about. He tends to get unhealthy attachments to his possessions. It's been a while since he's had a new obsession, and I think she may be the beginning of his based on our conversations. His last one was a punishment, and she paid the price because of his infatuation. I run my tongue over the silver hooped snake bites that Malice thought would be a good idea to get. Along with a shit ton of tattoos.

"Fuck!" The ball hits me in the face. I growl as I get up. My feet tangle in the blankets at the end of my bed, causing me to land face first into the rug. "Goddamn it!" I complain as I lay there with my face stuffed into the floor, arms sprawled out. I can't. I give up.

At that moment, Crew opens the door to check on me before slowly blinking and shutting the door quietly behind him.

Lifting my head, I yell, "Yes! I'm fine! Thank you, Father Dearest! I'll just lay here and *die!*" His low chuckle in the hallway is my only sign he heard me. Letting out a loud dramatic sigh, since no one is here to see me be a diva. I should probably get ready for the night. The freshmen downstairs are setting up for later. Someone will lock all the upstairs doors to prevent unwanted sexcapades from moving into our personal rooms. Most of the time, these parties begin with alcohol and drugs and progress to orgies everywhere. If not, then couples sneaking off into the trees to fuck like rabbits.

Every year, to start off, we have a party the day before class begins since it's a late start. More "Party at your own risk" because if they don't make it to class, it's their own problem.

Kicking off my blankets, I head to my computer to put on my "BDE" playlist to hype myself up for the night. Having to become easygoing to satisfy the masses wasn't as 'easy' as the word implies.

No one else could take on the role. Ben is too much of a playboy, wants to fuck everything that moves. Never underestimate a scorned woman.

Mal is too intense and doesn't play well with others. If anyone looks at him wrong, he thinks it's a threat and I mean that literally. He's also better off not discovered. That leaves Crew, a hard ass, control freak that a simple smile could crack his face.

Every year Bennett throws a 'back to school' party. The past couple of years it's been to mourn the end of summer. Tonight is about the upper classmen having fun and letting loose. A time to integrate the freshmen into the school. Let's hope tonight goes smoothly. Well… not too smoothly. The freshmen are in for a shitty night. I smile.

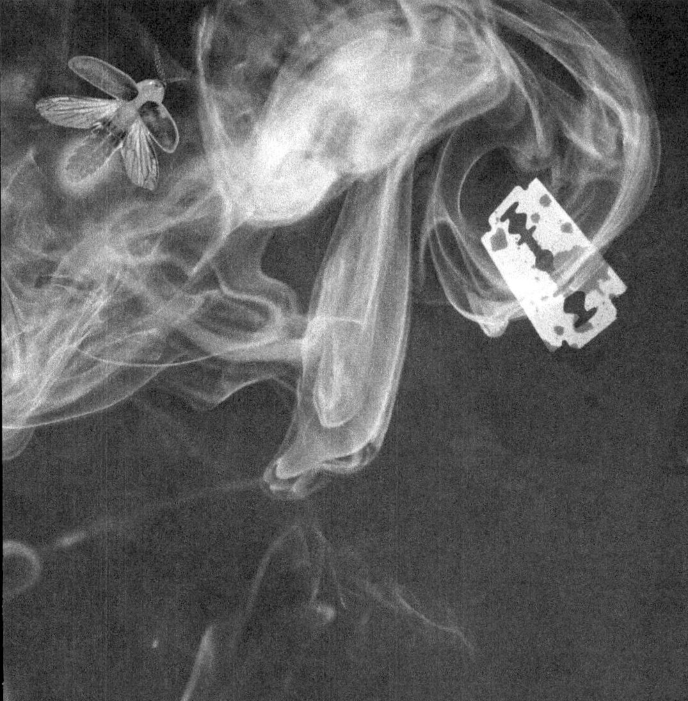

PRIYA

HAPPY ENDING – BAILEY SPINN

Blinking at my reflection, I flick my gaze to River behind me. She looks pleased with the outfit she chose for me from her closet.

The little bit of things I brought are… normal clothes. Jeans, sweats, hoodies and t-shirts. I've worn expensive clothing, hand-picked by my mom's designers, so the rare times I'm out in public I look 'presentable'. This? This would not pass her inspection.

"River…" I'm ready to let her know I can't go out like this, that this is unacceptable. The dress is a black long sleeve mini dress. The material is sheer but thicker where it comes to a sharp V that reaches the top of my belly button. My thighs look chunky because they're touching. My boobs are noticeably too small. And is that a pouch I see on my belly? I frown again at my reflection, then look at her while my insecurities thicken in my throat. My eyes sting with the countless flaws staring back at me. If I can see them, everyone can see them.

"Stop it right now. You look amazing! I don't know what you could possibly say to make me think otherwise." She spins me around until I face her, her hands steady on my shoulders. "We've known each other for two days. Does it seem like I'd do something like that?" Hurt flashes in her eyes as her lips twist. Arms crossed over her chest, "Say three nice things about yourself."

Taken aback, I don't think I've ever said one nice thing about myself. I study her. Her makeup is dark, with a thick winged eyeliner. She pairs her combat boots with a short leather skirt and a top that has silver studs forming X's over her breasts. Looking like an unapproachable bad ass dominatrix. She's just missing the mask and whip.

Looking around, unable to maintain eye contact. I start with what I know is true, "My eye makeup you did looks amazing, almost natural. Perfectly me. My hair looks like it's a silky wave in the ocean." My usual curly hair is tamed perfectly in big waves down my back, extra thanks to many hair products to help it hold. It conceals my bite mark from the other night. I look… good. The bags underneath my eyes are fully covered and my contour is on point. I think hard about something else nice to say about myself and come up short.

"And I'm lucky to have met you." I look in her cocoa-colored eyes once again, not able to convey my feelings into words, instead bottling it up. She rolls her eyes with a big smile.

"Fine, those were indirectly about you and the last one, not at all. But I'll take it. Next time will be better." She touches up her dark purple lipstick before handing me a light lip gloss, which I'm thankful for. Makeup isn't my thing.

Speaking of brown eyes… "Hey… on my way here, I saw a sign for a girl that went missing. Did she go here?"

She pauses in the mirror, straightening up to her full height, fidgeting with her outfit, her discomfort noticeable.

"Mm yeah, Megan." She leaves it at that, making herself busy in the mirror.

"What happened?" I inquire.

"She was here and then she wasn't."

All right, that wasn't vague at all. Why wouldn't the media or student be talking about a girl who went missing? Someone who went to this school, has a well-known family, or at least a wealthy one. The fact she doesn't want to talk about it makes it more important. I decide to push for more on a later date.

"Now let's go party and get fucked up!" Her enthusiasm is infectious, and the excitement flutters in my stomach. I may not like partying, but I like people watching. It makes spotting the sadness in their smiles easier. Maybe the fairness in their laugh. There's always something leaking through the cracks when someone thinks no one is watching.

Walking up to the metal barndominium, from what River explained, is a barn that's been fully renovated and furnished like a house. It was done her freshman year for the Demons to live comfortably for the next couple of years.

The barn has a white paint job, and the two massive barn doors are rolled open, exposing three large glass doors for entry, allowing partygoers to come and go. The party is in full swing, different colored lights illuminating different areas of the main rooms, and music filling the air even before we approach the doors. Money Longer by Lil Uzi Vert is blasting through the speakers. Entering through the doors, a majority of people scream the chorus.

I suppress a laugh because I'm sure almost everyone here has a mansion from their parents' money and nice ass cars that were bought for them. At least I'm not so far out of place. If anything, I'm overly dressed. Most girls are wearing little to no clothing at all. This must be a school thing they do because there's no way our parents would allow us to be seen like this anywhere. River is shaking her hips as she grabs and pulls me into the kitchen which, is easily seen in the open floor plan. An enormous island sits in the middle, littered with all sorts of bottles of alcohol. Fairy lights hang all over the metal beams that hold up the barn. I've been to countless mansions, but the idea that this used to be a barn has my mind going in circles.

"Drink?" a freshman girl wearing a neon yellow tube top and mini skirt asks. Is this what all freshmen are going to have to do? Taking another look around, I notice the bright color easily picked out in the sea of people all catering to needs. All the freshmen guys are in skintight speedos.

Grimacing, I avert my eyes to the girl in front of us. Everyone would know what they're packing, or not. Since it leaves nothing to the imagination. The cold outside wouldn't help their predicament. I stick with bottled water. While River is asking for a mixed drink along with a shot. Go big or go home, right? Because I'm ready to go home.

"Are you going to dance with me?" She screams over the music that switched to The Weeknd, a song about how he can't feel his face. Which seems pretty on par with the people doing lines of coke in the corner. The horror on my face must be evident because she laughs, twirling around a freshman girl and grinding against her to the beat of the music. I keep my post by the edge of the island to take in the scene. I count all the exits in case of an emergency. An automatic compulsion, courtesy of my lovely father. Aside from the way we came in, there's an exact replica toward the other end of the house where all the "fun" is. Drugs, topless girls and make out sessions are in full swing. My nose scrunches as I shudder with the thought of who's going to be cleaning the aftermath of this house party.

The cliques are seemingly spread out, not too much of one group sticking together. I've only been to the parties that require my parents to put on a good show. Champagne, hor d'oeuvre's, making connections to get in people's good graces, but nothing more. Never any dancing or good music, maybe drugs behind the scenes, but not out in the open like this. Oh, and everyone is wearing clothes.

One girl is in the corner by herself, swaying off beat to the music touching herself sensually, inhibitions lost in her own world. Whatever she's on… I wouldn't be opposed to trying.

I look back over to check on River to see she's switched up dancing partners to two girls that are wearing bralettes with some shorts that show their ovaries. She's smiling and singing to the song while waving her hands in the air. So unbothered that it brings a small smile to my face.

Continuing to scan the crowd, I stop when I spot one of the twins. The one who never smiles and fakes his emotions, plastering on false indifference. Probably because he feels everything tenfold, instead acting like nothing matters.

He's intently staring at me. Arms and legs spread to take up as much room as possible. A warning. "Don't come near me". That clearly tailored button-up shirt kisses the outline of his muscles perfectly, showing off how built he is underneath. The button up seems a little out of place here compared to the amount of skin showing everywhere else, but who am I to say anything? It's his house.

Accidentally, I make eye contact and pull back. That indifference I was talking about before is replaced with a twisted sneer. Making a poor attempt to hide the fact he gave a reaction, his jaw rigid from clenching that he could break his teeth if he did it any harder. The hostility startles me, wiping the smile off of my face from watching River dance. I redirect my attention next to him to distract myself from the heaviness in my stomach. Instead, I stop short at his womanizing brother.

Not concerned to conceal the disgust written on my face to see he has a girl in his lap that isn't Amber. His arms lay across the back of the black leather couch, holding a blunt. The girl throws her head back giggling at something he said while running a hand up his thigh, up to his fully unbuttoned shirt. This will not end well when his girlfriend gets here. That thought brings a smile back to my face. Karma at her finest. What comes around, goes around.

Where's that third little demon? Analyzing River to guesstimate how intoxicated she is, only to see she's still dancing her little heart away. Am I the only one who gets nervous and feels like I have to be responsible for the people I'm with? In charge of monitoring their well-being and making sure they're okay. Is it normal?

A hand reaches out and touches my arm, causing me to jump. I wrap my arm around myself before spinning around to see who is in my personal bubble.

One of the most gorgeous men I've ever seen. His blonde wavy hair falls into his eyes. My fingers twitch to brush it away to see the matching sapphire blue eyes so light it almost looks white. The freckles on his tan skin, show he's been in the sun a lot this summer. Probably from whatever adventures his family paid for. Let's hope he doesn't think I want to hear about them. Two wicked dimples that deepen as he smiles and talks. Along with two silver hoop piercings that hug his full lips, don't get me started on the neck tattoo that goes against his surfer aura.

"Huh?" His lips stop moving. I realize he's talking to me. My face heats. I halt my wandering thoughts and obvious eye fucking. He laughs like I said something funny. It's forced, faked. Who knows, maybe he thinks the reaction he draws from girls is amusing or possibly annoyingly repetitive.

"I asked how you like the party and if you're enjoying yourself so far." His voice is rich, smooth. Good enough to listen to in an audiobook and orgasm from it alone. He's wearing a white shirt with dark jeans that hugs him in the right places. Who says girls can't appreciate a male figure? I'm pretty sure I'm drooling.

"Uh… yeah, it's…" I dab at my mouth, looking for a word to not make me seem brazen. "It's definitely different." Translate to, 'I'd rather be anywhere else'. I'd rather read a book, take a walk, focus on homework… drown in my sorrows, sleep my pain away, contemplate my death. Not surrounded by people who only give a fuck about themselves.

He raises his eyebrow, obviously reading into what I mean. Perceptive as well. It's good to know he's not just a pretty face.

"I'm Priya."

"I know." He smirks. I suppose everyone knows of the new senior that transferred this year. "Do you want to dance?"

I refrain from making the same face I gave River when she asked a few songs ago. I frown and shake my head.

"I don't like dancing."

He's wearing more clothing than his partygoers, the same as the twins. What a way to go down. Too bad this is the third Demon. A Demon with the looks and body of an Angel.

"What did you say your name was again?"

"I didn't. I'm Saint D'Angelo." The way he says who he is, isn't as cocky as Bennett seemed to be earlier. It seems almost normal.

"I'm good, thank you. I'll probably get going soon." Attempting to excuse myself in a polite way. At least I hope it comes off as polite.

"So, not a good different then?" He asks, referring to my earlier statement about the party.

He was reading into my answers. He is more than a pretty face. Something about this situation doesn't sit well with me. Why is he talking to me? Why didn't he just stop the conversation there? There's always an ulterior motive with people and not knowing his makes me feel off centered. Cue the word vomit from nervousness.

"Honestly, we'll probably never talk again, so…" The likelihood of associating with the 'popular' group is slim to none. "No. Not a good different. I've only ever been forced to go to parties by my parents and it's never a good time." It's always ended up with my father's fists from some fuck up I did that night in his or my mother's eyes. "This is no better, just less clothing, more drugs and loud music. And I don't like people. 9 times out of 10, I don't get along with anyone, anyway." I say it aloofly, like the loneliness doesn't affect me, when it's quite the opposite. "The expectations are never ending and extend here as well. The end."

His eyes light up with amusement while his lips tilt in a half smirk. "The end?"

"Yeah, I'm done with my story." Trying to brush off the fact

I'm not good with people and most people don't tell people when they're done talking.

He looks about 5 seconds from laughing. Then unexpectedly I land face first into Saints chest as a fight breaks out behind us. His arms come around to catch me around the waist while shoving the guy away from me and into the guy who pushed him. He swiftly regains his balance while cocking his fist back to punch him. Blood gushes from his nose, pouring onto the ground. More people jump in, some trying to break it up, while others just want a piece of the chaos. The original guys are swallowed into the crowd of people fighting for absolutely no reason. This is what I imagine a mosh pit looks like. I've never seen one, but from what I heard, they're crazy dangerous.

Saint grabs my hand while I'm distracted and pulls me to the glass doors toward the back, away from the fight ensuing.

"Sorry, duty calls as host and all. I'll catch up with you in a few?" I nod once to brush off the commitment, because I fully plan on leaving before he finds me again. With a flash of his dimples, he disappears into the crowd. I lean against the cool glass when a flash of neon yellow catches the corner of my eye in the Demons' corner. The freshman that was dancing with River when we first got here is now in Bennett's lap, kissing her way up his neck. His hand traces the swell of her ass, up her spine when yet another voice comes to interrupt me.

"Hey New Girl, I came to see if you were all right. I saw you were in the middle of …all that. I couldn't get to you fast enough. But I figure I'd see for myself. I'm Oscar, by the way." His curly dark hair, perfect white smile. He's completely shirtless, showing off his abs followed by the arrogance radiating off of him.

Scoffing, "Of course you are." I mutter. It's always like this, "new girl this" or "new girl that". Who can get in her pants first? He must have seen my lips moving because he responds with a "Huh?" I toss him a fake smile, "I said, 'It's nice to meet you, I'm *Priya*.'" I lie, trying the emphasize my name so we can just skip the 'new girl' phase.

"Wanna step outside? It's quieter out there." He tosses me

what I'm assuming is usually a panty dropping smile, tugging me along with him. He reeks of alcohol and weed, and that never is a good combination for a partying teen. I shoot a brief look over my shoulder so I can throw an SOS out to River, but I don't spot her quick enough before the chilly September air meets me. I stand awkwardly on a porch that covers the whole back end of the barn. My body posture should read "uncomfortable" but he's either dense or drunk. He closes the distance while stumbling to playing with the ends of my hair much like Bennett did earlier. Only, it doesn't even come close to the same effect as Bennett's touch. I shy away from the unwanted contact as his hand settles right above my ass and pulls me flush to his front. He's ignoring every obvious cue I'm giving. Uncomfortable laughter, subtly backing up towards the party. Does anyone know how to read body language? Or did that die along with chivalry, too?

Grinding my teeth against the feeling of hands on my body, I realize he's the guy who's going to need more than a "No."

I'm on my own here, there's a couple people outside but not close enough to overhear me. The beginning of one of my favorite songs, "Swim" by Chase Atlantic. Whoever is in charge of this playlist is hitting all the right feels. This is perfect. I smile mainly to myself. I never said I couldn't dance, just that I don't like to.

Taking both of my hands, I gradually trace the length of each of his arms, leaving us skin to skin. He shudders from the welcome contact. Trailing my fingers lightly up his shoulder, and softly intertwine my fingers in the hair at the base of his skull. I sensually sway my hips slowly to the beat of the song. When his hands wrap around me, grabbing a hand full of my ass, I yank his head back with the fist-full of hair I now have. While pushing my breasts up against his chest, getting close to his ear to whisper.

"The last man who touched me without my permission… I set him on fire." Instantly, his arms drop from around me with a huge step back, eyes wide at the confession. The satisfaction of not being touched, accompanied by how horrified he looks, sends delicious chills down my spine. Before he can respond, the music fades as the grating voice of Amber Astor reaches my ears. I'm ready to go back to my dorm for the night. With that in mind, I head inside to tell River she can stay if she wants, but I'm over it. My people watching hasn't gone the way I wanted it to and I blame it on being new here, drawing curiosity and wanting to test my boundaries.

"Can all the fresh-meat make their way up to the front, please?" It comes out more like a demand than a question. About 30 students in neon colors stand in two single file lines facing the crowd.

"Perfect!" Fake cheeriness in her voice as she ushers other partygoers up with her. She hands one black permanent marker to each of the girls beside her that aren't wearing neon colors, then one to Ember and tells them to get started. Coincidently, Amber stands in front of the girl that was all over Bennett, whispering something in her ear and the girl's eyes well with tears.

The music is low, allowing only the bass of the song to be heard, while everyone forms a circle around the entertainment for the evening. Amber leads the way by removing the marker cap with her teeth before putting it on the end of the marker. The purpose of the girls' tiny outfits is quickly revealed as the body shaming begins. Arrows on her belly, thighs, legs front and back. There isn't a spot without markings leaving the freshmen looking ready for plastic surgery.

People around are laughing and cheering them on. Amber finishes up her disgusting display of pissing on Bennett's leg. Permanent marker everywhere, the girl is more marked than any of the other freshman. "Whore" is written across her forehead. I feel sorry for her. That's quickly forgotten when Amber turns around.

"We're just missing… one person." She stares at me, along with many other eyes. The discomfort sets in.

"You're new… aren't you?" A rhetorical question. People press in behind me, urging me forward.

"Oscar? Can you bring her up here?"

The air changes when he slowly creeps up behind me.

"Remember what I said outside? It applies here too. Don't put a fucking finger on me." I snarl. If he doesn't heed my warning, I have enough lighter fluid to light his ass up like a Christmas tree. Oscar throws his hands in the air to show he isn't touching me. My legs wobble like jello on my way up to the center of the room.

"Tonight, we're going to end off with a little self-reflection. Marker, please?" Then Amber leans closer to me as she did to the first girl.

"Next time, stay away from Bennett. He's mine."

Another Barbie hands her a red permanent marker. She uncaps while looking over my body, pondering the same thing we all do when we look in the mirror. Or maybe that's just me. She draws arrows inward on my lower thighs.

"There's no thigh gap… your thighs should be smaller for your height." I let out a harsh laugh. I've been told for years by my mother.

I grab the marker from her hand, tossing it somewhere behind me, followed by a yelp.

I mimic what she did, leaning in, "Let me make it easier for you. My boobs are too small, my ass is too fat, my thighs are too thick, I have bags under my eyes. I don't have an entirely flat stomach." I could go on and on. We're going to pick out my insecurities about my appearance? I'm a million times better at doing that than any fake ass girl who only wants attention.

"I don't want your pathetic man whore of a boyfriend who can't seem to keep his hands to himself. Do better." I whisper, giving her some girl -to-girl advice. I shove by her shoulder while I take my leave. Every single eye in the room is on me. I'm trying to hold it together because I'm about to snap.

This time, I don't bother waiting for River to let her know I'm leaving. Amber resumes her reign of terror on the poor freshmen who sit there and take it. The chilly air hits my sweaty skin again as I exit the barn.

"Priya! Wait!" I turn at the sound of River's voice and hit her with a scathing glare. She skids to a halt, hands up, yielding.

"Did you know?" I try to keep words from wavering and my face blank.

"What? What are you talking about?" This is the issue with people. They can hide behind hundreds of masks. Some are better at hiding their true nature than others. I scan her face, looking for any sort of guilt, remorse or responsibility only to come up short.

"I'm going back to the dorm." Ending on that, I turn away.

"Priya, I swear. Whatever is going on, I had nothing to do with it." She's eager to prove her innocence. I shrug. It doesn't really matter, does it? It happened.

I feel empty. The urge to burn the barn to the fucking ground to make me feel better about being insecure, but don't see it happening tonight. One day. Tomorrow should be better. She holds my phone out for me, looking at the phone and back to her, confused. She shrugs while scooting closer.

"Saint gave it to me when the freshmen hazing started. Said he was trying to find you. He found it on the ground." My only guess is that I lost it during the fight when I was shoved.

Tomorrow will be better. That's what I need to believe. Fake it until you become it.

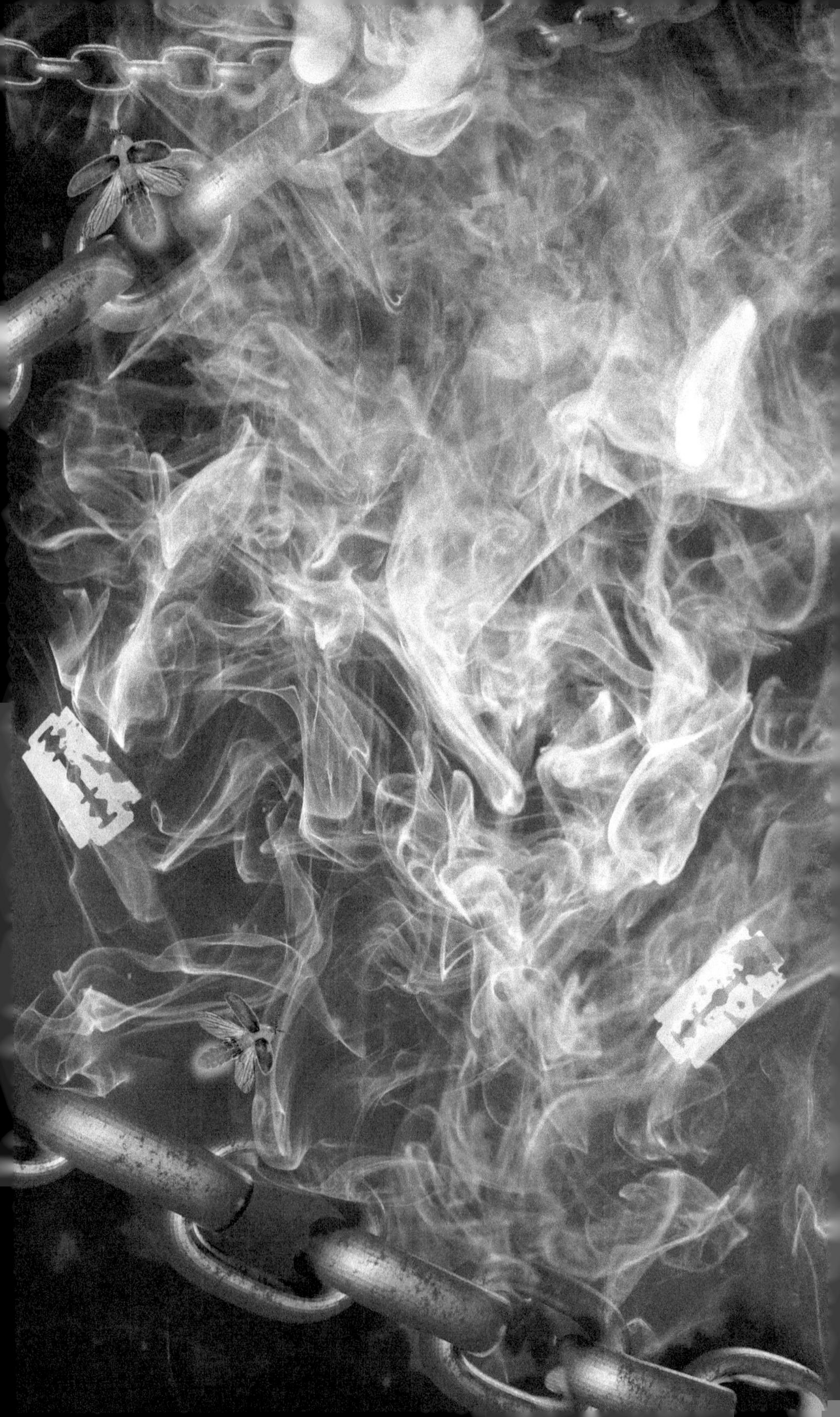

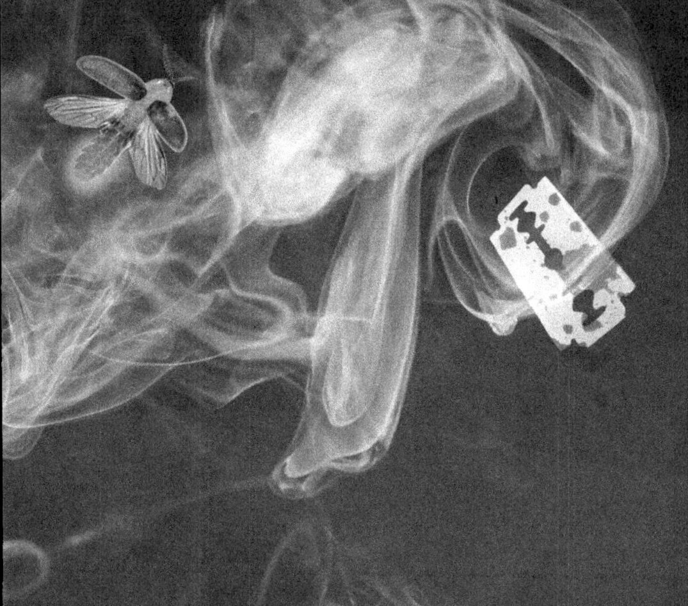

PRIYA

COPYCAT – BILLIE EILLISH

Eyes still closed, I unfortunately woke up realizing I didn't die in my sleep. No matter how hard I tried, I couldn't wash the sliminess of last night off of me before bed. Another day stuck in my miserable existence.

Stretching and yawning, I catch a whiff of coffee in the air. What the fuck? I jump up, my razor in hand, only to see River calmly drinking her tea, her legs tucked unseated her while scrolling through social media on her phone.

"Good morning, sunshine. Are you going to cut me with that too?" Ha. Ha. I appreciate the dark humor and the cup of coffee on the counter.

"How did you get in here?" I question. Since she shouldn't be able to, considering the card is usually stashed in my bra.

"Oh yeah, I'm good with computers." She holds up a replica

of my card in her hand. My brain is taking a second to wake up because she seems to be the only person in the world who is wide awake, dressed for the day and ready to have an actual conversation first thing in the morning.

"So…?" I gesture for her to continue her explanation, not fully awake.

She rolls her eyes, "'So' it's simple to snatch a spare keycard and reprogram it."

Yeah, it's 'easy'. For who?

"Do you have very many friends?"

She shakes her head but doesn't seem offended by the question. Normally, people don't have someone make a copy of your card to come and go as they please. But what do I know?

Zoning out, slowly nodding, I come to terms with this situation. If worse comes to worse, I'll cut her off and if that's not the case, then it wouldn't hurt to have a friend. Giving up the lecture of breaking and entering, I tell her to help me get ready.

"Who's that?" The picture I forgot to put back away lies on the nightstand.

"My sister." I say clipped, ending that conversation.

"Oh wow. She's hot." Swooning in her voice.

I chuckle, "Yeah, she is, huh?" I can't bring myself to look at her. And I never tell her she's dead. I don't think I'll ever be able to bring myself to say the words. Because saying she's gone would make it real.

"Hey, speaking of breaking and entering. Did you make that card today? Or yesterday?"

"This morning. Bright and early. Figured I could always be at your disposal." She bows as if it is a gift to be my friend and it makes me nauseous. I don't want to disappoint her when she figures out I'm not that great.

"Help me get ready for my first day of prison, Nosy Norma." I throw my pillow at her, almost knocking over her tea.

Looking at my schedule, it all coincides with Rivers, and I'm not sure if I should be thankful or suspicious. All but one, Psychology.

"Physical Education?" I huff.

"Yeah… P.E?" She squints at me.

"I know what it is. I completed all the graduation require-ments last year. Don't know why I have to do a fourth year of it." Sucking my teeth. I hated it then, and I'm sure I'll hate it even more here. It's the first class of the day. I thought seniors get seniority and some sort of special treatment for it being their last year. Thank God I don't wear makeup.

"We all get an extra 30 minutes to shower and get ready for the day again. If that makes you feel better. It's a requirement to shower afterwards. Leaves us shorter classes so, that's always nice." Miss Sunshine over here, looking at the bright side of running laps first thing in the morning.

I took longer than expected to actually get up and moving, procrastinating the inevitable, the first day at a new school. I grabbed us each a protein bar that was already stocked in my room for breakfast. Finishing my breakfast, we walk into the huge gym to get into the locker rooms. River hands me a lock from out of her backpack with a set of school standard gym clothes. What else does she have in there? Because it seems like she's more prepared for today than I am. With no one inside the locker rooms, I hurry to get changed before anyone says anything about my body or scars. River has seen me naked. I side eye her. At least she was an excellent date that night she stayed over, even made coffee in the morning for me.

Pulling my shirt down over my sports bra, an overwhelming amount of chatter filters in, lockers slam open and shut. There's a handful of freshmen in our class. The girl with permanent marker on her face, courtesy of Amber, is silent as she makes her way to the locker next to me. Her make up doesn't do a very good job of covering the arrows and lines nor the word on her forehead. A grimace makes its way to my face as I head out of the locker room with River.

"Amber went a little overboard with Lily last night." She whispers.

"Just Lily? The whole thing was absurd. She went 'overboard' because her boyfriend is a man whore who can't keep his hands to himself. Or if that wasn't the case, then say 'No'." I shake my head at the ridiculousness of it.

River shrugs her shoulders. "Everyone gets welcomed their first year that way."

"Yep! That explains it all." Sarcasm laces my voice. "Amber tried to pull that shit with me in front of everyone."

Anger replaces the look on her face.

"Ohmigod, no she didn't!" Nodding to confirm she *really* did.

"That's double fucked up. That's never been done before, or at least I haven't heard of it done to a senior."

"It came with a lovely warning of staying away from her boyfriend." Not mentioning Bennett's close proximity to me earlier that day is probably the cause. Better to keep it to myself.

"Priya," seriousness laces her tone as she looks me in the eye, "stay away from them. The Demons and the Angels. Not just because of Amber, they're all bad news. That girl you asked about, Megan? The word is the Demons had something to do with her disappearance. I'm not sure how much is true, but it's better safe than sorry. No one knows how capable a person can truly be."

That's the truth.

Walking out to the gym on a standing white board in a red dry erase marker is the teacher's name and what we're supposed to do.

"Mr. Riley - Warm up: 3 laps around gym."

A collective groan comes from over half of the class. I do a mental rundown of my physical health and it isn't very good. Well, it never has been, if I'm honest. My appetite has shrunk over the last nine months and the last time I had a drink of water was when it hit my lip in the shower.

On a more positive note, my mother made sure I ran constantly to lose weight if I ate something she didn't agree with. Three laps should be easy.

I start by pacing myself, getting a good rhythm going, a little slower than I usually would. I glance back at River and slow down a little more when I see her not keeping up. She smiles gratefully, gulping for air.

"I'm not a runner." She puffs. "Why sweat on purpose?" I'm impressed with her logic. "Who the frick thought that I would need to be running if I'm not being chased is beyond me."

Chuckling at her reasoning, "I think there is some quota the schools have to meet for our exercise each year, hence the reason for the mile." I heard it somewhere. Sounds legitimate enough.

"Miss Waaaaalton!" Her last name is drawn out in the way P.E teachers do. "If you're joking, you're not running hard enough!"

Wincing, I realize he'll probably make us run longer. We pass by him on our second lap and I do a double take. He looks familiar but I can't quite place him.

"River, who is the teacher? He looks like someone I know." I throw another quick glance over my shoulder in hopes of placing his face.

"Coach Riley? I dunno. He's been the football coach for the last three years. His family owns some oil rig company." That could be it, but not likely. Behind us, I see both Ambers whisper and look at me, or maybe River. The way they whisper conspiratorially makes me wary. I take my eyes off them for not even a second when my foot catches on something and I'm sprawling out across the gym floor. Blinding pain explodes from the front of my face.

"Ow, fuck. Ow." I moan into the ground until my hands come up to my nose, which is hot with pain and warm blood. The metallic taste of pennies coats the back of my throat. Gross. River runs up to me telling me she thinks I should go to the nurse. Then tips my head back to stop the bleeding. I gag at the taste of blood running down my throat. I'm going to puke. Both Amber and Ember are standing closer to me than I thought previously. Amber leans down.

"This is your last warning." She hisses, pulling back with faux concern. Apparently, the heart-to-heart we had last night was one sided and didn't quite resonate with her.

Riv gives me an 'I told you so' look and shakes her head,

opening her mouth to respond to the threat when Coach Riley appears.

"What the fuck happened here?" he questions. It makes me wonder if he's giving us the opportunity to come clean.

Amber chimes in, "It looks like she tripped." She forces a frown that's more like an unsympathetic pout.

"Come on." He grabs me gently by the elbow and leads us to an office with a metal door into a room covered in sports equipment. Guiding me to a chair, hand still holding my nose back up in the air. He turns to a misplaced sink in the office to wet a rag. He's wearing athletic shorts and a standard grey crewneck sweater. Even with the hoodie I can tell he is in shape. Muscled legs, strong hands, and perfect posture. Ew, that's my teacher. He's probably old and has a family at home, and I'm here drooling at his legs and physique.

He startles me out of my perverted train of thought, handing me the wet cloth. I tenderly clean myself up, careful of my sore nose in the process.

"Are you going to tell me what happened out there?" he prods.

"Amber told you, I tripped." Trying to blow it off, I'm not necessarily a clumsy person. My father's anger made sure I was a pro at walking on eggshells.

His face tells me he doesn't believe me. If he knows Amber, he's not saying anything.

"I can't do anything if you don't tell me the truth."

I stare at him. It's going to bug me to not know where I know him from. He's handsome in the classic kind of way. But nothing stands out about him.

"If you think I'm going to rat on someone, you're sadly mistaken. This isn't my first rodeo of being stuck with a mean girl." It'll be worse if Amber found out I snitched on her. What are they really going to do, anyway? A slap on the wrist? Suffering in silence seems to be the better option of the two. He drops his head like he wants to say more.

"You can head to the showers. Let me know if there is anything I can do to help."

"In the shower?" I joke to break the tension. His face contorts to one of horror. Whether from the thought of helping me in the shower or maybe because he is my teacher and I'm a student, but at least I'm quick to spot that he doesn't have a ring on his finger. I laugh at his face. It's funny to see him flustered.

Putting him out of his misery, "I'm joking! Calm down." From the corner of my eye, I spot a smile twitching on his full lips as he shakes his head. Then, I go out to face the humiliation of people who witnessed me get tripped. The unmistakable blood staining the front of my shirt.

I make a B-line for the locker rooms, trying to avoid people for the foreseeable future when I stumble upon Amber's other victim from last night. Lily leans against the sink, quietly crying in front of the mirror, staring at the word 'whore' written across her fore-head. Taking pity on her, I grab my bag with hand sanitizer and hand it to her as an olive branch. If Amber is going to be a bitch to both of us, we might as well stick together.

She glares at me from beneath her lashes. "What is this? If I wanted clean hands, I could just use soap and water like a normal person. Or is that beneath you?" Stunned at her outburst from me trying to be friendly because I felt bad, I have half a mind to walk away. Shaking my head, I realize from personal experience she's lashing out in anger from humiliation.

I clear my throat before speaking. "Have you tried getting it off with hand sanitizer? I don't think it will completely come off, but it should fade it enough to cover it up with makeup."

Her eyes light up with hope and a touch of apprehension. "Really? This isn't like some sort of trick and it's going to make it stay forever, right?"

Shrugging, I leave her to figure it out. I don't have a reason to be horrible to her. Not that she should have been all over Bennett to begin with. It takes two to tango.

She turns to the mirror with a sniffle and carefully applies the sanitizer to her skin. "I didn't know." She says quietly as I turn on the shower stall and grab a fluffy white towel from the rack. I don't have anything to say. Whether she knew Bennett's relationship status or not, isn't my business.

I let the hot water soothe my muscles and run down my face before I lather myself in soap face to toe, taking care to exclude my hair because it'll take forever to dry. The door opens and closes when she exits the locker room. I feel her absence in the stillness of the air.

I can be rather irrational. The emptiness of the room has a sinister feel to it. Shutting off the water, I dry myself and wrap a towel around my body.

"Hello?" Signal the stereotypical girl who gets killed in the locker room at her high school for being stupid and going out of her cornered stall. Is that a movie? Because I'm sure it's happened somewhere.

When no one responds, I make a game plan. I'm going to dry off, put my clothes on as fast as I can in order to get the fuck out of here. Pretty foolproof plan, right?

Running for my life, I grab my clothes and run back into a dry stall and begin dressing like my life depends on it. I tuck my shirt into my skirt, coming up short. What the hell?

My hands graze against the rough, tattered fabric of my shirt, its threads frayed and torn. The sleeves are just lines with vertical cuts through them. The bottom of the shirt looks like a toddler who got ahold of scissors. Stomping out of the stall, I figure I'll just wear my bloody shirt back to my room and change. That's also missing. Gritting my teeth, I get into my locker, only to find it empty. My eye is twitching because of course I would attempt to be nice to someone and in return, they fuck me over.

What would she have to gain? I was being fucking helpful! The urge to scream is prominent. I'll just go back to my dorm and it'll be fine. Fuck my backpack, my clothes, and my classes. Just as I go to open the door. There's a missing poster. The same one from the gas station posted on the back of the door. I don't know if it's exactly the same one, but it's the same girl. Megan Riley.

Folding it up and tucking it into the waistband of my skirt, I leave the gym. Lo-and-behold, Amber is sitting outside with her camera. A flash overrides my vision.

"Wow, nice bra, Priya. Is everyone invited to the show? Or was it just for Bennett?" Amber snickers.

I cock my fist back. I may not be a fighter, but I can practice throwing a punch right to her pretty fucking nose so we can both match. A black-haired ball zooms by, catching my arm.

"Let's not give the bitch what she wants. Which is you expelled on camera for punching her. M'kay?" River speaks lowly only for me to hear.

"She fucking shredded my shirt. All for what? Petty bullshit with her unfaithful boyfriend? I don't even like the prick! All I wanted was to finish this fucking school year in peace and she seems content with not letting that happen!" I rage, struggling to get out of her iron grip.

"Okay, well, let's get you covered up. Nice bra, by the way. Sexy. I pegged you for a Plain Jane, but the black lace?" She winks at me and leads me to a bathroom to change into a spare shirt of hers.

Sighing, I take it and change. "Plain Jane, huh?"

She cackles. "It got your mind off of it, though, right? Want to talk about it?"

I go into explaining about Lily crying, how I tried to help and when I heard her leave the room. Then I pull out the missing poster, hoping she'd shed some light on it.

"That's fucking creepy."

Thank you, I am aware of that. I lived it.

"So, why would a poster from four years ago pop up today?" I question.

"I don't know Pri… It's weird. Maybe they just wanted to scare you. And it worked, didn't it?"

Yeah, but that doesn't make sense. There's no connection between the two of us. We didn't know each other, not the same grade, and different birth years. It doesn't make sense.

"I think we should look into it." I push. There's something about Megan not being talked about or acknowledged that sparks my curiosity. This is the second time I've come across this missing person ad. If that's not a sign, I don't know what is.

Exasperated, she replies, "You want to look into a cold case that not even the cops could figure out? If the Demons had anything to do with it, you're as good as dead. Don't put your nose where it doesn't belong, Priya. People have died for less. You're my only friend here. Please, drop it." Her concern is endearing, but something about the events in the locker room rubs me wrong.

"Yeah, okay." I say, deflated.

"You're not going to let it go, are you?"

"No." I smile at her as she shakes her head.

"Come on, crazy, we got places to be."

Even though I heeded Amber's warning about Bennett Demonio, the Amber duo had already printed out pictures of me in my bra and plastered them all over the hallways, and on some social media site for the school by lunch.

In Psychology, I'm pulled out of class by none other than the douchebag that cornered me in the party to guide me to the deans' office.

"Hey, nice picture. Adding to my spank bank." His smug smirk tells me he had something to do with it. That's fine. He'll get what's coming to him.

"Thanks, Austin!" I say to get under his skin.

"Oscar." He says with narrowed eyes.

I know. I just don't want him to think his name holds any importance.

"Yeah, yeah. That's what I said." Brushing him off because guys who have big egos love that shit.

He leaves me at the dean's door and I knock, feeling like I was just here yesterday.

"Enter," says a bored voice from behind the heavy door. It

looks like he was in the middle of sitting here. I'm sure I'll be his excitement for the day.

"First day here and already causing problems, Miss Carter." His expensive brown suit doesn't mask the nastiness oozing from his pores. I do a dramatic 360-degree turn until I face him once again.

"I don't see any fires?" I question. Since that was the one stipulation he wouldn't tolerate.

"Ahh, no, but posting inappropriate pictures of yourself on the school website is frowned upon, don't you think? Or what about skipping second period? We take attendance here very seriously." Was I supposed to go to class like that? I would want everyone to see that? Is this guy joking right now? There used to be a show about this. Someone would jump out and say they're getting "Punk'd". I'm not a celebrity, but this has to be a joke.

Raising my eyebrows, I go to respond to tell him exactly what I think of arrogant pricks like himself. When he cuts me off.

"Saturday detention with me. I'll see you then." Then busies himself with some papers on his desk. The thing about men such as Headmaster Bush is that they never believe they are wrong.

By the time I get back to my room, I have homework in every class except gym. My hand aches from writing before transferring it onto the tablet provided from the school. I like to visualize it, see it then put down on electronics. Not only stare at a computer for hours on end.

Remembering the paper I put into the waistband of my skirt about Megan, I take a well-deserved break and do some research. Typing her name in the search engine only to have a window pop up as blocked, denying me access. Weird that a student who went missing here and now you can't search her name in the search bar. That's suspicious.

I pull out my phone that's not associated with the school network and try again. A minimum of five articles pops up when searching for information about Megan. I eagerly select the first one that comes up. It's the same flyer from the gas station and locker room.

> ***Missing Persons: Megan Riley***
> ***Sex: Female***
> ***Race: Asian/Caucasian***
> ***Age Missing: 17***
> ***Missing From: Port Clyde, Maine***

It goes on listing her physical characteristics, the standard on a missing person report. Backing out, I click on the article below.

"Teenager Reported Missing from Cox Academy," reads the headline.

"PCPD are growing increasingly concerned for the welfare and where-abouts of a teenage girl last seen on the school campus of infamous Cox Academy heading to her dorm. Megan Riley, 17 originally from Los Angeles, CA was last seen wearing a white shirt and jeans. Port Clyde police are asking for anyone with information to come forward and her family has put out a reward for her safely return. Officers are currently investigating close family members and friends. No suspects at this time."

My tongue runs along the outside of my teeth. Deciding to screenshot it to dig into it later. It's weird that her family asked for a "safe return". Did they know someone had her all along?

I back out of the website to see what else I can find. A recent headline from nine months ago, ***"Riley disappearance being ruled as homicide."*** Whoa. I click it and my phone glitches. An error page has popped up in place of where the article should be. What the hell? At least I screenshotted one page, that way I can try to track down any theories. A knock sounds at my door, and I quickly shut my phone off, knowing River didn't want me to dig into her disappearance.

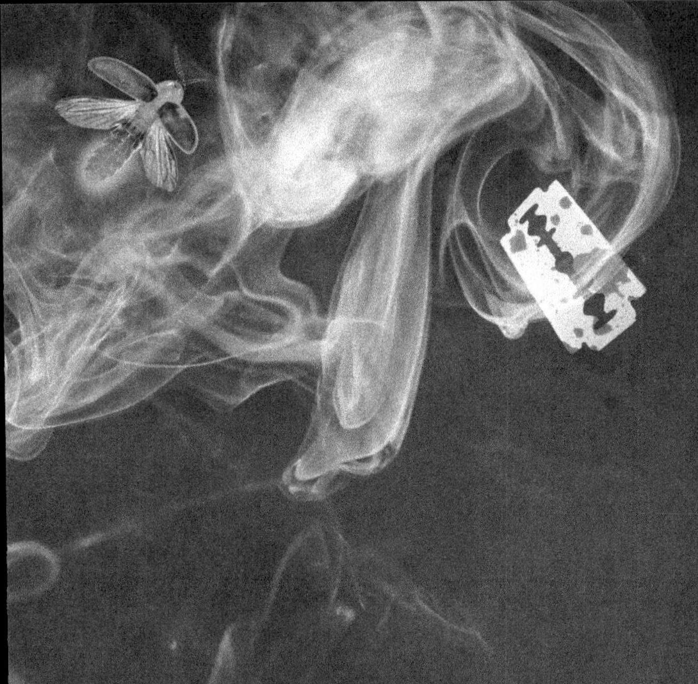

SAINT

ALL MY FRIENDS – THE WLDLFE

*D*ing. *Ding. Ding.* I jump up from my desk to find the source of the noise. I scatter blankets, pillows, clothes, and whatever the fuck else is lying around. Where the fuck is it? *Ding.* The phone continues to go off, signaling Priya is on it. I have it to set up to notify us of everything she does. It was easier than I thought to get my hands on her phone. The fight was the perfect distraction. Unplanned, but perfect. She didn't notice a thing. Not to mention the guys were proud of my sticky fingers. Not that I would fuck it up, just that they didn't think I had the balls to go through with it. The constant coddling to protect me from myself is getting to be too much for me. I'm treated differently and it makes me feel like I'm not a part of the team we created together. They think I'm fragile. Breakable.

Priya. I throw around her name a couple of times to see how it feels. She was unapproachable. Talking to her was like prying out teeth. How something that seems so innocent could be a devil in disguise? I'll never know. Well... I chuckle out loud to myself. Looks can be deceiving. I realized she didn't want to be at the party when she refused to participate in drinking, dancing, or mingling. Let alone talk to me.

After she finished drooling, she immediately stiffened and closed herself off with the resting bitch face she's had since she walked through the school gates. I smirk at the thought she doesn't find herself immune to us as she thinks she does. I find the duplicate phone underneath my bed, in a box. Leave it to Mal to think it's a game. I roll my eyes at his antics. He'll need to try harder and maybe shut off the sound next time. I click the lock button to unlock the screen and sit back and watch the software do its thing.

I watch raptly as she clicks onto a web browser. My heart drops in my stomach when her screen shows she's searching for the girl who went missing a couple of years ago. Crew is going to want to know about this, or maybe I need the reassurance that everything is fine. My palms start to sweat and queasiness forms as a memory tries to niggle from the back of my mind. Shaking my head, I send a group text to the guys downstairs to come up here.

Within three minutes, we gather in my room. Bennett on my unmade bed, Crew taking residence in the chair he's claimed as his own in the corner closest to the door.

"We have a problem." I state calmly when I'm anything but. I show them the phone with the articles she's currently scrolling through.

Crew shrugs unbothered, "Wipe it." Within a couple of seconds, all articles and websites that have to do with Megan Riley are erased from the internet as if it never happened. Everyone at this school knows the topic of the missing girl has been off limits since Malice had taken an interest in her.

"Was that all?" Crew states. Irritation claws at me. Before I can say something that would test all of our patience, Ben is there to break the tension.

"He means, was there anything else that she's been doing?"

"Oh, no. Not even a text message. But she did get detention on Saturday with Brian." Bennett looks at Crew, doing the twintuition thing. Being around them has me in on almost all their looks towards each other. I'm assuming Brian never let them know about Priya, like he was supposed to.

Bennett snickers, "Did you see what Amber did to her?" Crew responds to him by rolling his eyes and picks invisible lint off his crisp white shirt. "Child's play Ben."

Ben shrugs. "Yeah, but now there's a bet on who will sleep with her first. Some guy bet his Bentley Bacalar that it would be him. She'll be hounded constantly. All because I made sure we ran into each other in front of Amber the morning of her meeting with Brian. Nothing makes that girl jealous than me touching someone else." He sighs, like it is so hard to be fought over. I know the fucker gets off on that toxic shit.

"And then what?" I question Bennett to see what his plan is.

He shrugs again. "Amber will tear her apart without me having to do much. Just looking at her sends Amber into a rage. If she thinks someone is threatening her spot with me? She'd die for that shit. Not to mention she poisoned the last person she thought was threatening her position in the family."

"And does she have a spot here, Bennett?" Crew spits. Angry at the thought of being tied to her forever.

"No, of course not. She knows what this is. I'm just not ready to give up the free head any time I want."

It's my turn to roll my eyes at him. "You have slept with everyone at this school, teachers included."

"True, but hear me out. Her head game is on point, fellas. I also can't help that the cougars love me. What can I say? Look at this face." He grins, showing off his dimple, giving him a false look of 'boy-next-door' when he is more like the serial killer next door. Unaware they're stuck until they're too deep in his web.

"Saint, there's nothing to worry about with the Riley girl. Don't trip on it. There is no body. So, there is no evidence. Mal took care of it, and if there is one thing we can count on him for, it's protecting you. Has Priya's parents texted her at least?" I go to defend that Malice cares about them, in his own twisted way. He doesn't play well with others, but he has with them.

"Um, no. Nothing." I touch my lip piercing with my thumb. "Not even a phone call. I have it set up to record her calls. So even if we miss it, we still have it." He curtly nods his head and signals for Bennett to follow him out.

I sit back in my chair, causing it to creak under my weight. Now that I think about it, it is kind of odd she hasn't heard from her parents. All the research I did on her prior to her arrival depicts a happy family with two daughters. Dressed up to the nines for charity events, always near her mother, father, or sister, with a smile on her face. Her parents sent her here on a big donation in their name to make sure she had a place. She was a straight-A student all throughout high school, joined tutoring, chess and even the debate team at one point. I look again, seeing more articles on her sister than her. What am I missing?

CREW

ONE STEP CLOSER – LINKIN PARK

Storming out of the house, wanting to turn back to slam the door repeatedly as my times as I can to let the world know how vexed I am. My blood boils underneath my skin, heating me from the inside out. I refrain from it for the same reason. I don't want everyone to know I'm shaking with uncontrollable rage.

Ever since I was a young boy, venom has coursed through my veins, numbing any warmth within. At first, for no reason at all. It was just who I was. Bennett and I were the perfect opposites as far as twins go. Ben carries an air of contentment, a warm aura that radiates from him, sparking happiness in everyone. I, being skeptical by nature, have remained unconvinced. He thinks it's because I'm technically older, but that couldn't be far from the truth. I have always had to shoulder the burden of cleaning up after everyone's mess. Starting with our mother.

The day she died, I couldn't help but be relieved that she wouldn't have to choose between the drugs or her kids. I swallow the guilt that nags in the back of my throat. She chose. All the times I begged her to be better for Ben and she promised she would. Time and time again, I believed her broken promises. Thinking that one day it would get better. Each time, the relapse would be worse than the last until it finally caught up to her. Finding my mother's dead body fucked me up.

I expected once she was gone, it would be easier for us. I was wrong.

Someone separated Ben and me, which was uncommon for twins. He was sent to some fucked up couple with sick tendencies to harm little vulnerable, defenseless boys. And I went to a foster dad who would rather beat me until I was unconscious, wait until I healed, only to repeat the process. Now and then, Steve would get creative. His favorite punishment outside of his daily beating, was drowning me. Only to bring me back from the brink of death.

Suppressing a shudder at the thought of the grimy bathtub, I close in on Brian's room tucked behind the school. The building houses most of the teachers on campus. Being the dean means he has the biggest suite. An older building with grey stones, much like the school, completely remodeled inside. I open the double glass doors and head through a carpeted hallway. It smells like old books in here. Showing years of success, pictures of earlier deans' line the wall. Brian's room is at the end of the long hallway.

Taking a deep breath to lull myself back into the calm I'm known for, I turn the knob. The idiot left it unlocked. Walking in, I'm hit with the musky odor of sex. I know it's from Lisa, the nurse. I wouldn't call her a sex worker, but I'm sure the money we offered her had a hand in getting her to agree. Sitting down at the two-person table off to the side of his full-sized kitchen, I wait for the shower to turn off. Checking my pockets, I find what I'm looking for when he steps out of his bathroom, a towel wrapped around his waist.

I'm not like Bennett. I don't have time for the niceties and games he likes to play.

"Sit down, Brian." I say, emotionless.

He cautiously pulls out a chair across from me with his hands resting on the table. Good, he *does* know how to listen. He smiles weakly. I don't like to deal with him. Me coming to his room isn't a common occurrence. Glowering, I let him see my disappointment before swiftly pulling a narrow knife out of my pocket and stabbing it through the center of his hand. It's a clean wound, straight through, missing bones and anything else important. Brian's reaction is delayed a split second before I swiftly bring my other hand over his mouth to smother the scream.

"Shut the fuck up, Brian." He whimpers behind my hand.

"Were Bennett's directions too unclear for you?" I scold. Finally, somewhere to put the anger that constantly eats me. He shakes his head underneath my hand.

"Then why am I fucking here?" Slowly removing my hand, I allow him to speak.

"I-I was g-going to tell you! I swear," he stutters.

Not good enough. He should've told me the second she left his office. I jiggle the knife in his hand to let him know he's pissing me off. Clenching my jaw, looking away from his face before I put my fucking fist into it.

"I will fucking kill you, Brian. We had an agreement. First, you allow River Walton to change her schedule and now?" Letting out a humorless laugh. "I'm barely able to keep Ben and Malice from having a go at you. They want you fucking gone. I'm half tempted to let go of their leashes. I am the only reason you're fucking breathing right now." I'm not going to give my hand away and let him know I have a deal with his wife. Nor that he will probably be dead by the end of all of this. Having someone higher up that was easy to control from the sidelines was supposed to be the simple part. We're doing this for Ty. He was going to be someone. He was owed that much. We are in debt to him and his father.

"Here's what you're going to do, Brian. You are going to stick me into one of her classes since you can't manage the one, simple job you were given." I sneer. His name leaves a nasty taste in my mouth. He nods vigorously.

"Yes, of course, Crew." Brian gasps in between his pained panting. His face pales. Good boy, I pat his cheek. Finished with this conversation, I rip my knife from his hand and wipe it on his loose towel.

"Get a hold of Lisa. If she's even left."

The cool air washes over my face, doing nothing to stem the anger that holds a permanent residence in my heart. We need a job, and soon. I'm reaching a breaking point that I don't want to cross. The guys are probably as twitchy as I am to get back to work. I thought avenging Tyson would distract us, but it seems to be making everything worse. Pulling out my phone, I shoot off a text.

CREW

Any jobs?

ELIJAH

That bad, huh?

Rolling my eyes at his response, he always has to read into everything. Leave it to Elijah Cox to over examine a simple text message. He may not be my birth father, but he's more than a father than that deadbeat ever would be to us. Unfortunately, he isn't wrong. Regardless of what I show the world, he's always been able to see through it. Sometimes more than Bennett. The feeling that we aren't as close as we should be overwhelms me with regret.

I debate on lying to him, but then he'll just call.

CREW

Yes, it's that bad.

ELIJAH

Martin Pierce, 0000 River Road, Saint
George, ME. He's hiding out on a lot. I'll
send his crimes.

That's enough for me. I'll let the guys know when I'm done downstairs at the gym. We will get it set up. It's something we can get done this weekend. My phone dings with another text message.

ELIJAH

Love you, Crew

I look at it, shutting the screen off. I haven't been able to bring myself to say it. But he knows. He has to. *Ding.* Jesus Christ, should I just say it?

PRIYA

HOW TO SAVE A LIFE – THE FRAY

This morning, I asked River for a little time by myself. She was disappointed, but relented. There was no coffee first thing. No one sitting in a chair by the window scrolling through their phone waiting for my alarm to go off.

The room feels emptier without her. She brings life into a room without trying. I find myself missing the sunshine in the form of River. Her presence makes me less alone. I've been here exactly seven days, including the start of class and so far, things have been progressing smoothly. I'm up to speed on all the curriculum, thanks to my last school. The real reason I needed this morning to myself was to send a text to Addi. Since I've been here, I have mainly been limited to "I miss you", and "I love you" messages. Pulling out my phone, I update my sister on my life.

PRIYA

Cingulomania; a strong desire to hold someone in your arms. I believe I relate to that. I don't mean to send short messages. The school load was more than I thought it would be.

Things that are new lately. I almost punched that one Leticia bitch in the face. She was recording me when I came out of the bathroom, after someone shredded my clothes. She has some weird obsession with Bennett Demonio, he's cute enough. But not enough to risk my freedom.

I still haven't heard from mom or dad, but maybe that's for the best. River should be here soon, Iloveyou. Talk to you soon. - Firefly

Within the next hour, River promptly knocks on the door. A puzzled look on her face, a black envelope in hand.

"Where did you get that?" My pulse rises rapidly. I caught her red-handed!

She side-eyes me, "It was taped to your door. I pulled it off when you opened the door. What is it?" I'm unsure how to answer because I don't quite know either. This is the second one I've gotten. Grabbing it from her hands, I rip it open.

I watch you when you sleep. I haunt you during the day. You stare at me and see nothing but darkness. What am I?

River's head rests on my shoulder looking at the black paper matching the one in the bottom of my nightstand. She jumps back, "It's a riddle!" She says excitedly. I furrow my brows. A riddle?

"Yeah, I've seen these before. My brother and I used to read them all the time when we were younger."

"Where?" Thinking the envelopes are a normal occurrence and I'm overreacting.

"Online, duh. Or a book." she laughs.

"Not the envelope attached to the door?"

"Yeah, no. That's weird," she grimaces. Not making me feel any better. "Fear." River whispers. The hair on the back of my arms stands.

"What?"

"The answer is fear."

I peek my head out the doorway, looking both ways for any notable disturbances, only to come up short.

"You didn't leave this? Or see anyone outside my door?" She looks off to the side in thought before telling me she hasn't.

"Does it say anything else?" she asks. Showing her the envelope only has my first name on it.

"I'll see if I can hack into the dorm footage. Let you know what I find."

A weight is lifted off my shoulders. Hopefully, we can catch the person responsible. The headmaster won't do shit about it. I will though.

We're off to our first class. Psychology is first for me, while River has calculus. I'm happy to report I only have P. E every other day, as opposed to the standard every day.

River leaves me at the doorway of Mrs. Warren's class, and I take my assigned seat by the window, leaving the seat to the right of me vacant. She's an older woman in her 40s with her PhD in psychology. It's refreshing to be taught by someone who has worked in the field. Rather than someone who can only answer questions about the class. Mrs. Warren always dresses in a professional pencil skirt. Her hair is up in a tight 'no nonsense' bun. Glasses rest on the end of her nose as she goes over the notes for today's class. She's a fair teacher. Understanding when it comes to open and effective communication.

Her helpfulness at this school is unmatched. She's ready to

assist, whether it's through answering emails or addressing questions about assignments. The type of person who should be a teacher. Someone patient, compassionate, and dedicated to helping people learn. When asked about the topic of the day, a small smile tugs at her lip—a rare sight, considering her usual expression of irritation.

Getting myself comfortable, I lay out my things neatly. A chair pulls out next to me and a body plops down, startling me.

Well, well, well. If it isn't the third Demon that I've been fortunate enough to avoid, until now. His dark hair is perfectly tamed. The down-turned corners of his pouty, full lips reveal his irritation. There isn't a piece of clothing that doesn't have a hard ironed line in it. Crew Demonio is disgustingly tidy. I refrain from the temptation to crinkle his impeccable attire. My fingers tingle with the desire to mess up his perfectly styled hair. He's so perfect. It makes my skin crawl. This is what my parents wanted me to be like. Who the hell made him look like this?

"Are you just going to stare at me?" Crew huffs, waking me from my thoughts.

"I'm sorry. This seat hasn't had a single student since I've been in this class. And all the sudden there is. I think that's due for a little staring." I say defensively because he called me out. "If it makes you feel better, it's more of a 'why the fuck are you here' stare." Crew glares from beneath his lashes. Shrugging, just because we have to sit together doesn't mean we have to acknowledge each other. That is true until Mrs. Warren opens her mouth, and for once I'm not excited.

"Today, we start our semester project. We will work in pairs. Each pair will be picking a mental illness to report on. This will count for at least *half* of your grade in my class." My shoulders slump with relief. I read the syllabus for this class and got a head start on this project. Especially since it's a huge chunk of my grade. With or without the infamous Crew, I'm determined to pass.

Mrs. Warren starts with us. Before Crew can open his mouth, I let her know the topic 'we' chose. I've done most of the work already. He won't fuck this up for me. I'm ahead in all my classes and it will stay that way.

"We'll take DID. Dissociative Identity Disorder." Warren claps her hands together excitedly. Then moves on to the next group.

"Why did you pick that mental illness, Priya?" Crew quietly questions. His shoulders are tense. It's just a class, jeez.

"I already have most of the work done. I was prepared to do this assignment on my own. So, if you want to go over what I have done and add whatever is left to get some credit. That would be helpful."

"And if I don't?" He sneers. I seemed to have struck some chord.

Sighing, "Then nothing, Crew. I won't have you mess with the grades I try so hard to get and keep. Do it. Don't do it. I won't hold my breath. I'll finish it, regardless. It's up to you whether or not your name is on the paper." Taking out the assignment I already have done and printed out, I lay them in front of him. Crew grabs them, looks me right in the eye and rips it in half. I clench my teeth so hard that they're going to break at this rate. My fists form tight balls, begging to hit him. Through my blurry vision, I seethe. The seconds on the clock tick by. It's fine. It's not like I spent hours of this week working on that assignment, only for him to rip it apart. I'll print out another one. The bell rings and I hurry to go find River.

BENNETT

It's Friday night. Excitement buzzes through my veins while my brother sits Saint and I down at the kitchen island. Every article we're wearing is black, from head to toe. I don't want to brag about saying I planned our outfits, but I did. Malice is lurking in the background. It's been so long since we've been on a job. I have an abundance of energy, like a live wire. I can't imagine how everyone else feels finally to be free from the confines of this miserable, monotonous routine. We've made no progress with Priya and it's getting under everyone's skin. The fact she still walks around with her head high has my teeth on edge. I'll have to apply a little more pressure for some results. She needs to be pulled down a peg or two. I want her to pay for what she did. I want her broken. When Crew tells us about the gig for tonight, I forget my anger.

"Martin Pierce, 0000 River Road in Saint George. He's hiding out on some lot of land."

"Crime?" Saint asks. We all know it wouldn't matter what the offense is. We have signed, sealed, and will deliver his death warrant.

"Reoccurring sex offender. His recent victim is a 12-year-old little girl named Ellie. He kidnapped her for three days. Repeatedly raped her, before letting her go." He pauses. There is more. "He let her go in the forest. The police found her six days after her abduction date. Died from her wounds, starvation, and severe dehydration. The autopsy reported internal tears." My stomach rolls with nausea. Charles and Marie come to mind. Of a time when I was a defenseless kid with no one to protect me. Peeking over at Saint, he's not in much better shape. His face is paler than usual. Nodding, I get up, ready to take out this piece of trash.

"Everything is packed. We just have to stop in town to pick up the car." Of course. Crew would ensure that everything is ready to go.

We pull onto a dirt road. The ghost car is a standard older four-door sedan. Untraceable with counterfeit plates and insurance, in case we get pulled over. Worst-case scenario, we have to boost another car. Which would add to our fun 'night out'.

Having money definitely comes with some perks, but sometimes I miss the way our lives used to be, before mom died. Playing outside until the streetlights came on. Crew made a game to see who could steal the most food without getting caught. Another pothole has the guys jostling around. They're absolutely impossible to miss.

"You missed one." Crew grumbles from the passenger seat. My foot slams on the brakes in the middle of the rocky road, startling Saint and Crew.

"What the fuck, Ben?" Crew yells. Looking back in the

rearview mirror, Saint smothers a smile and shakes his head. I smirk, throwing the car in reverse. Gravel spins up from beneath the tires, losing a little traction. All of us go flying backwards when I hit the gas, bouncing from the deep potholes all over again. Have to make sure I hit the "one" I missed, according to Crew. Laughing like a maniac at the panicked look on Saint's face and the small smile on my brother's face. Their happiness makes my heart a little lighter than it has been in months.

Trees and bushes cover the overgrown pathway. The turn is barely noticeable in the dark. Driving slowly, I shut off the headlights. Better not to have him know we're here. It would ruin the surprise. My eye twitches when the rough texture of sticks scratches the side of the car, like nails on a chalkboard.

"Come on, you're getting ready to kill someone, and you're cringing at the noise?" Crew complains.

Giving him the side eye, "Your car deserves better than a reckless, heartless owner like you. Poor baby," I coo to the car, rubbing the steering wheel. We pull up to a literal abandoned shack in the middle of nowhere, about the size of our ensuite bathrooms. Stealthily, we get out of the car a little ways away from said shack.

My brother hands us each a pair of leather gloves. "Ben, you'll go in through the front door. Malice through the back." Leaving him to make sure our target doesn't get out from the sides. It's dark enough where mostly everything is a darker mass in the night. Since we're in such a dense area, I decided the best course of action was night vision goggles. Also, I just *really* wanted to try them out. Sliding them on, I bring down the binocular contraption. This is sick. I love it. Silently, we get into our positions.

Everyone has 30 seconds. It's an unspoken rule. I ready my weight against the center panel of the old wood door, decaying with time, and giddiness rushes over me as I push forward with my shoulder. The door splinters with a *crack*, making its way around the otherwise silent night. Wings flutter from animals that inhabit the unoccupied space. I wrinkle my nose at the smell of rotting wood, mildew, and human piss. Debris covers the entire shack. The room is a mess, empty cans of unidentified drinks strewn about in every corner. An old mattress that's blackened with age and grime lies on the floor, pushed up against the wall with a figure slowly sitting up. Disgusting. I open my mouth, but Malice beats me to it. He slinks from the darkened shadows. I remove my night vision goggles at the same time Crew flips on a lantern.

"Hello, Martin." Crew greets, followed by an ominous thud of our leather bag filled with goodies.

Everything after that was quick, the thrill of being in action after being dormant for so long. Malice grabs Martin by the back of the neck. While I make quick work of the rope Crew handed me when we switched cars. I bind the rope tightly behind his back, wrapping it around his wrists, following suit for his ankles, ensuring he can't get out. Malice enjoys the struggle too much as he tosses the trembling pedophile on the ground. He lands on his shoulder, screaming from the harsh impact. That will be the least of his worries soon enough.

"Do you know who we are? Why are we here, Martin?" Crew asks unbothered. Like Martin is wasting his time by being here. Martin shakes his head. Straight to denial, predictable. Who would admit they're a fucking predator?

Tsking, Crew continues. "You know the answer to at least one of those questions."

"The girl." Martin whispers.

A genuine smile splits across Crew's face. Happy with his admission. He nods to Malice, but Martin took it as a sign to continue.

"B-But her parents were asking for it. Who leaves their child unattended at a playground? There are monsters everywhere," he stutters but picks up with conviction.

My brother wears the matching scowl of my own.

"Monsters like you?"

The coward nods, not realizing that was the answer that sealed his gruesome fate. The zipper of the bag is loud over his labored breathing. I guess we're not the only ones dying of suspense.

"I'd give you the same courtesy you did for little Ellie. But unfortunately, *my* monsters are hungry."

Tension fills the air. I'm foaming at the mouth for it. The metallic tang of blood in the air. Unable to contain myself, I let out a whoop for what's to come.

Malice squats, impatient with Crew's mind games. He grabs a fist full of his hair at the roots and faces him towards us. The lantern's flickering light casts an ominous aura over Malice, giving him a sinister appearance. A demon coming to collect a soul.

A pair of pliers are placed in my hand. Where to start? I could take off his nails one by one. Hands and then feet. We purposefully left his face without tape to hear his screams. Beg us to stop for his life, just like Ellie did. My heart beats a little faster at the thought of a helpless girl begging for her mom. Or her brother, like I did.

Before I can pick a place to start. Crew eagerly lands the first punch square on Martin's jaw. His head snaps backwards, and he groans. Mal takes his knife and pushes it into the piece of shits skin. Only one gash, shoulder to elbow and fixates on the blood slowly trickling out of his wound, before dripping off of his elbow. Without fanfare he's dropped to the dirty wood floor. A steeled toe boot lands a perfect kick to his ribs. I cringe, that has to of broken something. My twin doesn't stop there. He beats Martin until he's an unconscious, bloody pile on the ground. His face is unrecognizable. Both eyes are swollen shut. Teeth are missing and his breaths are loud wheezes. His nose sits on his face at an awkward angle.

There's only one word to describe it. Beautiful.

Malice pulls out smelling salts, leaving Martin to startle awake. A smile stretches across my face. My turn.

The cold metal of the pliers seep through my leather gloves, sending a delicious shiver up my spine. His pinky first, all the way to his thumb, exposing the nerve-rich nail bed in its wake. Only to repeat the process on the next hand.

There is something about the way the fragile skin underneath the nail gives away that brings me pleasure. With each nail I pull, Malice leaves another cut on the man's skin. I don't know if he feels anything at this point, but I do. After his nasty toenails are done. I step back to admire our work. He's still alive, barely. He won't be as soon as Malice is done with him.

"Do you know who we are yet?" The thick British accent sounds menacing. A groan is the only response he gets. Mal hums his displeasure.

"We're the Demons." He slices, stabbing his blade into the bloodied leg before jerking it out, only to jab it into his right leg. A blood-curdling scream reaches all four corners of the dark shack.

"And we've come to collect your soul," he whispers darkly into his ear.

"Ooh, that one gave me shivers." I say to no one in particular. The man's wailing intensifies when the blade is yanked out once again. Aware he will not make it out in one piece. If I'm being honest, not even two.

While he's blubbering on the ground. Crew reaches inside the leather bag with our work tools to grab a bone saw. This elicits a weak fight-or-flight response from Martin. He struggles in Malice's grip to get away from Crew. I grab his hand in a death grip and apply pressure to his bloody fingertips to keep him immobile. The saw is the shape of an 'L', easily held. He grabbed his fancy one for tonight. The sound of the saw cutting through bone bounces around my brain as he brutally removes his pinky finger. Bloodied bone is visible through all the flesh parts, allowing us to see it clearly. Leaving us surrounded by the acrid scent of burnt skin and seared hair, fill my nose when I cauterize the wound to keep him from bleeding out too quick. The high I'm riding on is better than any drug could give me.

Without waiting for me to finish, Malice steps closer, letting me know he's ready to continue. Each strike pierces and cuts through Martin's flesh until his cries are silenced. There's something so peaceful after taking a life. The stillness that fills the air is incredibly calming. I could justify our actions by saying how horrible of a guy he was. How someone who rapes and tortures a little girl is scum. All of that would be the truth. But that's not why we do it. That's just a bonus.

Blood is present in every corner that the lantern light reaches, creating what would be a chilling scene to most. The transformation of Martin's exterior now matches the true nature of his inner self, the trash he used to be.

Malice's icy blue eyes connect with mine. I know what he's going to do before he even does it.

"Don't." I groan. He gives me a wicked smile, pulling the knife up to his mouth. "Don't you fucking do it, you nasty bastard." His grin reaches from cheek to cheek, bringing the knife closer to his lips, and licks one side of his blade. Blood coats his tongue and seeps into his teeth when he closes his mouth. "Mal!" I hiss, "you don't know if his nasty ass was clean. STDs?" Gagging at the thought.

Malice shrugs. "He didn't. I had Saint check when he looped the traffic cameras. Plus, it's a ritual."

A fucking nasty one. Mark my words, he'll fuck up one day and it'll bite him in the ass.

Crew pats my back. "You're on clean up." Come on! You have got to be kidding me. I barely got to play, and I get stuck with the dirty work. Grunting, I work on dismembering the body for transport. Starting with his limbs to isolate the torso. When someone moves the lantern, I notice a black envelope lying on the bed. If not for the light, it would've been easily missed. The envelope is the same color as the bed. I reach for it and rip it open. The message sends chills down my spine and not the good ones I've been feeling all night.

Saint, it's time to come home.

PRIYA

LILLITH – ELLISE

This isn't how I thought I'd spend my Saturday evening. Alone with the creepy ass dean. The big oak door seems more imposing than it did last time. Walking in it will be a bad idea, a metaphorical nail in my already snug coffin. What choice do I have? The mere thought of being sent back to Robert Carter brings back memories of the stifling spicy scent of his cologne and whiskey on his breath.

Knocking three times, I wait for his signature bored, "Enter" before going in. Detention seems like it's going to become a common occurrence if he's choosing to believe whatever nonsense comes to his doorstep about me.

Dean Bush gives me his back while at a small cart in the corner of the room. Without his eyes on me, I'm able to observe the room without him watching my every move.

Wood floor to ceiling bookcases, with an ancient appearance, adorn the four walls of the room, covering more than half of the space. Brian Bush doesn't look like the type of man to have touched a book in his life. What books could he have to fill the shelves? "How to be a Creep for Dummies"?

Rows of faux plants lining the shelves, their plastic leaves reflecting the dim light of the room. The air is stagnant and stuffy. I know little about plants but I'm pretty sure it's supposed to support the air quality.

As I walk over to his desk, I sit in the uncomfortable wooden chair with my hands resting on my lap. Clinking of ice hitting the bottom of a glass is the only sound in the quiet room. 5:10PM. We've already done nothing for ten minutes. The carpet muffles Bush's footsteps when he approaches his seat across from me. His amber drink, is already sweating in the stuffy room.

Ultimately, we engage in a staring competition to see who will break the silence first. A white ace bandage wraps the dean's hand, which holds the glass. A recent injury? If he thinks I'm going to say something first, he's wrong. My father controlled me all my life, telling me to jump and me saying 'how high?'. I'm a marionette in my household. I refuse to be one here at this school. Raising an eyebrow. I wait for him to speak. After all, the only reason I'm here is because *he* gave me unwarranted detention instead of standing up to the school's queen bitch.

"Priya." He addresses me calmly. I didn't realize we're on a first name basis. Bush takes a sip of his drink. Watching his thin lips press into the glass makes me uncomfortable. Being around a grown ass adult alone, drinking alcohol. Past run-ins with drunk men have made me cautious. Nothing good will come from it. As if he can feel my eyes on his glass, "Don't worry, it's after hours. I can drink freely outside of scheduled school hours." Yeah, that doesn't ease my anxiety at all. Thank you for nothing.

"For detention, we're going to sort out this reckless behavior of yours." Nodding along to appease him, his posture relaxes. I won't point fingers and blame the responsible party. But I'll clarify that I had no involvement in what triggered my behavior.

"Well, some questions might be uncomfortable, but please answer to the best of your ability." Wait, what? This isn't going where I thought it was.

"How is your home life?" Gauging his face when he asks. I determine he doesn't truly care. Nor is he my shrink.

"Fine." Giving him a bland answer.

"Everything okay with mom? Dad? Siblings?" My heart shrinks in size at the thought of Addison. He's being cruel because he knows what happened to my sister. As for my parents, it's always how it's been. I'm nonexistent until they need something.

"Yes." I grit out. He hums, finishing off his drink. Not noticing how quickly he drained his drink alarms me. Setting down the glass, he comes and perches on the large desk next to me. All the room on this polished tree, and he wants to be as close to me as he can be. Tension lines my body, high alert on his closeness. I stare straightforward, focusing on his empty glass, save a couple of ice cubes.

He's inspecting me. Picking me apart. For once, I don't want to know what someone is thinking when they look at me.

"You're pretty." He says lowly. His hand touches the black strings of my cotton hoodie I changed into before coming to detention. "Your lips are so full, a permanent pouty look. Did daddy pay for you to get that done?" I squeeze my trembling hands together enough to turn my knuckles white. Do I answer the only appropriate question he asked? Ignore it? Opting to remain quiet, I subtly shake my head.

"These clothes can only do so much to hide your figure, you know?" My teeth clench at what he's implying. Living with my father's unpredictable mood changes has trained my peripheral vision to be hypersensitive. From the corner of my eye, he adjusts himself in his slacks that I'm sure he's worn all day. My razor is in my bra. If he takes his dick out... I'll cut it off or I'll die trying. My father be damned.

The dean's finger lightly grazes my cheekbone before stepping away. Leaving behind a dirty feeling in his presence. Clearing his throat from whatever stupor he put himself in, he says, "I want, at the minimum, three reasons the Demons' have taken an interest in you. You can leave after." Confusion is the only emotion I've shown tonight and riddle me confused. A couple of life questions when this is what he wanted originally?

I'm not going to look a gift horse in the mouth. Asking anything more could make it seem like an invitation to continue his creepy line of questioning.

Bush drops a pen and paper in front of me. Three reasons they're interested in me.

They're not. My interactions with them have been minimal thus far. I don't know what makes him think otherwise. I get to work on my paper so I can get the hell out of here.

1. **I question their authority**
2. **They don't like being put in their place**
3. **I think they're self entitled assholes**

I drop the pen and storm out of the room.

PRIYA

As soon as I left Bush's office, I came straight to the dorm. Rubbing my book of matches doesn't bring me the usual feeling of peace. Clockwise, counter-clockwise. Repeat.

I need to do something. I pace the carpet back and forth, moving from one end of my dorm hallway to the other.

It feels like I need to run.

Away.

From something.

To someone.

My nerves are being stretched thin. The threads holding me together are fraying. It's times like this I *need* my sister. Her guidance, strength, even her grace to deal with these situations. She would know what to do.

My father is always haunting the corners of my brain. He never leaves me alone.

My sister's soul crushing absence.

Amber constantly coming after me with some fucked up agenda.

Bush's not so subtle perverted staring and touches.

The fucking black envelopes with their stupid riddles showing up out of nowhere with no explanation.

I want to scream and rage about the fucking unfair shitty hand I was dealt under the guise of a 'privileged life'.

My thoughts halt as I come to a stop outside of River's rainbow covered door. I'm battling with wanting to ask for help or trying to figure it out myself. My hand raises to knock, but I put it back down to my side. Can I do it? Can I be vulnerable? Every time I've tried, it's always bit me in the ass. I've begged for acceptance, only to have it thrown back in my face.

I'm so fucking fragile.

Showing my vulnerability will give her a chance to break me. The softest blow would be my undoing. Chewing my lip, I go with my gut feeling. Lifting my hand, I go to knock when the door swings open. River is in an all-black oversized adult onesie with bear ears on. Looking terribly cute and cuddly.

"Sorry." I mumble and turn away to go to my room. This was a mistake.

"Priya." She comes to stand in front of me, blocking my door. She's quicker than I gave her credit for. Her hip pops out, arms cross over her chest and eyebrows raised. Tapping my fingers, trying to get what I need out without sounding crazy.

"Spit it out."

"I need something." The worlds tumble out.

"Anything." The look on her face makes it seem like she means it. Like she would do anything I asked. Find a way to make it happen. Just like Addison would.

Swallowing my wariness, "I need a fire." Even the whisper sounds so loud.

She give me a curt nod. "Let me get my jacket and shoes. I'll take you somewhere."

Relief rushes through me. I need to get my stuff I hid in my room. Under the trash can, I pried up a floorboard to stash my lighter fluid and extra matches. It's a tight fit for the items, but with a little wiggling, it comes right out. Stuffing it in my black bag, I make sure I have my key card and my razor in my bra. Nodding my confirmation to myself, I go get River.

PRIYA

FREAK –LANA DEL RAY

A twenty-minute walk into the menacing woods later, River brings me to a clearing with a black hole about the length of me in the center. This is better than what I could've asked for.

"There are a couple of logs left. I mean there was last time I was out here," River says, walking over to the left side of the pit to point out the couple of logs scattered on the ground.

"Will you come with me to get more small sticks?" I ask timidly. I've never lit a fire for anyone but my sister. And after my last incident in the woods, I don't want either of us by ourselves. She comes over to me without hesitation, grabbing my hand, intertwining our fingers, and leads me to the edge of the clearing to the closest tree. A part of me wants to see her face. Is she judging me? Does she think I'm a psychopath, too? A weirdo? She hasn't rejected me thus far. That has to mean something, right? Doubt and insecurities plague me. The sound of a branch cracking echoes through the forest. Foraging has begun.

I try not to let my excitement show too much in fear of scaring her off. Like a busy bee, I flit from one tree to the next, gathering the different shapes and varying sizes of sticks. By the time I'm satisfied with the amount of firewood I have, my arms are full. My pockets hold any tiny twigs I could collect. Beaming, I throw my pile into the pit. River follows my lead, tossing in an arm full of branches. It's perfect. She keeps hold of one lone stick leaning against it, waiting.

"Now what?" She says, breathless from the exertion.

"Now? We burn this bitch up." My hands shake as I grab the lighter fluid from out of my bag. Covering the logs, branches and little twigs with it, the butane and isobutane bringing a sense of rightness to the world. To complete the process, I add the finishing touch by writing the name 'Addi' with the fluid. It's not like anyone is going to see it. But I'll know. She will know.

My hand digs back into the bag at my feet, pulling out my book of matches that have been dormant for too long. Shining stars peek through the canopy of the trees. It makes me wonder what happens when we die. Are you nothing? An angel? Reincarnation? Can we become a star? I think I'd like to think my sister is a star, able to shine brightly over the world. Finally, the comfort of rubbing the matches makes its appearance.

With the black match between my fingers, I strike it against the rough strip and observe as it transforms into a flickering inferno. It burns a few seconds before I toss it into the manmade pit. The sudden burst of heat and light fills the air when a spark ignites the flames. Creating a fiery ocean in the sky before settling down into calm waves. The trees cower away from the scorching heat of the fire. The heaviness in my soul slips away. Instant relief.

Letting the heat chase away the coldness in my soul for a few moments, I sit. River settles down next to me, handing me the stick she purposefully kept out of her pile. Gratefully grabbing it, I play with the fire. Running after the dancing flame with the stick, the crackling and popping sounds bring the much-needed comfort I've been seeking since my sister's absence.

"Ugh, I hate dirt," River states, breaking the comfortable silence we'd been in. The dirt didn't even cross my mind. The flames are more hypnotizing than our surroundings. I don't tell her that. She doesn't get the same satisfaction. Instead, I thank her by speaking her love language and lay my head on her shoulder.

"What happened?" At least she had an ice breaker before coming out with the question. Starting to shrug my shoulders and tell her I'm fine, she feels the movement and stops me.

"Don't. Don't patronize me." My lips purse to keep the lies inside my mouth.

"Everything." I whisper so quietly that I hope she didn't hear me. She takes my hand in hers once again. I can feel the unity in her grasp, letting me know she's here. So, I do the same thing and squeeze twice, "I'm here". She does it back. My heart clenches at memories threatening to pull me away from the conversation, into a happier time.

Drawing in a deep breath, I start with things I can get away without telling her everything. "I think the dean might be a fucking perv."

She doesn't deny it, just questions 'why?'.

I go into detail from beginning to end about our encounters. River stays quiet for a moment, in thought.

"What else? There's more. This doesn't come from one thing alone." She gestures at the fire that's still going.

I tell her about the envelope. How I *know* it's something bad.

That the same week someone left the missing person's picture of Megan Riley taped to the gym locker room for me to find.

"Could it be someone trying to scare you away?" It's not a far-fetched question, one I've asked myself more than once. It feels more threatening. Plus, where would they scare me away to? I don't have anywhere else to go. I'm alone, truly alone. I shake my head.

"No. Something is wrong. Call me crazy, but I just *know* it's something more."

"I had a look at the camera feed from our hallway." One answer to the many questions I have. "It's some guy. Wearing all black and a hat to hide his face from the camera on our floor. But, you clearly see him tape it to the door. I'll send you the video. Maybe you can see something that I don't."

Nodding, though, I doubt I'll see something she didn't. Another piece in my unsolvable puzzle. With no one tending to it, the fire is slowly dying. Believe when I say I want to, but I already feel bad for ruining River's Saturday night.

"So…" She draws out the word. "Fire?"

Smirking, I nod. "Yeah, fire."

"You're a … pyromaniac?" She asks, unsure.

I shrug, "I dunno. I've never actually been diagnosed. It's not as common in girls as it is in boys. But I like fire. A lot. Possibly more than most people should." River nods like it's a normal thing. And maybe it is here at Cox Academy. She did say 'everyone is here for something'.

"It's kind of why I was sent here." Admitting it to her feels like a sin. When she stays quiet, I take that as a sign to continue. "My sister." Tears clog my throat, thinking of the day I lost everything that mattered. "Two counts of involuntary manslaughter and aggravated reckless arson. Sentence pending upon completing this school year." I mock the judge's deep voice when he decided my fate that day.

It's quiet until I hear her gasp over the crackling of the fire, still fighting to eat anything and everything it can, like me. I ruin everything I touch. I'm unable to look at her. Disgust, shame, fear. I've seen it all already.

"What happened?" The words are gentle, not prying. Asking for my truth. I appreciate she doesn't jump to conclusions about what happened.

"I killed my sister." The confession tastes like ash on my tongue.

PRIYA

I might as well have lit the match and dug her grave myself. The broken ribs I was nursing that day were nothing compared to the broken heart I ended up with.

"What? No way." Her face scrunches up as she shakes her head, refusing to believe me. Pulling her shoulder away from my head, she stares at me. Only to go back to shaking her head in disbelief. "There's absolutely no way. I don't believe that. I've witnessed with my own two eyes how you talk about your sister. Tell me what happened." The only person who wants to hear the truth. *My* truth,

With a forced smile, I gaze back into the flames.

"My parents don't like me very much. They never have, even as a small child. Constantly trying to pit Addison and I against each other." I believe their intentions were to get her to hate me as much as they did. "But it never worked. Addison was more of a mother than our mom was to me." Telling her this was to stress my sister's importance to me. "She was an overachiever. Regardless of how they treated us, we wanted them to accept and love us. She was a cheerleader, dated the 'hottest' guy at school, did volunteer work for the community. All around, she was just the kindest person you could know." I could be romanticizing her death and that's a different kind of stupid. This little bit of hope is keeping me alive. It's hard to think about any of the negative things people did when they die. It's usually focused on everything good they have done. But Addi has always been my hero, before and after the incident.

"They wanted me to be more like her. So, by joining extracurricular activities like her, I thought it would make them happy. Chess - boring, by the way. And soon after I added tutoring. On one of my days, I had to tutor a boy having trouble in history class. I'd never met him, but it was my easiest subject. She knew I was having a bad day. Worst one in weeks." It was the same week my dad had hired a new private doctor after the first one reported the abuse I was being subjected to. The doctor drew the line when my dad had broken one of my ribs for the first time by kicking me too hard. Addison didn't know the extent of it, but she tried to make my life a little easier by letting me rest.

"My sister offered to take my tutoring session. I should've said no. Sucked up whatever I was going through and went." Maybe things would have ended differently for her. For me. "When I dropped her off, I was supposed to pick her up and hour later, and she was going to take me to my spot to burn some things. Let off some tension. When I got there, the library was up in flames." My eyes sting from remembering feeling like my chest had caved in. The hopelessness that followed the shattering of my heart.

"The library was in flames. After they put out the fire, two bodies were found." Deciding its best to disassociate from her death and push through the story. "Both were burn beyond recognition. A male and female, later confirmed to be my sister and the boy she was with. It was a closed casket. Our parents made sure only immediate family could attend her funeral. It wasn't posted, talked about, or even mentioned that she had died." My parents thought it was best to not make it known to the public. They said it would ruin their perfect image, but I think they were in denial about losing their star child.

Everyone acted like the world hadn't lost meaning. As if her death meant nothing.

With a sense of release, I let out a deep breath as the weight on my shoulders disappears. All the people I've talked to assumed I was guilty. They were never interested in the truth.

River's brows furrow. "Wait… That doesn't make sense. You say it like you weren't there." Shaking my head, I should've been, but I wasn't.

"Then who set the fire?"

According to everyone else and the paper I signed. I did.

"All I heard was that there was a fire accelerant spread around." My gaze goes from the dying fire to the accelerant I have.

"There's no proof? You weren't there but because you like fire, it was you? Did anyone check cameras? Ask if they even saw you there?" The only acknowledgment I give is a half shrug of my shoulders. Not one person asked. I don't know if my parents told the lawyers about my obsession with fire and they made a deal. Or they didn't do anything at all.

"In my parent's eyes, I'm guilty." Shock overrides her other questions at the admission.

"W-What?" she stutters.

"Yep."

"My parents would never do that… They love me." She blinks and bursts out laughing. My shoulders shake with laughter. That's so fucked up that it's funny. Tears slide down my face from laughing so hard.

"That's fucked up." I say between wheezing fits of laughter.

"I know! I'm sorry! I didn't want you to think it was something I could relate to. Because I have never been through it. I couldn't resist. It was a tense moment for me. Maybe not my finest," she says while wiping tears from under her eyes.

"Thank you."

She squeezes my hand, pulling me up to my feet.

"Let's get back. These woods are creepy at night. I always feel like I'm being watched. And the fire is pretty much out." The scent of charred wood lingers, marking the end of the once roaring fire. A pang of longing hits me before I follow River's lead out of the woods, sparing a look into the forest. The looming trees seem to stretch out their boney fingers, beckoning me to come back. Their long arm-like branches are reaching for me. Back to the pit.

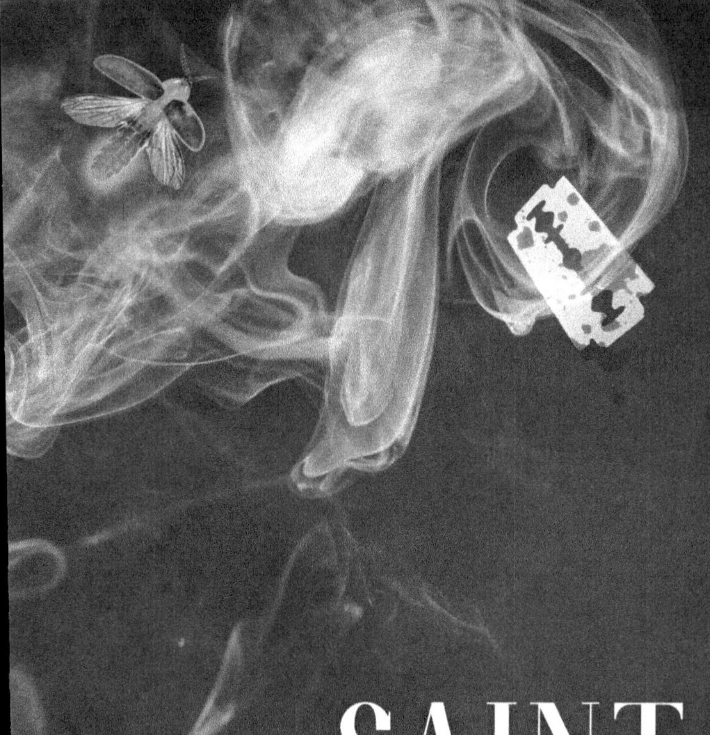

SAINT

BAD THINGS – CULTS

These days, I spend more time in my room in front of the constant hum of my computers, searching for anything that will point me in the right direction. Bennett brought up the need to push Priya a little further. All of us can agree that we're not happy with the results this far. It's been almost a month at this point and there's nothing to show how we've promised to honor Tyson, our best friend. My eyes wander from the glowing computer screen to the photograph of the four of us, like a bright patch of color against the dark surface hanging on the wall, flanked by heavy curtains. The summer when we were 16 and carefree. Now, everything feels like it's falling apart without him. He was our glue. He saved us, and in the end, we couldn't save him. Sadness tugs at my heart, but I push it away. Actions speak louder than words.

"All right?" Malice questions to see if I'm okay and when I don't answer, he continues. *"Are you daft, mate?"* I make a face at Malice, thinking calling me dumb will get me to answer. Just because he's taken the role of protector, doesn't mean he's always pleasant. He hates being ignored.

My hands rub up and down my tired eyes as I make my way to my perfectly made bed, thanks to Malice and his need for cleanliness. Malice's insistence on cleanliness has resulted in a spotless room, with everything meticulously dusted and clothes neatly put away. He left my blue thinking ball on the nightstand. The only thing that is messy is the computer desk that I refuse to let him touch.

Lying back on the king size bed, the navy blue down comforter welcomes my body into its embrace. "No. I'm stuck. I feel like I'm failing Tyson and the boys. No matter how hard I look, I can't find any new information. Everything is about her father's successful career, her sister's achievements, the charity events that they've thrown. I've even hacked into her old school database. Not one mistake in the past four years. She's like a fucking ghost." Agitation shows through my usual calm when I throw a pillow at the wall. It lands with a soft, unimpressive thud onto the hardwood floor.

"Did you mop the floors?" The lemon scent in my room is more noticeable now that I'm not staring at an electronic device.

"Yeah, throwing a wobbler will help you figure it out." He ignores me. The disapproval of my behavior is evident with his bored tone.

"What the fuck else am I supposed to do, Mal?" Gritting my teeth to ask because it's what this fucker wants. He knows something.

"I'm glad you asked, mate. You're stuck behind a computer when she's just a walk away. Instead of getting all cheesed off, go observe her." He brings up my irritation and says the simplest thing. *Observe.* Meaning…

"What have *you* found out, Malice?" I implore.

"Bloody hell, all this revenge plot. But you blokes have no idea what you're doing." Smug satisfaction rings in his voice. Nothing better to him than being one step ahead. It's annoying. He's supposed to be

on our team. *My* team. Instead, he's playing games with me. *"All right, I'll tell you* something. *But after that, take a look in the mirror. You're knackered. All work, no play, makes Malice a dull boy. That's how that saying goes, right?"* Rolling my eyes at his clearly botched proverb.

"Have you seen her eat?" Trying to picture the few times I have seen her in the cafeteria, it's always something light. A salad, eggs, seafood, maybe some chicken now and then, but she always has a glass of water. I nod. He's waiting for me to connect the dots myself. She hates good food? No, Mal wouldn't waste his breath for that. She's obsessed with her figure? My fingers tap against each other, callouses rough against the next, starting at my pinky. Thumb to pinky, thumb to my ring finger, and so on. Eating disorder? It's possible. It's small, but it's something.

An idea strikes me. I jump across the bed to grab her cloned phone off the charger to go through *old* messages. We assumed since she was away from her family, there would be an influx of text and calls, but that hasn't been the case.

I pull up her text messages. Her most recent text is to her sister. Clicking on the thread, I start from the most recent message and scroll up. If circumstances were different, I'd probably feel a bit sorry for Priya. Hundreds of text messages from Priya to her sister go unanswered. The ones of her pleading with Addison to just talk to her or give her a sign that she's listening make my stomach sink. Others act like she's giving a daily update about her life. Some messages are angry and filled with hurt. Most of them are simple 'I love you's, that go ignored. Damn, she must've done a number on her sister to be iced out completely. Months and months. Not a single reply. Not a "fuck you" or "Don't talk to me", just radio silence.

Her next thread is her father, Robert Carter. He himself is a shitty human being and politician, currently in the run for senator. He's always been a greasy shitbag. It wouldn't surprise me if he was an even shittier father. He never sends a text longer than one word. There isn't a single word of affection for Priya. Daddy issues?

The phone dings in my hand, alerting me to a new text

message. I watch in awe at the accuracy of my software and programming work with ease. A little pride thrums through me. Priya adds a new number to her contacts. River. I've seen the two girls smitten with each other since Priya's arrival here. It's no surprise that River's hacking and computer skills *almost* rival my own. It would suck to see a fellow techie become a casualty in a war she has no part in.

Priya goes to River's message. She sent her a video. There's a man in all black with a hat covering his face from the view of the camera, so I can't tell who he is. At first, I think it could be one of the guys, but this is something they'd tell me. Whatever he tapes to the door has Malice bugging to come out. Blinking twice, I can feel the switch flipping. The world switches to silence and my eyes fall closed.

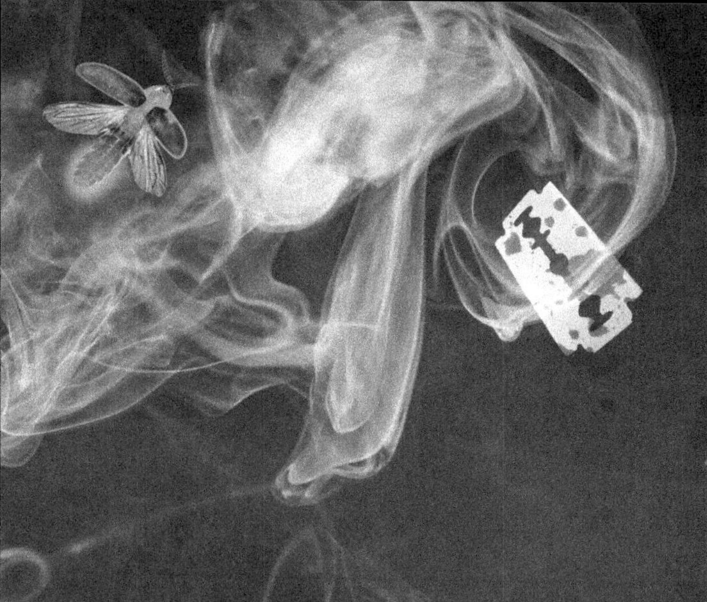

MALICE

AN UNHEALTHY OBSESSION –
THE BLACK ROBINSON SYNTHETIC ORCHESTRA

D o I coddle Saint a bit? Probably, but he'll forgive me. He always does. He has to. We can only exist together. I needed to nick sometime with Priya while I can. The outside in October is parky if someone's not used to it. Zipping up the black hoodie, I throw on the hood to keep up my anonymity from the cameras. I keep to the tree line to avoid any unwanted eyes from seeing me. The walk to her dorm room is fairly quick. For the past four years, I haven't been allowed to be around females. It was unanimous with the Demons that it would be in everyone's best interest for me personally to stay away. When I was ordered to 'scare' her, it opened a door I assumed had been nailed shut. But with Priya, she's a special case.

There is so much I want to know. What makes her tick? How much does she know? Maybe she's just as misunderstood as I am.

That's why the information Saint is obsessed with finding is right in front of him. But I want to hear it from her pretty mouth. She has secrets, and I crave to unravel them.

Hidden behind the building, the side door provides a discreet entrance for the janitors to enter without having to encounter the spoiled rich kids. Swiping my master key card, I got from the dean's office. The red light flicks green. Although the lights in the female dorm lobby are dimmed during the night, they're still bright enough to allow for clear visibility of anyone walking through the halls. To the right are the concrete stairs that go up to the third floor. I won't take any chances of being seen by some nosey girl who hears the elevator ding. Plus, I don't think Saint is prepared to be thrown into something he doesn't quite understand yet. He'd be miffed, for sure. When considering the idea, there is a slight smirk as I contemplate how enjoyable it could be, like a fish out of water.

The time on my phone says it's a little after 1AM. She should be sleeping peacefully in her bed. The stairs don't leave me winded, reminding me that the time I spend at the gym is well worth it. Pulling my hood tighter to my face, the stairway door creaks open as I spot the room I'm looking for.

The soft carpet cloaks my footsteps, making it much easier to sneak past her nosy friend's room. Taking the key card out from my pocket again, the lock turns green. Slowly turning the doorknob, I hold my breath, not wanting to ruin the fun by waking her. When it stays silent, I slink inside. Her friend is none the wiser.

Inhaling the room's aroma, it smells like her. The fragrance of coconut and wildflowers brings back memories of my childhood in London, playing in the meadows, inhaling their sweet scents. I was quite fond of that smell. Her dark wavy hair lies sprawled across her pillow, while both of her hands are underneath her cheek. She's wearing what looks to be an oversized white T-shirt for pajamas. The face of a vengeful angel. Even during sleep, her brows furrow, keeping the constant frown she wears. The weight of her heavy lashes casts a shadow from the moonlight on her high cheekbones, concealing her haunted gaze from the world. If I pull her hands down a bit, it would appear she was praying.

Speaking of hands, I grab a zip tie from my coat and ever so slowly slide the black pointed tie behind her wrists. She doesn't move a muscle. Her soft breathing remains undisturbed. Fishing it through the hole, each groove clicks as it gets tighter. I'm not ready to tighten it all the way yet.

First, I need to obstruct her vision before she knows who I am. Her room is too clean. The way I clean Saint and I's room. No personal belongings other than her clothes. I'll be back to inspect it all soon enough. Stalking to her closet, I grab her school tie to use as a blindfold.

Here's the tricky part. Do I blindfold her first? Risk her waking and getting her hands out of the binding? Or tighten the binds and risk her seeing my face? Decisions.

Staring at my Little Monster, I decide I'm not ready for the fun to end. If she wakes, it'll be easy to subdue her. The last two items I have are a roll of tape, in case she gets too loud and attempts to call for help and my small blade I take everywhere with me.

Carefully, I put the tie gently around her eyes and double knot it. Not my best work. As I run my fingers through her hair, it feels soft as silk. I want to make a pillow out of it. That's a thing, silk pillowcases. A whiff of coconut reaches me and I realize it's her hair products. In the room's stillness, a shrill hiss pierces the air as I fasten the zip tie, pressing harshly into her skin.

If. No. When, she struggles it'll cut into her skin and leave beautiful marks showing I was here. We'll both know what it's from.

With each intake of breath, her chest rises and falls frantically. I know what comes next, so I slap my hand over her mouth to smother the scream, predictable. Grabbing my blade, I set it against the throbbing pulse in her neck and wait for her to settle.

"'Hello, my Little Monster." Her struggle stops. A smile creeps on my face. Fear. "I'm here for a chat. Can you do that? Or do we need a repeat of what happened last time?" A small nod conveyed her fear, the sharp edge of the knife an obvious reminder of her vulnerable position.

"I'm going to remove my hand, and when I do. I want your silence. Understand?" When she nods, I slowly remove my hand. She continues to stay silent as she was asked, despite her shallow breathing. Maybe I could train her.

"Atta girl, love." At the praise, her body relaxes a fraction. She would claim it's because she's no longer being strangled. But I saw how she reacted during our last interaction. Her words can lie, but her body cannot.

Dragging a chair over from the window, each thump of my boots coming closer make her flinch. I lean back and sprawl out to make myself comfortable. I'm not sure how long we will be here. I can't see the color of my chair, but I hope it's not pink. Unless it's the shade of Priya's face when she gets angry. I would like it then.

"My mates seem to think you can solve an issue we're having. But I think differently. They're not seeing the bigger picture. I don't believe you're capable of the cruelty they say you are. Not in that way. What do you think?" I say thoughtfully. It's more politeness that has me asking her opinion, because whatever she says won't change my mind. She lies still for a few moments, gathering her thoughts.

"What is the issue I can solve?" Her voice is hoarse from sleep. The urge to tell her, to hear her reaction, is hovering in the back of my mind. Revenge, an outlet for their guilt.

"Not important." I wave my hand at her like she can see. "But what I am interested in is *you.*" Her breathing picks up again. We will have to work on her dramatics. I've only threatened her once.

"W-why me?" She questions.

"You're broken." My answer is simple. Saint and I, we love broken things. He likes to fix them, and I like to break them. We're two peas in a bloody pod.

She shifts uncomfortably. "There are plenty of broken people. Go find them."

If only it were that easy. She's too far into the heads of the Demons' and she doesn't even know it yet. Poor girl.

"You don't eat very much." It's a statement, not a question. I don't need her to act coy.

"Oh, so you're here about my eating habits? That's why I'm tied up? It all makes sense now." She snarks, making me grin. I like *this* Priya.

"I admit, I'm curious." The room stays silent.

Oh, we're playing a game?

My knife hovers an inch away from the top of her nightshirt. She's unable to see what I'm doing, so she stays frozen. I cut a line down the collar at the center. Not enough to leave her exposed, but so she's aware of my intentions. Her breath hitches when my knife skims her skin, leaving a barely visible, thin red line on her chest.

"If I answer your questions, you'll leave? You'll stop?" she hastily utters.

I remove my knife and take a seat on the bed. I want to be near her. Inside her skin. "Yes. That's the idea of a chat, love. We talk. But I can see you're not very good at that."

Huffing out her disagreement, "Most of the 'chats'", she makes air quotes in front of her face with her bound hands. "Don't have the person they are talking to blindfolded and tied up." She looks so pretty like this. Helpless.

"The eating." I push.

"Yeah, okay. I don't eat a lot." Her words are sharp. I want to understand her.

"Why?"

"I don't want to get fat." It sounds rehearsed, something that's repeatedly been said. The urge to touch her hair again becomes an impulse I don't feel the need to tame. It's so bloody soft.

"Why?"

"What are you? 5? Because my mom says it would make me look disgusting and unattractive."

"When we were playing in the shadows together, I put my hand over your nose and mouth. You went somewhere in your head. Where?" My eyebrow twitches as I glare at her small frame lying still on the bed. I like to think fondly of our time together, but that's one thing that drives me mad. I rather dislike being ignored and dismissed.

"Hmm, I don't know, maybe because you were fucking suffocating me!"

Shaking my head, I disagree. "No, you fought me. Or at least tried to." Remembering her poor attempt has me chuckling.

"But when my hand covered your face, you stopped. Went rigid. Something happened. What was it?" She ignores my question. I stop petting her hair to grab my knife. Slicing the shirt down to where the tops of her breasts peek out.

"I don't want to answer that." Cede to her request knowing it will come out eventually.

"Who are you?" She asks.

"That would take away all the fun, Little Monster." Sucking my teeth at how eager she is to end this. After our last job, I find Priya takes the edge off the bloodlust a bit.

"Why do you keep calling me that?"

"Because I see what lurks beneath all the sadness." I tilt my head to study her. The shadow of her true self. The dark and twisted wants and revenge that simmer under the surface. My monster likes to ask questions she won't like the answer to.

"You're ugly inside. Just like me. The loneliness you hide behind self-isolation in fear of rejection. Your hidden abuse comes out when a sudden movement comes from the corner of your eyes. Anger you use to deflect from your sadness. I see it all. You can hide from the rest of the world, but you can't hide from me, love." A lone tear leaks from her eye. I bend down and lick it, savoring the taste of her sadness.

"Save your tears for me." She'll need a reason. "Every time I find out, you're crying. I'll carve a letter of my name into you." Patting myself on the back, that sounds comforting. A win-win for both of us. If she cries, eventually she'll have a permanent mark of me. One she could never rid herself of, no matter how many times she washes herself. By not crying, she'll save her tears for me. Before anyone knows, she'll already be mine. It'll be too late to take her away.

A monster needs an owner.

She sniffles, attempting to hide her tears.

"How did you get in?" She whispers.

"River isn't the only one who has ways to get in. But I'm here with a warning for you." She waits.

"It's going to get harder before it gets easier. Don't yield to the oncoming obstacles. You're *mine* to break Priya Carter. Forgetting that would be a grave mistake on your part. I'm not the forgiving type." Bending down, I place a kiss at the center of her chest, where the moonlight reveals the slightly raised red mark of my knife on her pale skin. While simultaneously sliding my hand underneath the pillow where her head lies and grab her razor.

"One last thing. Who left you the black envelope?" I whisper into her ear.

My nearness throws her off. "I-I don't know. I thought it was you." Interesting. Not admitting or denying it, I place the razor blade into her hands so she can cut herself out, leaving me plenty of time to get back home.

PRIYA

NO ROOTS – ALICE MERTON

PRIYA

Our word for the day is, agathokakological (adj.) – something that possesses both good and evil.

I think I met someone who embodies this word. You probably wouldn't approve because you never thought anyone was deserving of my time. Or maybe I'm delusional from the lack of sleep and I'm hanging on by a thread and making excuses, so I don't have a mental breakdown.

Is it too late to runaway?

I'm joking… kinda. This place is locked down like Fort Knox.

lloveyou.

F og covers the school grounds as if someone left their Halloween machine out. The chill of the air seeps into my bones. Arms of the woods peek out against the mist, looking for unsuspecting souls to grab and pull in. Last night left me feeling and looking like a zombie. Autopilot has me going through the motions. River is her chirpy self. Not even the strong coffee she made me this morning has put a dent in my brain's fuzziness.

I love her, but I can't keep up today. She reminds me of a toddler, talking a mile a minute.

I wonder what Mother Dearest would say about me today. I barely managed my curly hair into a low, slicked back bun with money pieces out. River said I looked cute, but I'm second guessing. I should go back to the dorms.

My mind wanders to the cause of my tiredness. Irritation duels with my exhaustion. What type of psychopath breaks into someone's room, ties them up "just to talk"? I sleep at night knowing my room was a community area for breaking and entering. No matter where I'm at, I can't seem to get privacy. But there is a difference. No one that has been in my dorm room has laid a hand on me in anger.

A pang of sadness hits me when I think that…he might be lonely, too. He mentioned knowing about how it feels last night as he laid out my truth, exposing me.

That's still not a normal way to make friends. River breaks into my room but doesn't touch me.

His questions made me more uncomfortable than when he pulled me into the woods. I don't like when people notice things about me. Significant details and then throw them in my face, showing me my imperfections. Could he be the eyes I've felt watching me?

He'll be back. He only asked a couple of questions. There has to be a way this could benefit me. He was kind enough to warn me about something. No idea what he was talking about, but it's the thought that counts.

River bounces in front of me, pulling open the cafeteria door to guide me to our table. What time did I wake up? 1:30 or 2AM. Next time he decides to have a heart to heart, it better be on a weekend when I don't have to wake up early. River places an order on the tablet and hands it to me. Staring blankly at the screen, I don't know what I want.

"Maybe try some French toast this morning? A sugar rush will help for a little." I bite back a retort. If I ever see my parents and my mother thinks I put on weight. I shudder at her wrath. She would make me throw it up or run off the weight until I pass out. Settling for ignoring her suggestion, I go for an assortment of fresh fruit. It has natural sugars in it, that should help. I hope.

My first class is psychology this morning, and to say I'm far from excited is an understatement. Dealing with my silent and broody partner. Crew sucks more energy from me than being exhausted ever would. We've had at least three more partner assignments since then and he refuses to do any of the work. Leaving me to figure it out by myself, causing me to pull late nights so it doesn't affect my grades.

A waiter comes and sets River's stack of pancakes flooded with syrup in front of her and in front of me, the "assortment" of fruits I asked for is a piece of lettuce. Glaring at the waiter in a white dress shirt and slacks, I barely keep my cool. River must read my mood because she jumps in.

"Uh, that's not what she ordered. She orders almost the same thing every day."

"I-I'm just doing what I'm told." His eyes won't meet mine.

"By who?" The question comes out more snippy than I intended. The waiter shrugs and scurries towards the kitchen, making himself scarce.

"What the frick?" River whispers, stunned, looking past me.

Oscar and his little buddies. What an unpleasant surprise. The last interaction I had with him he wanted nudes.

"Carter." He puts his arm around me, causing an involuntary flinch. Slowly, I grab my fork and bring it underneath the table.

He laughs it off. "I'm sure you've heard of the bet going around?" I look at River, who looks sheepish.

"No." I say, trying unsuccessfully to shrug out from underneath his arm.

"River!" He puts a hand to his chest in mock shock. "You didn't tell her? You naughty girl." Tsking, he returns his attention to me. Whispering low in my ear. "The bet is who can fuck you first. Proof gets half a million dollars and a classic Bentley. So, what do you say? Want to make a video? I'll give you half the cash." His brace straight teeth, purposely messy dark hair, doesn't do it for me. Nor does the disgusting way he just propositioned me for sex. People really make bets like this? Everyone here has deep pockets. There isn't one person who attends this school as a student who would need either of those things. His arm reaches across my body to my exposed leg of my skirt. With a tight grip on the fork, I bring it up from its hiding place in my skirt, pressing it where his balls would be if he had any.

A quick stab of the fork into his balls, he hisses while jerking away from me. I lean closer, so our audience doesn't hear.

"Oscar." I say with a sickly sweet smile. "You have three seconds to get away from our table before I puncture your tiny balls for propositioning me with that nasty bet." My lips touch the shell of his ear. "Don't forget what I told you the night of the party. This is the second time you have put your hands on me without permission. I *always* keep my promises." Tapping his chest, he releases the breath he was holding when I pull away.

He laughs, but his eyes hold a promise of retribution. "Let's get out of here." He stands and his friends follow suit. "I bet she's only a prude in public. But she's nasty in the sheets." He winks, making me bristle. Empty threats won't do. I'll have to act on my promise.

I turn my eyes back to River, raising my eyebrows in disapproval of this type of secret keeping.

"I was going to tell you! The time just never felt right. I mean, how do you tell someone there is a bet about being the first person to sleep with you?" She cringes.

Shaking my head, I don't have the energy to deal with this today.

"I wanted to protect you from it." She admits. It thaws my heart a little at the cold shoulder I'm giving her.

Relenting, I answer, "River, things like that are important for me to know. What if he and his friends cornered me by myself?"

"I'm sorry. I didn't think of that and if I would have thought it was something serious to consider, I would've said something. I've never seen him act like that before."

"Then help me get back at him." It's more of a test to see where her loyalties lie. She nods excitedly. Something to preoccupy me, a little revenge.

"Do you know who is fucking with my food?" I ask River, crossing my arms. She looks in the corner to where the Demons' lair is. I don't need to look to know they're staring. I can feel their eyes on the side of my face.

The bell rings, letting students know they have five minutes to get to class. Gathering my black bag, I wave River off and go to my class with the broody Demon who was in on my breakfast fiasco. River and I part ways after breakfast. Or her breakfast and my rabbit food. As she makes her way out through the entrance, I enter through the side door that leads to the lengthy hallway. The rhythmic clicking of my heels on black and white polished tiles echo through the space. Tracing my fingertips over the rough, weathered wainscot paneling, I'm reminded of the depth of this place's history. I wonder if there are any secret passageways. *That* would be worth exploring.

In the middle of the hallway, I come across school photos. Only ten individual photos hang on the wall showcasing the short span of the school's life. There is no sign of the Demons' presence in the photo from last year. The two years before that the Demon boys stand in the center of the crowd that gives them wide birth. The twins wear matching scowls, arms crossed over their chests. Standing on the left side is Saint with a half-forced smile. To the right of the twins is a darker skinned boy who has an arm thrown over one of the twins' shoulders, pulling him in towards himself, wearing a beaming smile that reaches his eyes. The closest person to them in both is Amber Astor. Go figure.

The last picture I look at was taken three years ago. The boy's freshman year. Saint's eyes focus to the right of him, a smirk lining his lips.

Holy shit.

That's Megan Riley!

While everyone is staring at the camera, these two are staring at each other, happiness written on Megan's face. Did they have a thing? We're they together? Did the Demons' have a hand in their disappearance like River suggested?

River! Oh man, I've got to tell her! There's no way she wouldn't want to know what I've found out. The curiosity would kill her and maybe then she'd want to help.

A door closes in the distance, causing me to jump and turn towards the noise. Once again, face to face with Oscar. This time, I'm alone.

PRIYA

JESUS CHRIST – BRAND NEW

It crosses my mind that I may have jinxed myself while talking to River. Bringing life to the worst situation I could be in. In a hallway, by myself, with Oscar. A smile lights up his face. Not the smile that gives you butterflies in your stomach. One that sends a cold sweat down my spine.

Halting, I do a 180-degree turn to go the other way. Preferably to a bathroom. Footsteps quicken behind me. His hand wraps around my elbow when I am yanked into the bathroom, pinned against the wall by his forceful grip on my elbow, the icy surface sending goosebumps all over my body. My eyes frantically search for anything near that I could use as a weapon, coming up short in the bare bathroom.

"Not so mouthy now that you're alone, are you?" His forearm rests above my head while his other traces the buttons from the bottom of my school shirt, up to the top button, before flicking it open.

How do I keep getting myself into these shitty situations? I make to walk away, hoping he'll let me. That he's just trying to scare me. He snatches my bun and yanks me toward him, pushing my face against the cream and vanilla wallpaper. A grunt leaves me at the impact.

Using all the leverage I can gather and shove us backwards. Struggling against the smothering smell of bleach, I desperately search for an escape route from this confined room, growing smaller by the second. The movement caught him off guard, giving me the wiggle room to lurch for the small bathroom door.

Back at square one, my hand fails to find the knob, leaving me even more uncomfortable than before. My head slams against the unforgiving wall, sending sharp pulses of pain through my body. His bulky hand clamps onto my arms. The sound of my frenzied breathing fills the room while my cheek meets the rough texture of the wall. His labored breathing fills my senses, the powerful aroma of cigarettes mingling with the stinging odor of bleach in the bathroom.

Struggling to get out of his hold. I move my head and arms at the same time. His hand grips my hair at the roots, slamming me face first into the wall. The impact of hitting the drywall echoes through the room, each thud intensifying the dizziness. I yelp. Darkness distorts my vision.

"Stop fucking fighting me!" He hisses. "You're going to give it up. My family is going bankrupt. Any money would help. So, you can fight me and make it unpleasant or lie there and take it! Either way, it's happening."

My skull feels like it's going to split open from the constant pounding. The force of his yank causes my shirt buttons to burst open, revealing my bare skin on the wall. Ripping the shirt down to my elbows behind my back, he stops. He's saying something, but I'm trying to find a happy place away from here. As I remain mute, his rough hands forcefully turn me towards him. A veil of fury clouds his features.

"Who did you let fuck you?" Spit flies from his mouth, hitting me on the cheek.

"Hmm?" His hand is a blur when it connects with my cheek, causing my head to snap to the side. My mouth fills with the unmistakable flavor of blood, leaving a trace of metallic bitterness on my tongue. My father made sure that this was an injury I was familiar with. I suck the blood from my lip.

"The fucking bite mark, bitch. Don't play stupid." The bite mark. I slowly throw it around in my head for a moment. Remembering where it came from.

"I didn't sleep with anyone."

He shrugs, cruelty lines every feature in his face. "Since there's no video, mine will work." His hands grab roughly at my breasts. Throwing my head back into the wall, I stare at the vaulted ceiling. Tears swim in my vision, fighting back the urge to cry. Oscar's hands roam down my ribcage, into the sides of my pleated skirt. I will not give him the satisfaction of my pain.

I pray.

Please, please Addison. Please don't let them take this from me, too.

Closing my eyes, his hands drift lower. An agonizing sob leaves my throat.

The bathroom door bangs open, ricocheting off the wall. My eyes stay closed. The invasion on my body stops abruptly, and the hands disappear.

"What's up, Demonio?" Oscar asks nonchalantly, different from what it was seconds ago. Gone is the rapist asshole, back is the friendly frat guy.

"What are you doing, Bush?" His voice sounds deep and dark. Was it always like that?

"I was about to score that car and the money." Oscar sounds cocky.

"Yeah? Well, rape wouldn't count." Anger rolls off him in waves, taking up the limited space in the room.

"No, we were just having fun. Right, Priya?" I open my eyes, shooting him a venomous glare. He thinks I would cover for his ass? Turning towards the bathroom doorway, I come face to face with Bennett. His white button-up shirt is still intact, unlike mine. The soft fabric drapes over each bulging muscle and curve, hugging his body tightly with every movement. His hair looks like he *actually* rolled out of bed, unlike the look Oscar was going for.

Humiliation overwhelms me. I can't imagine what I look like. Weak, pathetic, like some whore who gives it up in the bathroom during class. Hoping my state will convince Bennett that I'm not here willingly, I plead with my eyes. From the top of my head to the heels on my feet, his scrutinizing look burns into my skin. His lips pull down slightly at the corners, showing a faint reaction to my disheveled appearance. His full hazel eyes with long lashes soften at the corners a fraction.

"She must be into some kinky shit." Bennet says. Oscar's lips turn up, smiling. I choke on a whimper while the silence looms between them like gas waiting to be lit by a spark. My adrenaline is pounding. I don't think I'll survive another round of Oscar.

"Get the fuck out of here, Bush." He says calmly, like this situation doesn't bother him. Oscar makes a quick escape, muttering a 'Thanks', on the way out without so much as a glance back at me.

Bennett strides over, replacing where Oscar stood moments ago. His frame towers over me by almost a foot. A couple of inches taller than Oscar is. I look up at him, hoping to give the false impression that I'm stronger than I feel. His hand cups my cheek as his thumb pushes on the split lip I'm sporting. Hissing in pain, I pull back.

"Don't I get a kiss for being your knight in shining armor?" His voice cuts into the silence with a smug smile. Gone is the kindness his eyes held before when they looked over at me from the doorway. I'm shaken by his question.

"How about a swift kick in the balls?" I say bitterly. I was just cornered in a bathroom and almost raped and he wants a kiss? My cheeks flush with fury, my shame temporarily forgotten. Bennett's hand goes to the nape of my neck, pulling at the hair to angle my face up to him.

"You will give me one kiss. Or I'll have him finish what he

started. Your choice." His tone tells me he's unbothered either way. What option do I have? I have lost almost every choice in my life, one way or another. What's one more?

"You're a fucking prick." I whisper. Afraid my voice will shake, showing my fear. His arms encircle me, putting a hand large enough it spans my waist. Then pulls me aggressively towards him, closing the little space we had. He leans down. The smell of fresh mint washes over my face as his breath mingles with mine. His eyes darker than they were before, as he lazily studies my face approvingly before glancing down at my gaping shirt. A mischievous look plays in his eyes. His lips hovering less than a centimeter away from mine. Giving me the illusion that it's *my* choice.

Clumsily, leaning forward, pressing my split lip into his. They're full and softer than I expected someone else's lips to feel. I've never kissed anyone before. I give him the bare minimum, a peck before pulling away. His eyes narrow, shaking his head.

"No princess, I want to feel the hatred you're not trying hard to hide. I want a real kiss."

My breath catches at his low, sensual voice sliding across my skin. His hand slides up my neck, stopping at my pulse and squeezing briefly before he cups my jaw, tilting my head up towards him. The action contradicts the hardness in his eyes.

Do it and get it over with. Wetting my lips, I push forward with the last of my courage, crushing my lips to his. His tongue licks the seam to coax them apart. Hesitantly, I part them slightly to allow his tongue to explore. I follow his lead and our tongues intertwine, filling my mouth with the sweetness of mint and the buzz of excitement. His movements become frenzied, taking over the kiss. Hands grip my thighs, lifting my feet off the floor. Automatically, my legs wrap around his waist to keep from falling. Using his body to press me against the wall, my thighs try to squeeze shut to relieve the aching that's building. Something hard presses into my center. He's hard. For me. A moan escapes me when he rubs it against my pussy, making my panties wet.

Bennett pulls away panting, looking down at his jean clad hard on rubbing against me, "Fuck, that's so fucking hot," he growls.

That's when I start overthinking. He knows I've never done this. I don't know what I'm doing. Does my breath smell bad? Why should I care? This was a deal. Panic seizes me when I realize this is just a game. His game.

Pulling his head toward me by the messy strands, I bite his lip. Hard. He drops me immediately, recoiling. His eyes widen at the sight of blood from his injured lip.

Nodding, satisfaction fills me that we have a similar wound.

"That was your kiss. Take it or leave it." My arms cross over my chest. He laughs and shakes his head.

"Okay." He steps out of my way, allowing me to leave the bathroom. Before I make it out the door, he reaches out and softly grabs my elbow.

"Do yourself a favor and don't go to the dean about this." Wanting to give him a piece of my mind and tell him where he can put his advice, he cuts me off before I can get a word out. "He's the dean's nephew. This isn't the first time he's done something like this." My jaw snaps shut. I nod my head, the message loud and clear. Because of who Oscar's uncle is, there won't be any consequence for his behavior. It runs in his family.

In an attempt to shield myself from prying eyes, I pull the torn fabric around my shivering body. There shouldn't be many people out since everyone is in their first period of the day. My feet rush to carry me to the safety of my room, where I release my pent-up emotions through soft cries and regret. A pity party to wonder why this shit always happens to me. When can I just… *be?*

BENNETT

I t's uncommon for me to respond to texts from the guys, yet alone send a group text. But what I walked in on warrants a meeting. Don't get me wrong, I hate Priya for what she did in California, and I want her broken just as much as Crew and Saint. But rape? Even hers goes against everything we stand for. We torture and kill people like that for a living.

Oscar is lucky his uncle is on Crew's payroll, otherwise he would've been dead long before this incident. He's always been a pushy shit, pestering girls when he wants something. He's never been on our radar because his activities never interfered with our agendas. My thumb absentmindedly rubs my lip. Oscar has over stepped and put his nose where it doesn't belong. Near Priya Carter.

My mind goes back to when I heard her scream in the bathroom. I stood there, listening. I thought she'd handle it on her own. The sound of that sob was so gut-wrenching that I've only heard it once before. She sounded every bit of broken that I wanted her to be, but not at that expense.

The last time I heard something that horrifying was when my mom had brought some John home for work. She thought my brother and I were sleeping, but I wasn't. I heard everything. Each piercing cry, muffled whimper, and desperate prayer echoed through the room. As a young child of 8 or 9, I lie motionless, tears silently streaming down my cheeks, unable to react. Promising my mother retribution for the pain he caused her. I didn't know there were some things that could never be healed. Until I lived through it myself.

The side entrance to the barn is within arm's length. It's the entrance only the guys and I use. Unfortunately, that doesn't mean its location is unknown. Amber's crazed voice reaches my ears before I'm able to hustle inside.

"Bennett!" My shoulders draw up to my ears, shielding the precious organs from hearing loss. I know what this is about.

Turning around on one foot to face her, I put on a cheery smile, "Amber!" She's brought her eerie replica, Ember. Ember Callahan. Same shade of blonde, same makeup, their school outfits even styled and paired with the same black Louboutin heels. Good thing Ember doesn't talk much, if at all.

"Don't start with me, Bennett Demonio! What type of bullshit was that?" My eyes flinch against the screech. Is she a fucking banshee?

"What?" Playing dumb will only piss her off further. She gets in my face.

"I saw you kissing that freak, Bennett!" I smile in her face. Amber is a lot of things, beautiful, wealthy, jealous, and predictable. Shrugging off her observation only sets her blue eyes blazing with rage. She raises her hand to slap me. My reflexes are faster than that. After all the time we've spent together, she should know. Then again, most of that time is spent looking at the back of her head.

My grip tightens on her wrist. "I let your crazy ass get away with a lot, Amber. Telling the school I'm 'yours' when I let you know up front what this was. But if you *ever* attempt to put your hands on me again." I pause, letting the threat soak in. Her lip wobbles, but there are no tears. She plays this game as well as I do.

"I did it for you." She whispers.

"What the hell are you talking about?" I knew what I was doing, getting Priya to kiss me. I timed it perfectly so Amber would walk in. Stirring the pot. We didn't see any reactions worth mentioning, so I push for more.

Amber remains quiet. Shaking her, I ask again. "Amber, what the fuck are you talking about?"

"I thought that if Oscar scared her a little, she'd leave. Or at the very least, leave you alone." My eyebrows draw down in a glare and my nose wrinkles.

"You got Oscar to try to rape her?" Pushing her back, I turn around and storm inside. I didn't think Amber was that vile. I'm all for her games of making people's lives hell if it isn't mine.

"Took you long enough." Crew says, standing at the kitchen counter, his arms crossed. His tie lies on the counter, wrinkled and forgotten. He had already unbuttoned the top of his shirt, letting the cool air hit his skin. Saint is sitting on the stool in front of a laptop. Because he doesn't have at least three monitors in his room. What is one more that he can bring everywhere with him?

"Yeah, was dealing with some shit. Anyway, I found Oscar Bush attempting to rape our spoiled princess."

Saint looks horrified, as expected. Crew, on the other hand, looks the opposite. He has no expression. That may be his usual look, but he's never hidden his emotions from me. Glancing at Saint, I try to gauge his reaction to my brother's lack of.

"Was she crying?" Saint says. What an odd question to ask.

"Um, yes. Understandably so. Considering when I walked in,

his hands were in her skirt, and she looked like a DV victim." Saint's eyes change briefly before looking back at his laptop.

"And?" Crew replies jaded. "Did you let him do it?"

"Fuck no!"

He shakes his head. "Maybe you should have," he says so quietly I almost miss it. I wish I did.

Most of the time, my brother and I don't see eye to eye, but our morals have always been the same. Saint sits mutely, not a word or a sound. I know mainly, Crew and I lived the same life. Struggled in the same way, especially with mom. But this? This is a new low.

"We want her broken. This would've done it."

Old resentment I have comes bubbling to the surface.

Oh, I see what he's implying. He believes this would make up for Tyson's death. That this would be the wash to make us even.

"Yeah? You think so, Crew?" I shove him against the counter, getting in his face. "Did I fucking deserve it when I was younger? When Charles would fucking stick things inside me while Marie videoed it and I begged them to stop? Did I deserve it when I said 'no' and he'd make me get on my knees for the hell of it? What about when he would whisper in my ear and tell me I 'liked it'. That I 'wanted it'? And when I refused, he put me in a fucking closet for days! All the times I cried for my *brother* to come fucking save me from that hellhole." My voice is hoarse from screaming. Bringing up the incident where he couldn't save me completely changed the course of the conversation. That has nothing to do with Priya.

"Fuck you, Crew," I spit. "If this is how you're going to play the game. I'm fucking out. Tyson is rolling in his grave right now, hearing those words from your mouth. He would be disgusted. I know I am."

Walking back to the side entry door, I rip my keys off the rack to my Aston Martin. The one girl who doesn't talk back and piss me off. The only way I'm going to come back and not murder Crew is if I go for a drive.

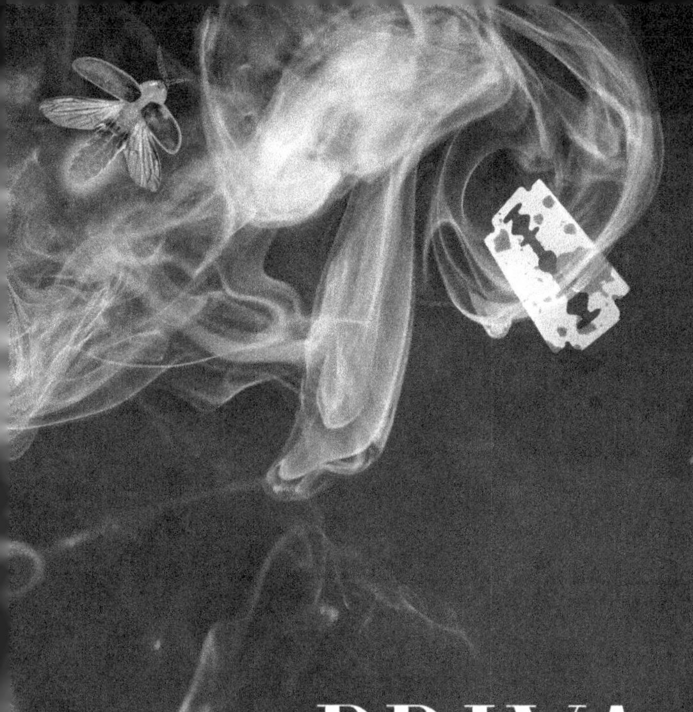

PRIYA

BABYDOLL – ARI ABDUL (ON REPEAT)

Nighttime used to be the most terrifying time of the day for me. Dreading when my father would come home from his office. No women occupying his time. No one to talk politics with and no friends to plot the world's domination with a bottle of whatever whiskey he drinks. That would be the time he would deal out whatever punishments for the day he saw fit. He called it his "most creative time". Nowadays, it's the only time I get a reprieve from my mind.

It's a little after 1AM when I decide to take another shower. My day was mostly filled with a continuous cycle of tears, screaming into my pillow, followed by sleeping. Texting River, asking for space when that was the last thing she wanted to give me. The threatening to barricade the door if she wouldn't give me time seemed to do the trick. She wants to take care of me. That's not something I'm used to. I've convinced myself that I need to figure this out alone, even when I have the support to help me through it.

I spent the last part of my day thinking about why I wasn't scared of the guy in the woods and why Oscar was so much more terrifying. Was it the beating he had delivered beforehand? It reminded me of my father. Luckily, my father had the perception that I was too repulsive and undeserving of any physical contact besides hitting me.

In the woods, at first it was relief, the knife, the thought of death. Then it turned exciting. Not once did he raise a hand to me in anger. I didn't have to face him. Not really. He's like a dark secret I hide in the deepest parts of my heart and soul. A darkness... a shadow that sees through my bullshit. The clarity in which he sees me may be worse than either of those things combined.

The smell of coconut lingers in the steamy bathroom as I rinse the conditioner from my hair. The fog in the bathroom is so thick it's like a physical barrier that separates the shower from the rest of the room. My skin is bright red from the heat of the water and the force of attempting to scrub off Oscar's nasty hands from my body. Even now, long after he's gone, the faint lingering of his grip continues to haunt me. My skin, once a bright red, is now morphing into a muted shade of plum. The piercing sound of my tormented wail echoes through the empty room.

My mind won't shut the fuck up. I just want silence. Why? The last bruises from my father just fucking faded! Why can't I just be left alone? I grab the new bar of soap I found under the marble countertop and turn back into the waterfall spray from the shower, wishing it could be a pressure washer. That could get rid of it. Scrubbing strenuously, I'm determined to loosen his hold on me.

Maybe I'm not meant to be happy in this life.

As darkness completely envelopes me, I can't help but let out a shriek. There are no windows in here for privacy reasons, but that means it's pitch black. The confined space, mixed with the unilluminated room, makes my heart rate spike. Did the entire school go out?

If I find my phone, I could call River. The utter blackness makes me disoriented. Not knowing which way is up or down. Guiding myself by touch, I feel my way to the open lip of the shower to get out and find the door. Only to be met with a wall of hot flesh. The sharp sound of my piercing scream echoes off the walls, filling the room. Oscar. He came back to finish the bet.

"Hush, Little Monster. No reason to lure anyone in here. I would have to kill them for seeing you naked." The light British accent is distinguishable, even through the ringing in my ears. Gulping. It's best not to tell him River has already seen me naked. The sensation of his calloused fingers trailing lightly down my arm sends goosebumps all over my body.

"Don't touch me." I grit out between clenched teeth. My body is confused already. It doesn't know what it wants.

"You're touching me," he says matter-of-factly. My fingers trace the hard planes of his warm body stopping on the puckered skin on the sides of his Adonis belt. Digging my nails in and squeezing the exposed skin as hard as I can. I *need* someone to feel my pain. To hurt as bad as I am, inside and out. Instead, I get no reaction. Not a grunt or hiss of pain.

My Shadow's thumb softly traces my lip before pushing the split bottom lip harshly, returning the favor. The feeling of shame and regret lingers as I flinch away from his probing touch, my breath catching in my throat. The wetness on my cheeks from my tears is distinguishable from the hot shower that beats down on both of us. The saltiness on my lips reminds me of the sorrow I failed to wash away.

"Why are you so gutted?" Another emotionless question. This time, regardless, if he wants a genuine answer. I'm desperate enough to give him one.

"I-I can't get h-his hands off of me." My voice breaks, the pain unfiltered. It's more than that, it always is more, but right now this torments me.

"Show me."

I have reservations about what I'm considering doing. What else do I have to lose? I'm at the point of physically peeling my skin off if I scrub any harder.

I'm tired of being the victim in my own story.

Perhaps what happens in the dark will never come to light.

Still unable to make out where he is entirely except for a darker figure in the darkness. I let my hands lightly trace up his body, trying not to touch him but wanting to find his hands without patting around. The Shadow's body is smooth in the no hair sense. A distinctly rough sensation spreads through my fingertips as I trace the outlines of his disfigured skin. Some scars are barely raised. Some feel like someone has taken chunks of skin deep enough to leave nerve damage. Different shapes, sizes, and textures cover his body.

How bad are they in the light? My fingers brush against the hard muscles of his broad shoulders, my nails scrape down the rough texture of his arms, and finally softly grasp his calloused hands.

"Above my elbows, when he grabbed me and forced me into the bathroom," I whisper. When his fingers close around my forearm, I gasp. My pulse quickens, and he holds my arm aloft. My skin tingles when a warm tongue traces where Oscar's fingers pressed into my arms, igniting a sense of longing I haven't felt from my Shadow. A sharp intake of breath is audible over the splattering of the water hitting the tiles. He nips at the skin, leaving a new mark in its place. It's nowhere near the amount of pain I crave.

My heart physically aches. The Shadow is rewriting the meaning of my abuse with new marks.

Then my hands move to my ribcage. His hands follow. Kneeling down, the musky smell of leather and the smokey tang of burning firewood infiltrates the smell of coconut. He is silent, like the shadow I've made him out to be. My hips remain anchored by his powerful grasp. The warmth of his tongue and sharp teeth trail down either side before halting. Waiting for direction. My breathing becomes faster, more rapid. My nipples pebble despite the hot water beating down on us. This is turning me on.

If I tell him where else, it could progress. Would he tell me 'No'?

"He stuck his hands down my skirt." I gulp, knowing he'll be going lower, overwhelmed by the sensation of his tongue tracing along my hipbone and anticipating his teeth sinking into my flesh. He bites to the point of pain. I moan. The warmth radiating from the bite cocoons my entire body. Pressure builds up, sending tingles from head to toe. Everything feels sensitive, like electrical pulses going through my body.

"Okay?" he taunts, a smile in his voice as he stands. Taking the heat I borrowed with him, leaving me shivering. Reality washes in. Stumbling backwards, I sink down until I reach the tiled floor of the shower. I don't know what he came here for, but he'll leave. Everyone does. My chest tightens. Dread floods out the euphoria, causing my hands to shake. I want him to leave so I can do what I need to do to pull myself together. My razor.

He could fix this. Looking into the darkness where I think he is, "I don't want to be here anymore." Hoping that it's communicating what I really mean.

I don't want to be alive anymore. I'm tired of hurting and being hurt. Death has to be sweeter than what's in the future for me.

The soft padding of bare feet grows louder as they draw near, halting in front of me. Dipping down, his breath dances over my slick skin and his hand softly moves a stray piece of hair away from my face, turning my head upward.

"Death would never be so kind to you, my Little Monster." Bitter tears slide down my cheeks. "I'm a result of Death's influence and he has selfish motivations for wanting to claim you as well." Sitting with the realization that I will be stuck in misery for the rest of my pathetic life. With my luck, I'd attempt to kill myself and survive. Every. Fucking. Time.

"Put your hands behind your back," he commands.

"Why?"

"I made you a promise last night. I intend to keep it. Let's call this your first test of obedience. If you move your hands, I'll bind them and leave you here naked for someone to find you." Aware he isn't one to crack a joke. I place my hands behind my back, holding my wrists and leaning against the wall to pin them in place. The angle sends a zing of pain up my arms.

"My blade is a lot thicker than your little razor." I stiffen. How the hell could he know about my dirty little habit?

"You can bite me if the pain is too much. But do not move your hands." Nodding to the dark, I stay still. This is what I need. It will take the pain away, at least for a little while.

With a sharp jolt, the cold metal blade connects with my thigh, sending a tremor of excitement down my spine. It's away from where I usually cut myself, giving him a blank canvas. The initial sting is what I'm used to. Until the blade pushes a little deeper.

"Fuck!" I growl. This is different from doing it to myself. I want to move away from it rather than to it like usual. It still brings the release I crave. His hand moves quickly downward before lifting again. Starting at the same point, making two diagonal cuts. I focus on the sting from the first incision he made as he positions for another horizontal line like the first.

This time, I'm expecting the bite of the knife gliding through my skin effortlessly. Bringing my lips to his skin, I bite down. Hard. Just like he did to me during our first altercation. My intention is to mark him and make him bleed. This way he can't forget me, even if he wanted to. Like the rest of his scars, this one will be permanently etched into his skin. He lets out a low, sexy groan. Pain. Pain turns him on. As the pressure intensifies, my thighs squeeze together, causing a wave of sensation to ripple through my core. I need more.

The blade moves away from my thigh. His wet hair brushes against the side of my face when he leans in, tasting the raw wound on my skin. I release a hiss at the soreness from the contact. This is 15 shades of fucked up because this is more erotic than I could've ever dreamt of.

"Good girl. Don't touch yourself. I'll know." There's a hint of a smile in his voice.

"Thank you."

"For?"

"For coming back."

The unmistakable sound of a door opening, allows a sliver of moonlight to sneak through the crack before it shuts, leaving me in total darkness once again. The room feeling bereft of life. My heart sinks to the pit of my stomach at the realization that he's growing on me.

What feels like 20 minutes later, the lights in the bathroom flip on. My eye squint, readjusting to the sudden harshness of the bright light. The floor is marked with a trail of blood that leads to the door before it disappears on the other side. On my thigh is a letter 'W' or a "M' about an inch and a half wide and long. The water sprays onto my new wound, causing me to wince, washing away the traces my Shadow left with only blood.

CREW

MEET YOU AT THE GRAVEYARD — CLEFFY

The cool, smooth touch of the old white marble fireplace in the corner of my room brings back memories of our first family vacation to Europe, when Elijah Cox proudly showed us off as a family for the first time. It held too much sentimental value for me to leave it behind. Not that I would ever admit it to anyone. Ice clinks the side of my glass as I slam back the rest of the amber liquid in my glass, savoring the burn as it goes down.

My scowl sweeps across the sterile walls and bare furniture of my four-year dwelling, devoid of character or warmth. A black leather platform bed takes center stage in the room, emanating a luxurious but cold aura. The barn's A-frame has been replaced with a towering window, filling the room with natural moonlight.

Nightstands and a dresser provide practical and stylish touches. My fist clenches against the whiskey tumbler.

Pathetic. Eighteen years of life and nothing to show for it.

Failing to contain my rage, I fling the empty glass towards the blazing fire, shattering it into sparkling shards. Enjoying the sound it makes as it hits its mark. As my footsteps reverberate through the space, I reach for the bottle on the side table and forego the shattered glass scattered on the floor. Settling right back into the leather chair that's molded to my body from countless hours of staring at the fire.

Any time I'm struggling, it's as if Ben has a second sense that's in tune with mine. The more time we spent together, the more the four of us effortlessly synced and found a harmony. Echoing footsteps bounce off the wall and stop, taking up the seat next to me. Without looking up, I know the second part of my soul when it enters the room. The fire crackles as it finishes its destruction on the wood before beginning to eat away at the next victim in its path. No thought or remorse for the damage it makes.

Holding the bottle by its slender neck, I take a slow sip before setting it on the ground. Bracing my forearms on my knees, I focus on the crackling fire, attempting to communicate my feelings to Bennett.

"I'm sorry, Bennie." I rarely use his childhood nickname unless I'm mocking him. Using it now, I pray it tells him I'm being sincere. I keep my emotions to myself. But for my brothers? It's unnecessary. We are all we have. Without acknowledging me, he snatches up the bottle and takes a mouthful, the sound of liquid sloshing loud emphasizes my sparse room. Him staying is acknowledgment enough.

Clearing my throat from the emotions trying to claw its way up, I continue. "I'm sorry I couldn't save you. I tried. Regardless of the battles I was facing, there wasn't a day I didn't try." Emotions aren't something we all share very often. It's something all four of us keep buried, but in order to earn his forgiveness, he'll need my honesty. The truth.

"Steve," The mere mention of his name brings a bitter taste to my tongue, causing the remnants of tonight's drink to churn in my stomach. Trying again, I want him to understand. Our time away from each other wasn't something either of us have relived together, agreeing ignorance is bliss.

"Steve wasn't a kind man. He beat me constantly. You're aware of that much." Bennett's slight nod shows me I have his attention.

As I steel myself to speak, the sound of my shaky breath fills the tense silence between us as I build up the courage to reveal my past as he did earlier. "My punishments were always the worst when I tried to find you." I admit quietly as he studies me. "Those days, he would push my face into the bathtub that he would fill with cold water and hold my head underneath. I'd fight with everything I had, but between the starving and daily beatings, there wasn't much left. When I could no longer fight, the feeling of a knife being twisted in my chest would become overwhelming and I'd start inhaling water until I lost consciousness. He would resuscitate me. Over and over again until he got bored. The cycle never stopped. In the last moments when long awaited peace would wash over me it would be apologies to you. For not being stronger, for giving up, for being tired. And every time I came back, I would fight. For you. I knew I couldn't leave you here." That's not the worst of it, but he needs to know I never gave up on him, not even in my darkest moments. "My biggest regret was letting him know you were my one weakness."

The fire is still going strong. No chance of dying out anytime soon. But its warmth does little to stave off the frigid feeling of the bathroom, cornered by Steve's toothless sneer and soulless black eyes or the heavy weight of his hands on my body. The plaid flannel he always wore with a greasy white shirt. At one point, he shot me up with heroin, using the same needle he used for himself. And if that fucked me up, I can't comprehend what kind of damage it does to someone long term.

Bennett's discreet sniffling pulls me out of my nightmares. I'm on my feet, squatting in front of him before I realize I'm moving. I pull him toward me until his forehead meets mine. We sit like that for a minute, understanding and acceptance passing through the bond we have. Kissing his hair, my hand wraps around the neck of the bottle, bringing it with me before taking my seat next to him.

The heavy oak of my bedroom door creaks open. Cue the third person in our makeshift quadruplet. Saint walks in with a black hoodie and jeans on. His blonde hair is damp from a fresh shower. A faint smell of coconut trails after him. Taking his seat beside Bennett, all of our eyes fixate on the vacant fourth chair that will forever stay empty. The heaviness of his absence fills the room, adding to the already somber atmosphere.

"I miss him." Saint says softly. Leave it to him to make us face our emotions head on. Nodding, it hurts too much to admit he's gone.

"Yeah, me too," Bennett adds in with a wistful smile. "Remember all the plans he had for us? He wanted to live together until we were old. Build a house out in the woods for the four of us with a house on the property for dad. All these ideas for drug addicts and children in need. That damn humanitarian." He laughs. The organ where my heart should be aches and it only spurs my hatred towards Priya. Someone robbed him of those dreams. He will never get to live them out with us. He'll never live to graduate, have children or get married.

"Remember the first-time dad caught us street racing? Man, the cops bringing us home. He almost popped that blood vessel in his temple that throbs when he's mad. I swear he was going to need an ambulance. Ty spouted some bullshit about the cops chasing him." Saint lets out a belly laugh, reminiscing about our childhood shenanigans. Happiness teases the edges of my heart, seeing Saint and Bennett laughing together.

Raising my glass to our dead best friend, I toast to his empty chair, something we would say when we did something reckless that could get us killed. "To Death and back." Each of my brothers' voices echo after me, taking a drink to seal the deal.

PRIYA

The plushness of the bed dips beneath my hips, the weight of someone joining me on the soft mattress. Inhaling through my nose, the smell of burnt coffee mixed with lavender and honeysuckle that I've come to associate with River fill my lungs. The dreary grey light of the cloudy day shrouds my room in a dull haze. I hope to gauge her reaction to my solitude yesterday. The scowl on her face speaks volumes, while the lingering scent of burned coffee hints at her retribution.

"I thought lavender is supposed to be soothing. The daggers you're glaring at the side of my face are anything but." Closing both my eyes again to avoid whatever wrath this kitten is aiming at me.

"And it would be if you didn't avoid and shut me out." She sounds snappier than I've ever heard her. An uncomfortable feeling makes itself known in my gut. The lingering regret of my actions hangs over me, leaving a sour taste in my mouth. With Addison, I could tell myself I was protecting her. Even if the truth is that I didn't want her to know how truly broken I am. That excuse won't work with River.

"River..." I start.

She holds her hand up to stop me. "I don't believe you truly like solitude, Priya. I think you're afraid of being disappointed. If you don't want to talk, then we can not talk about anything together. If you want to cry, I can cry with you. You don't have to do this alone."

My senses heighten when I hear her sniffle and immediately sit up, apprehensive at the sounds of sobs. The uncomfortable pressure tugs at my thigh. Forcing myself to ignore the burning pain. Without her usual bold winged eyeliner, her eyes are noticeably hollow and heavy from lack of sleep. Her usual milky and honey skin tone looks sunken and dull rather than bright and full of life.

Was I really so selfish that I didn't even consider how I was affecting her? Gently guiding her towards the fluffy cream blanket on my bed, I enclose her in a snug bubble of warmth and comfort. Pushing the black longer bangs that frame her face away and behind her ear. I share with her the events of yesterday after we went our separate ways.

Her face is animated as I go into detail, reliving the terror of yesterday for what I promise is the last time. She gasps in horror, her brows furrow in anger, fist clenched on her stomach, fully engrossed in the story. She weighs each bruise and mark he left on me before ultimately settling on sadness.

"I'm so sorry, Priya." Weeping into my still damp hair from last night's shower. I shrug in response to her apology. I don't blame her. There is nothing she could've done to prevent it. They say, 'good things happen to good people'. Maybe I'm not a good person. Or could this be my karma for a past life?

"You can't heal from your hurt if you don't admit it's there, Pri." Her breath tickles my skin. How do I say I'm so tired of falling apart? Most days I don't know which way is up or down and I'm just free falling, hoping for the best. The mask of pretending everything is fine is the glue that keeps me intact, but I'm afraid it's wearing thin with each blow.

River clears her throat before I spiral any further.

"Did I tell you why I was sent here?" Shaking my head at the sudden change in topic. "Do you remember the family friend who would sneak into my room that I told you about?" Nodding, I remember her talking about it the first night I met the Shadow.

"When I was thirteen, I killed him. I was so tired of it. One night, he went too far. The day before his last visit, I put a knife in my nightstand. I still remember his smell, the taste of him, even the exact time it was and how long it took him to stop moving." I'm stunned. It's safe to say the kitten in my arms has sharp claws and enough rage to kill a person. Shocked, silent, I don't know what to say. No one should have a chance at life after hurting a vulnerable little girl and live to talk about it.

"Good."

Her body visibly relaxes in my hold.

"He threatened to kill my parents and do the same thing to my little brother that he did to me if I told them what was happening. Said he'd make me watch what he did to them before killing me. Apparently, he had friends in high places because they pushed to have me put behind bars, but my parents got me in here instead."

How fucked up is that? An act of self-defense from a child and people want to put her behind bars. If I had the same upbringing as Addison, would I feel as entitled? Remembering Amber's name for her it makes sense. Not that it's warranted. It's a little fucked up.

"I'll help you kill him."

Whoa, wait a minute. My eyes widen at the dark turn of events. Pulling my stare away from the blank white wall, I lean back to look into her eyes. She's dead serious. I don't know where my ray of sunshine went this morning, but she's cast in rain clouds. Or it's the opposite. She's a blazing inferno, like the sun.

I don't think that Oscar doesn't deserve to die, but I didn't want to drag River into what I had planned. If it wasn't for Bennett Demonio, he would've gone a lot further. How would I even go about planning a murder? Am I capable of committing one? I don't have the first clue on how to hide a body. This isn't the same as hacking into video feed or cloning a keycard. Opening my mouth to tell her my reservations about committing a new crime on top of my pending charges, my phone dings with a notification.

"We will put a pin in this and come back to it. With or without you, it's happening. I just thought it would be polite to give you the opportunity for vengeance." She states nonchalantly. "Your phone has been pinging all morning. I was nice enough to ignore and not read it." Looking at her freshly painted black nails and then at me. Yes, I'm sure it was quite the struggle for my nosy friend.

Rolling my eyes, I click on the notification in my school email. Coach Riley is requesting a meeting with me in his office. If there's anything I've learned in my short time at this school, it's that nothing is a suggestion. I wasn't planning on going into class today. Hence the reason I'm still in bed instead of getting ready for the day.

Sighing, I set my phone down and go into the spacious walk-in closet for a school outfit. Not wanting to chance getting detention with the dean again. Why can't I just have one day where I can recoup from my life? While getting dressed in the closet, I yell to River about the email, then decide she'll just look anyways.

Before putting on the pleated skirt, I notice the makeshift bandage I made last night has held up rather well. A tight bandage encircles my thigh, coated with soothing ointment to protect the gauze hiding underneath. That's how I usually take care of those injuries. I'll need to change it at some point today. The soft fabric of my skirt conceals it seamlessly, leaving no trace of its presence. Unless someone is looking up my skirt. I shudder at the thought. It wouldn't be surprising at this point. A school for criminals, a perverted dean, and his disgusting nephew, and to top it off the Shadow man. What's next?

"I brought you a cinnamon roll!" River calls out. My nose wrinkles as I tally the calories and carbs I know are inside something so sweet. I've been doing well with limiting my calorie intake since I'm not running as often as I did at home. She's just being nice. How would she know what I won't eat?

"Thank you!"

I hear her scoff as I exit the closet. "You need to eat, Priya. This is the only thing I could take from the Hall this morning without the kitchen staff being suspicious. You should've seen the chef peeking around the door at me. Hey, did you know your account has been locked down with 'specific dietary instructions'?" She uses air quotes. "What did you do to piss them off?" Them being the Demons.

Blowing out a puff of air, "Honestly, I don't know. I ran into Bennett when I first met the dean. Didn't immediately fall down to my knees at his charms. Crew hates my existence, along with everyone else. Saint seems decent enough." Forgoing about telling her about Bennett getting me to kiss him.

Picking up the sickly, sweet treat she brought, I take a bite while making eye contact to show her that I am eating. My eyes close as I savor the burst of flavor on my tongue. The sugary icing is so sweet, I moan my agreement to it… and River. It's so good, but I really shouldn't indulge too much. I've gone longer without eating thanks to my parents. My mother's punishment of choice was always to play mind games, withholding food, isolate me from my sister, and keeping me on the edge of my seat waiting for my father. She never directly put her hands on me. I wonder why that is.

"Ready?" Standing and grabbing my things. Hopefully, after I see the coach, I'll come back and work on my schoolwork. Take the rest of the day off from the outside world.

"Okay, but can we go back to the Hall? I'm still hungry." Sticking out her bottom lip, pouting. I wanted to avoid people. The feeling of everyone staring at me makes me uncomfortable. I'm not sure how fast word travels around school. River knew about the incident before I even told her.

"What? That was our first fight. I thought we should make up with something sweet after being sour. They say the stomach is the way to a woman's heart." Giving her a slight nod, I agree. No reason for her to go hungry after she did something thoughtful for me when I hurt her feelings. She lets me stick my arm through her elbow while she leads us out the door, acting like nothing is out of the ordinary and I couldn't be more thankful for it. I don't want to be coddled and handled with gloves. That would frighten me more, waiting for the other shoe to drop.

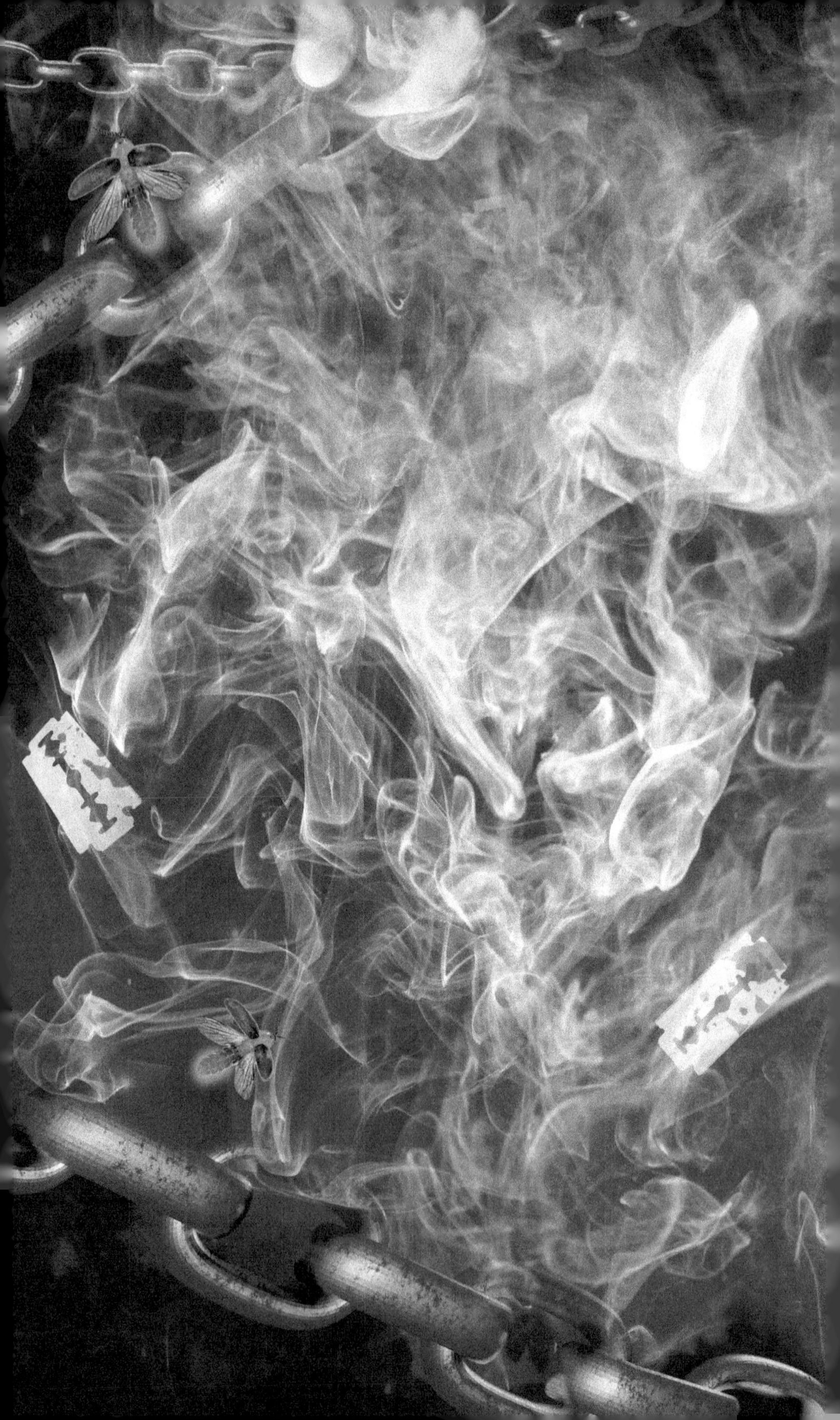

PRIYA

With a skip in her step, River leads us to the white-clothed tables, showcasing tiers of mouthwatering breakfast delights. "I just want to grab something from the buffet table quick and we'll go to P.E." she calls over her shoulder. Trailing behind her at a much slower pace, a nagging feeling creeps up on me. Call it paranoia, but I can't shake the feeling that everyone is staring at us. More specifically, at me.

Despite my instincts, my eyes cannot resist shifting from one face to another. Because of my habit of avoiding eye contact and trying to keep my head down, I don't recognize most of the people here, even after a month. Except Amber leaning back in a chair in the Demons' lair with a cocky smirk on her foxlike face. Her siren eyes tipped up in delight. Her minion Ember is sitting next to her with a vacant expression staring across the cafeteria

The atmosphere is crackling, making the air feel heavy a tense anticipation. The absence of the usual chatter from the students in the morning creates a peculiar silence. Could it be from that bullshit with Oscar? Chancing a glance at River, she seems undisturbed by the eerie silence, filling her space with her own musings about breakfast.

Treading carefully, I walk toward the end of the buffet to wait for River. That was my second mistake this morning. The first was getting out of bed. With my back turned toward the onlookers, I find it easier to focus on River prancing around the food. Out of sight, out of mind.

The piercing stares from the Demons sitting at the table consume my mind, as well as the hundreds of onlookers who wait with bated breath. Sensing the shift in the air, a menacing presence settles behind me. My senses go on high alert at the sudden prickling sensation at the base of my neck. The Demon's action has caused an energy shift that's emitting a nearly equal amount of animosity as my father.

As he moves my hair to one side, exposing me. I shiver from his freezing hands. He gives off a predator-like aura and I'm trapped like a prey in a standoff. Running would only spur him into action. While I search for a spot to focus on in the cafeteria, I become captivated by the refreshing aroma of crisp linen. Crew.

Softly, his lips brush against my cheek. "I want you on your hands and knees."

Initially, I thought he was being sexual. The guy I sit next to in psych class is now deliberately trying to make my life miserable by publicly requesting a blow job in front of our classmates.

"Crawl to Bennett." I jerk back like I've been slapped. My cheeks heat and I don't hesitate.

"Go fuck yourself." Pulling myself away, he manhandles me, grabbing ahold of my arm that still aches from Oscar's unwanted hands. Gritting my teeth and staring straight towards an exit. It's only a couple of feet away. It would be relatively easy to leave.

"Crawl." He demands shoving me back in front of him. The way he says it is nonnegotiable.

"No."

Before I can escape, he pulls my back flush to his front, leaving no room for movement. I can't stand it when other people put their hands on me, and it seems like that's all that's been happening this week. It provokes an itching sensation on my skin while a sweat breaks across my body. My eye twitches. Trying to find my only friend in this chaotic mess, I notice River and Saint standing side by side. He turns her to face me and Crew.

A stoic expression has replaced Saint's usual sunny demeanor. Absent are this trademark dimples, and his eyes have taken on a darker hue of blue. His usual open demeanor has disappeared. His straightened spine gives him an inch growth that is impossible to ignore. He looks wrong, wicked and evil. One arm is thrown over River casually, as if they're old friends when their faces read the opposite. She looks scared. Folding in on herself, she crosses her arms over her chest, creating a defensive barrier. Saint only slightly shifts, showing off a narrow knife pushing into where River's lung would be located. What the fuck is happening right now?

"Or…?" Asking for clarification on the escalating situation.

"Or I'll make sure he stabs your little friend and let you watch as she suffocates from the blood filling her lungs. Then you will know the loss of a friend, too. Crawl!" he bellows. When I go to open my mouth to ask what the fuck he's talking about, he kicks the back of my knee, making it buckle. The stone floor is unforgiving as my knees smack against its rocky texture. My breathing comes in pants. Our audience is blurring along with the edges of my vision. River lets out a resounding shriek, her white button-up shirt stained with seeping blood. Her eyes plead for me to help her. And I can't.

Tossing my bag in River's direction, I steel myself. Wishing more than anything this was Hogwarts, and I was a witch so I could burn him to death with my glare alone. That doesn't happen, but I would find a way.

When my palms touch the cool ground, the sensation of humiliation spreads through me, burning my cheeks. My arms tremble with a shaky weakness, as if I might faint at any moment. Alternating, lifting one arm and the opposite knee, and then repeat on the other side. The length of this crawl of shame looks distorted. Each stride I take makes it look longer. I keep my head raised but my gaze is down. I can't stomach the incessant giggling, the constant sound of video recordings, and the hushed conversation that fills the room.

With my attention focused on Bennett's coal black slacks, I stop, instinctively grabbing his knee to steady myself as I rise. My grip tightens, my fingers curling into claws, desperate to draw blood like he did to River. He may not hold the knife to her right now, but he's every bit as guilty as Saint. They all are.

His eyes narrow, knowing my intentions. He tsks at me like a petulant child that needs to be reprimanded. "Sit." Fury courses through my veins. I want to kill him and his brothers. Rip his eyeballs out and cut that condescending smile off of his face. River yelps and I release my grip on his knee, sitting on my heels.

"Good girl." His eyes darken at my obedience as his hands pats my head like he's praising a dog. From the left of Bennett, something gooey hits my ribs, followed by Amber's cackle. Icy hands encircle my throat, placing something around it with a click locking it into place. My hands strain against the unyielding choker, refusing to budge, no matter how hard I pull.

"Every bitch needs a collar." A chair scrapes against the stones before both sets of feet leave me on the ground, hyperventilating. Panic rises and fear takes hold. Get it off, get it off! I can't breathe. In and out, in and out. My vision blackens at the edges before someone sits in front of me. Strong arms scoop me underneath my legs, while another supports my back.

"God damn it, Carter." The only thought is I want out of his arms. It's too much touching. My demons are nipping at my heels, begging to have a turn.

"Please," I whisper to whoever is carrying me. "Put me down." The walking ceases, but the arms stay banded around me. "Put me down!" My anger comes back in full force. The person gently sets me on my feet. For once, someone is listening to what I'm saying.

"Thank you."

"Sorry, I wasn't even thinking. Are you okay?" Nodding. What is he going to do if I say "No"? Nothing.

"What happened out there?" The athletic shorts and school crewneck give away who it is before I reach his face. His dark eyes are filled with concern. Coach Riley stands in an empty hallway with me, while his thin lips are tipped into a confused frown. Even though he's not conventionally attractive, the baseball cap adds an air of anonymity to his appearance. Someone I'd pass on the street and not be able to point out again.

"What does it look like?" I scoff. Where were the teachers at, anyway? Is he supposed to believe River was held at knifepoint while I had to crawl to Bennett in front of the entire school, then be collared like an animal? Doubtful.

"I just wanted to check on you. I noticed you caught the eye of the founder's adoptive sons. My intentions were to warn you, but I can see that I'm a little too late." He grimaces, obviously staring at my new accessory.

"Yep. Consider me warned. See you in class." The gym is the opposite way from where he took me, in the other direction.

"Priya, let me walk with you." Okay? That's not odd. We're usually cool in gym class, but that's as far as that's ever gone. "I care about you. And I don't want to see you get hurt."

He cares about me? This man knows nothing about me. I attempt to read his intentions. My bullshit-o-meter needs calibration because I cannot tell what's real and not.

"I mean, as I do all my students." Amending what he said. To know, he thought, he needed to clarify intrigues me a little. I'll bite, but only because I don't want to be caught alone in the hallway again. I learned my lesson. Standing a little too close for comfort, we head toward the gym, talking about his lesson plans and his home life. He mentions his parents divorced three years ago, and he has a younger sister. The way he talks about her reminds me of Addison. I need to text her.

Opening one of the many oak doors that leads up a winding flight of stone steps, I follow after him. The clicking of my heels is loud in the old, confined, stone hallway.

"You remind me of her, my sister. Headstrong, determined, sarcastic," He laughs, remembering something. His voice holds longing when he speaks about her. "She was also a troublemaker. Caught the attention of one of the Demons. I can't imagine what it's like to have the wrath of all three." Coach Riley studies my face, looking for something, but I'm not sure what. "I believe that was her downfall." Side eyeing him, I'm not sure what he's getting at.

"If you think I've intentionally gained the eyes of all three Demons', you're sadly mistaken. Whatever issues they have with me are one sided." Or they were. Until they brought River into it and degraded me in front of everyone in the school. I chew on the inside of my lip and rub the burning sensation in my sternum. River.

"I would hate to see a beautiful girl like yourself be mixed up in the wrong crowd is all, Priya." Pursing my lips, I can visibly see he doesn't want to listen what I have to say, like most of the male population.

"Coach Riley, I appreciate you helping me out back there, but I am not your sister. I can handle myself."

He smiles to himself before looking over at me. His expression seems a little too friendly for a teacher, but he's not giving me creepy vibes yet.

"Yes, I can see that. Please, call me Mason."

"All right, Coach Mason. Thank you for walking me to the nurse's office." I dismiss him.

I'm not going to go into Nurse Lisa's office. When Mason is out of sight, I rush as quickly as I can in heels through the castle's dark and gloomy hallways into the even more grim morning to find River. The compulsion to check on her is consuming.

PRIYA

Feeling a sense of urgency to see River, I kick my heels off at the elevator doors, and sprint down the hallway to her rainbow decorated entryway. Unlike the last time I was here, I don't hesitate to knock. A part of me is worried I lost a friend during that debacle.

Her door cracks open, revealing her brown eyes rimmed red from crying and darkened with pain. For the second time, I want to reach out and touch her. I'm probably the most awkward person when it comes to comforting, but River's brokenness calls to a forgotten part in my heart.

"Can I come in?" I aim for gentle and not pushy. She sighs and, with a resigned shrug, opens her dorm door.

At first glance, her room doesn't match her sunny personality. But it does match her gothic appearance, the room is painted in a sage green making all the shadowy black items stand out more prominently. A matching green canopy lined with fairy lights hangs above the bed, giving a sense of otherworldly comfort. Tons of live greenery of plants bring life to the otherwise morbid room. Pinned spiders and butterflies line the walls. Small coffins that look like décor and I secretly hope are empty give off a Halloween theme. It smells like her, lavender and honeysuckle. She's made herself at home.

River's silent as she sits at the end of the queen size black iron bed and grabs a knitted pillow to cover herself with. It feels like she's closing herself off from me. That could be my insecurities speaking for me.

"I'm sorry, River." My hands reach for hers, but I pull it back in case she doesn't want to be touched.

"He knew." She whispers brokenly. Slowly, giving her time to object, I climb on the bed and pull her towards me, hugging her tightly. This was supposed to comfort her, but I need this hug just as much. Deep sobs wrack her body. I'm out of my depth here. Not one to show my emotions in front of others, I usually go numb. Her reaction is the complete opposite. How do you comfort someone? Should I Google this?

It will look bad if I pull out my phone to do just that. I rub her back as she clings onto me crying into my shirt. Should I ask?

After my arms tingle with numbness and my shirt is soaked, her sobs turn into sniffles. Reaching over to her side table, I grab a charcoal-colored tissue out of the box and hand it to her.

"He knew about how I got here. Details he shouldn't know." She halts, staring at me. "Did you tell him?"

My eyes widen at the accusation before realizing she's genuinely asking. Even though they weren't far away from me and Crew, it's plausible that he whispered something low enough that only she could hear.

"Of course not! We've been together every minute since you've told me. I would never betray your trust like that!" My initial emotion was to lash out. Angry that she thought that low of me after I've spilt my secrets to her and trusted her. She's hurting.

I've done this to her plenty of times since we've met. She's not trying to take it out on me. Mentally patting myself on the back for not jumping headfirst into my emotions, I let her work through whatever is going on through her head.

She nods woodenly.

"I'm sorry." Apologizing again because I can't help but to think this is my fault. The Demons are angry with me. They used her against me to comply with their outrageous games.

"Are you okay?" She asks, getting the attention off of her. We're at an impasse because I don't want to talk about what happened, either. The feeling of needing to downplay my feelings is tempting, but I think she wants to run away from her own mind by focusing on me.

"No. Not really." My pride is hurt. Shame is second on that long list of why I'm not okay. Admitting is the first step, right? "They threatened to hurt you if I didn't do it."

Her eyes zero in on my new piece of jewelry, then on my bare feet. Too tongue tied to do anything but touch her own throat. Her gaze makes the collar feel more like the shackle it is. Renewed humiliation washes over me, causing me to look away from her to stare at the black velvet curtains.

"It's locked. But why?" she whispers, her brow creasing. She's worried for me. This time, she has a right to be, because I am too. Voicing it out loud, with my track record, would jinx me.

"I don't know." I say honestly. "Originally, I thought it was because they're egotistical assholes who can't stand to be questioned. Then, I thought it was because I shut Bennett down. My bluntness towards Crew in psychology, even." Shaking my head, ceaseless questions batter my mind. What do they want from me?

"The Demons' have never directly interfered with anyone, Priya. Something is wrong. This is more than just mean girls like Amber. During my time here, they've kept to themselves." My fingers grab my matches from the side of my pleated skirt. I do my ritual to calm myself so I can think.

"We could always just ask them?" Her cocoa-colored eyes hold an air of innocence. My face flushes red, remembering being on my hands and knees.

"Yeah, River. Let me go ask Crew why he did that. I'm not worried about him finding a new way to humiliate me." Sarcasm in full force as I throw my hands up in exasperation. Pinching the bridge of my nose, I close my eyes. None of this is her fault. It's mine. Somehow, someway, I have offended them enough to earn their ire and drag River into it. I want to know why, but not at the risk of going through that again.

River pulls out her phone while I'm deep in thought. She gasps at whatever it is she sees. Anxiety pauses my thoughts looking over at River. Her hands shake as she passes me her phone and I frown.

On the school's student gossip site, which I refuse to get because of this type of drama, is a clear video of me on loop. Crawling on my hands and knees. Starting from Crews feet, following me zoomed in on my ass is my black thong on display for the school. Rolling my lips onto my teeth, I nod. I knew there would be a video. I could faintly hear the chatter from everyone around me. Scrolling down with my thumb there are now memes about me. Disgusting comments under each post.

OscarBush @ AmberAstor "I knew she was
cock hungry!"

Biting my tongue, I manage to hand it back without throwing it.

"I think things are about to get a lot worse for us." Hopefully, for her sake. It's just me. By the way Saint had no issue in involving her in whatever game they're playing, I doubt it.

"You know what always makes me feel better? Plotting revenge. Rome wasn't built in a day, but I'm pretty sure it was destroyed in one. Don't fact check me in case I'm wrong." She plays with the string over her black throw blanket. There is the River I have come to know. We could always burn this place down and never have to worry about it. That would leave me with Robert.

My phone vibrates in my hand. An email flashes across the screen.

"Detention," I mutter. He couldn't really say more than a few nasty words to me, right? "Plan world domination later. I'm going to go take care of this."

"Fine, I'll start without you." A cute pout lines her face. Chuckling, I leave the room to talk to Bush, who seems intent on helping the Demons' make my life a living hell.

PRIYA

Marching into the dean's office, I do without knocking. On the way over here, I've worked myself up over the injustice of being targeted by him. It's as if he sits there constantly monitoring the students' school website, fixated on any mention or wrongdoing associated with my name. My father, my mother, the Demons', Amber, and the dean, everyone conspiring against me.

As I push the door open with more force than needed, I briefly lose my resolve when I notice the nurse rubbing her knees while Bush casually zips up his gray trousers. It's easy to put two and two together to figure out what's going on. I may be inexperienced, but I'm not naïve. I understand what oral sex involves. Strands stick out on the sides of her messy, dark brown hair, as if someone had run their hands through it. She hurries past me, touching up her smeared maroon lipstick and avoiding eye contact. Before rushing out into the hallway and shutting the heavy door behind her.

"Miss Carter. You're earlier than expected. Take a seat." His tone holds a note of irritability at the unexpected interruption. My steps are slow and measured as I take the seat across from him. Considering the amount of funding this school receives, I'd expect them to invest in comfortable seating. Not chairs that make my bones grind against the wood with every subtle movement I make. My chilly hands clasp together in my lap as I wait.

Bush straightens his suit as he sits. "What was so important that you had to interrupt my meeting?" The unbothered tone he has is grating on my nerves. His "meeting"? His dick down the school nurse's throat during school hours seems *super* important.

"I wanted to discuss my detention."

"Ahh, yes." He says, patronizingly, "Your little…" Bush looks up, searching for a word. Everything about this guy is shady. The detentions, the questions, the double standards. Call it my sixth sense, or just dealing with people like him all the time, but I'm right.

"Inappropriate display in the cafeteria this morning." My jaw drops open on its own accord. This guy must be kidding right now.

"You're serious?"

"It's becoming quite bothersome to keep tabs on all your transgressions."

There's an easy fix for that. Stop. "Get your head out of your ass and do something about the menaces running this school." That's what I want to say, but it'll only get me into more trouble. If there is anyway to get out of these ridiculous detentions, I'm going to have to up the stakes. Time to go with the next best thing: blackmail. I've never resorted to it before, but it's not beneath me.

"What would everyone think if they knew you were fucking the school nurse?" Exuding a sense of calm and confidence in my threat. Checkmate, sleazeball.

Bush's eyebrows shoot up at my boldness. Like everyone else, he probably underestimates me. With a smug glint in his eyes, he leans back comfortably in his wingback chair.

"You want to know something I found interesting?" Refusing to take his bait, I stay silent, observing his coiled posture, mirroring a striking cobra. He's going to tell me, anyway.

"I received a call from your father after our last visit." The pause he takes lets me know he wants to keep me in suspense, because my father would never willingly call anyone about me. "Told me to let him know if I had any additional issues with you and your behavior. He wouldn't have a problem coming here and setting you straight." The statement alone makes my confidence falter. He searches my face. What he must see causes an evil grin to spread across his face.

The usual darkness that intertwines and drags me to face my grief is now a chill seeping through my bones with the phantom ache of his fists. All the air has left my lungs. The facade of my calm composure is cracking. My nails dig into my thighs, hoping the sting will bring back some resemblance of control.

"Now, since you're here early, we can get started on detention. Unless you were planning to go back to class?" Giving him a brief nod of acknowledgement, I wait for today's torture session.

Leisurely, he makes his way next to me, just as he did last time. This time, my guard is much stronger. He will not throw me off again. He reaches out with his repulsive hand, making me instinctively recoil as he tries to touch a loose strand of my hair.

"I once heard about attention seekers like yourself. That any attention is 'good' attention." He sucks his teeth. "If you need attention so badly, I wouldn't mind giving it to you." I flinch at the husky tone his voice takes. Red flags are waving in front of my face. My stomach turns at the thought of him using my father as a threat for this. Would I choose the evil I know? Or submit to threats?

"Don't worry, Priya. We'll get there." There's an unspoken promise in his voice that makes my skin crawl. "I had a ladder brought in here for you. My shelves are in need of some dusting, especially the top ones." His eyes are like mud caking my body as they look me over. He nods his head towards the shelves, and I take the hint. Last time, he only kept me for the hour. I hope he'll need the office for another student and cut my time short.

"Start from the top down."

Biting my tongue to keep myself from telling him how much of a pervert he is. I stomp over to grab the ladder out from behind his desk. I'll begin at the farthest corner and hope my detention will end before I get anywhere near him.

The ascension of the ladder feels more like a death march. His gaze seems to penetrate through my skin, leaving a trail of discomfort with each step. There's one exit out of this dungeon, and it's right next to me. Worst-case scenario, I throw myself off the ladder in heels and make a run for it. Potentially stab him in the eye with one of them. Filled with thoughts of revenge, I direct my energy towards tackling the dirt and grime that's accumulated on the highest shelf. The dust on the books confirms my earlier suspicion that they are purely decorative and have never seen a scrap of daylight. What are the qualifications for running a school? Chancing a peek over my shoulder, his eyes are zeroed in on my ass. I cringe and wrinkle my nose in response.

"Fucking pervert."

"What was that?" There's no way he heard what I was muttering under my breath. It seems that he interpreted it as a indication to come closer. My eyes dart to the doorway. I'm only a couple of steps up on the ladder. This jump wouldn't hurt… much.

He's close enough that the metal steps of the ladder dig into my back, in an attempt to get away. His sausage fingers run over the buttons on my school uniform. My stomach rolls. Much like his nephew did. Right as he's about to speak, the door to his office swings open. He startles and skitters away. In the doorway stands Saint. Unlike Bush, his mere presence in the room is enough to dominate the entirety of the office. It's suffocating and dark, like it was this morning. Remembering the terror on River's face as he pressed a knife into her side, my jaw clenches.

Saint hums, taking in the scene before him, looking between

the dean and me. His steel-blue eyes hold a dangerous calm. His tongue runs along the piercings in his lips, drawing my attention away from his stare.

As the words, "You-You're dismissed, Miss Carter." left Brian's mouth. The tension in my posture leaves and I practically skip down the ladder, my heel catching on the last step. Thrown off guard by the abrupt presence of a hand reaching out, I quickly react by instinctively throwing myself out of harm's way, eager to put some distance between myself and the perceived danger. The hand, quick and firm, grabs me and pulls me behind a wall of a man, herding me towards the door. An intriguing combination of leather and wood emanates from Saint bringing back a vague memory that I can't quite place. My shoulders lose the tension I've been carrying since walking into Bush's office. Whatever connection my mind is trying to make, I quickly dismiss it to get away from Bush.

Once I make it back to the safety of my room, I shut and lock the door behind me, pressing my forehead against the cool metal of the barrier that hides me away. As if that's kept anyone out this far. The moment I inhale, my muscles automatically become tight and rigid. It…smells wrong here. Like when walking into my room after Addi had been in there, I could smell her long after she left. Or forgetting to take out the trash. When food is left out on the counter when leaving in a hurry. There's a smell here that doesn't sit right.

Upon opening my eyes, my arms go limp. The energy I had accumulated from the headmaster's office is sucked out of me completely with the chaos that has consumed my room. Papers scattered everywhere, and furniture overturned. The bed, which once used to be cozy and inviting. Now lies in disarray. Its stuffing ripped out and scattered about. Small strips of shredded bedding fill the room, and feathers from the cream colored down blanket settle on every surface. Someone has ransacked the kitchenette, tossing now, opened food packages haphazardly. There goes the last of my food. The Demons' haven't let up on my personal rations of rabbit food and fruit for dinner. Hunger grumbles in my stomach, aching at the thought of discarding carelessly wasted food.

My eyes fixate on the closed closet door. A lump forms in my throat, and I struggle to swallow it down. My sister's sweaters. I have more at my parent's house, but these were her favorite. The threadbare hoodies that are timeworn with love. She mostly slept in them. She was always cold and shivering, even with the heat on. These articles of clothing are the most precious things I own. Pictures can be replaced, but objects that hold her scent or that her skin has touched cannot. The odds of someone missing my closet after destroying my room are slim to none.

The room's vibrant colors seem to drain away as I reach for the doorknob. My focus shifts to what awaits me on the other side. The unsettling creak of the door is magnified by the surrounding silence. I'm already regretting bringing something so important with me here. In our house, we left her room untouched, a constant reminder of her absence. Forever frozen in time, the way she left it.

My heart pounding, I utter a silent prayer before forcefully ripping open the door like a Band-Aid. Quick and painless. Only, it's not. Inside, ripped clothes lay in tatters, while someone had recklessly thrown crimson liquid around, coating everything in its path, including the formerly immaculate carpet. My eyes bounce back and forth, scanning the destruction, hoping to spot any trace of the three hoodies. Faded white, beige and baby pink. My hands shake as I reach into the trash thrown around the closet. I search through the pile of clothes, frantically sifting through anything that resembles her hoodies, discarding everything else in the process. My body trembles, heat covers me from the inside out. Where the fuck are they? Anyone who came into my room wouldn't know the significance of these clothes. Turning around in a circle to see if I missed something, I squint when I see the safe. Only touched once when I first got here. It's unlocked and barely cracked open. A sinking feeling settles over me, like a demon leaning over my shoulder, filled with excitement that has me breaking out into a cold sweat. That means someone knew the combination *and* knows it's my sister's birthday.

"Open it", a voice whispers in my mind, spooking me even further. I'm procrastinating. Whatever is inside isn't a good thing. At a snail's pace, I open it. Inside sits my sister's precious hoodies, unscathed from whatever disaster struck the room. Relief loosens my shoulders. They're okay. It's short-lived with the black letter on top, lined with my name in red calligraphy. Gingerly reaching in to not touch the clothes with my red stained hands. I carefully pluck it off the top, then settle back on my haunches to open it.

Whoever did it was kind enough to save one of my most prized possessions. Could it be my Shadow? My painted fingers massage the oncoming stress headache. My Shadow doesn't seem to be the petty type. Destroying my things is too childish for him. Now, destroying my life? That would be more his pace.

With trembling fingers, I open the flap,

I'll always ensure the well-being of my possessions.

Yeah, that's not creepy at all. I'm thankful for my things being saved from the carnage and all, but not enough to truly be in debt to someone over it. Is it too much to ask for someone to be a decent human being?

I should ask River if she can look into the hallway cameras again. The worst she could do is tell me no.

PRIYA

Hey, can you look in at the cameras again?

Her response is instant like her phone was in her hand.

RIVER

Yeah. What am I looking for?

Do I start with whoever gave my room an extreme makeover? Or who left the letter? It could be an answer to both.

PRIYA

Someone broke into my room. It's destroyed.

Not even five minutes after I've begun to sort through my things, the door to my room swings open. River stands in the doorway, her hands fly up to her mouth. Windblown jet-black hair and chunky combat boots, I can't help but imagine her running here, her cheeks blushing with a rosy pink hue from the wind.

She splutters incoherently before she's able to form words.

"What in the actual fuck?" The words sound foreign in her mouth, like she wasn't made to say curse words. It brings a smirk to my face. I'm corrupting her heaven bound soul. Instead, I nod and continue to put everything into garbage bags for house-keeping to take. Realistically, this is their job they're paid to do, but helping speed up the process wouldn't hurt.

"I've already got ahold of the office, the cleaners, and the people who are supposed to be in charge of the dorms. They should send you money to replace all your things. I also took the liberty of sending the dean the video of Oscar and Amber breaking into your room. But I didn't send him the one of the guy dressed in all black coming in before *and* after they had left. I thought you would want to see it first."

My eyes narrow at the phone in her hand before she tosses it to me. Watching the video, my face flushes, my knuckles turn white from the death grip on her phone.

"Whoa, okay killer." She plucks the phone out of my hand, caressing it gently.

Both Amber and Oscar were in on it. In each hand they carried a gallon of red liquid before Amber pulls out a key card for my door and opens it, both slithering in like snakes.

"Does everyone have a fucking key to my room?" I say between clenched teeth. River's face pales and she shrinks back from my anger. I understand River's need to have a friend, and I even appreciate it. Without her I would have no one, but a small part of me can't help but to wonder if her having an all-access pass to my room started a trend.

Surveying my dorm, my bones grow weary. What am I going to do? Sleep in the tub? I haven't looked in there. I don't want to. The room pales compared to the disgusting thoughts that flood my mind. Everywhere I look, there is red liquid–pooling on the ground, seeping into the torn bed, and smeared across the countertops. Where do I even start? River stands with her hands in her hair, looking as perplexed as I feel.

There's a part of me that thinks River is in on it. The timing of her arrival every time I have a problem or she's already there. It could be the paranoia from the dean. It has to be. Blaming River for my bad luck isn't fair. She could easily say the same about me. I'm sure her life wasn't this exciting before I came. I'm dragging her down with me.

"Why don't you stay with me until your room is back in order?" she proposes. My eyes dart over to the floorboard that appears untouched. My stuff. I'll check on my contraband and see if I can make room for my sister's clothes in there.

"Just let me get some things and I'll be right over." I like River, but I hope we don't tire of each other. 24/7 with anyone sounds like hell. She loves being around people and I need peace and quiet. Some things can't change, no matter how hard you try.

CREW

Nothing compares to the satisfying feeling of accomplishment. Well, that's not true. One of the top items on that list is the jobs we receive from Elijah. My lip curls into a smile as the warmth of the whiskey slides down my throat.

"What's for dinner?" Bennett unceremoniously jumps on the sectional across from me, disturbing my peaceful inner thoughts. His feet prop on the arm of the couch. The obnoxious behavior makes my nostrils flare. He walks around stepping in God knows what all day. And he couldn't even take his shoes off before he did it. It's ridiculous how frequently I have to tidy up after him as if he were a toddler. How difficult is it to place your filthy feet on the floor?

"I'm not your mother. Figure it out." He sits staring at me like

I've grown a second head. "And get your damn feet off the couch!" I growl. A wide grin lights up his face, just like when we were kids, and he would get caught doing something that would get him in trouble. That's what he wanted. A reaction. He's bored.

"Go play with Amber." I roll my eyes at his childish behavior.

"She's mad at me right now," he pouts, crossing his arms over his chest. We both know he doesn't care if she's upset. A snap of his fingers and she'd be right where he wanted her. In his bed or on her knees right here in front of us. Time, place or audience is irrelevant. What would cause him to not want to play with his favorite toy?

Quiet footsteps halt in the hallway as Saint emerges, his presence a rare sight after spending most of his time locked away in his room. We should check in on him. Saint's normally icy blue eyes are dull and hollow. He slumps down next to Ben on the couch, his body moves sluggishly as he rests his head on the back of the cushion.

"What's for dinner?" He asks.

"What do you want? Do you want to order in? Or I can make something." The look on my brother's face is priceless. His eyebrows raise, jaw hangs open, and his arms extended in disbelief.

"Are you kidding me?" He says through maniacal laughter. It takes everything in me not to laugh with him. What can I say? Pay back is a bitch. I rest on the loveseat, feeling the stiffness from not using it often, and act clueless.

My brows furrow with a mock frown. "What do you mean? He's hungry, Bennett. Am I just supposed to let him starve? What kind of monster do you think I am?" Saint lazily peeks open one eye to observe the show. Bennett jumps up and paces back and forth in front of me.

"*I'm* hungry," he emphasizes. A smirk pulls at the corner of my mouth.

"Take out tonight. But can you make tamals soon?" Oh, Bennett is going to lose it.

"Yep." I reply, taking another swig of my whiskey and

releasing an audible sound of satisfaction. The sound of Saint's snickering in the background is the final straw that unleashes Bennett's verbal rampage.

"Crew! I've been begging you to make mom's tamals forever! Saint asks one time, and it's 'yep'? Why does he get the special treatment? He has a condition, not a fucking disability! You can't possibly think he's prettier than me because we share the same face!"

He thinks he's the only one who can get under my skin. But fails to realize we're twins. Regardless of the time spent apart, I'll always know him better than he knows himself.

He obsessively rants about loyalty and food. I've blocked him out. There's nothing he could say that I haven't heard already. Saint pulls out his phone from his sweatpants to order our food for tonight. Wherever he goes, he knows our orders by heart. After finishing, he lets us know when it'll be here. Since he's finally made an appearance out of his hole, I figure it would be a good time to talk about this morning.

"This morning proved to be eventful."

Ben stops in his tracks. He spins on his heel with a devilish smile in place of his running mouth. Even though Bennett prefers to watch, having an audience turns him on just as much. Throw in someone who is attractive? That's a wet dream come to life.

"That collar was a nice touch, diamonds?" He praises. While I can hear the questions about my intentions at the same time.

"I won't have a pet who looks like trash. The entire student body was a witness to our not so subtle claiming." I wave off his concern. I would've been fine with a shock collar around her neck. Then she'd be more compliant. But that would be less appealing to look at.

"Malice did well today, keeping River in line." Saint nods. Malice is unpredictable at best, so knowing he was able to control his urges was a win.

"Actually, there was one thing I did want to talk about, something I found in her old messages."

Is that why he's been absent lately? Looking for more information? My heart swells at the thought of him being able to help and not feel like a hinderance to our cause. He needs to feel wanted and being helpful does that.

For a second, I was worried he had found out about the letter and that was the cause of his absence. Malice has a tendency to push Saint to extremes, claiming it's his job. Sometimes I'm not sure if we have the same definition of the word "protection".

Facing him, I give him my undivided attention. His appearance is haggard and drained. Guilt eats at my conscience, at pushing him too hard for more than he's ready to give. We don't know what could trigger him to become dormant, leaving us with Malice for who knows how long. He might be helping, but what is it going to cost him? Saint wouldn't come to us unless he really thought the information he had would be beneficial.

"You know how we couldn't really find much on her phone? No one has reached out to her since her arrival at Cox." I gesture for him to continue. "Well, like I said. We couldn't find anything. We were waiting. So, I decided to go back. Back before the incident and reread old messages. I started with her fathers. The only text she's received from him that wasn't a one-word response was something about her grades." He rubs the back of his neck. "There was some sort of threat there. But nothing to reveal exactly what it was."

"You think her father made her burn the library down at the academy?" Bennett ponders.

Saint's head tilts, and he plays with his black lip piercings, something he does when he's deep in thought.

"Not, exactly. No. I think Robert Carter is a little more messed up in the head than just politics."

Abuse? I want to ask, but he seems unsure of the answer already. He'll continue to beat around the bush if he doesn't have a definite answer.

"The point is, whatever threat was there is directly connected to her grades. I think that's where we should hit next."

Tilting my head, "That's perfect. We're partners in psych. I'll put something in place to make her fail. It'll get a reaction from Robert and possibly a confession."

Saint stands ready to go back to his room. "I'm working on one more thing. I have a theory, but I need a little more time to research it before we can use it."

Perfect, everything is finally coming together. Let's see what makes our pet tick.

Mrs. Warren has a reputation for being quite solemn. She reminds me of the social worker that was on me and Bennett's case after our mom died. No room for nonsense, a very straightforward woman. Told us we were more than likely to be separated, giving us no time to grieve our mother while losing each other.

Mrs. Warren's crow's feet tell a story of a life filled with smiles, though their presence has diminished over time. Cox Academy has drained her spirit, like it does to everyone. Elijah had different intentions when he saved this place from ruin. He was determined to offer teenagers a fresh start and a chance to make positive changes in their lives. A means to break free from home and the burdens that are tied to money, allowing us to simply enjoy our youth.

With Elijah grieving for his son, he's been MIA from the school. Everyone grieves differently, and for him, his way of coping is to avoid places that remind him of Tyson. No one can blame him. The happiness that Ty brought with him is irreplaceable.

This woman is the only one who is not desperately trying to suck Bennett's dick. The reason for that is her joyful marriage to her wife, Lauren, of nine years. She is the most competent out of all the teachers' here.

The sound of her heels clicking on the other side of the door pulls me out of my musing. Abruptly ceasing when she unlocks the classroom. One of her brows raise, the only sign that she's surprised to see me. Her outfit exudes sophistication, a charcoal grey pencil skirt, and a blouse crafted with the finest silk. Her wardrobe consists mainly of a pencil skirt suit, the classic attire often seen on women in corporate settings. She looks every part of the word "professional".

The empty room amplifies the sound of her heels as she sets her glossy black briefcase on her desk in front of me. The classroom arrangement mimics a college like setting, featuring a series of desks that gradually rise, resembling steps. However, the only exit is the entrance. Relaxing back in her chair like we're old friends and this isn't our first interaction.

"Mr. Demonio, to what do I owe this pleasure of yourself in my seat? Have I warranted your wrath?" The air is thick with her mocking tone, fueling the anger within me that strains to break free. She is not to blame for this. Keeping the same indifference I always wear.

"I think we may be able to help each other, Mrs. Warren." She doesn't look at me, instead reading today's lesson. When she leans over to arrange her computer, the scent of maple drifting in the air. She's pretending that my appearance hasn't unsettled her, but I can see through her act.

"And what could possibly give you that idea?"

"I need you to fail Priya Carter. Mark this upcoming assignment as a zero." It sounds like I'm casually inquiring about her career in the field, rather than unjustly failing a student. She stands there for a few seconds staring at her computer screen, unblinking, trying to process my request.

"Why would I fail Miss Carter? She's an excellent student. Her work is almost always one hundred percent in my class. It's common for her to complete her assignments early, sometimes by several days. She participates and is more knowledgeable than half of my students."

What I am hearing is "no". That answer doesn't have a place in this conversation, nor in my vocabulary. Fortunately, I hold a high regard for her as a teacher. It took Saint longer than usual to find something I could use to get her to consider my offer. There are some minor things from her teenage years, but as a woman of 40, she's clean. At the end of the day, everyone has a price.

"How's Lauren?" Her hands freeze on the keyboard.

Composing herself, she clears her throat and shifts her weight from side to side. "Are you threatening me?"

"Absolutely not."

"Then what are you implying, Mr. Demonio?"

"I know about her diagnosis. Cancer, stage 3?" It's rhetorical. She purses her lips and nods, subtly avoiding eye contact.

"What if I told you I could get her into one of the best treatments? A trial treatment that's been promising. Dr. Kahn's."

"I would know you're lying. I've pulled every string and called in every favor I have to get my wife into that treatment." The tension in her body reveals her anger.

"Dr. Kahn owes me a favor." Leaving it vague, it doesn't matter to her or her wife the schematics, only that she's accepted with a chance of surviving a silent killer.

"I can't live without my wife," she whispers guiltily, peeking at the picture of the two of them on her desk with their Golden Retriever. I agree with her putting on a sympathetic face. I don't know, not truly. I know what I would do to protect my brothers. She takes a step back, searching for the truth in my face. I'm not sure what she sees, but she agrees reluctantly.

"If I do this, she'll have a place in the trial?"

My eyes lock on hers as I utter, "You have my word." A deal with the devil is a dangerous game to play. It's not like she has much of a choice. I don't want Mrs. Warren to be a casualty in this war, so I gave her the illusion of a choice. Something that would benefit her, the one thing she holds dear in her life.

She sniffs and her deep brown eyes gloss over. She's seemed to age at least 6 years since we've started talking. Her wrinkles are more prominent than they were before, even through the Botox. Her bun isn't as meticulous as usual. The lines of worry etched on her face and her cautious movements betray her frazzled and wary state.

Personally, I've never witnessed someone battling through

cancer. Most people glimpse its impact on someone's appearance or even in a brief encounter. Still, few people have the chance to see firsthand the day-to-day effects on their loved ones and themselves. I'm not sure what's worse, watching a loved one wither away and die or a sudden passing with no goodbye.

Getting up from the comfortable chair, it groans in protest. I take a moment to straighten my freshly dry-cleaned school uniform. "I'd like results today, if possible."

She's quiet until I reach the door. "What is your issue with Miss Carter?"

She wants to justify her choice in picking her wife over a student. Not bothering to turn around to show the resentment I drag around with the mere mention of her name.

"Worry about Lauren, Mrs. Warren. Priya is not a concern of yours." She's mine. In every sense of the word and meaning.

PRIYA

There's nothing worse than waking up and immediately feeling like the world is going to end. There's a sense of urgency coursing through my veins, leaving me restless. I tried to tame my hair, but it seemed to have a mind of its own. It's a wild, frizzy mess. My heart was racing as soon as I woke up in a place I was unfamiliar with. I convinced myself that I'd overslept and dashed around like a chicken with its head cut off. Unable to finish one task before starting a new one.

Then River makes her morning appearance, popping her half done face of makeup from the bathroom, questioning why I'm up so early. Apparently, waking up more than an hour earlier than usual. Our routine is a comfort that's become more important to me than I initially expected. A sharp pain interrupts my thoughts.

The Demons' are putting the 'fast' in breakfast. Since the incident of my public humiliation, they have yet to let up on my eating restrictions. The hunger pains that usually bring me comfort are growling at the aroma of food in the morning and at dinner.

Normally, I manage to steer clear of food during the times my mother puts me on a fasting regimen. It seems damn near impossible here. How long can I survive off of fruit and a piece of lettuce? I've stooped so low that I devour the meager piece of iceberg lettuce I'm given each morning. Disturbing.

River and I go our separate ways after she walks me to my psychology class. The flustered feeling I had this morning is still hovering over me. The door snicks shut behind me, along with the faint whispers of a couple of students who have arrived early for class.

I reach the seat that was assigned to me on my first day here. The moment I sit, the desk objects with a loud creak, making me wince. Since I've left home, I have no way of knowing whether I've gained or lost weight without a scale. The compulsion of wanting to check is worse than wanting to eat.

Today, Mrs. Warren wears a beige skirt suit. When she clears her throat, the rustling of notebooks and shuffling of chairs subsides, signaling the beginning of class. On time, the *dong* of the bell on the highest tower drones out my wandering thoughts. Right before the door shuts on the last student walking in, Crew Demonio dramatically enters the room, commanding everyones attention. The idle chat of students decreases and eventually ceases as Mrs. Warren begins today's lesson.

"As you all are aware, the class was assigned group projects for the end of the semester. Some of you turned it in early and others will wait until the last possible second. I've been grading those who have turned it in. The grade you receive will be the grade you get. No 'do-overs' or extra chances. Everyone has had ample time to prepare."

Good, one thing to check off my list. I've dedicated countless hours working on my paper about Dissociative Identity Disorder. A rare disorder that affects less than 2% of the population. I find it unhealthily fascinating how a human mind can split. It's not easy finding information on it. And no thanks to my lazy partner who refuses to do any of the work.

Unable to control my emotions, an overwhelming sense of loathing settles over me. I chance stealing a glance at my tormentor. The collar is a tangible symbol of the suffering he's caused me, always present and impossible to ignore. Everyone saw it and no one did anything to help. Me and River had spent our free time trying to get it off. She even watched a video on how to pick a lock, which proved to be unsuccessful.

Crew sits in his desk chair, leaning back with a relaxed posture, completely unfazed. Why should he be? It's not like he was going to help do the project. The blatant ignoring me was a dead give-away. My nose wrinkles. He's giving… entitled brat. It's an ick. All because his daddy owns the school, he and his adopted brothers believe they have the authority to mistreat anyone they please.

My fingers skim along the diamond collar he placed around my neck. Every day, it feels like it gets tighter, until one day it'll constrict around my throat until I suffocate. Whenever I think about the spectacle they created, anger looms threateningly, ready to cloud my vision. It's better to sweep it under the rug. Screw Crew and the other Demons.

Opening the school laptop, I pull up my grades and anxiously scan through the numbers. So far, so good. Scrolling through the first five classes, all scored in the high 90 percent range. The lowest grade is a 95. That is until I get to my psychology grade. In an instant, my heart plummets and the sound of rushing blood fills my ears. I worked my butt off for this project, losing sleep and sanity to make it perfect. Earning the grade I deserve. It's one percent from failing, a 60. I'm so confused. Did I turn in the wrong assignment?

Clicking through each graded paper until I come across my failing assignment. I was so confident in my research paper that I turned it in early. Mrs. Warren's voice drones on in the background, but I'm hyper focused on what the hell is going on with my grade.

I click open the assignment with the rubric pulled up on a separate tab. Checking and rechecking. The paper that is turned in is mine. I matched the grading rubric to a T.

"What's wrong, pet?" Crew's warm breath feathers across my cheek, bringing me back to my senses. Irritation heats my body at his gloating voice. Glaring from under my lashes, choosing to ignore the taunt. Mrs. Warren climbs the stairs with purpose, her footsteps growing louder as she approaches our section of desks.

"Is something the matter, Priya?"

"Yeah, actually, I was wondering about my grade for the term project."

Her eyes quickly flick to Crew, then back to me.

"Yes, I was going to speak to you after class about that." Her voice is more tense than usual.

"What about it?" I question.

"Mr. Demonio reached out to me via email, stating you've been noticeably unfocused lately. He didn't want to throw you under the bus, but you didn't help nearly as much as you should've. I have to say it was disappointing to hear. Not like the student I've come to admire." She shakes her head. "I hope that this experience will demonstrate the importance of contributing equally when working as a team. Do not expect others to do it for you." Then she continues up the steps, checking in on other students.

My mouth gapes open, stunned silent. Whipping my head towards Crew, he looks amused. A smirk creeps up on his usual stoic face.

He sucks his teeth. "I guess you should've done your part." His nonchalance to tanking my grade has me fuming. My face and ears burn hot.

"Are you fucking kidding me, Crew?" I snap. He brazenly ignores me while he scrolls through his phone. Looking at him, then back at his phone in his hand, I make a rash decision. Ripping the phone out of his hand, I chuck it toward the front of the classroom. With his gaze fixed on it, he watches as it sails through the air, then it crashes onto the floor with a resounding smack.

There is no doubt in my mind that it's ruined. A large part of me hopes it will be unusable and it'll take a couple of days for a new one to come in. His jaw clenches while his nostrils flare. He has yet to look at me, and I think that frightens me more than whatever will come out of his mouth next.

The room has gone silent. To be fair, it was an impulsive thought.

"Go. Pick. It. Up." He says between heaving breaths. I do the same thing he did to me. Looking towards the front of the class at the board with today's lesson plan, I ignore him. Grabbing my pencil and copying what tonight's homework will be since I didn't pay attention when she was addressing the class.

Crew snatches the pencil from my hand and throws it, just like I did to his phone. So, what do I do? Acting unbothered by his childish antics, I pull a pen from my black bag and resume writing. Once again, he reaches over and rips it from my hand, hurling it across the room.

A laugh escapes my mouth before I can stop it. He's so mad. He thought I would throw a fit over him throwing something I have an endless supply of? Despite fishing for a reaction, I can't help but to smile like this is a game we're playing. All of this is childish, on both of our parts.

"Are you done?" I say, laughing.

A vein throbs in his neck and his eyes are burning with a fury that is only focused on me. He clenches his fists on the desk. Gone is his previously relaxed posture as his body leans towards me, invading my space, trembling with barely contained rage. His body language is showing me something I've only seen thousands of times before. He wouldn't put his hands on me. Or at least not in front of witnesses. I shift from hip to hip in my chair. Would he?

His hand unclenches as he jumps at me, snatching me up by my hair. My eyes water at the sting from the strands being ripped from my scalp. Suppressing a whimper, I gather my courage and lock eyes with him, matching the intensity of hatred. He's the one who started this. In front of everyone, he forced me to crawl and wear a collar, and now he's using his authority to manipulate my grades. He can't even fathom the amount of anger and hate I hide underneath "Robert's perfect daughter" routine. Baring my teeth at him, I give him a peek of the feral girl who hides underneath my skin.

His eyes narrow before he barks out the order, "Now!" Ignoring my silence, he roughly tugs at my hair and brings his lips dangerously close to my ear. "This will get worse for you, Priya. You thought crawling for us like the bitch you are was the end of it?" He chuckles darkly. "That was only the beginning." The threat sinks into my bones, making me heavy with exhaustion.

There will be more. That's his promise. From the corner of my eye, I glance toward the front of the room. Well, as much as I can. He has me by the hair, with my back towards everyone else. It's the same as before. No one moves to help or tries to put a stop to it.

Bennett had it wrong. They're all sheep. Too scared to do anything. If I give in to him now, what will that show everyone else? That aggression makes me compliant? Shaking my head to tell him no, his free hand comes up to my face, gently stroking my cheek, a contrast to the tight grip he has on my hair. The feeling of tenderness has me relaxing into his grip a fraction. Warm fingertips dip to my thudding pulse before dropping to the back of my collar, pulling it backwards, cutting off my air. My hands claw at his wrists to get him off. Too much of this reminds me of my father.

I want his hands off me. My vision blurs at the edges, darkness creeping in from the lack of oxygen. I can't get a deep enough breath and it's getting uncomfortable.

"Are you going to pick it up? And if your answer is anything other than a 'yes, sir', I'll kill you right here in front of everyone. And not one person would tell a soul." Quickly nodding, he loosens the grip on my collar.

"Yes, sir." I sputter out spitefully while rubbing the circulation back into my neck. He lets go, taking a step back from me. I don't turn my back on him until I make it towards the steps with jerky movements that lead down to the teacher's desk where his broken phone lays.

The room swarms with dizziness. I want to scream, releasing all my pent-up frustrations. Punch him in the balls and make him kneel at my feet in pain with tears in his eyes. I have no clue what I did to the Demons to make them hate me so much, but game on.

I pick up his shattered phone. The sharp edges scrape against my fingertips and stomp my way back up the steps to our desks. Not one person is looking at us. They fix their eyes on their computers. Even the teacher has left the room. Some good 'authority figures' we have.

Once I'm face to face with him, I hold out the phone. Just as his fingers are about to touch it, I deliberately release my grip, causing it to plummet to the ground. The sound of the cracked screen breaking further fills the air, missing his outstretched hand by inches.

"Oops," I murmur. To anyone else, it would sound apologetic, but to him, we both know it's a sign of disrespect. His honey-colored eyes darken at the open mockery. Words have never scared me more than the silence. Like a mouse trapped in the sights of a cat, my heart pounds and I hold my breath as I cautiously try to escape his overwhelming anger.

His hand encloses around my wrist, twisting it behind my back and the other returns to the roots of my hair, shoving my face into the desk. The force of my stomach hitting the wood top knocks the wind out of me. The heat of his body presses in behind me. With our bodies intertwined, I can't help but to notice the sensation of his slacks grazing the back of my exposed thighs. His weight presses in, flattening me against the surface of the wood.

Sometimes, I just don't know when to admit defeat. Maybe it's the years of being my father's punching bag and being forced to stay silent. Maybe it's never being allowed to voice my feelings, thoughts, or opinions. It could be many things that make me proceed to push his buttons.

"Fuck, you're heavy." I wheeze, suffocating under his weight. Who would have thought someone who looks slim is not as light as a feather. His dick presses into me. Not very hard. If you ask me.

"I'll fuck you in front of this entire room. Keep pushing me, Priya."

Priya. Not pet or bitch. I think that's the first time he's used my real name. He must mean business. Second, what is he going to fuck me with? He's either soft or the size of a pill, the ones you don't need water to swallow with.

"No, you wouldn't want anyone to see the size of your mircodick. It would hurt your fragile male masculinity." With each passing moment, he pushes harder against me, the grip on my wrist becoming more aggressive, until a sudden coughing fit comes over me. The choice comes down to breathing or acknowledging the pain radiating from my wrist. If he kills me, I won't have to worry about either.

The door to the classroom opens and shuts. Mrs. Warren's brittle, steady voice breaks the silence of the classroom.

"That's enough, Mr. Demonio." Her stern voice cuts through the tension in the room. He lets go of me, chuckling darkly, and I slump over on the desk.

"Just wait, pet. There won't always be someone to interfere. You've just made it worse than it had to be," he whispers, patting my head condescendingly before walking away.

My legs won't hold me up. It could be from the lack of food I'm getting every day. Or the fact Crew wants to kill me. The bell dings and I gather myself. Tears sting the corners of my eyes as I stumble down the stairs and out the door. Karma is a bitch, Demonio, and her name is Priya.

BENNETT

S kipping class is an art. Unlike most people, I have the finesse for it. Or I'm just willing to take one for the team and sleep with the teacher. Either way, it requires skill. No one wants a lousy lay. With a quick swipe of my hands on the filthy rag, I slide it into the back pocket of my jeans. There's a certain satisfaction that comes from the scent of motor oil and fresh car parts.

Giving the old girl, Mindy, a loving pat, I shut the hood of my Aston Martin DB4GT from the first series. The keys jingle in my hand while I put them into the ignition to carefully maneuver her out of the garage. I sink into her seat. The rich, nostalgic smell of ancient leather and wood wraps around me, like a hug, a feeling of comfort and familiarity.

The gear shift is like an extension of my hand, blending seamlessly with my touch. God, she's the most perfect specimen ever to walk this earth. She never talks back, always tells me when something is wrong and how to fix it. Well, she never has to let me know. Her upkeep is my top priority. Never picky on food and doesn't yell at me. The smooth vibrations of the engine purrs beneath me, creating a sense of harmony between man and his machine. That's poetic.

This was the first project Elijah and Ty worked on with me. The bonding for us turned into a hobby for me. Fixing up cars is my emotion dumpster. Pissed off, sad, even happy.

It makes me wonder where I would be if we had never met Tyson and his dad. I'd like to think that I would run my own personal chop shop, but I wouldn't be able to bring myself to destroy some of the beautiful one-of-a-kind cars that I've come to know personally. That would break my heart, for sure. Ben & Bros Auto. Ben & Co. Auto…Yeah, that sounds nice.

The music in my car startles me as it blares in my ears. Before reversing out of the garage Elijah built for me, I can't help but to laugh at myself. Technically, there's not supposed to be cars here, too many issues with kids sneaking out. That's why even at 18, most teenagers have to rely on someone to pick them up or plan with the admin building to go into town. Being Elijah's son has its perks.

Parking Mindy in her designated spot. The satisfying click of the locks as I bid her farewell make me wish I was on the road. I'm dying to go out for a drive soon. The sensation of the wind against my face, combined with the soothing hum of the motor beneath my hands, gives me the thrill I crave.

"Goodbye, my baby. I'll see you soon." Blowing Mindy a kiss while I walk back towards the school. Just as I tear my eyes away from her polished headlights, a shrill screech echoes through the air.

"Bennett!"

An embarrassing shriek escapes my lips. Until I see Amber's face screwed up into an ugly glare, aimed at me.

"Ahh, Amber. What's up?" I keep my eyes on the castle as I walk towards our place.

"Are you avoiding me?" She flips her short hair over, her eyes narrow to slits. That will obviously get me to spill all my secrets. I hope the grimace I'm hiding stays that way.

"Uh, no?" Yes. She's like a vampire, sucking the life out of me. The ruby red lipstick she wears is actually the blood from her victims.

"My parents are coming to this years 'Parent Day'. They want to meet you." She skips happily next to me, her hand stroking my bicep. Shit, I've been avoiding her dad for the past three years, wanting to never meet him. Every year we go home to dad for a weekend to catch up, visiting Ty or take on another job. My stomach rolls at the thought of her involvement with the Priya and Oscar situation.

As I scratch the back of my head, I rack my brain for a solution, fully aware that my brothers and I decided to stay this year, hoping Priya's family comes.

"Um…" I let the 'm' drag on for as long as possible, to buy myself time to avoid answering. Has she always been this way? Cunning and vindictive? I looked the other way because it didn't interfere with my life or getting pussy. It makes me second guess her as a person. She knew we were only a fling. I never gave her the impression I wanted to be more.

My saving grace is my brother stomping into the house, slamming the side door behind him. Perfect.

"I'll catch you later. Something is going on with Crew."

"Oh," she looks around before lowering her voice conspiratorially, "I heard Priya started some drama in psych." Side eying her, I shrug her off of me. What else are brothers for? If not to get me out of situations I don't want to be in.

Trying to escape Amber's bony fingers is overwhelming. With a swift movement, her hand finds its way into the waistband of my boxers, wrapping around my dick, sending a jolt of pleasure through me. Despite the restriction of my jeans, she persistently tries to stroke me. Maybe a quickie? I scan our surroundings for a better place to bend her over. There's no way I'm laying her down here and doing that face-to-face shit.

Her lips kiss up my neck, causing me to harden in her soft hand. Did I say it was bony before? I meant soft, in the way she strokes me from root to tip.

The sound of glass shattering breaks the trance I'm in. Crew. Grabbing her wrist to stop her, she fights me, continuing to rub along the length of me. A jab of fear makes my heart stutter as a cold sweat coats my skin.

"Stop, Amber." She ignores me, fighting against the grip I have on her wrist. My foster parents flash behind my eyes. Feather light fingers brush against my skin. Heavy breathing and the distinct stench of alcohol permeate the room.

"That's enough, Amber!" Blind panic causes me to shove her away roughly, using all my strength. With a lack of grace, she tumbles and lands in an awkward sprawl on the grass. Anger over-whelms my guilt for putting my hands on a woman who may or may not deserve it. Narrowing my eyes at her, my lips pull back into a sneer.

"Do you know what the word 'stop' means, Amber?" My voice comes out low and dangerous. Fists balled at my sides to hide the trembling. Her bottom lip quivers as she nods.

"But Bennett, you always like it when I touch you."

"I like to fuck people, Amber. Don't get it twisted thinking I'm only interested in you. You knew what this was the first time you spread your legs for me. Playing dumb will only get you so far." I scoff and shake my head, looking away from her, afraid I might do something I'd regret. She isn't as coy as she pretends to be.

Her usual flawless face transforms into what she really is. The hatred in her eyes tries to burn me to ashes where I stand. Brushing off her skirt, she gets up without saying a word and stomps away.

Finally, once I'm in the house, I want a shower to clean off the memories that are ghosting my skin. No one tells you that trauma will always find a way to haunt you. It's one of those things that goes unsaid and can only be understood once it's happening. At least I'm not like Malice. That guy destroys everything he touches. On another note, I think Saint is still a virgin. Anytime the topic comes up, he changes the subject. When I get bored enough, I'll look into it. Deflect.

Heading up the stairs to the bedrooms, I follow the smell of fresh laundry and asshole, straight to Crew's bedroom. The room looks like a guest bedroom, with only a bed, nightstands, and our four chairs. Oh, and that little area where he keeps his alcohol. Other than that, I wouldn't assume someone lived in here. It's lonely.

Sadness weighs me down as my steps become slower into my brother's room. A thick syrup runs in my veins instead of blood. Does he really have nothing sentimental enough to have in here? There are no pictures of our family, even Ty. None of his accomplishments in his life. There is nothing. Not even dirty clothes are on the floor. An idea chases away the sadness. I'll get him a custom shirt or blanket with my face on it. That way, he's never alone and when he misses me, because everyone does, he'll still have me.

With that in mind, I bust open the bathroom door. Thick clouds from the shower pour out of the doorway, filling his room in a misty atmosphere. I leave the door open so I can breathe properly. I tiptoe over to the foggy shower glass, to not disturb the silence. The shower hides his features, leaving only an outline, which means he might see mine if he pays attention. I'd like to think of myself as a ghost, invisible and barely making noise.

I bring my finger up to the glass and draw a big heart before using my entire hand to wipe away the center and place my face there for Crew to see.

Putting on my cheesiest smile and batting my eyelashes, I ask, "Can I join you?"

Instead of scaring him and making him jump, he freezes, still as a statue. He's almost a replica of myself. Sudsy bubbles cling to his mocha- colored skin from his soap. Except scars line his body from his time with Steve. His back is the worst of it, though. It looks like he was whipped. Raised scars crisscross on his back, a constant reminder of the trauma he endured. Crew always talked about getting it covered with tattoos like Malice did for Saint, but I think a part of him is afraid.

It's better to ignore it, then to bring it up. The other night was a once in a lifetime opportunity to hear about it. I wasn't going to miss that.

I wonder if he washes his hair with laundry detergent since he always smells like clean linen. So, I ask him, just making naked conversation on the other side of the glass with my 'big' brother.

"Or here's a thought. I wash my fucking clothes, dirtball. Get the fuck out of here." He resumes washing himself, rinsing the bubbles away before starting on his hair. My lips purse, giving him a look that says "Really?".

"Dude, we have the same equipment. Don't get all shy on me now. Your body is a temple or what?"

His body heaves as he lets out a long sigh. "I'm not in the mood to put up with your shit today, Ben."

It's possible Amber was right about what she heard. Before I can ask, my phone dings in my pocket, a text from Saint.

"Dear brother, we are being summoned." I say in a posh British voice, mocking Malice. He grunts a response.

"Is that a 'yes', 'no', or an 'okay'?" If I can press his buttons, I will. Bad day or not, who else will give these guys a laugh? They're not funny. I'm the life of the party.

"I need a new phone." He mumbles, shutting the shower off by pressing a button on the wall. The steam has mostly cleared out, so I can see my hand in front of my face. The only thing that's changed about him is the vein in his throat throbbing, and that only happens when he's livid. He's still the same old grumpy guy we know and love.

I wait for him to elaborate on the phone situation.

"She threw it."

Unable to hold back my laughter, I die. Tears are coming out of my eyes, and I struggle to breathe as my chest tightens. Why the hell would she do that? Does she have a death wish? Oh my

God but imagine his face when she took it from his hands and threw it. I bet it was good.

My eyes connect with his dark honey-colored ones, and I laugh harder. His scowling expression is so intense that it looks like he has a unibrow, while his arms remain tightly crossed against his chest, clearly not finding this situation as hilarious as I do. Wiping the tears from my face and take a much-needed breath. "Oh, fuck." I say, while sighing. "I needed that, thank you."

"Are you done?" He replies, short and snippy.

"Huh? Yeah." This time I'm able to swallow the laughter that threatens to come up. Clapping him on his wet shoulder, I make sure it hurts a little.

"Let's go see what Saint is up to."

He follows me out of the room, towel and all. We can hear Saint talking to Malice before we reach the door. The harsh hushed whispers seem like they're in a disagreement about something, which is extremely unusual. I gauge Crew's reaction to see he's slightly alarmed at this development. Stepping on a creaky floorboard outside his door, the talking stops. Crew opens the door and walks in like he owns the place. Drama queen, I swear. Everyone thinks it's me but get a load of this guy.

Saint is laying on his messy bed, head hanging off the end with his squishy blue stress ball in hand. Pillows are strewn around on the floor, giving the room a messy appearance. The other half of the room looks like Crew came in here and tidied up. How long has it been since he's left the room? It smells a little stale in here, like sweaty balls. At least he has actual clothes on, jeans and a white T-shirt. The bags that were under his eyes a couple of days ago are long gone. He looks much better, refreshed even. Since my brother always takes the chair closest to the door, I have no choice but to sit in the computer chair.

Saint jumps to stand on the bed, "I found something!" His excitement reminds me of a puppy excited to see its owner. Crew's eyebrows raise at Saint's eagerness. Me? I'm foaming at the mouth to see what our little techie found.

"Okay, remember when I said I had a theory I was working on?" We both nod.

"Okay, okay, well. If you look up the articles for the fire that was set in the school library, you'll find hardly anything on it. Remember how dad didn't want Ty's death in the paper? What if the Carter's didn't want theirs in the paper either? The messages stopped coming on the same day of the fire. There was no public funeral."

I'm unable to keep up with Saint. He's talking a million miles a minute. He lost me after the first sentence. Casually, I glance at Crew from the side of my eye. He appears as confused as I do. I don't want to bring Saint down from whatever high he's on, so I leave it to the party pooper.

Crew holds his hand up, effectively stopping Saint. "Now let's try again, in English this time. Take a deep breath."

Saint's shoulder slump as he recovers from whatever the fuck that was.

"All right, you know how dad made sure there was barely any coverage on Ty's death? What if he wasn't the only one pulling strings? What if there was another death that the Carter's wanted to cover up? We thought it was just to keep Priya out of the papers for burning down the building. It wasn't making sense to me. Why did the texts and calls to her sister go unanswered?"

He looks at us for an answer. I'm caught off guard because I thought it was rhetorical and he was going to answer it.

"Her sister hates her and the fact she killed someone is unforgivable?" I question.

Saint's finger goes up in an "A-ha" gesture. "That is what we thought. But we were wrong. Her sister is dead. She killed her sister *and* Tyson in that fire."

A gasp leaves my mouth and my eyes stare at him in horror. She killed her sister? Oh, that's fucked up. Why? This brings me more questions than answers. Who would kill their sister and why was Ty collateral damage?

"How are you sure?"

A smug smirk that's more like me than him sits on his face. "I thought you guys would say that. So, I made sure to fact check everything. At first, I was confused. No mention of it in the media. No funeral. It's the type of messages she would send her sister that got me thinking. I used the cloned phone to place a call to the cemeteries in Los Angeles. Eventually, after many phone calls, I got the right one. They immediately recognized the number and who it was. I played the part of a surprising boyfriend and got her plot number and confirmation of Addison Carter's gravestone."

"You're sure?" Crew asks, coming out of his shocked stupor.

"Absolutely, Exhibit A." He does a grand gesture towards his computer. Addison Carter's grave sits there on the screen. Some generic shit on the headstone. My body faces the computer screen entirely, with my back to my brothers. I look up at the ceiling when my sinuses sting and attempt to sniff it away before someone calls me out.

I don't know what kind of fucked up person could kill their sister. Thinking of Crew or even Saint being killed makes me queasy. Maybe it's the times we have almost died or the tight bond we have. My brothers would never die by my hand. The guilt would eat at me for the rest of my life. I hope it does to her.

A plan forms in my mind.

"I know what we should do next."

PRIYA

The morning mist hangs heavy in the air, lending an extra dose of eeriness that adds a deep chill in my bones. The forest surrounding the dorms and school seems like something out of a horror movie. Dense, tangled trees and ominous silence. Something is lurking, ready to snatch us from this life. Obviously, I mean me personally, because no one else seems to feel that way. Students chatter happily on the way to Theodore Hall for breakfast, as if the world was completely at peace.

There are people struggling to make ends meet? Not a problem here. We use money to wipe our asses.

World hunger? Not us, we never go hungry.

The thought of food instantly triggers my stomach to growl. I raise my water bottle to my parched lips, drinking greedily to soothe the relentless ache of hunger.

The effects of not eating are taking a toll on me. I'm always tired, but now I'm waking up tired. The cold I usually feel might be because of the change in weather from California, but it's like an ongoing desire for warmth. I don't want to inconvenience River by constantly adjusting the heat in her room. I'm already always there.

She is without a doubt the ideal roommate someone could hope for. We have established a schedule over the last three days. She still doesn't understand boundaries because whether I'm peeing or showering, she's telling me a story or rambling about her day. It distracts me from my emptiness, mostly.

My room is supposed to be complete today, so I can reclaim a little privacy. There is no mention of any improvements to the locks or security measures. Amber and Oscar are still walking around with a sense of superiority, noses stuck in the air. Either way, the space and isolation will be a welcome reprieve, a cool-down period. It's been a whirlwind of events since I set foot in this place.

River pulls out my chair for me at our table.

"Thank you, kind sir." I say in jest.

Her smile stretches from one cheek to the other, lighting up her entire face. "Someone has to do it. None of these assholes would be caught breaking a nail."

River's voice trails off as her eyes wander over to the breakfast buffet. The one I've stopped going to because the chefs interfere and give me a piece of fruit instead of eggs Benedict, Belgian waffles, or French toast. Another swig of water for the hunger.

"What?" I ask River, who is uncharacteristically quiet.

"I don't know… Something seems off."

I stiffen. Off like Amber and Oscar? Off like the Demons? There are a lot of things that can be "off".

"Behind the buffet, there's a projector. That's never been there before." The need to run away overwhelms me. I'm ready to bolt. I cast a worried glance over my shoulder, noticing the Demons. My stomach clenches tight at the meaning of their sudden interest in breakfast.

Could it be from breaking Crew's phone? I retaliate one time and they've rained hell down on me.

"River, I want —". Before I'm able to tell River I want to leave, Bennett heads up to the projector that's lit up a neon blue on the wall. His walk is calm and confident, his hair a tousled dark mess. The front buttons of his school uniform unbuttoned and his tie nowhere in sight. Not surprising considering the Demons' law is the only law.

River sits in a stupor, pulling me closer to her. She gently pries my clenched hand open, intertwining her fingers with my sweaty one.

"Good morning, Cox Academy!" His charismatic voice booms throughout the room, bringing every conversation to a stop. He playfully winks at the group of girls closest to him, sending them into a fit of giggles, like the schoolgirls they are. I'd roll my eyes, but they're glued to Bennett Demonio's face.

"Sorry to interrupt everyone's lovely morning. We thought a brief presentation would wake everyone up." He looks at Saint, who clicks something on his phone and the screen changes. My breath hitches, getting stuck in my throat. My heart stutters, the color drains from my face when I see the tamed curls of honey colored hair and the same baby blue eyes that our father has. I avert my gaze from the person I've spent over half of a year avoiding staring at.

"A show of hands. How many people in here know who this well-known daughter is?" Mostly everybody's hands shoot up in the air. He points at Amber Astor to answer.

"Addison Carter."

Bennett snaps his fingers and points at her.

"Right you are! Addison Carter died in December. Does anyone know how?"

Everyone murmurs at the latest news. No hands go up. No one knows my sister is gone. The sound of her name spoken aloud sends waves of spears shooting through my chest. A punch in the chest, worse than when my father would hit me. The thought of hearing these despicable people mention my flawless sister's name is so unbearable that I would rather crawl on my knees and endure the humiliation of my collar any day.

"No? Not surprising." His face is the perfect picture of sorrow, but I don't for a second believe he cares about her or her death.

"In December, before winter break last year, there was a fire at her school. It was said to be so out of control that even the firefighters couldn't control it." My vision blurs with tears that threatened to spill over. The rigidity of my spine softens as my shoulders curl in on themselves, knowing the vise that gives me a sense of relief has taken the one person I value most in the world, my sister. "They had to let it die down before seeing if there was anything left of the people inside. Two people died that day." River's hand squeezes mine in comfort but fails. "Another student and Miss Carter. Now, people, if we put two and two together, we can surmise that none other than Addison Carter's sister, Priya Carter," He points at me, his dark eyes shining with hatred so palpable I can taste the bitterness on my tongue, "is here. Our little Pyro Carter, if the psychologist was right."

"Murderer!" someone yells.

"She killed her own sister!"

"Pyro Carter!"

"Couldn't take the heat of being second best, I bet."

The thundering rhythm of my heartbeat overshadows the relentless barrage of taunts and insults. Dizziness overtakes me, the world blurs and fades from my view. Pressure closes in around me, a tingling sensation on my face. While the rest of my body stays numb. A hand rubs up and down my back while whispering.

"Breathe, Priya." I want to scream that, "I'm trying!" but nothing comes out. I need to get out of here.

Nothing these people are shouting at me isn't things I haven't told myself daily. This all-consuming guilt I live with. I hate myself more than they ever could. They think I don't wake up every morning wishing I was dead? The only reason I haven't done the job myself is *for* my sister. All of this is for her.

Old wounds are reopening, the gashes pouring into my misdeeds and wrongdoings that swirl around in my head.

It should've been me.

My legs buckle as I stand to run out of the Hall. The edges of my vision darken before completely taking over.

PRIYA

My mind is active before my body stirs. The firm mattress is oddly unfamiliar, a stark contrast to the soft, plush ones I've grown used to during my time at Cox Academy. Lying on clouds has become a part of my routine, their softness sucking me into drowsiness. The air has that new store smell, unused, but there is a musky scent on the pillow I'm using. Every swallow is like sandpaper, and to top it off, my tongue is dry as fuck. Did I fall asleep with my mouth open? I groggily contemplate opening my eyes, but the lingering sensation of grittiness deters me.

I need to face whatever is going on, but procrastinating doesn't seem like a bad idea. What the hell happened?

My mind tries to sort through the last thing that I remember.

The woods outside of the school were like an omen of my bad day to come.

Addi. Knots twist in my stomach as my heart settles in the pit. Despite my eyes being shut, the sharp stinging in my nose as tears well up in my lashes, threatening to push their way to the surface.

Murderer.

The Pyro killed her sister.

Jealousy.

Lies float around me, battering my mind. I loved my sister. I would trade places with her in a heartbeat. A part of what they're saying isn't wrong. I shouldn't have let her tutor that boy that day. I should've sucked it up and went. Maybe things would have been different. Maybe she'd still be alive.

My sniffles are loud in the room's silence. Suddenly, a floor-board creaks beside the bed. Mid-sniffle, the sudden sound of someone's presence shatters my illusion of solitude.

A voice breaks the stillness, attempting to sound gentle. "I know you're awake, Priya."

The effort feels forced. I might as well face whatever comes next. There's no use in hiding. No matter if I thought keeping my eyes shut would take away the reality.

Peeling my eyes open, Coach Mason Riley sits at the foot of the bed. Without thinking, my eyes sweep the area, seeking possible ways to escape. The door between him is definitely not an option. There's no way I would make it there before he grabs me. He's the gym teacher, a fit one, not the ones that get the job because they're the coach of the school's unsuccessful team.

Propping himself up on the bed, he leans back, his muscles bulging with rigidity. My eyes dart towards him momentarily before darting to return to the nearest window. It's stands out from the majority of the windows at this school, which are expansive and reach from floor to ceiling. It's what I would consider a normal size window. Small enough that I can push each window panel to the center to open each side. What are the odds they open?

I refocus my gaze on his face, desperately seeking any indication that he hasn't trapped an innocent 18-year-old girl in a room with ill intentions. A faint smile appears on Mason's lips, but his eyes betray a hint of sadness. Forced, like his voice was.

"Where am I?" I start with the simple questions, hoping to hide the nervousness that's tightening its grip on me. It'll buy me time if he thinks I'm compliant. If I start off aggressive, he might get defensive and do something rash. At least with Baldwin, I thought I could take him. Mason is much smaller than he is. Quicker. The situation makes me less confident, not knowing why the hell I'm here in the first place.

"In the teacher's dormitory, I figured a safe place to gather yourself would be better." He looks at the ceiling, avoiding my gaze, but that doesn't seem to stop his cheeks from getting red. Is he blushing?

"Why?"

He angles his body towards me, giving me a better look at his face. His cheeks have a noticeable pink hue. Filled with curiosity and anticipation, his dark eyes bore into mine. His face is smooth and clean shaven, his jawline free of any stubble. He wears sweats and a fitted T-shirt that stresses his muscular physique. His Adam's apple bobs a few times before responding.

"I was worried about you." He averts his gaze as he says 'you'. Am I in the Twilight Zone? What the hell is happening right now? The way he's behaving is making me on edge and uncomfortable. Coach Mason's body constantly shifts and unable to remain still. I draw my knees up close to my chest, bringing the white blanket with. I scoot higher to the wall to put some distance between us. This room is smaller than mine, and I can feel it as the walls close in from all four sides, making him too close for comfort.

A weapon. I need a weapon. The way he's acting and sitting has me backed into a corner with no escape. Scanning the room, I notice the worn-out furniture and scattered belongings, confirming that it's definitely lived in. Books lay on every surface available, even the floor. Haphazardly strewn in corners, the clothes create a cluttered and untidy appearance. The closet door is wide open, revealing the dark recesses of its interior. The back of it reveals it's noticeably smaller than mine. I'd think the teachers would have nicer, if not the same luxuries we have. Life isn't fair, though.

I could always bash his head in with a book …If they weren't all paperbacks. Multiple books, maybe?

"How are you feeling?" he asks, inching closer.

Amazing, I loved everyone discovering my sister's death via presentation from Bennett.

Bennett.

I scowl as boiling anger shoots through me. I thought my revenge would be on his twin, but he will be my sole focus. Right after I get out of this room.

"Sorry, it's a little messy. I figured you'd need some space to hide out after that fiasco." He grimaces, looking around the room. Fuck the room. I got a dose of revenge to administer to the Demons'. I shrug, because I don't mind. It's not my living space, it's his.

"Where's River?" I clear my throat, past the uncomfortable knot forming.

"Your little gothic warrior princess?" He chuckles at his joke. "She's sitting outside the door at her 'post'. Refuses to move until she can see you." Relief washes over me, loosening some of the tension I was holding. I'm not alone with Coach Riley, technically.

"Could you let her in? Please." I tack on please, to make it seem like I'm asking permission. He purses his lips with a disappointed look but moves toward the door, stepping out and shutting it behind him.

The sound of hushed, raised voices reaches my ears. Each sentence causing one of them to get louder.

"She's not yours! If I find out you touched her, I'll kill you myself. You won't have to worry about my brothers." River's voice hisses.

Brothers? I thought she had one younger sibling. Mason murmurs something too quietly for me to hear before River is bursting through the room, like a Bat Out of Hell, causing me to jump at her obnoxious entry.

"Thank God!" She jumps on the bed, landing next to me and pulling me into a hug, her comforting lavender scent soothing in this unfamiliar space.

"Are you okay? No, don't answer that. I know you're not. Did he touch you? At all? Anywhere?" The bombarding of questions has me quiet. I don't know what she wants me to answer first. No, I'm not okay. But I won't admit it out loud. If he touched me. Someone carried me here. It's safe to assume it was him.

"What happened?" I ask.

She breaks eye contact with me, avoiding the question. Her jaw locks shut as she picks at her chipped nail polish. Suddenly, the chatterbox wants to remain quiet. I pull out of her embrace to look away from her. She doesn't get to come in here asking questions and not want to answer any in return. I can feel her react to my shifting demeanor as she presses closer to me.

"Honestly?" I throw a glare her way and press my lips together. I've never asked her to sugar coat shit before. She sighs, "You were crying, then it turned to screaming and next thing you know, you fainted. Shortly after that, Coach Riley came in like Captain Save-a-Hoe and picked you up off the floor, whisking you away. I insisted he take you to my room, or even yours. He was set on taking you here." She looks around just as I did. Her nose wrinkles at the mess. "Not sure why."

Her eyes soften when they look back at me. "I'm sorry."

"Why are you sorry? You didn't do it."

"No, but still. Even if they knew the truth, I don't think they'd believe it. They seem to have some narrative about who you are and what you've done. The truth wouldn't matter." Her soft hands run through the strands of my hair, untangling knots on the way down.

My throat clogs with emotion. "I want to do something. I want them to hurt as much as I do." The admission is freeing. It is what I want. Even if it makes me as evil as they are. It is a longing so powerful that it trumps my need for oxygen. It's bad enough to hurt me, but it's even worse to bring my dead sister into it. Anything but her.

A Cheshire Cat smile slowly creeps across her face, mischief glinting in her coca-colored eyes, making her look a tad bit impish. I'm still getting used to this devious side of River.

"I think I have the perfect plan for Bennett."

"I'm listening."

"One thing he always talks about is the 'love of his life'." She rolls her eyes. My first thought is Amber. "He is one of the very few students who are allowed a car here. He parks it in the teachers' parking lot. Talks about it all the time. His classic Aston Martin he built from the ground up. Maybe…" Her melodic voice trails off, but her smile lingers, accompanied by a knowing look.

I know what she's insinuating without her having to finish. I'm burning it. This will be the last time they fuck with me. Energy renewed, I jump from the bed, the blanket revealing my disheveled clothing. It's going to be my best fire yet. My flames have a nice date with his car tonight. The sooner the better.

"I'll take care of the parking lot cameras. He's going to kill you." She snickers behind her hand.

"I'm already dead." Priya died the day my sister did.

PRIYA

For once, the outside world doesn't bring my close friend, dread, along. Instead, it welcomes me with a sense of tranquility. That could be because River insisted on coming with so I'm not alone. We're both dressed head to toe in black with matching black beanies, she swears we had to wear. Personally, I think our dark hair would have blended in fine with the night if we tucked it into the beanies. But she begged. It's hard to say no to her most days. That's false, I don't think I've ever directly told her the word 'no', now that I think about it.

River leads the way to the teachers' parking lot. Since we've come up with a plan, I've had tunnel vision. Counting down the minutes until I could act on my need for revenge.

There's a keycard to open the gate to get outside the school's premises, like a prison. The light silently blinks green when she holds the key up to the locking mechanism, doing a silent fist bump and a dancing wave with her arms before holding the gate open for me to cross through.

I don't need to be raised like the people here to know nice cars when I see them. Even as 'sheltered' as I was, I still had access to the internet and movies. Still allowed to see the outside world. In my household, at least, it's better to be seen than heard. Scratch that, being invisible and silent has always been better for me.

There are BMWs, Skylines, Audis, Porsches, even a few Lamborghinis sprinkled in the mix. River said a "few". I'm wondering what that word means to her, considering the lot is the size of a football field. What catches my eye is the black Aston Martin with two car spaces on each side, ensuring it doesn't get scratched. My heart flutters in my chest at the sight. There are only 75 of those made in the world. I'll fact check that later to be sure.

"That's it."

My eyebrows raise with a whistle. Damn, that sucks. For him. As I take my bag off of my back, a wide grin spreads across my face and adrenaline courses through me, making my hands tremble. Marching towards this beauty's funeral is bittersweet. I've never had the chance to see one in person. I'm honored to be the one to destroy it.

Running my fingers along the glossy black paint, I can't help but admire the polished, mirror like finish. It could be a dark blue. The color won't matter after I'm through with it. Maybe I could steal it. Where would I keep a whole ass car when I have no cash to my name? Cards are traceable.

No. He deserves to have this taken from him and sullied like he did to my sister's name. Now we can both lose something we worship and love.

Where to start? With cautious precision, I navigate around the car, my steps gentle and almost noiseless, from the back to the front. The only noise that accompanies my footsteps is the gentle shifting of rocks beneath my boots. River props her hip on the hood, letting me take my time. Automatically, my fingers find the comfort of my match book, rubbing the edges.

A loud crack shatters the peacefulness of the night, causing the windshield to shatter into web like cracks and the crickets to fall silent. The car rocks from the impact. I stand, stunned, my mouth forming a perfect 'O'. I stare at River with wide eyes.

Rapidly blinking, I pinch myself to make sure I'm not dreaming.

"Where the hell did you get a baseball bat from?" I whisper-yell.

"I found it. Handy, huh? You were taking too long." I stare at her, and she stares right back. A lightness in her eyes I haven't seen before. My lips clamp together, and I put my hand over my mouth to stifle in the manic laughter that threatens to spill out. Her eyes widen before she looks at the bat in her hand and bursts out laughing. It doesn't take long before our cackles become the dominant sound in the air. My hand grips the car in order to keep my legs from falling out from underneath me. Who the hell finds a bat and brings it with them? She is crazier than I am. She must've pulled it out of her ass. The thought is so amusing I can't help but laugh harder.

Tears are streaming down her face, her hands grabbing her sides that ache from laughter. I know, because I'm doing the same.

"Okay, okay." She sniffles, inhaling some much-needed air. "Back to the task."

I drop the familiar black bag, my constant companion, onto the ground with a satisfying thud. My hand delves into the depths of the contents, desperately searching for what I need, my fingers clumsily fumbling a few times for the lighter fluid.

This beauty deserves a fresh, unopened bottle for her glorious demise. One to ensure it's completely ruined. The car's weight moves a little as I clamber onto the hood. Popping the seal on the red cap, I pour the liquid all over the top of the car, the sound of it splashing against the surface echoing around us. I swiftly jump off and move towards the hood of the car where I was standing, feeling the oiliness of the substance on my skin. Per my MO, I write Addison's name. Remembering who I'm doing it for, gives me a little more strength for the possible fallout. I'll deny that I had anything to do with it.

Stepping back, I take a moment to admire my handiwork. The two-seater car is pretty small. I don't want to risk the flames only damaging the frame. I want it all.

"I need inside." I tell River, my eyes fixated on the interior. River's footfall seems deafening now than it was before. A quick smack to the corner of the window has it shattered entirely. The breeze brings the strong, acrid odor of the liquid to my nostrils as it penetrates the air. I start my process by treating the driver's side, meticulously coating the seat, steering wheel, and then moving on to the dashboard. Then, with the urge to speed up the process, I empty the whole bottle inside before tossing it in the passenger's footwell.

Dusting my hands off and pulling my head out of the broken car window, I look at River.

"Ready?" Giddiness makes my voice rise. A simple nod and a slight retreat is her response. My unsteady fingers struggle for my matches, the thrill of the moment making it difficult to focus. With an unsuccessful first attempt at the match, I throw it inside to get rid of the evidence. It lights on the second try.

The interior quickly ignites, sending plumes of smoke into the air. A shiver runs down my spine as I stand in awe, goose bumps prickling the back of my neck. My body goes slack as soon as the fire spreads, the tightness in my chest gradually eases, while the tension in my shoulders disappears. The weightlessness of every burden I carry vanishes. Bliss, even if only for a fleeting moment. This brings a sense of steadiness to my heart, as if all the chaos of the world has faded away.

Peace, that's what this foreign feeling is. Maybe.

This is what I would expect it to feel like, so that's what I'll call it. I send a silent thanks to Addi for giving me this. If anyone is looking out for me, it's her.

The car's interior is a fiery inferno. The heat radiates and scorches everything in its path. The flickering flames, escaping through the broken window, eagerly lick the exterior of the car. Damn, this is a masterpiece. Baldwin's SUV seats have nothing on the way this makes me feel. My eyes search out River, who is as entranced as I am. She must feel my eyes on her because she looks at me immediately, coming to stand by my side.

"You really did it." Her voice drips with awe. Of course I did. This is a win-win situation for me. Revenge is best served with a blazing hot appetizer. Something like that.

Her hand links in mine. I squeeze hers and in return she squeezes it back. I'd like to think my sister sent someone here to help stave off the loneliness I've felt for so long. That even in death she would take care of me. I would for her. When I go to hell, I'll still find a way to her and make sure she's okay. Tell her I love her one last time. A small smile graces my lips. I'm happy I could know unconditional love, because that's what I was able to give her.

River's grip turns painful, her knuckles going white.

"We've got to go." Urgency laces her voice. My eyes flick to the fire and then back to her. I want to see this through. There's still so much left.

"What? Why?" My brows wrinkle as she looks behind her. I strain my ears, searching for even the faintest sound. A guttural roar comes from the other side of the gate we came through, making me jump.

"Run!" She yells.

My legs are carrying me before I can register what's going on. I gain on River just as she cuts through the dense woods, our footsteps crunching on the fallen leaves. Despite the tree obstructing our path, we maintain our pace without missing a beat. Undeterred by the branches smacking me in the face, I push forward with more determination. My breaths are quick and uneven, a stark contrast to my usual steady rhythm as I struggle to find my pace. Oh fuck, a cramp.

Leaning against a tree, I take a moment to catch my breath and scan my surroundings, my ears tuned in for any faint footsteps. My pounding heart is the only thing I can hear, which doesn't help. The effort I put into running makes my lungs burn, each breath is a stab in my ribs.

The forest is alive with the sound of snapping branches, every footstep leaving a trail of destruction in my aggressor's wake. A squeak escapes me as I bolt like a rabbit from one tree to the next, hoping to lose him. Would I have time to climb it? I've never climbed a tree in my life, but I'd try right now.

The thrill of successfully evading my pursuer dissipates as I unexpectedly trip over a protruding tree root, excruciating pain shoots through my twisted ankle. The pain is fleeting, overridden by the adrenaline. I scramble to my hands and knees. A fierce roar tears through the forest, followed by the jarring impact of a bulldozer slamming into my side, leaving me breathless and dazed. My diaphragm spasms. This is going to be the longest minute of my life.

"Pause." I wheeze, grabbing my stomach.

The pressure of hands wrapped around my throat, their firm grip around the warm metal collar making it increasingly difficult to breathe. Obviously, he doesn't know what the word pause means because he fast forwarded, and I wasn't ready.

"I'll fucking kill you, you stupid bitch!" Spittle hits my cheek while baring his teeth. Oh, it's Bennett. Not really the most ideal for this situation. My eyes focus on what they can, since his hold isn't loosening on my neck. His nostrils are flaring and his chest heaves, his breath hitting me directly in the face. Seems I'm not the only one out of shape. My dad has choked me harder than this. He'll have to try harder to impress me.

In the dark, his eyes appear as deep, black voids, reminiscent of the Demon he's rumored to embody.

My voice comes out as a squeak. His grasp loosens and I cough, drawing in a much-desired breath of air. With his hatred solely focused on me, I reach out my hand for something I can weaponize. My chin lifts as I hold my head up high, easy considering his hand placement.

"You fucking deserved it, you piece of shit! Tossing my sister's death out there to a pack of hungry piranhas for the latest gossip.

Like she was *nothing*. She will be remembered by how she died because of you. Not for who she was." My hand finds purchase on a stick. I spit at him.

Unfortunately, it falls flat, landing on my chin. Not what I was going for, but a distraction all the same.

"You're a fucking murderer. You deserve to die and I'm going to be the one to grant you that mercy," he growls in my face.

Oh, I want to die. But not by this asshole's hand. I'll go out *my* way and not a second sooner. My Shadow's words niggle in the back of my mind.

"Death would never be so kind to you." Not today. My Shadow's words echo through my head.

Using all my strength, I raise up the stick and strike him in the head.

Smack!

"Piece of shit!" I repeat.

Smack!

"Keep my sister's name out of your filthy, lying mouth!"

Smack!

It dazes him for a split second. All it did was successfully piss him off further. My limbs failed to convey the strength of my words. Self defense is clearly not my strong suit. He redoubles his efforts, his hands squeezing tighter, forcing my head to collide with the forest floor. Light flashes behind my eyes with each impact. Not the heavenly kind or the light at the end of the tunnel. The one when seen from a sudden explosion. The contact with the uneven ground sends a sharp jolt of pain coursing through my head, spinning and twirling like I'm back on the teacup ride from that fair Addi and I went to years ago, where I got sick and threw up. I might now. My neck rises from the ground, only to collide with a sharp rock.

I bite my tongue to stifle a scream. Years spent with my dad coming into play. Do not show him weakness. My eyes squeeze shut, keeping my tears at bay. It's probably not that bad. I've had worse.

His hands fall away, and I sputter for air. Choking on the very thing I need, nice. Wincing, I drag myself towards a nearby tree.

Where the fuck did he go? My eyes dart around the dark to find him kneeling on the forest floor, his hands up in surrender. His intense, pitch black eyes pin me with a piercing glare. Behind him stands River, who I thought at least got away, with a knife to his throat.

"River!" He says pleasantly. The low growl in his voice that he used with me is gone. Back is the charming playboy façade. "That's a dangerous toy you have there. Why don't you put it down? This has nothing to do with you. This is between me and the little Pyro." His glare returns.

Where did she get that knife? She's a magician tonight.

"You don't get to hurt my friends, Ben." Her voice is low and deadly, void of emotion. She's capable of murder, since that's the reason she's here. But would she do it for me?

"She's not your friend, River." He growls, switching back to the asshole he truly is. The more enraged he becomes, the more the knife buries itself into his throat, leaving a crimson stain beneath its tip. I feel like I'm witnessing something important, but the oxygen hasn't fully returned to my brain, so I'm just a bystander in this conversation.

"Do you know what she did?" He seethes, still staring at me.

River shakes her head sadly, the only emotion she's showed thus far toward him. "No, Bennett. Hatred, revenge, and lies blinds you and your brothers." He stops pushing against the knife. Searching my face for something.

"What do you mean?" His voice falters and cracks. For a second, he looks like a broken boy, looking for answers. He's like me. River's head snaps to me, remembering she has an audience.

"Go home, Priya. I'll take care of this." She says it so gently, a contrast from the night we've had. Somehow, my legs manage to get underneath me. The last thing I want to do is pass out in the middle of the woods. I wince, the world spinning in circles again. My hand grips the closest thing next to me. A tree. The bite of the bark on my palms keeps me grounded, limping my way back to my dorm.

MALICE

The room has an off-putting smell that lingers in the air. The fragrance of wildflowers has faded, now overpowered by the fresh scent of new furniture and clothes she purchased to replace the belongings destroyed in her room. Another one of Bennett's "great ideas" that fell flat. Sometimes, I wonder if she experiences emotions differently, like I do. Her reactions to most of the things happening around her are subtle, almost nonexistent.

The resistance of the hardwood floor makes the new sitting chair scrape against it, creating an unpleasant noise while I position it across from her bed, near the vent. Opening effortlessly, the vent reveals the carefully hidden camera I placed before her arrival at Cox, remaining untouched. Good girl. Curiosity killed the cat. As unaffected as she seems with the Demons' scheming, I don't think she'd be too pleased with my cameras. It's keeping her safe.

Well, her finding out would be fun. When anger consumes her, she transforms into a fiery kitten, spitting and hissing. There's always been an unexplainable tension between me and animals, as if they could perceive something about me that others couldn't. But she'd be my favorite animal. A sudden low thump echoes once in my chest, soon giving way to a serene, steady beat.

The cameras have a few blind spots, but not in areas that raise concern. One points at her bed. The camera abruptly cuts off, leaving the kitchenette hidden from view. In the loo, an additional camera was installed, aimed at the shower and vanity area, intentionally excluding the toilet to ensure privacy. To monitor any movement near the front door of her room, I positioned the last camera above the closet. It would be crazy to not know who's coming and going while she's away.

My teeth grind at the thought of the mysterious man dressed in black who's been leaving her cryptic letters. Deep down, I have a feeling of who is sending the messages, but the identity of the messenger remains unknown. Once I capture him, I'll be able to extract more information about *his* location. He's my lead. The moment the Demons uncover what I know, it will feel like stepping into one of those scandalous novellas that Bennett is so fond of. Dramatic.

With a grating sound, the chair slides back across the floor as I return it to its rightful position. To hide the tainted mess, the decorators set out to rearrange the room, their goal being to convince others it was now completely "new and improved". I did Priya a favor by putting it back to the way it was when we first met. Everything else was in my control, except for the frustratingly unchangeable colors. The new down comforter has a soft, off-white color rather than the cream color I had grown accustomed to. The designers stuck to a selection of neutrals.

On the bright side, when I rip her virginity away, these sheets will be a perfect souvenir. Where would I display it? The living room for the rest of the Demons to see? Just thinking about their reactions brings a smile of satisfaction to my face. Who will be lost in the plot first?

With a click, I shut the blinds using the controller, plunging the room into complete darkness. The door creaks open. A thin beam of light from the hallway slices across the floor, illuminating the bed in the center of the room. Her silhouette engulfs the doorway before enveloping us in a suffocating darkness. Can't chance ruining the surprise of who I am. This makes it more fun, the guessing and wondering. There's a part of her that isn't curious about my identity. She likes the anonymity.

My superior scotopic vision is a skill that sets me apart from the basic human. It doesn't make me inhuman, but it makes me better. I find it simple to transmit sensory signals that create real visual perceptions. After spending all my life in darkness, I adapted.

Like a hunter stalking its prey, I keep quiet. I walk with a gentle tread, my steps almost weightless for a man of my size, deliberately hugging the edges of the room where the darkness offers the most concealment.

She uses her cellphone as a makeshift flashlight, searching for her bed in the center of the room. Her movements are hesitant and strained. The light casts eerie shadows on the walls, but never shining directly on me. As I approach her from behind, she freezes in place. Ahh, she's aware someone is here.

I pounce, using her fear to my advantage. Even though I consider her to be different, I still expect her behavior when I cover her mouth with my hand. The other dips under her black hoodie, pressing her warm body close to mine. I bury my nose into her hair, hoping to catch a sweet dose of my childhood, a simpler time in my twenty-eight years of life. What I smell causes me to pause. There's a faint hint of flowers and coconut underneath the powerful scent of smoke and lighter fluid. The aroma reaches my nostrils, a wicked smile stretches across my face.

"You've been busy, love." At my voice, her body relaxes. Her trust is dangerous for both of us. I'll only be her damnation. "Fuck, you've got me bloody hard as a rock. You smell like sin and bad choices, Little Monster." I push my hardness into her. The friction of the jeans creates a pleasurable pain, making me groan into her hair and her breathing speeds up. Fear and arousal can often be confused with each other. I hope it's a combination of both.

Her self-preservation pleases me, she should fear me. But a darker part of me, needs her to need me. Crave me like the very air she breathes. I want to be so deep in her mind that there isn't a second she doesn't think about me the way I've been obsessed with her.

"Tell me what you did." She won't yell for help. She wants me here. I quench the loneliness she hides so well. We can both be lonely and misunderstood together. She's mine.

My hand moves down to cup her throat. I want to feel her pulse quicken when she tells me. My fingers skim on her new necklace of ownership.

"The diamonds suit you." She leans into me.

"I-I burned down one of the Demon's cars." The admission catches me off guard, and I burst into a full belly laugh.

"Which one?"

"Um," she shifts her weight from foot to foot. "I think it's safe to say it was Bennett's."

Oh, this is too good. I can only imagine his face. He always assumes he's untouchable. Even the cockiest people need to be humbled. Ben honestly thought she'd sit there and take it?

"Do you know why I'm here?" She hesitatingly nods.

"You owe me something." She nods again. There's nothing more refreshing than not having to repeat myself. I warned her what would happen if she cried for anyone but me. "Strip."

She stumbles a bit when I release her from my grasp. When she gets her balance, she stands there for a second. I can physically see her weighing her options. Priya doesn't enjoy being told what to do, but she will listen. Or I'll make her. The Demons aren't the only scary thing in the dark. I am. Their blood thirsty chained dog, thanks to Saint.

The gentle sound of the zipper interrupts my spiraling

thoughts. Her black jeans slowly coming undone, her thumbs deftly sliding into the belt loops as she lowers them down her curvaceous thighs, revealing her voluptuous, round arse adorned in a black thong. She slips them down further before stepping out of them completely. In her actions, there was an unintentional sensuality that made her vulnerable. She's still facing forwards, refusing to acknowledge my presence. I've noticed her do that a lot, zoning out when she's somewhere she doesn't want to be.

I step up behind her, lining up our bodies together. My hands trace the path from the "M" I left on her skin, applying added pressure to the spot I plan to mark. The raised texture of her old scars, remnants of her secret battles, has become a personal comfort of mine. When I touch her, her shoulders slump slightly, revealing her insecurities. My hands move to the next area, palming her ass, my grip bordering on painful. She stays silent. Scars or not, her body is like running my fingers through still water, smooth and silky.

I want to be the one to mar the smoothness of her beautiful skin. My name all over it, ruin the perfect little doll she pretends she is. Bring out the monster that she hides so well.

"Bloody hell, you're perfect." Perfect to ruin. To cut and bleed. Her body curls in on itself, seeking protection from the world, from me. Irritation pricks at me when she ignores my compliment. My hand leaves her body and plants itself into her hair, ripping her back into a confident posture while resting her head against my shoulder. Rarely do I offer praise, but the relentless disrespect aggravates my already frayed nerves. She yelps and tries to pull away, but I hold tight, rubbing the sticky strands that are usually soft between my fingers. I'd know the feeling anywhere. Blood.

"Bennett," she whispers. I hum. Grabbing her by the hair, slamming her face first onto the bed, leaving her legs suspended over the edge, ready to obey my every command. Last time I let her face me, she thought she'd be clever and bite me hard enough to scar. I tattooed it, the outline of her teeth indents. Secretly pleased with her returned affections. But she won't get that chance again.

I yank her down to the edge of the bed by her hips.

"Don't. Move." I snarl. Allowing a little bit of my inner demon out. She lies motionless, a rag doll waiting to be played with. Her long legs snatch my attention. I trace the curve of her body as she's bent over. Her panties hug her swollen pussy lips. I've barely touched her and she's wet. But how wet?

My boots echo in the room, letting her hear my approach. I shove her hoodie all the way up under her arms, baring her hourglass figure. My hands meet her hips and my grip turns painful enough to leave marks on them while I yank her into me. A gasp leaves her at the feel of my erection nudging into her heat that seeps into my jeans, a zip away from plunging into her.

Not yet. She's not ready. My jaw locks at imagining her bouncing on my dick, her ass jiggling at the impact of my hips colliding with hers with every stroke. Her moans and whimpers as she begs me to keep going. She'd feel me for days afterward. I wouldn't be gentle with her. I guide her hips, angling them up so her back is arched, and that sensitive bundle of nerves is exposed to me.

I assumed, but I need confirmation. "Are you a virgin?" I make sure each word hits her clit. Her breaths become rapid, her legs shift impatiently.

"Does i-it matter?"

Yes, it matters. Every person who's seen her body or has had her compliance in the bedroom matter. I'd slice away the part of them that believed they were entitled to touch her. What gave her the right to allow them the invitation to her body? My hands trace up her spine to thread into her hair, ensuring I grab where her wound is and pull, snapping her head backwards.

"Ow!" Despite her obvious pain, she's cheeky enough to say it through her sniffles. I purse my lips. The desire to inflict pain on her simmers below the surface, tempered by a sense of restraint. That's unusual for me. An idea strikes me. One I've never done it before, but if it doesn't work … No, it will.

In one fluid movement, I stand and rip the belt out of my dark jeans with practiced ease. I pause to feel the smooth texture of the worn leather against my fingertips. The fact she can't see what I'm doing causes her to shake. She instinctively pulls away at the sound. Interesting.

"Tell me." I say with a calm that belies the bloodlust raging inside me.

She averts her eyes with a slight turn of her head and focuses on the way she came through.

"Whether or not I am is none of your concern." She snaps.

Playing hard to get? Let's see how far that gets her. She tenses as I remain silent, but I swiftly loop the belt around and deliver a firm, balanced swat. A warning, because it can always get worse. With a mixture of shock and fear, she unleashes a startled shriek and desperately tries to crawl towards the headboard to create more space between us.

"What the fuck?" She yells, while rubbing the pink welt on her ass. It's barely anything. Trust me, I've committed worse deeds than this.

"Tell me to stop." I say. She remains silent, refusing to admit defeat. I would stop, only for her. When she doesn't answer, we continue. "Hands down, lay down."

"No."

No? She's really taking the piss tonight.

"Lay down or I'll fuck you with my knife before I finish carving you for everyone to see who you belong to." The threat gets her compliance. Her hand drops from her arse, resting next to her head.

"Answer me." No response.

This time I pull the belt back farther. The sound of it slicing through the air. Three more swats that land perfectly across her rounded cheeks. They jiggle on impact, making me bite my knuckles, holding back a groan. I don't want her to know the sight turns me on. Is this what's considered an "apple bottom?" Shaped and colored like an apple? Bloody hell, this is a sight. One more wouldn't hurt… me.

The metal of the belt jingles when I raise it again. Her knuckles turn white as she fists them into the blanket, readying herself for the next blow.

"Virgin." She pants. "I've never been with anyone." Good to know.

It whooshes through the air. The impact causing her to let out a squeal and sink her teeth into the bed. Dropping down to my knees, my hands gravitate toward the curve of her arse. While it may seem like I'm trying to comfort the hurt I've caused to some, my indifference remains unchanged. It's because I want to feel my marks on her. I'm curious to know if my actions can help me understand and share her relief at receiving pain. It's like a constant need, an addict looking for their next fix.

With every strike, her skin got hotter and transformed into a unique shade, creating a mesmerizing kaleidoscope of colors. Each welt has its own distinct color–the first a soft, rosy pink, the second set a rich, dark red, and the last one a bold scarlet hue. The strikes were fast and continuous, each one blending seamlessly into the next. It'll bruise. Every time she moves or sits, she'll remember me. That's exactly what I asked for.

My fingertips delicately glide along the seam of her thong, caressing the most sensitive part of her. Her body writhing to get away, clearly uncomfortable with my touch. From this angle, the black fabric soaked, its color deepening to an even darker black. I take a chance testing the boundaries by pulling her panties to the side exposing the glistening lips that are no longer hidden by flimsy fabric. My middle finger touches her stiffened bud before dragging down to the opening of her pussy, sticking in only the fingertip she clenches around nothing. Her pussy weeping for more. There is no way she's as turned on as me. Just a taste?

No. I said she wasn't ready, and she's not. Not yet, anyway. I pull out my push dagger, the one that has been with me through all of my kills. Always cleaned after each one, letting me bask in the memories of each drop of blood spilt. Recently, it's only been hers. She's been able to stave off the constant need of death.

I'd like to think I'm helping her. A therapist to talk through problems with. A diary to pour her heart out to. Or maybe even a God who answers her prayers. The knife's sharp point connects with her skin, making an indent before I pull it down. She sucks in a breath between her teeth and forces her body to relax. It's no easy feat. A strange man comes into her room to cut her when she fucks up. I'd like to think we're closer than that. Then her thinking I'm just some weirdo who breaks into her room at night.

She… makes me feel things I've never felt before. Things I was never given the opportunity to feel. I'm not sure if that means anything because I've never really had anyone. Saint, Crew and Bennett are all BFFs. The way they interact with each other, the way Saint talks about the twins, isn't something I've ever experienced. I've never really thought about it like that, so it's never bothered me how alone I am. It's possible she helps fight off my newfound loneliness.

"Do you think we're strangers, Little Monster?" I whisper into her soft skin. She makes a strangled noise. "I'd like to think we're more than that." My unoccupied hands trace the belt marks, hoping she'll move, and my dagger will go deeper. She doesn't. "I'd like to think we have a connection." The knife sinks into her flesh at an angle, cutting down, opening beautifully under my direction. "That what this is, is deeper than the surface level shit you feed everyone else."

I ready the blade again, making an upside-down V. It slices through like butter. The last line goes in the center of the V, completing the letter. My breath catches at the sight in front of me. It's hard to control myself around her. Everything about her is so inviting. I place my face down at her knee level, the drops of blood racing each other down her pale freshly shaved legs.

"I think you were made for me." My tongue touches the drops of blood, her skin sweet as the flowers she smells like, and lick a strip up to her new mark. My mark. I suction my lips over the wound, sucking at her like a vampire starved of blood for the last century.

"You're so sweet." I say, licking the blood from my lips and sucking her wetness off my middle finger. The combination is deadly.

She's not as broken as she was the last time in the shower, begging to die. Don't get me wrong, she'll always be broken in the way that attracts darkness to her. But she won't always want to die. I don't think she knows what she wants. She lays stock still, no answer, no movement.

"Stay here."

"Okay." Her voice comes out breathless and husky. Should I kiss her? Isn't that what people do after first or second dates? My mind is whirring with questions of what the "right thing" to do is. This is new to me. I need to research "How to take care of a pet". Yeah, I'll do that.

I keep the lights off when I go to get her supplies ready on the counter that she uses to clean herself up. Then I remember the head wound I viciously pulled on when she wasn't listening. An ice pack is my next step.

After I'm done with my bathroom task. I stop to admire her in the same position I left her in. Bent over the bed, bloody and bruised. The image brings a smile to my face. She does listen. Every pet needs guidance, and that's what she'll get. The freezer suctions closed after I grab the ice pack. I place it gently on the bed next to her right hand, letting the coolness seep into her skin.

"Make sure you ice your head. That's going to be a nasty headache." I stroke her hair twice, pushing it away from her face. "Sweet nightmares, Little Monster, dream of me." I decide against the kiss. That's a pretty big step for us. It should come naturally.

When the door softly shuts behind me, I think of everything we still have to do together. The tension I've been carrying during our separation is fully gone. My thoughts are clearer than they have been in days, all thanks to her. Now to the more pressing matters at hand. The guys are getting suspicious. Saint more than the others. The twins think that Saint has just been shut in his room finding helpful information.

The truth is, I've been a bit of a naughty boy lately, fronting more than usual. Saint is the one who is asking more questions. Eventually, I'll have to tell them the truth.

PRIYA

"Ow, ow, ow." I hiss as the sunlight hits my eyes, the pounding of my heartbeat in my head. Pain radiates through every inch of my body. Carefully, I press my fingers against the back of my head, where most of the pressure is building up. For the past hour, I've been contemplating getting out of bed. I instinctively bring my hands up to my eyes, desperate to block out the overwhelming light. I fumble for the remote control that seals off the outside world to create a pitch-black haven within these walls.

On the first try, I miss it completely, and my fingers graze it on the second attempt. With a sense of resignation, I release my grip and allow my hands to go slack, grabbing a pillow to cover my face, accepting defeat. I would scream if I could, but that would only worsen the pain.

A feminine throat clears in the room's corner.

"God, is that you?" My hoarse voice croaks out. The remote lands on my chest with a smack. "Ow, bitch. Definitely not a merciful God."

"The nurse is on her way up here. I suggest you change your clothes. You're halfway naked and on top of that, still smell like fire from last night." She tsks. River, sweet, sweet River. There's something I need to ask her. A sharp pain interferes with whatever thought I was working on.

"I think I'm dying." I groan. This feels like one of the beatings my dad gave me when I accidentally embarrassed him by thanking the waitress for helping at a charity event.

It's kicking my ass. Speaking of my ass. I wiggle side to side on the bed, shrinking away. The rough fabric against my sore asscheeks mixes in with a dizziness that overcomes me with each movement, makes it unbearable. I forgot about this part. It's been a while since I've had to nurse a concussion and an ass whoopin'. Even without a doctorates degree, I know that Bennett left me some brain damage.

Saliva fills my mouth and I know what comes next. With a jolt, I propel myself out of my bed, making a beeline for the nearest trashcan, my body wracked with dry heaves. My feet kick at the floor as I gag. My palms sting at the feel of the trash can scraping against them. Fuck, I hate this.

The cool lip of the trashcan presses against my cheek. I've been sitting here for hours with my eyes closed. I don't feel great, but better. There's a light tap on the door. River's footsteps lightly clunk on the hardwood floor to answer it. My throbbing head worsens with each soft word spoken at the door. I need quiet.

"She's been dry heaving for the last twenty minutes and hasn't moved from the trashcan." River says. "Babe, get into bed so the nurse can look you over and excuse you, at least for the day."

On my hands and knees, I turn to make my way back to the bed, the trashcan in tow. I look pathetic but I have to admit, Bennett did a number on me. River's soft warm hands pull me up into the bed, taking my hoodie off and throwing it somewhere in the room. The softness of the down blanket is cool against my skin, covering my breasts from the nurse's view. Why wear a bra with a hoodie? I'm a part-time member of the itty bitty titty committee. The other half of the time I'm ashamed of my body.

"All right, Miss Carter, can you tell me what you're feeling to start off with?"

I list off what I know. "Dizziness, even when laying down. Speaking to you is making my head feel like it's going to explode. Dry heaving in the trash can. The light hurts and I want some fucking peace and quiet."

"Okay." Her fingers tapping away on a tablet, the *click, click, click* alone is loud enough to make me flinch. "Sorry, dear. Just have to put notes into your file." She touches me and I shrink away. If this is Nurse Lisa, I know what that mouth was doing the other day. I don't even want to think about her hands. Sweaty old man balls. The thought makes me gag. River readies the trashcan for me.

"Do you know what day it is?" She asks. I want to say it's Saturday since I'm still in bed, but River wouldn't be over here that early in the morning.

"Friday?" I question. She hums and doesn't correct me. What does that mean? Yes or no? Never a straight answer with these people.

"Do you remember what happened?" My eyes pop open and look at River, who's only noticeable from the glow of the tablet in the nurse's hand. Her eyes widen a fraction before shaking her head. Yes, I remember the most amazing and successful fire I've ever created.

"No." I lie.

"Have you ever suffered from memory problems prior to this?"

"No." She nods and types notes into her little handheld computer. She leaves the screen on to illuminate her face as she talks.

"I think you should take the next few days to recover. Lots of sleep. Limit your screen time. Keep it dark. Over the counter meds are all I can offer. I can't prescribe anything. I'll make a note to the dean to excuse you for classes. And I'll send one full meal up here." With that, she gets up and lets herself out. The promise of food makes my stomach rumble. I'm starving. What if I throw it up? That would be a shame.

"He really got you, huh?" River grimaces. I don't need her to tell me I look as bad as I feel. Everything fucking hurts, aches, movements, lights, and voices.

"What happened?" My voice cracks. I'm going to lose it, thanks to last night.

"What do you remember?"

Okay, Nurse River. The need to roll my eyes at her is there, but the thought of a dizzy spell prevents me from doing so.

"Um, vaguely setting the car on fire, Bennett finding me. I don't remember exactly how I got to my room. That parts a little fuzzy." I remember bits and pieces of the Shadow man being here. But I keep that to myself.

Staring at the comforter covering my legs, I'm suddenly transported back to that moment. Where he eagerly shared all the "juicy" details about my sister with everyone. I shrink deeper into the bed, wanting to hide. I clench my fists tightly, feeling my nails digging into the raw, open flesh of my palms as I fight back tears. He told everyone I killed her. The stinging in my eyes prompts me to lift my gaze to avoid crying hysterically. There's a lot of shit I can take, but my sister didn't deserve to be remembered that way.

"I brought some prescription pain pills. Open up." My eyes stay closed when I stick my tongue out. Today I'm choosing to take the help where I can get it. "I think… today we will spend it sleeping and relaxing. I'm going to get my headphones. Just because you have to be in silence doesn't mean I do. But I will suffer missing two days of school for you." She winks at me from the door before leaving me alone. I want to close my eyes for a little, and then I'll deal with everything later. I still need to tell her what I found out about Megan.

CREW

The car rocks from the force of the trunk slamming down. I throw the work clothes Bennett requested on top and lean against it while waiting for the others. Someone must have texted Elijah for a job because I received a location close to here less than 30 minutes ago. Unfortunately, it's not unexpected that pedophiles exist in nearby towns.

What caught me off guard is knowing one of my brothers went around me to ask for a job instead of coming to me. It's unanimous among all of us when we need a release. I fidget with my black t-shirt. The thought of us falling apart fills me with unease. This isn't an obstacle I thought we would ever face.

The crunch of gravel being stomped on draws my attention, followed by another set of footsteps approaching us at a leisurely pace. Bennett's body is shaking when he reaches for his clothes, ripping them off the trunk, shrugging them on. I observe his tantrum with wide eyes as he storms to the driver's side of the vehicle, the sound of the door slamming echoes around us.

In a matter of seconds, Saint lazily saunters towards the back passenger's side door. I'm about to question him about what's happening, but he shrugs nonchalantly and climbs inside without waiting for me to speak. This is a fucking weird night.

With a sudden jolt, the car comes to a stop and smoothly shifts into park, strategically parking a couple of houses away from our target's location. The entire drive over here lacked the usual hype Ben brings. There were no cracking jokes, music, or excitement for tonight. Only the screeching of the tires as he took turns too quickly and Saint in the back gripping the "Oh shit" handle for dear life with every acceleration of the motor. The car turns off, and he puts the keys in his pocket, leaning his head against the headrest of the driver's seat. His eye's almost swollen shut, and a dried, crusty line of blood along his neck.

"Bennett." I look at Saint for help. Saint raises his palms towards me and mouths, "No idea."

"She burnt Mindy." He sniffs and wipes his nose on the back of his hand. There is only one *she* that would fuck with any of us. The car is so quiet that I could hear a pin drop. My eyes flit from Bennett to Saint.

"She burnt down your car?" My words come out strangled. That still doesn't explain the black eye. She's a hundred pounds on a good day. Is she alive?

"Yes!" He snarls. "I showed up too late, and Mindy is fucking destroyed. The car that Dad, Ty and I built. Fucking gone! The little bitches took off into the trees before I could catch them." He huffs.

"Your eye?"

"Well, she didn't quite get away."

As Ben begins his story, I can't help but notice Saint's intense focus. His eyes locked on his every word, as if not breathing would guarantee he didn't miss a single detail. I swear he purposely leaves us in suspense.

"I put my hands around her throat and almost squeezed the life out of her. When she wouldn't shut her mouth, a couple of bashes into the ground definitely did." Saint has stopped breathing completely, his posture tense, ready to jump at any second. At him? Out of the car?

"Is she…?" Saint asks softly, not wanting to say anything too permanent.

"Oh no," he chuckles humorlessly. "Your little techie managed to sneak up on me before I could finish the job. Spouting some shit about we 'have it all wrong' and when I didn't let her finish, she punched me in the face! I would've taken a knee to the balls before she fucked up my money maker." He throws a fist into the old dashboard. Saint's body returns to his usual casualness, losing the tenseness he had moments ago when he thought Bennett had killed her.

"So…" Saint says.

"So, she limped off somewhere. It's difficult to talk shit to a tiny girl who has a knife to your throat. She's stabby." He absent-mindedly rubs his neck, feeling the cut like he can still sense the knife.

"You let River get one over on you?" Saint snickers, settling back into his seat. "Amateur."

Ben ignores him, popping the trunk, a signal he's ready to move forward. Saint sensing the hostility slinks out to meet me at the back of the car. He looks to me for answers before nodding his head towards Bennett. I shake my head at him, not knowing what to tell him. We both take a second to take in the surrounding area.

The suburban neighborhood is a camouflage for blending in seamlessly for a pervert. The houses merge together with their uniform shape and size, but the vibrant colors and well-maintained landscaping add individuality. People would consider this the perfect picture family home in a friendly neighborhood.

The streetlights cast long, eerie shadows that creep towards the edges, obscuring the view beyond the illuminated sidewalk. That's where we will stick to. The "Neighborhood Watch" signs, the nice pristine lawns, and the luxury cars create a deceptive sense of safety. Cookie cutter life is the word.

All of us are in our signature work attire, a sea of black. It's easier to blend into the night and the color easily hides blood. I hand out a pair of leather gloves for each of us, the scent of new leather wafting through the air. Gripping Ben on the arm to give him his, he snatches them from my grip without looking at me and jogs across the street, disappearing around the dark corner of the two-story house to the back door.

Saint wrings his hands in front of him, the leather squeaking as he frowns at the front door.

"What?"

Malice usually joins us on these outings. After years of friendship, we've learned what his tells are. Sometimes it's as simple as zoning out by staring off into a distance and other times, if it's negative, a wince.

It's very rare that Saint would be fronting right now with no switch in sight but calling him out might make him more antsy. He shakes his head, brushing off the question before waiting on me to make the first move. He sticks close to one of us on these jobs if he comes with. I wonder if he's just as confused as we are that Malice is absent.

I follow Ben's lead, sticking to the shadows. The house is devoid of life. It stands in stark contrast to its surroundings, with no light to be seen. It's wrong, especially when every other house on the street has their porch lights switched on. Saint rummages through his hoodie, searching for his lock picking kit, his gloved hand gripping the doorknob cautiously. With a silent twist to the right, the door opens effortlessly. His brows crinkle as he examines his hand, then turns to look at me, wetting his lips with a quick swipe of his tongue.

Something is off. The house stands ominously, its silence serving as a haunting invitation. From the entryway, the rooms appear stark and empty, with no evidence of anyone living here. The distinct odor of the fresh paint and lacquer is the first thing that hits me. Someone has been busy with renovations.

The sound of heavy, booted footsteps stomping down the wooden staircase, ring through the house as I maneuver Saint behind me, pressing him against the wall for safety, my heart beating a mile a minute. Responsibility weighs heavily on my shoulders, over everyone in our small circle, but Saint especially. I want nothing to stall his progression from how far we've come since we were kids. If I can protect him, I will. Even if it's from his own mind.

"Crew. You're going to want to see this." Ben's voice is devoid of emotion. "I cleared the house. It's fine." He adds. Both of our bodies relax. With Saint close behind, I make my way up the staircase. We enter a sparse home office tucked away in the loft area. The pungent smell of a recently lit cigar lingers, overpowering the fresh paint. Behind the desk, a naked man stands with his limbs stretched out in a star position. I drop the bag of toys I brought on his desk and creep closer to observe the man we were sent here to kill. Holy shit…

"That's Brian." Bennett mutters from behind me. Brian Bush's lifeless head hangs heavily on his chest, immobilized with his limbs stretched out, while a black envelope is securely stapled to his hairy torso. Upon closer inspection, I notice the fine layer of dust that settled on the bookcase behind, evidence of recently drilled holes. As I lift his chin with my pointer finger, I can't help but notice the sickly grey complexion and the careless, bloody mess left behind by the peeled-back skin on his cheek. The sight of burn marks on his abdomen, the flesh still puffy and raised, indicates the intensity of the burning object. In addition, his fingers have been cut off at the second knuckle and cauterized. This was done out of anger. It's sloppy.

"It appears we have mail," I say. Ripping the black envelope off of Brian's chest. We all collectively neglected and pushed it aside last time, placing our focus on Priya. It should've been more alarming that it was at a job, but now it poses a problem by making another appearance in a place it shouldn't be.

They both fixate on the glaring elephant in the room. My twin rubs his hands over his bruised face, giving the letter a tired look.

"Honestly, I totally forgot about the last one. I figured it was a hoax the first time. Outta mind, outta sight type shit." We both wait for Saint to say something. He simply stares at it, his mind transported to another time.

"Who is it addressed to?" Saint asks without moving his eyes.

Bennett's hand moves at lightning speed, snatching it from my grasp.

"You." His eyes scan Saint's face to see his reaction. Acknowledging him with a nod like it's what he expected. Ben opens it. His eyebrows raise and he faces it towards us to do the same.

I know something you don't know.

The words are taunting. Childlike. Saint's eyes refuse to look at it.

"Saint?" I press. He glances at it briefly, then down at his hands.

"Yeah?"

"Well, what do you think?" Bennett asks impatiently.

"It's him." He whispers. The discomfort in my gut is prominent as I recall the way Saint was when we were younger. A dirty, malnourished boy with bruises littering his body. His father thought his shoulder length hair was too "feminine" back then, so he shaved it. We learned from Saint that he believed he was being punished for something he'd done. All of us brushed it off, choosing to prioritize his happiness over delving into his personal life. Not even the school tried to save him. It's disgusting how many kids are failed by the very system that is designed to protect us.

Bennett shakes his head side to side, disagreeing and in disbelief. "Nah, man. You're trippin'. There's no way." He laughs, but there's an underlying tension in the sound.

Saint's complexion is ghostly pale, all traces of his usual tan have vanished within a matter of minutes.

"Ben. It's the same *black* card, same red writing that he used to have me deliver to his victims' families. The pose, I remember it so vividly. He used to make me chain them up. But I've never seen him choose a man." He swallows hard.

My brother scoffs at the ridiculousness of what he's implying.

"Impossible. We killed him. All four of us." He looks at me. "Right?"

I don't know how to answer. I thought we did, but something has me second guessing. Saint's eyes bulge out of his head, never closing. His head shakes in a constant back-and-forth motion.

"I…thought we did," I say.

"There was no body. We tied him to his bed and set it on fire. There wasn't a body. We should've checked." Saint says over and over again, squeezing his eyes shut. Ben and I stand silently, taking in the sight of him.

"Saint. I swear to God if you don't shut the fuck up. He's been dead for years. Me, Crew, Ty *and* you, killed him." His tone is harsh and defensive, but anyone who knows Bennett knows it's because he's scared.

Saint ignores my brother in favor of pacing. His restless steps echo throughout the room. The veins in his neck visibly pulsate as he repeatedly jerks his head from side to side, as though grappling with an internal struggle. What the hell is going on with everyone today?

"I need to tell you guys something," he says, still pacing. We patiently wait. "Malice doesn't want you guys to know." I stand taller, crossing my arms over my puffed chest. Throughout our entire time together, we've maintained an open and honest relationship between the five of us. I never thought Malice would be the one to break that with how important Saint is to him. It was a red flag when we heard them briefly disagreeing before they stopped as soon as we entered the room.

"What?" The question comes out harsher than I intended. I'll blame it on the bomb he just dropped.

"Priya, she's been receiving the same letters."

"What the fuck do you mean, 'receiving the same letters'?" I grit out. I'm trying to be patient because, according to him, he's not supposed to be telling us anything.

"Fuck man, I can't." His eyes screw shut tightly, tugging on his hair before taking a deep breath. "She's gotten a few of these letters. Malice and River have been working on it separately, of course. There's footage of a man in all black coming to deliver them. Priya thinks it's Malice fucking with her, so she isn't that concerned. Tosses them into the nightstand next to her bed and doesn't think about them again. Not that we've noticed."

There's a lot to unpack here. The secrets a breach of trust, and while I understand Saint isn't solely to blame, I expected better from our connection. I was foolish enough to think it was anything more than that. Where do his loyalties lie? What about Saint's? Why would Priya think it's Malice? I scoff, allowing the indifference I wear for everyone else to wash over me. Emptiness fills my chest, strangling my usual rage into a box that I can deal with at a later time.

"What do you think, Saint?" I say calmly.

"I don't know. I've been trying to tell you guys, but he's kept me busy in our room looking for shit on Priya. I thought he was helping." He stops pacing to stare at both of us. "This is my father. I can feel it. Something had to have gone wrong that night. It's been eating at me every time I see you guys. Not to mention I don't know what he's hiding from me. There are bigger spaces in time I can't remember. He doesn't fill me in anymore. I'm lost, and it's making me insane."

"What do we know about the letters?" Ben asks quietly, refusing to look at Saint. Opting to stare at the dead, naked school dean instead.

"Whoever is delivering them isn't my father. He wouldn't chance being surprised a second time. He's been inside her room and through her things. Mal thinks he wants her. He doesn't know why." His pacing slows and he plays with the hooped piercings on his lip.

"We could put cameras in her room." Ben suggests. The first time we got lucky. Saint lived with him and we could plot his death with Elijah to cover it up for us. This time? I don't know where to search for his piece of shit father.

"Why now?" I ask, "It could've been anytime in the past four years he could've reached out. But he chose now."

"Priya?"

I nod my agreement to whichever one of them said it while I stare outside through the window overlooking the quiet street. The only thing that has changed is her. He's going after her. What's his endgame?

"Is she in on it?" I question.

Saint shakes his head. "No, she's clueless. I told you she thinks it's Mal."

"Yeah, well, you also failed to fill us in on this recent development of your guys'." Bennett sneers. Saint cringes under our stares of scrutiny. This changes things for us. All of us.

"We can bring her home?" Bennett proposes, looking at me. It seems I'm not the only one who took Mal's secrecy to heart.

"No."

"Think about it, Crew. If she's at our house, there's no way she can receive a letter without us being here to intercept it. Catch the guy. This goes beyond revenge." His feet tap the ground, letting me know he's nervous. "I may not like Saint 95% of the time and Malice even less, but no one deserves what he had to go through."

"No," I say with finality. It's not happening. I will not allow someone who killed one of our best friends to live in the same house as us. As Ty did.

"Put some cameras around her room and we will go from there. Saint, call Elijah and see what the fuck happened." I'm curious to know why he's been sending us to locations that Saint's father has been finding. Is there a leak? Did Elijah turn his back on us? Bennett's hand slams on the desk to get my attention.

"If we lose another one of our 'brothers' that you claim you love because you're so blinded by revenge. I'll never forgive you. You will lose *everyone*." He promises as he storms out of the room, down the stairs, slamming the back door on his way out. Everything is falling apart. It's all connected to her. We should just kill her. That would give me back my brothers. What's left of us, anyway. Tyson dying was because of her stupidity and because of that Elijah won't come around anymore.

Saint is pulling away from us because Malice is forcing him to keep secrets and stay busy. If Saint is keeping secrets from us, it's safe to say that all our goals may not be aligned. We did all of this to have her here to now protect her? That's what it feels like. Where is the justice?

PRIYA

A gentle whisper carries my name. "Priya."

Choosing to ignore it, I roll over and sink deeper into the fluffy comforter, enjoying the warmth and coziness.

"Priya." What will it take to shut it up? The headache has dulled to bearable and I'm not throwing up, so that's a plus.

"Priya!" As the seconds pass, the voice becomes increasingly louder, making it impossible to go back to sleep.

"Hmmm!" More of a 'What the fuck do you want?'

"Someone was at the door." That jolts me upright, instantly wide-eyed and alert. River is standing beside the door. She looks small, her arms holding herself in the shadows of the moonlight. Carefully, I slide my hand under the far pillow, feeling for the familiar shape of my razor blade. It isn't much, but it's all I have.

My bare toes touch the frigid hardwood floor, sending a shiver down through my body. Cautiously, I tiptoe towards the door, fearing that it might betray me with a creak. My Shadow man wouldn't hesitate to make himself at home in my room but he's also never visited when I had a visitor.

With a quick glance through the peephole, I strain to make out any details in the dimly lit hallway. Since there are only two of us on this floor and we don't have any friends aside from each other, very few people come up here. I grip the handle of the door and steel myself against whatever is out there. The door gently opens, freeing the lock and opening silently.

The hallway is eerily empty, creating an unsettling atmosphere that is new to the space. The lights aren't flickering or out entirely, so there's a silver lining. From my room, the elevator sits diagonally across, its buttons glowing brightly. It reaches the first floor, and a soft ding fills the air. I don't want to jump to conclusions but what are the odds that it's the person leaving my floor? A part of me feels like the older horror movies that have the stereotypical dumb blonde wanting to go see. The other part of me that's overly cautious knows I should stay put.

Just as I'm about to return to the room, I notice a black envelope taped to the door. They've been more frequent lately. I figured the Shadow man just didn't want to admit the truth when he asked me about them and didn't deny it. I'll ask him about it next time. No way he's doing whatever he wants until he comes clean with me. Determined, I rip it off the door and tear it open. My heart skips a beat and my brow wrinkles. The ominous letter feels heavier than usual.

You were so easy to find :)

My nail catches on something taped to the back and when I flip it over, the walls of the hallway close in on me. The blood drains from my skin and my lips part in silent terror. A picture of my sister's headstone stares back at me. In messy handwriting it on the bottom of the Polaroid shatters my mind. "She's gone because of you."

The vicious poison of hopelessness has finally settled into the cracks of my soul, no longer able to be held off by my sister's memory. I thought by gaining a connection with the Shadow or even River I could stumble through life. I let *hope* weave it's way into my heart that I could carry on without my sister.

My fingertips trace the glossy tombstone holding my sister's name. Addison L. Carter. I choke on my breath. A sucker punch seizes my lungs. No…not a punch. An echo of it, the aftershocks that leave me with the clarity I've been running from.

Murder.

Pyro.

Bitch.

Pet.

This will never end.

"Priya?" River's soft voice calls out snapping me out of my trance. I shut the door double checking it's locked before reassuring River that it's safe.

"Who was it?"

"The hall was empty," I say quietly, crawling back into the warmth of my bed, hoping she won't see the decision I made out in the hallway written on my face.

I leave the corner of the blanket pulled down for her to join me. I lay on my side to give my sore ass a reprieve from being laid on. "What time is it?" I yawn.

The bed sinks with her weight, but she doesn't lie down. "3:30AM."

Damn, I slept a whole day away. I feel slightly better, thanks to River sneaking in a real pain pill. Maybe that's why I'm so drowsy. Why is she even awake at this time?

"Pri? Can I ask you something?"

I swallow the lump forming in my throat. Even if I were to say "No, go to sleep." She'd still ask.

"Yeah."

"Why aren't you like the other girls here?"

The sensation of my eyebrows coming together causes my eyes to squint and the moonlight to become a blurry haze.

"What do you mean?"

"Like, you're not as stuck up as I would assume someone who has never had to work a day in their life would be. You're not belittling and bringing people down."

"Is Amber bothering you, Riv?"

"No, it's not that. When I first heard I was getting someone on the third floor with me, I thought you'd be someone like Amber and you're not what everyone expected." This feels like judging a book by its title or whatever they say. I don't know what to tell her, so I shrug.

"You don't wear the same name brand clothes as they do."

"That's because my parents didn't allow me to wear name brand clothes."

"Why?" she asks quietly.

A sigh involuntarily escapes me, craving to steer clear of these types of questions. I thought shit got deep at 2 am not 3:30.

"I don't know, River. My parents said it was a privilege I didn't deserve. I only got name brand things whenever I was needed to go to an event or show my face to the public with them."

"You don't talk like them."

"No one ever really talked to me but my sister. She's all I had to go by. So, I'm not sure if that's a good thing."

"You're really quiet. The way you carry yourself is different. The etiquette and manners seem off compared to what I've seen since my family came into money."

She's just a chatty Kathy tonight. I'm quiet because my dad would beat me more than usual if I spoke out of turn. I have nothing to be stuck up about. Everything I love and cared for is gone.

"Go to bed, River." I throw the blankets over her and turn over. This conversation makes me uncomfortable. I'm not used to being put on the spot and asked questions like this. I've never had to explain it to someone before. My sister just knew. She watched me live through most of it.

My sister. The thought makes my stomach turn. Someone needs to remember her the right way when I'm gone. Or maybe if we're together it wouldn't matter anymore. They could remember us or not and it would be okay because my life would've been what it was always supposed to be. I'm nothing without her.

"Are your parents coming to the Parent's Day?" She's not taking the hint. I huff at her incessant badgering.

"No, River. In case you haven't gathered it yet, my parents don't fucking like me."

"Oh."

She wants more from me. Prodding isn't something she usually does, leaving me to wonder what's going on that's sparked the sudden interest. A part of me feels guilty. Maybe she just wants to fill the silence with talking and I'm just shutting her out and leaving her alone. Something people have done to her before and that's the reason she's more timid tonight. I don't want to be that person.

With a sigh, I give in and turn around to face her in the dark. She's staring off into space, not really here with me. Fuck, I'm such a bitch. Who am I to think she buries her trauma and not relive it every night? Whenever we're together, I always end up dozing off before she does, and to make matters worse, she didn't have to stay here and monitor me.

"When is Parent's Day?"

"The weekend after Halloween."

My eyes dart to the kitchenette, where a school calendar hangs on the wall. Halloween. My birthday, the first one without my sister to make it worth more than another day. I don't want to spend one year without her… I could make this my last birthday. River's gasp breaks through the sinister thoughts.

"Ohmigosh! There's going to be a Halloween party this year. Well, there is every year, but it'll be your first one here. They're legendary! We have to go! The theme for last year was a goth-ic/Victorian era. The year before that was Alice in Wonderland,

and in my first year here they did a haunted house theme. The Demons are assholes but they know how to throw a party."

I've never been to a Halloween party. I've seen the trick-or-treaters walking around our street before. But most of the time I'm roped into some "important" political dinner for my father. He's been trying to get his greedy claws into a senator title the past couple of years. Every year he swears it'll be the year. Reminds me of when people talk about their favorite NFL team, and still don't win.

"I've never been to one," I say nonchalantly. Despite the cover of darkness, her widened eyes shine bright white, showing that her previous thoughts have vanished. Plotting, I'm sure.

"Priya!" she shrieks, causing my head to throb. "You've never been to a Halloween party?"

I wish this time her excitement was contagious enough, but the only thing I can think of is wanting to go to my first one with Addi. She would have loved to have gone. To satisfy her love for holidays, she would dedicate her room as a sanctuary, filled with festive decorations that were banned from the rest of the house.

"This year, it's a black light circus/carnival themed! It's going to be amazeballs."

"Please feel free to *never* use that word again." I giggle at her ridiculousness. Her chilly hands grab at my unusually warm ones that were tucked under my cheeks and hold them. She looks at me. Her eyes betray the seriousness she's trying to project with mischief.

"We have to go together. Nonnegotiable."

"Riv, that's really not a good day for me. I'd realistically just like to stay and relax. Plus, who knows how I'll feel by that day? I can't miss something I've never had." My words may convey one thing, but the true meaning runs much deeper. I've never celebrated my birthday and anytime I've had hopes, my parents ruined them. Forgetting or ignoring the fact I was born that day. I don't want to hype myself up over having a "good" birthday.

"Oh, we're going. There is no way you won't be back in class on Monday, Miss Straight-A student. I was just hoping by giving you a choice you'd choose correctly. You didn't. I would start looking for an outfit. Everyone dresses up. That isn't an exaggeration. I already have my costume in mind."

Fine, I'll bite. "What is it?"

She playfully smacks me and tells me it's a surprise. I roll my eyes and wince at the movement. I need to go back to sleep to sleep off this concussion. Nothing a little sleep won't fix, right?

River finally settles back down into bed and cuddles up close to me. I've never really felt like a big sister before, but River makes me feel that way. Even with her head laying on the pillow next to me with her eyes closed, I can still feel the excitement vibrating from her.

"Go to sleep, River." I scold. She pretends to snore like she's actually sleeping. I pull the comforter around her shoulders and tuck her in before pushing a piece of her dark bangs that falls over her eyes behind her ear and close my eyes. If this is going to be my last birthday, I can have a last hurrah. Sleep tonight and plan a kick ass outfit. My decision has me feeling the peace I've longed for my entire life. There's just one little thing…

"Hey, River?" Her fake snores stop as she peeks an eye open. "I haven't really had the time to tell you about my recent discovery. A lot of things have happened back to back," Oscar, the Demons. It never really seemed like the right timing to reveal to her what I found out. "But that day in the hallway before…" I swallow around saying his name because the thought of Oscar Bush makes me want to vomit, knowing I haven't retaliated in the slightest. "Anyway … I noticed the student photos of the school and three years ago when the guys were freshmen, Megan Riley was here too."

My eyebrows draw together when her body tenses next to mine. I haven't even said what I was going to say yet. All the times I've brought up the missing girl from the gas station to River, she's reacted negatively. I know I'm not Nancy Drew, but it is suspicious.

"She looked cozy with Saint. At the least, friendly. For the rest of the years, everyone keeps a noticeable distance from the boys.

That's weird, right?" I ask for reassurance that I wasn't crazy for thinking that way.

"Mmhmm."

I shrug and shake my head, clearly not getting anywhere with her on this topic. For the last time I drop it. It won't matter anymore anyway.

SAINT

Resting my head on my computer desk with countless open tabs, I absentmindedly squish my blue ball. Its pliable texture offers a soothing sensation. The tabs contain a mix of Priya's texts, searches for her sister, and still photos capturing the man in black. I pause my squeezing, and like a vacuum, the goo inside the ball sucks back, regaining its normal circular shape.

It's kind of strange the differences between the sisters. In siblings, there's striking similarities they inherited from their parents, but Priya looks so out of place with her family. It could be she looks like her mother. Lacking the coldness that her mother carries. Some would call it ruthlessness, but I know better. Even pretty faces can't hide the wickedness lying underneath. Malice's attention to detail is rubbing off on me.

I throw my head back and let out a groan while staring at the ceiling. Everything is falling apart before our eyes. I understand why the twins are upset with me, but I'm not completely to blame. It's Malice. As long as I've known about him, we've been on the same page. I never asked him how long he's been here, but I remember he started chatting with me around the time I was almost 14. I don't understand where the divide is coming from.

No matter how hard I try to talk to him, he consistently ignores me, withholding any information he comes across. He's just gone silent, like he's never existed. The part of me that has relied on him to be there when I need him feels abandoned, like I felt as a kid. My knuckles rub my chest where it aches from the memories it threatens to bring up. I want to demand answers. Why did he leave his phone out for me to find? I saw the cameras he placed in her room. That part I left out to the guys, in fear of them turning on me. They never have before. Maybe they would've understood.

Whenever I recall the intensity of Crew's stare, my throat tightens. It hurts to think that even after all this time, he looks at me as if I'm someone new. As if he's suddenly seeing me in a different light. He trusted me, and Malice broke that. All for what? My hands rip at my hair in desperation, hoping to pull out an answer. Just think. Think. I repeat to myself while smacking my hand against the top of my head.

Malice has never turned on me before. He's a calculated, manipulative bastard. For some reason, Priya Carter holds his attention. Long enough that his impulsiveness hasn't led to killing her or… hasn't yet. It's not her beauty, that would be too narrow minded for him, there's always a bigger picture. On autopilot, my hands detach from my fisted hair and swiftly navigate towards the screens, where I effortlessly retrieve the camera feed he had cleverly installed in her room. There's no code because, as he says, "I have nothing to hide."

The cameras have a night vision feature that automatically activates at a specific time. Even at 04:00, her room is illuminated in a clear, grey and white hue. Angled perfectly at her bed. She doesn't look too beat up as I thought she would from having Bennett strangle her on Wednesday night. River's arms and legs are flung across Priya's, like little animals snuggling together for warmth. It's almost cute. Protective.

Time passes as I watch them sleep soundlessly without a care in the world. By studying her, I hope to decipher the hidden motives behind Malice's actions. He's only ever been obsessed with death, how to bring it, cause it, extend it. My lips pull back in a rarely seen sneer. And here he is, allowing her to breathe the same air as us, knowing what she did.

Maybe I'm totally misreading it. It could be that my father is alive, causing me to doubt everything I know. But that doesn't explain how he would know she's receiving letters from him before us. So many questions without answers. My phone vibrates with a notification, a group text for a meeting downstairs. The weight of anxiety settles in my chest as I make my way down the steps, my hands becoming clammy.

Are they going to push me out? Could Malice really ruin the bond between me and the twins?

The kitchen is quiet when I enter, my steps slow and cautious. No one lifts their head to acknowledge me, leaving me surrounded by an uncomfortable silence. Crew leans against the counter, purposefully creating a physical barrier between us, dressed and ready to go to classes. His arms remain tightly crossed over his chest with balled fists, the unmistakable "go fuck yourself" vibe emanating from him.

Clearing his throat, Bennett takes the lead, acutely aware of his brother's simmering rage. His anger is a suffocating weight, longing to punish us for our deeds. The air is heavy with tension, so dense it could be severed with a blade.

"Regardless of whatever is going on here," he gestures to the house. Meaning between all four of us. "We can't allow any of these money hungry assholes to know there is a weakness. We keep a united front. So, with that being said." He claps his hands with excited energy. "The Halloween party."

He waits for a response and falls short, his face falls betraying the act he was putting on. We can see he's trying to be happy-go-lucky when we're clearly anything but. He purses his lips while leaning back onto the kitchen island in front of me.

"Okay, well, I've come up with the theme and have already made some calls, so everything is in order. I'm thinking about circus/carnival/Blacklight. What do you think?" He'd use any excuse to throw a party. Holidays, birthdays, even professional sport wins.

I smile, but it's strained. They'll both see through it. "Sounds good." What's the point in doing the fun banter we usually do? Ben gives me an eye roll, the leather of jacket his jacket creaks when he crosses his arms.

"Really, Saint? No snide comment?" He lets out a heavy sigh, then looks at Crew for input, but he still refuses to engage with us. Admitting it doesn't make me feel like running away would be a lie. For the first time in a while, I find myself doubting that everything will be all right as long as we stick together. What a time for us to be pulling away. The only monster that's worse than Mal is my father.

No.

The word monster is too gentle of a term to use for him. He would be the devil in the flesh, risen from the depths of hell, hoping to bring it here on earth. The sting in my eyes forces me to divert my gaze from the family I chose. I'm so alone.

"Is that all?" Crew asks Bennett, before storming off down into the basement. Probably to blow off steam, or his anger with me. I have that to be thankful for. He's never once put his hands on me in a rage. I glance at Bennett to see him already staring at me. He shakes his head, dropping his eyes to the floor.

"Fix it."

My ears take a minute to adjust to the lack of sarcasm he usually aims at me. It's well known between the three of us he doesn't like me, he ignores me and at best, tolerates me. Crew thinks he's jealous of our relationship. Specifically, that I took Crew away from him. To hear him say he wants me to fix things with his twin is a conundrum. Playing with my piercings, I find myself questioning his true intentions and reflecting on his expertise in manipulation. My head turns to observe him, taking in his upright posture, piercing black eyes. It's only 7am, yet he's already dressed as if he has somewhere important to be. Maybe this is affecting him more than I think.

"I can see those little wheels turning in your head. He's *my* brother. If he hurts, I hurt. The way he's showing that is his anger. Well, that's all he's good at showing. But you?" He lets out a low whistle. "You did a number on him. You were one of the first people he let in, besides me, of course, and whether or not you think so, you betrayed him. Malice did." He grabs Crew's car keys off the counter and makes his way to the side door. "Better you than me, though." And there it is, the asshole sarcastic comment I was waiting for.

The door slams shut behind him. One thing that would make Crew happy is cleaning the house to his standards. I'll start there and hopefully find the balls to talk to him before this gets any worse.

PRIYA

The weekend flew by in a blur, mainly sleeping and listening to River's laptop play low in the background. I've woken up to breakfast outside of my room every morning since the nurse came. I'm not going to test the Demons when it comes to life's necessities. At least, not yet. Anyone who thinks it isn't possible to survive off of only one meal a day with a sprinkle of snacks here and there would be wrong. I'm not saying it's healthy, but that's the one thing that has followed me from home. People watching what I'm eating. Soon enough, it won't be a problem.

I'm still not 100% from my run in with Bennett. My throat is a little tender to the touch, but I'm more than capable of going through with school. My psych grade isn't the best since Crew ruined it. Just because my parents don't speak to me doesn't mean they're not watching and waiting for me to fuck up. If my parents catch wind of it… I don't want to imagine the consequences. I've never thought to test the boundaries on how far they would go. Especially when I already try my hardest to get their approval.

All my schoolwork that I've missed during my absence is sprawled all over my bed. Starting one assignment only to move to the next and back again. My door shuts with the distinct clumping of combat boots to dull the chatter in my head. The coffee machine turns on while River makes herself at home in the new chair angled towards the bed in the far corner by the window.

The Shadow Man's chair. I press my lips together to prevent myself from asking her to pick a different spot. One of the few things I will miss after my birthday is him. He's been the only person who's never judged me, even at my lowest. I have no doubt that he'll be fine without my presence. I've never had someone be so horribly sweet to me. The difference between him and the other villains in my life, he soothes the hurt he causes. I never realized how much I've needed that. In such a short time, I came to rely on him to help me see through the fog that constantly follows me around.

He offered me an out the other night. I would never take it, but that's more than my father ever gave me.

And River. I've stopped trying to complete my homework a while ago, there's no use for it. My eyes slide to her as she stares out the window, sipping from a white mug she's declared as hers. Her full lips caress the lip of the cup, closing her eyes in soaking in the faint rays of sunlight, dark lashes fan her face, hiding her doll-like eyes. Her upturned nose and porcelain skin tell nothing of the horrors she's faced. I'll miss River too.

I've been telling myself since I made the decision that being gone won't affect her as much. That's what I say to fight off the guilt. Despite our short time together, she's made an impact on me. She's been a friend when I didn't think I needed anyone. Listened when no one would, held me when I cried and never left my side. She's healed things in me I never knew were broken. This is how I want to remember her.

"Why are you smiling at me like that?" She asks with a raised eyebrow.

"I was just thinking about how grateful I am for you." My voice cracks and warmth spreads through my chest. Her eyes soften at the corners as she places a hand over her heart. "Tonight is the Halloween party. Are you excited?" I change the subject to avoid her prying for more than I want to give.

"Yeah, the workers finished putting everything together last night! Did you see it?" I shake my head. The only thing I saw was most of the male carnival workers check out the young girls, flirt and whistle at them. One tried to approach me on Tuesday, and I made a run for it. Wishing I had a rape whistle to blow in his face.

Classes were excused today by the stand in dean. Now that I think about it, I haven't seen or heard from dean Brian in a while. I'll take that as no news is good news. Earlier this week, my outfit was delivered. I'm beyond excited about tonight.

In the bathroom lays my costume I went all out for. I've decided a sexy clown would be my big bang. My life has always been the bud of a bad joke. The bruises I have will be an excellent addition since it's Halloween and I won't have to hide them with hoodies that press down on them. Tonight is about setting myself free.

PRIYA

With each step towards the evening festivities, the cold becomes more pronounced, causing a tingling sensation on my exposed skin. The air crackles with an electric energy, making me restless and jittery. Nothing can touch me right now. Ignoring Oscar's offensive comments about my outfit and the judgmental stares from other girls, I carried on with my head held high, eyes straight forward.

River talks animatedly, painting a vivid picture of elaborate costumes and spooky festivities of previous Halloweens. Her attire is reminiscent of a broken doll, with frayed edges and cracked porcelain makeup. The short, tight black dress and a white-collar clings to her curves. By applying white eyeliner on her waterline, her eyes take on a larger, doll-like appearance. The attention to detail in her costume was clear in the realistic cracks she painted onto her forehead and cheek. She said it will light up under the black light like the sky on Fourth of July. I misunderstood the assignment for tonight. All of her make up will light up, while mine is invisible until I'm under the black light.

A red and white stripped tent dominates the once wide-open center of the campus appeared to be held down by fairy lights that connect at the top. We enter under a dilapidated, flickering sign that reads "CARNEVIL," casting a wicked glow. With the lights missing in the first four letters, the word "Evil" is more conspicuous and eye-catching. Circus Psycho by Diggy Graves is playing somewhere from the middle overlapping with regular carnival music that cuts out now and then. It's giving horror movie vibes.

Carnival workers are dressed in orange jail jumpsuits with prison numbers on the arm, wandering around. Based on their appearance, it seems like they focused their decorating efforts on their head and above. The lack of budget restrictions allowed the student body to fully express themselves through provocative or scary costumes.

There is so much going on, I don't know where to look first. My mind is numb as I try to soak in my last night here. Some rides make me pause because they seem as weathered as the sign we entered through, producing creaks and groans with every twist. The combination of cotton candy, deep-fried foods, alcohol, and perfume created a sensory overload as their scents mix. Black lights, dangling from every angle, bathe the designated party area in a surreal glow, accentuating the food and game booths. River was accurate in stating that she would be glowing. Her eyeliner, lashes, and previously unseen cracks on her body are all neon in the light.

"Whoa. I have to say I'm a little impressed." She says as she stares at the now visible white black light makeup I drew on.

River attempts to break away from me, but I hold tight to her arm. She slows down long enough to ask if I'm okay. And I am. I've never felt better than I do right now, knowing what's coming by the end of the night.

"It's just a lot."

She graces me with a small smile and pulls me closer. It's so crowded that if River were to be two steps ahead of me, the hoards of people surrounding us would swallow her. I'm not saying we'd be kidnapped but, I would kidnap River if I was a weirdo. She's cute and innocent, people are drawn to that. A fog machine completely obscures the ground in front of us, making it impossible to see our own feet.

"Have you ever had a funnel cake?"

When I don't answer, she rolls her eyes and tosses her head back while dragging me to a dirty-looking booth. The woman behind the table is wearing a zombie costume. The black 3D voids on her face and sketched teeth appear vividly under the lights. River orders for us. I watch with my mouth agape at her pouring batter into a deep fryer. My mouth waters, it smells so delicious, but the calories… I stop myself before I dig myself into a hole I can't get out of.

Tonight. I can do whatever I want. Be whoever I want. Eat whatever the fuck I want. To distract myself, I force down the bile that threatens to surface and take another moment to observe around me. Spread out around us are various attractions, and one in particular catches my eye. It has the appearance of a colossal devil, with Venetian masks adoring its entrance. The chipped paint on the masks adds an aged and enigmatic charm, while the menacing fangs from the top and bottom give a sense of foreboding. Just next to it, there's the Mirror of Horror's, and a little further, a haunted house.

The booth beside us is providing tarot card readings.

"The main tent is closed until 11:30, so that leaves us with about an hour to explore. Where should we go first?" She says through a mouthful of food. I'm like a deer caught in headlights. Someone has to decide for me. My eyes pinball from one place and person to the next.

"Um…"

"How about we start with a reading? It's all bullshit, but it could be fun?" Without waiting for an answer, she drags me with standing in line. There's only one person in front of her. Lily, the girl I helped in the gym locker room, and then she proceeded to cut up my clothes.

River's eyes narrow, shooting her a venomous glare while her nails dig into my arm. I don't think there's been a moment up until now she's been alone. There's always someone with her or when she catches sight of us, she scurries away. I wouldn't want to be Lily right now.

She's dressed up as a kitten. The light from the front of the dark tent makes her nose and drawn on whiskers stand out. The leather bodysuit she wears fits her tightly, and her knee-high boots with platforms make her taller than River by at least 5 inches. To say River is not intimidated would be an understatement.

"Bitch," River says under her breath as the tarot reader calls for the next person. There's a sign near the tent flap that says, "One At A Time". River sees it the same time as I do and cringes.

"We could go somewhere else?" She offers. I'm not going to rain on her parade. I'll find something else to do while she gets the reading. There's not much a tarot reading could tell me about my short, bleak future that I haven't already made a decision on. It would be pointless.

"It's fine. We can meet up at the Devil's mouth when you're done? I'll go get a lemonade or something." She bites her lip, looking at the tent, then behind me where I offered to meet her when she was done.

"Next!" a high-pitched voice yells when a crying Lily rushes out. What the hell happened in there? It looks like the reader killed her cat with the way she's crying.

"Okay, but you better be there." She tacks on a "please" before disappearing into the hole of the tent.

I take my time meandering through the large mass of people and enjoying the fresh air. Until a whiff of tobacco hits me in the face, causing me to gag. Fresh-ish air. With each step, the refreshing breeze against my face is a stark contrast to the suffocating fumes of secondhand smoke.

I wonder what death will be like. I've thought of a couple of ways to go out. Weighing the pros and cons of each. The only acceptable way would be to suffer as much as my sister did.

As long as I've been alive, I've been fighting for something. Acceptance, love, happiness, surviving another day. It's freeing to finally be done. No more conflict. Whatever awaits me on the other side has to be better than this. It isn't just the Demons. It's the constant fear and guilt that hovers above my head. That isn't living.

"Miss?" A hand waves in front of my face. I blink at the carnie, the sounds of laughter and creepy carnival music filters through my haze. "Go on. Or get out of the way. You're holding up the line." His costume is simple, only a clown mask.

"Oh, sorry. I don't have any money on me." I murmur and feign searching my non-existent pockets, restricted by the tight corset, attempting to leave the line that I'm holding back. He huffs and crosses his arms.

"It's all paid for. Everything is free tonight, courtesy of the school's founder." Then I'm being shoved forward into the mouth by the people complaining behind me. Throwing a look over my shoulder, hoping to catch River so she knows I didn't ditch her, I'm swallowed whole by the Devil. It's a lot more imposing up close, the teeth extended canines of it are about the length of my body. Some areas of the white teeth have chipped away, revealing the faded pink color that was once a vibrant red. As I walk, the floor feels uneven, the tongue of the devil sinking beneath my heels. The walls have a rippled effect, causing me and others to stumble occasionally. It's like walking up a set of stairs, miscounting and stepping on air. The lights cut off and ear-piercing screams sound out around me.

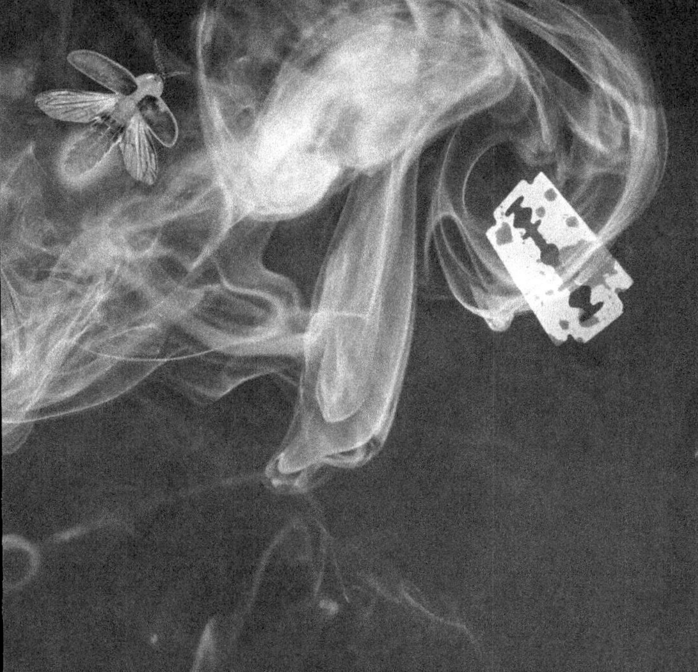

BENNETT

"Good evening, my fellow ..." I trail off. "What the fuck are you?"

Crew rolls his eyes and continues to check off items on his list for the main event tonight. Technically, it was supposed to be my job since I planned it, but Crew took over like the control freak he is. I have no complaints because this is the boring part.

"A ring master," he says. Not paying me any attention going down his list. No. No fucking way.

"Um, no you're not."

"I clearly am, Ben."

"*I'm* the fucking ring master. You… you're the Wish/Temu version of it." He shakes his head. "How the hell did you manage to copy me? I kept it a secret."

"You clearly copied me," he tells me, turning away to speak

with one of the acts of the night. The audacity this guy has. I jump in front of his face, cutting off the conversation mid sentence. He huffs and attempts to sidestep me, and I follow.

"Admit it." I press.

"Great minds think alike. I don't know what to tell you. Go change."

He has to be joking. His dismissal of me is telling me he's not. There's no hidden laughter or jokes. He's serious. If there was ever time for a cat fight, it would be right now.

My eyes narrow, thinking of a way to fuck his life up. There are no boundaries I wouldn't cross to force him to see he's wrong. Brother or not. I don't believe in coincidences. Before I can speak my mind about him and his bogus ass costume, a woman walks up. Beautiful figure, curvy in all the right places. She has that charcoal look on her eyes. What is it called?

What really draws me in is the full beard she has. I'm impressed. I can't even grow one that full. It comes in patchy.

"Smokey eye!" I shout. Both of them look at me. "You're the bearded lady?" My voice raises, betraying my excitement. "Oh, my god. Is it real? How do you get it so full? Can I touch it?" My hand reaches towards her and my brother smacks it out of the air with a dirty look. The woman smiles at me, despite my intrusive questioning.

"Yes, it is real. It's medical condition. But I figured if I make good money off it." She shrugs. Her thick Russian accent makes her roll her 'r's in English. Wow. This is amazing. She saunters off, hips swaying in the black lingerie she's wearing.

"Whoa," I whisper.

"Get a hold of yourself. Abuela had one just like it." Crew rolls his eyes. He thinks everyone is dramatic, but we all got it from him. How is none of this amazing to him? It's a *real* circus.

A huge part of this was because I have never been to a fair, circus, or carnival. Call it a childhood dream come true. The outside of this tent doesn't do it justice for what's inside. Tiers of seating stacked on top of each other to make room for tonight's acts. People are practicing. There isn't one area on the main floor that isn't busy. Some people are just helpers, the ones who put everything together, seats, food and drinks. With everything almost done, it leaves barely any room on the floor for the most astonishing stints.

A knife thrower, motorcycles, acrobats, fire breathing, even trained animals. A leopard trailing after what I assume is its owner. Free. No leash, wandering around. A. Leopard. Would Crew let me get one?

"Hey, where is Saint?" Crew asks nonchalantly from behind me. The issue with my brother is he likes to pretend he doesn't care. If he is bothering to ask, he does.

"I don't know. He was here earlier helping with the stands." He hums his acknowledgment. "Did you need him for something?" I ask.

"No."

"So you were just … asking?"

He ignores me. Pretending to look at his bullshit list. I don't know how much is on it, but there's no way he has that much left to do. From the corner of my eye, I spot a man in a suit walking towards us. Everyone here is in costume, so when a man walking in wearing something so outrageous is sure to catch everyone's attention.

"Crew?" I smack him on the back of the head to get his attention.

"What! Bennett?"

"Who the fuck invited this guy? He went with a Dior suit, but if you ask me, I think he should've gone with a Brioni Brunco. Can't go wrong with that." The man continues towards us, his nose held high, glaring at everyone like they're beneath him. It's that politician look, the one that's ambitious and untouchable with that comb over and maintained beard. The Russian woman's was way better. What holds my attention is the transformation my brother has made.

Gone is the spat we had. His posture is poised and ready to attack. My eyes look back and forth from the suit guy to my brother. Immediately taking up residence to the left of my brother,

I brace myself for whoever this is that has him on edge. Regardless of what's going on between the three of us, I'll always take my brothers' side.

I'm definitely missing something. Do we know this guy?

"Robert Carter. What brings you so far from home on this lovely Halloween evening?" Crew's smile is almost too charming to be believable. Oh, shit. Carter? As in Priya's father?

Robert's glacier blue eyes narrow, taking us in from head to toe and looking away from us. I can tell he finds us lacking. He adjusts his Cartier cuff links and checks the time before speaking.

"I heard all about the Halloween festivities put on by the founder's adoptive sons and couldn't miss it, could I? Besides, it's my daughter's 18th birthday." He says with a vile smirk.

It's Priya's birthday? Am I the only one who is out of the loop here? Crew purses his lips but remains quiet.

"Where is my darling daughter?"

"You don't know?" Crew asks.

"It's a surprise visit." He shrugs. "Aren't there supposed to be three of you? Where is the third musketeer?"

"Probably fucking your daughter." I sneer. There's four of us. Or he's just a fucking idiot that didn't do his research. His face turns tomato red while he sputters for a comeback and falling short, choosing to storm away, his tantrum in tow. God, that guy was insufferable. Crew fixates on where Robert made his exit, fists balled at his sides.

"So… are you going to come enjoy the rides with me?"

"No. And neither are you. This is your show."

My jaw drops open as he shoves the clipboard into my bare chest and walks away.

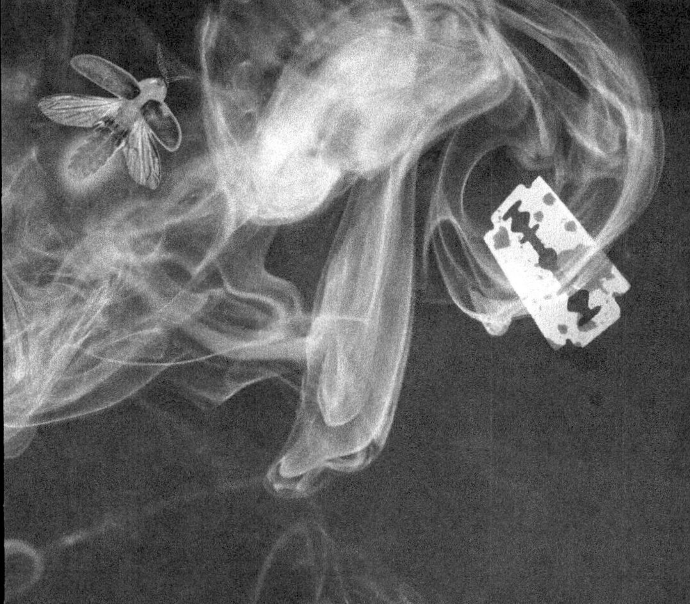

MALICE

MY CHEMICAL ROMANCE – MAMA

No matter how loud the room is, I'll always distinguish her high-pitched shocked scream, even if it was barely a whisper. She's like a beacon in the night. A lighthouse that guides the mentally insane towards her. She calls to the darkness that people are embarrassed to admit they have.

Evil doesn't discriminate, it lives in everyone.

The carnie shut off the lights at the attraction when I handed him a crispy one-hundred-dollar bill.

'Everyone has a price', is what Crew would say. It seems he knows a little about how people work. If the worker of the attraction I'm stalking had said no, I would've considered killing him. That word is unwelcome in my vocabulary.

The vibration of each scrape of the metal baseball bat against the ridges of the Devil's throat feels pleasant in my arm. I'm a considerable distance from the frightened crowd of people at the opening of the mouth of 'Hell's Half Acre' maze.

Their screams die down from the initial shock of the complete absence of light. The steady thump of my steel-toed boots resonates through the metal throat of the Devil, growing closer and louder with each step. The locked entrance will be enough to send some people running back towards the group to keep up. I couldn't have Priya Carter slipping through the cracks and escaping.

The sound of hurried footsteps reaches my ears, gradually turning into hesitant, cautious steps, numbering no more than ten following close behind. Among the group, a guy leads the crowd with his overconfidence, dressed as a shirtless pharaoh and donning the distinctive neme headpiece with lappets.

He steps deeper into the throat of the Devil, his sandals scuffing on the ground, closer to me, taking charge to lead the group through the windowless maze of metal tunnels that lie ahead. Rats in a maze.

"What was that?" A meek bunny asks, clutching onto her friend's hand.

A chorus of "Shh!" and "Shut up!" Ring out. My steps never falter. The bat grinds against metal, emitting a piercing screech that would make most people cringe. A few muffled whimpers escape from behind people's hands. I inhale the stench of their fear, metallic and bitter, with a hint of rubber from the tongue of the false mouth, so potent in a small space. The people who realized the locked door have trickled in towards the small group gathered 6 feet away from me. I stop. The screech and pounding of my footsteps with me. It remains silent.

Only heavy breathing surrounds me. The last woman, in stiletto boots, slowly tiptoes her way into the back, her steps timid and hesitant, arms tightly crossed over her stomach. The foreign sensation of my cheeks lifting underneath my mask intensifies at the same time as my heart thumps, completely mesmerized by her presence. It's unlike her to show anything other than deceit around so many people. The dark always brings the truth to light. Something along those lines.

The pharaoh who has proclaimed himself the leader cautiously makes his way toward me, unaware of my proximity, stopping 3 feet in front of me, perfect hitting range.

How much force would it take to hit him hard enough for his head to fly off like a baseball? It's unlikely but an exciting experiment. I'll have to pocket that idea for later.

He squares his shoulders, standing taller when nothing happens. It would be easy to believe he was unafraid, if not for the relentless thumping of his pulse trying to jump out of his throat.

"See? It's fine." The pharaoh laughs weakly, turning his back to me and facing the small herd that's accumulated. Saint's piece of shite father was right about one thing. It's a mistake to turn your back to a predator. I prefer the fight, but no one ever said life was fair. "The noise was probably further down. It's Halloween. We're supposed to be scared." He scoffs. Just as he takes the backward step that invades my personal space, I swiftly remove the bat from the wall, swinging at his tibia.

A satisfying *crunch* on impact. The sounds of the bone breaking sends a shudder of pleasure through my body. His wail is a little more feminine than I thought it would be, disappointing. My lips purse, holding in a manic laugh. He sounds more lady-like than the girls in here do. Before his dramatics end, a horde bursts through, trampling over him. I suck my teeth. The people who wanted so badly to follow him to safety left him for dead. Well, not literally. I have no interest in killing him when what I want is inching quietly towards me, using the wall for guidance.

Gently, her fingertips glide over the grooves in the wall as Priya scans the darkness, her eyes straining to see, making her way cautiously around the outskirts of the people huddled together.

She takes careful steps, trying to mask the sound of her stiletto heels clicking against the floor. I tilt my head, a smile still playing on my lips at her feeble attempt to be sneaky, but it's immediately overshadowed by her outfit. Or lack thereof. Clad in a black corset, her breasts are lifted and appear larger than her natural size. To complete the ensemble is a black thigh harness, which fastens the all-black lace tights in place, leaving a sliver of skin bare on her upper thigh. Her straightened hair is purposefully in messy pigtails that frame her heart-shaped face. The diamond collar left by the Demons adorns her neck, signifying our ownership. I bite my knuckles to suppress a groan, skin breaking beneath my teeth. She looks edible. What is she supposed to be?

The clatter from the bat dropping halts her mid step. Her breath quickens, and she puts her hand over her mouth to smother it. It wouldn't matter. Not for her, anyway. She's the reason I'm here.

"Happy Halloween, love."

She releases a shuddering breath, removing her shaky hand from her mouth, her shoulders relaxing at my voice.

"Shadow?" she whispers.

Shadow? That's new. It's safe to assume that she'd come up with her own name for me, getting off on not knowing who I am. She crosses her arms and pops out her hip, drawing my attention to her long and slender legs. This differs from the way she was holding herself moments ago.

"Are you going to hit me with that thing, too?" She asks. Her eyes search for me, talking to the opposite side of where I am. It's how I would imagine someone who was newly blind to look around. Lost.

"Is he dead?"

"Who?"

"The guy you assaulted for no reason!" She hisses like she cares.

Oh, him. I'd almost forgotten. I look him over, his chest rising and falling. He must've fainted from the pain. Pansy.

"He was cocky." I shrug.

"Are you wearing night vision goggles?"

A topic change to something she's more comfortable with. Avoidance is key with her.

"No."

"Then how can you see me?"

"I thrive in the dark." I tell her. Keeping it short and simple.

She scoffs, throwing her hands up in the air before taking slow measured steps past me, hand back on the wall for help. My hand shoots out, grabbing her wrist, forcing her to stumble to a stop. My grip prevents her from breaking her ankle without help.

"Where do you think you're going, Little Monster?"

"Uh, the fuck out of here to find River." My grip loosens as she shuffles forward. She's always with River. Stays with River, eats with her, spends most of her time with her. My eyes narrow while I press my lips together, not wanting to anger her further. We're long overdue for a chat, River and I.

"You claim we're so different. But you didn't bother to check on the guy who was just trampled by people?" I ask smugly. She stops again. I can see the war going on in her head, the lie on the tip of her tongue. She doesn't want to admit she's anything like me, but her actions prove otherwise.

"He wouldn't have thought twice if it was me," she says quietly, stepping past him and continuing to move deeper, her heels clicking confidently.

"Best hope I don't catch you." I say in a singsong voice. The metal bat drags on the ground to let her know I'm coming. My body trembles at the thought of catching her off guard and having fun with her.

"You owe me some answers, Shadow Man. You don't get jack shit until I get what I want." Her tone is flippant but the way she was biting back a smile tells me she'll play with me, anyway.

PRIYA

DECODE – PARAMORE

Time seemed to stretch as I stumbled, disoriented in the dark, running my hands over metal walls, tripping over air, until I finally grasped the fact that the obstacle in my path was none other than a solid metal door. There was no way I was turning back to face the Shadow Man after that bomb ass exit. With my luck there would be cameras, and the person monitoring would die from secondhand embarrassment.

Once I undid the latch, the room I entered filled the endless hallways before me with a red ambiance, as opulent dark red drapes adorned every wall and emitted a distinct "store new" scent. Even the ground had plush red rugs. I believed one of those paths would ultimately lead me out of this maze. That's what I've been walking through ever since. One dead end after another. Each corner more frustrating than the last.

While making a left turn, I collide head-on with a singular floor mirror, the frame is aged, once where it was golden is now a dark copper color, golden vines wrap around the frame reads "Timent Veritatem" whatever the hell that means. My eyes dart around my figure, taking in the sight of my clenched fists tightly pressed into the sides of my short, poofy skirt, before averting my gaze. The tightness in my jaw intensifies. My teeth ache under the pressure. The thought of looking at my reflection is enough to make me nauseous.

I'm pathetic. I can't even look at myself. Wiping my sweaty palms on the skirt, my nostrils flare in response. I take a deep breath to face the mirror. I quickly glance, seeing my black corset reflected back at me. Keeping my stomach sucked in, my brows furrow.

Weak.

Scared.

I'll be able to see exactly what I am. Every flaw. Every insecurity. Every bit of ugly I am reflected back at me, mocking me. Offering me one final motive to put an end to my miserable existence.

One last time. I can face what I am, just like everyone else has to. I don't get to make a life-changing decision and runaway like a scared little girl now. Addison wouldn't. She'd pull up her big girl panties and handle it with the grace she's always had.

But I'm not her. She was always stronger than me. In every sense. My sister would never let something hold her back from doing what she thought was right. Even if it was hard. My nails puncture my palms as I gather the strength to meet my gaze.

There. I did it. My eyes travel from my shoes, up my legs, and settle on my stomach, before I finally find the strength to meet my own eyes in the mirror. The girl staring back at me doesn't look anything like the person I once remembered. There's a big difference between slapping something on in the mirror and staring into my soul.

I hate her.

The girl in the mirror is someone I would gladly kill and not think twice about the consequences.

Her face is gaunt. The cheekbones and jawline are so prominent that it's impossible to ignore. Hollow and tired eyes, with noticeable bags under them. Her hair, once radiant and glossy, now appears lackluster and devoid of its former shine, a stark reminder of how everything has changed in the past 10 months.

Ugly.

I've spent my life trying to be who everyone wanted me to be. Only to be picked apart from the outside in. And I complain about them but I am my own worst critic.

Disappointment.

She's so dumb to think anyone could care about her. She let hope seep into her soul, only to be crushed by reality.

Unloveable.

She looks so tired.

Our eyes sting with tears, a physical manifestation of the pain we have endured for months, even years. She looks like the type of person to suffer in silence when she's barely getting through the day. One who would intentionally starve herself for days on end hoping to go down a pants size.

Fake.

And I hate her. I hate us and what we've become.

I don't want to be here anymore. I want to be done. Maybe I'm sick, mentally. Maybe there is help for me, but I don't deserve it for what I let happen to the one person I swore to protect. I don't deserve happiness. I should've died with her.

In the silent corner, my panting is the only sound that breaks the stillness. Our brows furrow in unison. I raise my clenched fist and lock eyes with the girl in the mirror, only to realize there's someone watching my emotional unraveling.

Do I pretend I don't see them? Hope they'll go away? Or acknowledge them? It seems a little rude to be watching someone and not at least let them know they're not alone.

Lowering my fist, I turn to face the intruder with both hands on my hips, ready to give them a piece of my mind on their snoopy ass behavior.

As I open my mouth, they're closer than they were seconds ago. It's easy to tell it's a man by the broadness of his shoulders. He's dressed in all black head to toe, minus the Ghostface mask from that horror movie. In the mirror, he seemed so far away, at least to the end of this corridor. Could it be a trick of the mirror? But that wouldn't make sense, since there was nothing unusual about my appearance.

I step back, hitting the mirror, realizing I've cornered myself. This has to be a part of the attraction.

"Could you tell me how to get out of here?" I ask casually. The act of crossing my arms over my chest gives me a reassuring feeling of control. Safe.

Mask guy doesn't respond. "A simple 'No' would've been fine," I grumble, walking to slip past him. His gloved hand snaps out, catching me by the arm. A gasp escapes my mouth at the sudden touch.

"Can I help you?" I say through gritted teeth. The anger I felt earlier comes back tenfold. What would be a better way to get rid of it than putting a handsy carnie in his place?

His face ducks close to me. A whiff of gasoline and leather hits me. He reminds me of…

"Shadow?" I squint and tilt my head. He's taller than I thought he would be. How tall is he…6'11? Whatever he is, is a giant. During my darkest days, that smell remains a constant companion, engraving itself into my memory. He mimics me, tilting his head. The way he stays silent causes my heart to race, second guessing myself. I'm a little over the games tonight. I nod, coming to an agreement mentally.

"Let me go." I demand. Yanking my arm from him, but he holds tight.

"What's wrong, Little Monster?" His voice is calm as his other hand cups my cheek, forcing me to look up into the solid black eyes of the mask. The longer I stare, searching for answers from a mask of a man I don't know, my eyes fill with tears. This is what my life has come to. Spilling my heart out to a stranger.

"Have you ever felt so twisted up about something? You know what you have to do. But you're scared?" I whisper. A single tear traces a path down my face, relaying the exact words my sister uttered one year ago. His hands are painted all black except the fingertips where it's worn from use. Using his thumb, he slowly wipes it away. I swear I can feel his eyes dissecting me.

"I can fix it. Do you want me to?"

I nod.

"Say it."

"Please." My voice cracks as I pour what's left of me into my plea of release. The rough brush of the pad of his thumb moves from my cheekbone to my lips to smear the lipstick I'd carefully applied earlier. My eyes involuntarily flutter shut, savoring the sensation. A touch that isn't out of anger. One that doesn't cause pain.

"Turn around."

"Wait."

My heart aches at the thought of saying goodbye to the closest thing that has brought me peace since my sister died. I need the closure of knowing what he looks like. Closing the distance between us, I press my body against his, feeling the comforting heat radiating from him, warming me to my core. I'll miss this. The silence his presence brings to my mind. I place my trembling hands on the cool plastic of his mask, sensing the steady rhythm of his breath beneath my touch.

"I want to see you. Just once."

He accepts with a tilt of his head.

With my eyes closed, I stand on my tippy toes to pull it over his head, paying attention to the warmth of his skin when my fingers brush against it before I let it go, dropping it to the carpet with a light thud before resting my hands on his chest above his heart.

Thump thump.

How isn't his heart beating out of his chest like mine is? What if I know him? What if revealing his identity to me means he'll tell everyone what we do? What I allow him to do to me.

Thump thump.

Does it matter?

Steeling myself to be disappointed, I stand a little taller knowing it won't matter after tonight. And open my eyes.

PRIYA

My hands follow the black drawstrings up to the opening of the hoodie. I lift my eyes to follow the path of my fingers as they trace up his throat, the brushstrokes of the painting creating the illusion of a smaller neck. The bones are meticulously painted white, while the gaps were filled in with a solid black color. Black contours around his jawline, making the white paint stand out.

A frown pulls at the corner of my lips, the excitement I had deflates at the second costume underneath the mask. I was hoping it was a hoax, but unfortunately, it's not. The rest of his face is painted like a skeleton. The fake teeth drawn on cannot conceal his full lips. He uses black paint to rim his eyes, creating the illusion of empty eye sockets. I take my time tracing what would be his lips, cheekbones, to closed eyes. When he subtly leans into my touch, my heart flutters nervously in my chest.

I'd happily be his canvas for the rest of my life. If all the hurt he brought me was glossed over by whispered sweet nothings and soft touches. If I could mean something to someone, just once. A dull ache forms in my chest with the knowledge I could never be what he deserves. There is pain in wanting something I could never have. There is no happy ending for me. I can't be fixed.

Right on cue, his eyes, devoid of emotion, spring open and bore into my soul. There is no smile, just eerie blankness. It chills me to my core.

"Your eyes have no reflection."

"I know."

"Why?"

"I was born that way. The way you were born to display every thought across your face." His eyes flit to every corner of my face. "Why do you cry? Are you frightened?"

"No."

"Do you know who I am?"

"My salvation." With my hands under the hood of his black sweatshirt, the texture of his hair is greasy as I tug on it. Rubbing my fingers together. I pull my hand out and examine the sticky black residue of hair grease. I arch my brow in question. "You wouldn't make it easy. Would you?" I shake my head.

"You don't like what you see, Monster?" He asks, slightly cocking his head, scanning my face. Monster. Is that what he is? I wouldn't put it past him to deflect his issues on to someone else.

The face painting dips down beneath his black hoodie, not giving a thing away. No visible tattoos, scars, not even his skin color.

"A skeleton?"

"Or Death."

I purse my lips. "Did you do this on purpose?"

"I knew you'd want to see me eventually, yes. People are predictable."

Cue the red flag.

"Not giving me a thing to work with here."

"Turn around."

I pay no attention to him, fully immersing myself in the pleasure of tracing the dark shading on his face, adding a touch of realism to the skeleton's features.

"What are you doing?" His voice strained. I'm making him uncomfortable? Good. It's about time someone gave him a taste of his own medicine. What I'm doing is driven by my selfishness, regardless of whether it aligns with the truth.

"I want to remember you," I whisper softly.

His brows furrow. "Remember me?"

I nod. Even though I can't pick out any real characteristics about him. This is the real him. He's not hiding in the shadows. I can physically see him, touch him, feel him. And that's enough. It has to be.

"Why?"

"Why not?" I retort.

With a firm grip, hands swiftly twirl me around before firmly pressing me into the heart of the mirror. Clearly done with that conversation.

"Bend over."

"No. I have questions." They don't matter. I'm just buying myself time with him before my night is over.

"So do I. I'll start. Why were you crying?"

I shrug. Choosing not to answer the question is more convenient than facing self-loathing once again. That is until he tugs on my ponytails, my head still sore from Bennett.

"Ow." His hands wrap around my hair twice before tugging again. I'm unsure how he feels about the 5th amendment, but I remain silent. Instead, I bend over and use my hands to maintain a distance between myself and the mirror. Releasing my hair, he takes a step back and kicks my legs further apart with his boot, putting a strain on my calves. I watch with bated breath as his painted hand starts at the ankle of my boots, lazily trailing upwards. I suck in a breath the second his hand contacts my bare skin. Squatting down, he flips the skirt up and positions himself at my hip level. I observe his every move as he reaches into the hoodie pocket, revealing a black sharp knife shaped like a 'T' with a gleaming blade.

With rapt attention, I watch him trace the cuts he made with reverence. The cold, metallic blade glides along my inner thigh, causing me to involuntarily squeeze my legs together, resulting in an unintended cut. With a huff, he delivers a sharp slap to my inner thigh, causing a shooting pain that forces a hiss to escape my lips.

"Don't move." He moves his head between my legs. In the mirror, his piercing gaze locks with mine, while his skilled tongue explores the sensitive area behind my knee, soothing the worst of the sting. He hums and his eyes shut, sucking until it's numb. I'm sweating. Is it hot in here?

"Fuck, you're so sweet."

I gulp. What do I say? Thank you? The knife's point goes directly below the 'A'. The first line is horizontal. It matches the ones I make on myself. Shutting my eyes, I savor the pain caused by the kiss of the blade. The knife comes to an immediate stop, remaining motionless at its last position before making an unexpected vertical turn.

"You're exquisite."

I squeeze my eyes shut tighter to drown out his lies and savor the moment. "I believe we were made for each other, that I've spent my entire life searching for someone who completes me. One who understands me, who could accept me. I've walked this life alone, content. Searching for relief in others' pain, just to find you."

There's nothing more I want than to believe him. Instead of responding, I choose to embrace the pain, sinking further into its depths to silence him.

"There are no words to describe the power you hold over me. Timent Veritatem," he says, "It means 'They fear the truth'."

When he halts, a fiery sensation fills the void where the blade once was, causing me to spin around and gaze at him with wide-open eyes.

Shadow's brow creases. I assume it's because I didn't allow him to finish his normal routine. There is still a lifelessness in his eyes. How freeing would it be to live a life where I didn't have to feel?

Crimson blood trickles down my leg, saturating the ebony lace of my stockings. I fixate on his face to hold back tears as I lower my hand to the freshly carved letter. I gather as much of the blood on my hand as I can before smearing it onto the drawn teeth of the skull. The taste of me on my fingers makes him groan as his tongue wraps around them, a warm drop of blood sliding down his chin.

The firm grip of his hand on the back of my knee guides my leg up and over his hip. I'm not surprised when he grinds his erection into me. Memories of the shower flood my mind, and I realize what truly aroused him - not pain, but blood. I lean in and lick the warm, coppery taste of my blood from his chin, taken aback by the involuntary sigh that slips from my mouth.

It's not entirely unpleasant, but it's lacking the "sweetness" he claimed it had.

"I-I want you to be my first." I wet my lips, staring at his, a fluttering in my chest takes flight. His smile is blinding in the red light. A warn feeling buzzes through my chest knowing I've pleased him. Even if the smile is rehearsed, he still put it on for me. I was worthy enough.

"Priya?" A soft feminine voice calls out.

MALICE

Priya freezes in my arms, her breath hitching before she pushes herself away from my chest, hastily smoothing down her skirt to conceal the fresh addition of my name. Everything I had been working for was within my grasp. Tonight was the turning point. She would have no choice but to embrace the idea of me.

"Priya?" River's voice grates on my nerves, disturbing our bubble of contentment. She's far enough away that we still have time.

"Stay with me." I tell her. Priya glances up at me with her doe eyes. The faint smattering of freckles on her face seemed to blend into the reddish hue of the light. Catching her bottom lip between her teeth. I can't fathom a reason she wouldn't immediately respond with an enthusiastic "Yes". When I pull her lip free from the abuse she's inflicting, my brows crinkle in concern.

"There's nothing or no one who could keep me away from you, Priya. Not even you."

"Priya?"

Always lurking around the corner. I wouldn't put it past her to have waited for the perfect opportunity to intervene. River has always been adept at manipulation, effortlessly playing the innocent card even when the evidence is stacked against her. I don't buy that coy act she puts on, having everyone wrapped around her finger.

She turns the corner of the red draped maze, coming to a sudden halt. Her body freezes, and her eyes widen when she spots the closeness between me and Priya. A black dress from the 50s adorns her, lending an air of vintage sophistication to her appearance. The detailed cracks drawn on River's skin, mirror the shattered pieces of her past. Exposing the hidden ugliness that still lingers within.

She put her hair into rollers to achieve that big wave girls do with their hair. Fixated on Priya, her eyes hold a certain intensity, mirroring the way I often find myself staring at her.

If I could kill her without jeopardizing my relationship with Saint or incurring the wrath of the Demons, I would do so. She's a nuisance.

"Priya? Is everything okay?"

My eyes narrow on her. I growl, letting my lip curl up at her insinuation that she wouldn't be safe with me. I'm not the only one who has been hiding things from our Little Monster. I can practically taste the bitterness of her words in the back of my throat. But Priya is quick to intervene.

"Uh yeah. He was just going to show me the way out." My jaw clenches as I stare at the side of her perfect profile, concealing her affections like she didn't lick her own blood from my lips a moment ago. I adjust myself. Fuck, are blue balls a thing? I haven't encountered this situation before, but I suppose there's always a first time for everything.

River's eyes, wide and observant, capture the area where I've cornered Priya, along with the lone mirror behind us. Then, her gaze locks onto me, her eyes sparking with recognition. She knows.

"I think I've got it figured out." She summons Priya by extending her arm. Spots dance in my vision when she effortlessly goes to her side. "Just keep going straight. I'm going to have a word with the… worker."

My monster's body tenses before I hear her suck in a breath and release it through her nose. She throws me a look over her shoulder at me, smiling shyly, "Thank you for everything." I keep my eyes locked on her until she fades away from sight.

My arms spread wide for a hug and a faux welcoming smile stretches across my face. "River!" I say with Saint's American accent that I've learned how to perfect over the years for when it suits me. "I've missed you."

"Really, *Malice*?" She hisses, taking a step towards me. "I've already threatened Bennett. She's off limits. I know you abide by your own laws, but please. I'm begging."

I roll my eyes, "What are you on about?"

"You!"

"What gave it away?"

"I know my brother."

I hum, tapping my chin. "Last I heard, you abandoned the family." It's not openly talked about. The abandonment issues River has developed over Saint letting her go live with a good family after the Demons 'killed' their father. The Demons and Elijah Cox decided to let River live out the normal life she deserved. Unfortunately, River followed the boys here. She wasn't about to be left behind. She wanted in on whatever they were planning. The twins refused to have her involved in their little agenda to do with Priya Carter. So, River weaseled her way in the only way she knew how to. By befriending the object of the Demons' obsession, putting her right into the thick of it.

"You guys are still my family, Mal."

This is manipulation perfected into a form of art. Attempting to manipulate me with emotions when she had already confessed that I only adhere to my own principles. If I killed or kept Priya, it wouldn't have anything to do with her request.

"I'll pass it along." I won't. It wouldn't matter. They all have a soft spot for her. "I'm being summoned. See you around, River. And if I were you, I'd keep my mouth shut."

"Please, not her."

"We've already chosen." I shrug.

"Did you forget what happened to the last girl who was in your guys' orbit?" She lets out a laugh that lacks humor. "Megan Riley is dead because of you." Despite the red lights, her brown eyes remain piercingly dark, unable to hide the fiery anger within them.

My nostrils flare as I step into her face, bending slightly to put us at eye level. At 5'7 she thinks she can intimidate me. It almost makes me laugh.

"Let's not forget *why* I had to do it, River." I spit her name. "It was either her or *you*. Saint wouldn't have been able to live with himself knowing what your father was going to make him do to you, so I shouldered the burden for him, like I always do." She recoils away from me. "I. Saved.You." I punctuate each word, so it sinks in. Her eyes drop to her feet, unable to meet my eyes. As she should.

I don't feel guilty for being the bad guy. Someone has to be. I nonchalantly wiggle my fingers in the air, dismissing her.

A gasp sounds from the end of the hallway. I freeze at the small audible sound from the corner where Priya Carter disappeared around a minute ago. With a slow irritated blink, I direct my glare to the new source of issues. River running her mouth for Priya to hear.

That's something I'll have to deal with later.

River swiftly takes off to follow our Monster down the hallway, disappearing into the red-carpeted abyss.

Me and Saints phones ping one after the other with notifications from the twins, letting us know that Priya's father made an unexpected appearance. This night just got a lot more interesting.

With our hood and mask firmly back in place, I make my way towards the red and white tent I last left the twins in. Off the bat, I spot Bennett dressed in a ringmaster costume fawning over a woman with a beard. Inches away from petting it. He says something and instead of laughing, she rolls her eyes. The closer I get, I overhear him asking about her tips for a full beard. This bloke can't grow one for the life of him.

"For fuck' sake, Ben. Leave the poor bird alone!"

"Malice! Where have you been?" He hiccups.

"Are you taking the piss?" I rip the clipboard from his hands. On it is a drawing of a beard. I can only imagine why he drew that. With a nod to the bearded lady, she dips out of sight.

"Where's your brother?"

"He was asking the same about you earlier. Where'd you slither off to anyway?" Bennetts jab about being a snake isn't as subtle as he thought it was. They haven't seen me since Saint spilled the beans.

"He left after we ran into Robert Carter. Then poof. Gone with the wind." He giggles at his joke. My teeth grind against each other, giving me comfort in the pain. Leave it to Bennett to fuck up a simple task like finishing the checklist Crew left him. It's out of the norm for Crew to leave his irresponsible brother in charge of something so big.

"I know that look and I don't need to be babysat, Malice. It's you everyone should be worried about." He attempts to poke me in the chest but misses.

"Let's go find your brother, you wanker." There's something off about him disappearing and we're going to find out what it is. "Which way did he go?"

Bennett points towards the back of the massive tent, the flaps fluttering in the light breeze from outside. "Now that I think about it, that's the same way Priya's dad went." He burps and doubles over. "I don't feel too good." Fucking lightweight. "I wanna talk to you about something real quick." The asshole sits down on the ground crisscross apple sauce and pats a dirty spot next to him. Time is of the essence and he's wasting it.

"I know what you're thinking and I'm not moving until your grumpy ass shits down." He laughs, "I mean, sits down. Same thing."

Taking a deep breath, I play along with his shenanigans. I won't get far otherwise. "All right, Ben?"

"No. You really hurt my feelings. Our feelings." I blink slowly. He's joking? This is going to be a long night.

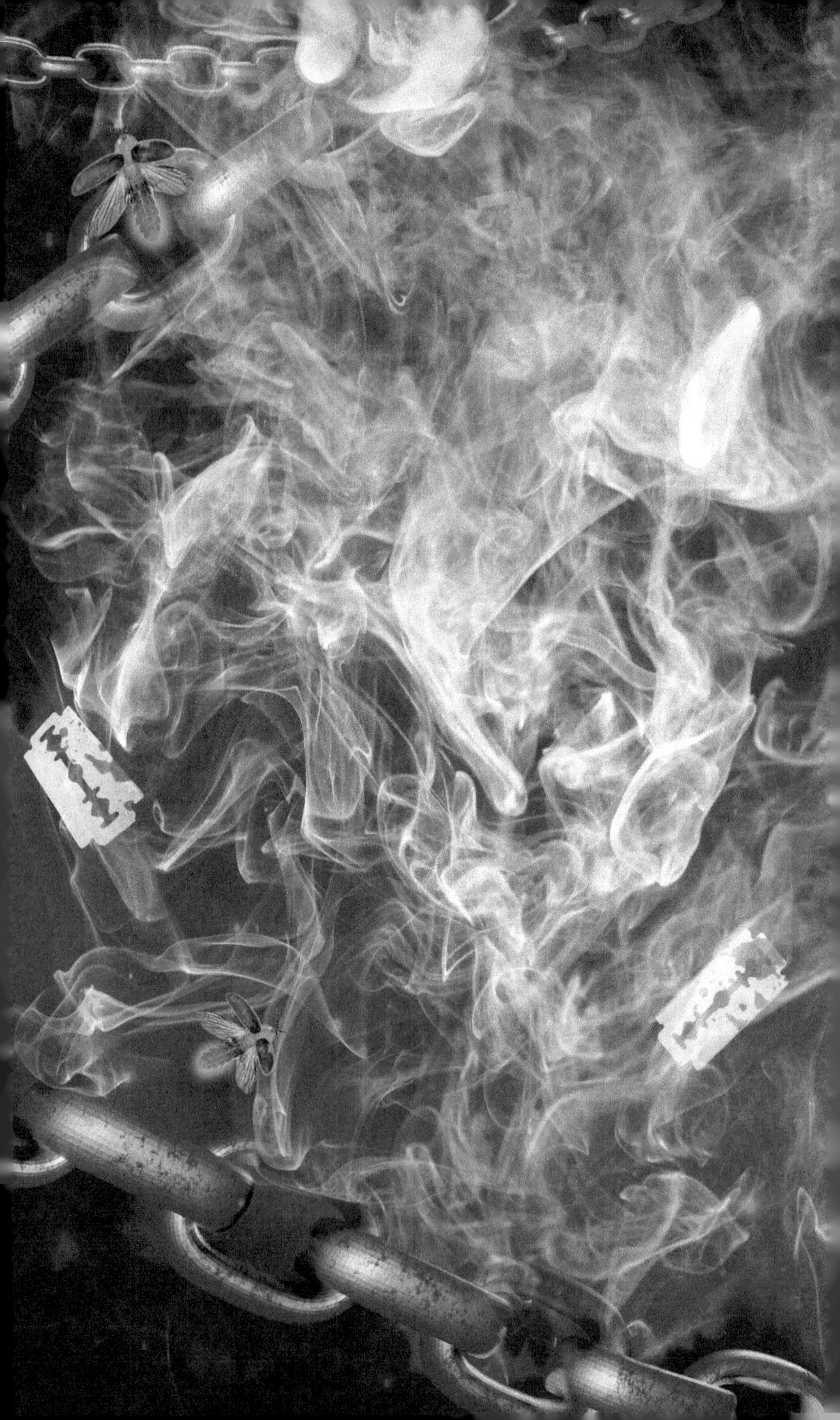

PRIYA

PARAMORE – I CAUGHT MYSELF

The night loses its comforting embrace with the new knowledge I've gained about my Shadow and River. Usually, I listen to River whenever she tells me to go. She's been at Cox Academy a lot longer than I have, dealt with the Demons' presence more often than me. I've never thought to question it. River has been nothing but kind and welcoming to me since I have arrived. But what threw me off was the way she tensed up the night I told her what I had discovered about Megan Riley. All the times I've asked or brought it up, she's brushed me off by changing the subject or warning me away from it. Intuition told me to stay behind and listen to her and the Shadow Man.

That's because she knew. She knew what happened to Megan. I was unable to catch most of their hushed argument, but I heard what I needed to hear. From both of them. A confession.

The dwindling chirps of the crickets matched the waning energy of the night, while the biting chilly wind seemed to carry with it a sense of deceit and confusion that infiltrates my thoughts.

When River finally caught up with me, I brushed her off by telling her I wanted to go home. With a soft ding, the elevator doors open and I exit. River faithfully trails behind me. On the other side of that door, I can almost hear the serene silence beckoning me. I just need to get there. The hallway seems to grow longer the more I walk.

"Pri—"

"Thank you for everything. I mean it." I cut her off mid-sentence, attempting to mask my annoyance with a feigned cheerful expression.

"Priya. We need to talk."

Without thinking, I instinctively cross my arms over my stomach. Avoiding eye contact, she keeps her gaze fixed on the floor as I impatiently tap my foot.

"D-did you hear?"

"Yeah." Enough of it, but it would be stupid to tell her how much I heard. I would rather her rat herself out, thinking I heard it all.

"How much?" She wrings her fingers, twisting her hands. "I was going to tell you."

I scoff, avoiding her first question. "When? Just like you were going to tell me about the bet?" She had time. The perfect time was when she admitted to murdering her rapist. Maybe throwing in that she knew what happened to the missing girl everyone refuses to acknowledge would have been a perfect time.

She shrinks away from me, "No, I mean it. It just never seemed like the right time."

A laugh escapes me. "Right… I've heard this before." Screw this, turning my back on her like I should've when she showed up at my door the first day we met. My hand reaches for the knob, the cool metal beneath my fingertips.

"He's my brother!"

In an instant, my hand freezes, and I spin around to face her.

"S- I mean Mal is my brother." She corrects.

Mal. My Shadow's name is Mal. The name doesn't suit him. Struggling to find words, my mouth moves in silence while tension coils within my muscles.

"Your brother? Are you kidding?" I shake my head. "You said you had one little brother."

"I do…" With a gesture, I motion for her to go on. There's more. "But I also have older brothers."

"I've told you everything and you couldn't even have the decency to tell me I was fall-" I stop myself from revealing anything more. "That he was your brother?"

This is the red flag I wanted to ignore. She mentioned it to Mason after Bennett outed my sister. I was reluctant to accept the fact that she might hide things from me. That she would come to me when she was ready.

My truths, my sister, I poured my heart out to her. Leaning against the metal door, I clutch my chest as a sudden, sharp pain shoots through me.

"Did you know?" My voice cracks. Our eyes meet, tears well up in hers.

"Priya, please! Let me explain! It's not what you think!" Behind her hand, a muffled sob breaks free.

"You knew about everything. Every time I cried. You were there holding me. After Oscar tried to," Unable to stomach the words, "every bad thing that happened to me… You were there. River… I gave you a piece of me that not even my sister had." Each word is a knife, piercing through the cracks in my heart, intensifying with every second that passes. "I trusted you." My lip wobbles. Tears stream down her face, smudging her makeup in dark streaks.

After everything… It was all a lie. Is the Shadow man in on all of this, too? Not just Megan Riley, but the horror and humiliation I've been facing.

Did I let myself become blindsided because I wanted to be worth something to someone so badly? Weak. I'm fucking weak. I knew better than to trust anyone, and I did it anyway. How could I be so stupid? I let her inside my heart.

Pathetic. No one can replace Addison.

With an uneven step, I fumble for the key and finally unlock the door. Before I'm able to take a step in, she tugs on my arm.

"Priya! Please! I'm sorry!" I'm unable to hold back my tears any longer.

"Me too, River. I would've done anything for you." I've been hurt by everyone in my life. Walked on, tossed to the side and discarded, and I refuse to die allowing people to think I'm okay with it. "But fuck you."

Throwing myself into my room, I slam the door in her face. Collapsing to the floor, I curl into a ball, clutching my legs and muffling my cries as I release a scream so powerful it could shake the very foundation of the room. A scream that could bring the roof down. That spoke to the world of my pain. One that bore the same scars and disfigurement as my own wounded soul.

Why me? Can't I catch a break? Why can't I be good enough for once? My cheeks flush with heat, and it spreads to my ears, then descends from head to toe. With legs trembling, I summon the courage to complete my mission. A haunting stillness descends upon me, extinguishing the flames of anger and pain.

Friendship heartbreak is something I wouldn't wish upon anyone. It's worse than a boyfriend breakup. But nothing is worse than losing a best friend and this will be the second time. The last time.

"Alamort," I whisper, "To be half dead, or exhausted, but it can be used to mean 'to the death'. That will be our word for the day, Addi." I wait for a response, a sign that she's listening. If there is nothing after death, then she can't hate me for what I'm about to do. After all, that's what I am. Barely existing, hanging on by a thread.

When the tears dry on my face, I stumble through the darkness, navigating my way to the bed by tripping over the rug that peaks out from underneath the frame. On my hands and knees, I reach for my black bag, holding the contents that I need to end my shitty existence. Whoever said that misery loves company lied.

A dim light switches on, stretching to the edges of the bed, enough to shine on my bag.

"Priya. I've been waiting for you."

The unfamiliar monotone voice of a man causes flight or freeze to kick in as a wave of icy coldness floods through my veins. My heart thunders through my ears.

"We're long overdue for a chat. You can call me… Mr. K."

ABOUT THE AUTHOR

Jaine is the epitome of a bookworm. She doesn't just read, but feels the books on a deeper level. She cries with the characters, laughs with them, even does the same facial expressions simultaneously. Though her work is, of course, a fictional story, each character is woven with real conversations she's had and a dash of the favorite parts of her three sisters making them her babies. However, her most significant achievement is being a loving mother to her vibrant five-year-old son, who is the center of her universe. When she's not reading or writing she can be found conquering her day with her dry sense of humor and quick wit or bugging her mother and fiancé with her next "big idea".